Sing Me a New Song

Joyce Bentley, although living in Darwin since her marriage, is a Mancunian born and bred, and a member of the Manchester Literary Club. Of Irish descent herself, her grandparents emigrated from Ireland at the turn of the century to become a part of the Manchester Ancoats scene. A keen local historian, she is a tutor in creative writing for the Open College North West. She is the author of a biography of Constance Wilde and *Proud Riley's Daughter* (1988), also published by Pan.

Joyce Bentley

SING ME A
NEW SONG

Pan Books
in association with Sidgwick & Jackson

First published 1990 by Sidgwick & Jackson Ltd
This edition published 1991 by Pan Books Ltd,
Cavaye Place, London SW10 9PG
in association with Sidgwick & Jackson Ltd
9 8 7 6 5 4 3 2 1
© Joyce Bentley 1990

ISBN 0 330 31208 1

Printed in England by Clays Ltd, St Ives plc

To my dear friend Ann Redmayne

Chapter One

They were walking along the deserted country road toward Dublin, she with a bright scarf over her dark hair, he with one knotted about his throat. The summer morning conjured up memories, and stirred in each a different mood.

Tessa noticed a clump of bushes, windswept and forlorn yet suggesting a wild majesty. The ragged leaves sparkled with a lacework of gossamer webs, and slivers of sunlight touched the wild berries, highlighting the gradient shades of crimson and purple. The colour and sparkle held an element of magic which reminded her of their wedding.

Finn's gaze went to where the distant turf had been cut, and the underside of the bog, as black as Lipton's treacle, glistened and gleamed. I'll not be digging the likes of that again, he thought, never, ever again! Now they were on the run from it all; on the run from the past; from the awful memory of the day the peat bog had overflowed its banks into the remote valley in which he and Tess had lived. Thank God I reached her father's croft in time to rescue her, he thought, as he had done so many times since; for life without Tess would be no life at all. To everyone else she was Tessa, except to her father, who had preferred the baptismal Teresa; but to Finn she had always been, quite simply, Tess.

He was on the run too, from the curse of his aunt. He shivered. The aunt, having worked her way into his thoughts, now gripped them and would not let go until he had relived the invocation. He saw her gaunt figure, arm outstretched, gnarled finger pointing, breath coming sharp.

1

'So, you're leaving the Aunt to take up wid a girl! By God, you'll rue the day!' she had shrieked. 'Nothing will go right. Bad luck will follow you, bad luck will be upon you!' He had turned to run out but her fingers clawed at his sleeve. 'Bad cess and good riddance! A curse on you, Finn Collins! A curse! A curse!'

A feeling of rebellious triumph ran through him. So much for the Aunt – it was she who had perished in the disaster! He and Tess had both mourned for the others of the community who had lost their lives, but now he could not get away fast enough. They were off to a new life. He and Tess, his love, his darling, his girleen. Ah, was he not the proudest of fellas?

His eyes, as darkly blue as the butterflies on the bog asphodel, dwelt fondly on Tessa, on the tendrils of hair which, escaping the scarf, were being teased by the wind, first curling about her ears, now nestling about her throat.

Was it the combination of dark hair and blue-grey eyes, he wondered, that gave her the look of a young woman regal born? Or perhaps the high cheekbones and smooth, wide forehead? She was quite tall, and although only eighteen moved like a goddess. The swing of her walk was brisk, the swish of her skirts graceful. And, as though these accomplishments were not enough for any mortal, he reflected, she could also – unlike himself – both read and write.

Her father, God rest his soul, had been so proud that they called him Proud Riley. He had wanted a better life for his daughter and now it was Finn's aim to fulfil the old man's ambition.

Thoughts of the present merged momentarily with those of the past. Sure, as long as he lived he would never forget the time when he and Tess, in the aftermath of the disaster, thought themselves done for, banjaxed, finished . . .

Covered in bog-slime, intensely cold, ravenously hungry, and hopelessly lost, Tessa and Finn wandered over the mountainous terrain, looking for a little softness, a little lightening of the sky. But the clouds, almost as dark and threatening as the Great Bog of Ennabrugh, stared bleakly back.

2

'If we ever get out of this Godforsaken place, will you marry me?' he asked, as they stooped to drink by a stream. 'I love you so very much . . . Oh, it's no use,' he groaned. 'No one will find us now. And if the Authorities are looking for survivors we've already wandered too far . . . '

Then she told him about the baby their first act of love had already started. She had not wanted to tell him yet, not until they had found safety and shelter but, with the future looking so bleak . . . And then, suddenly, the future was no longer so bleak. The fact of the baby went to his head like a shot of poteen. Getting to his feet, he caught her by the waist and swung her round, and would have danced a jig if either had had the strength. All at once, everything became more positive. Survival was no longer in doubt, but merely a matter of time. It was then, as if summoned by sheer strength of will, that he saw a movement in the distance.

Tessa followed his glance to see a raggle-taggle procession on the skyline, flanked by hordes of ragged children frolicking like hares.

'Tinkers!' They stared and held their breath. Was it a mirage? A figment of their starving imaginations? 'God save us!' exclaimed Finn. 'It's Spider Murphy returning to his winter quarters!'

The barrel-shaped silhouette which Tessa had thought never to see again appeared on the landscape swinging seductively from side to side, leisurely drawn by a long-tailed pony.

'Finn, there's two of 'em. What do you make of it?'

'It will be Martin Jarvey, begod! Him and Kate!'

Only a few months before, at Ennan Fair, Finn's friend Martin had left the valley to marry Spider Murphy's daughter, Kate, and in so doing had adopted the tinker way of life. Finn had always admired his friend's self-assurance, and the thought of meeting him again now bolstered his own.

'Did he not say it wouldn't be long before he got a van for himself and Kate? No more living in tents and rigs for them. Isn't he just the boyo? Oh, Tess, thank God! And aren't we in the luck that it's Murphy? The tinkers always repay a debt of honour and don't they owe you, Tess, for finding Kate when she got lost, and curing her asthma with the goat's milk? Besides,' he went on, looking at the bleak, mountainous moorland, 'we can't do other than throw ourselves on their mercy.'

'But Finn,' she exclaimed, looking down ruefully at their appearance. 'We're black with the bog-slime and as unfragrant as your pigs used to be. C'mon –' she seized his hand ' – let's find a deeper place downstream and wash some of it off.' As they walked, she added in a lower tone, 'Martin will have to be told that his da and uncle drowned with the rest.'

'He will so, and I'll do it.'

Gasping with the coldness of the water, the first flush of optimism was replaced by memories of the tragedy until Tessa caught sight of the mist descending from the mountains.

Down it came, wreaths of it, reeling and swirling; cutting down the visibility and threatening to obscure the direction of the tinker cavalcade. Eyes round with disbelief, Finn swore, and grabbing Tessa's hand tried to outrun the mist. Stumbling and staggering, panic now filled their every step. The tinkers were their only chance of staying alive. Finn thought of the child he had fathered, of the girleen who was its mother. Surely God in His goodness had not saved them from the overflowing bog to perish like this? He shouted until he felt his lungs would burst, and prayed that the wind which hurried the mist would also carry his voice to the tinkers.

'Finn . . . ' Tessa, overcome by fatigue and suffering from exposure, had fallen to the ground. It seemed as though the mist had caught up with her and was trying to wrap its grey folds about her head. Then she heard his voice strong and cheerful.

'They've seen us, Tess. And isn't it Martin himself on the way with a donkey! Rest easy, love,' he said as he gathered her shivering body in his arms, murmuring words of comfort with terms of endearment. He stroked her wet hair and smoothed it away from her face. 'Oh, you're so cold . . . Tess, listen to me: you'll soon be warm, Kate will look after you.' He continued talking, as to a child. 'And when I find work, sure I'm going to buy you the warmest Connemara shawl that money can buy , . . ' His voice sounded like music; the grey mist slowly unravelled

4

itself from her head; she imagined herself nestling into the warmth of the loveliest shawl and slowly . . . slowly . . . closed her eyes.

The following two days were an odd mixture of noise, movement and hours and hours of sleep, punctuated by careful tending. Tessa gave herself up to the ministrations; to being washed and clad in clean dry clothes; to sipping broth; being fed a mixture of herbs before dozing off into oblivion again.

She surfaced to reality and found herself in Spider Murphy's winter quarters. He and other travelling families had taken over the one remaining wing of a large and derelict house. The floor was flagged and the long, narrow window apertures, from which the glass had long since gone, were blocked up with stones and the cracks stuffed with old rags. A great peat fire burned in the middle of the floor, and along the wall hung a row of chickens grabbed after dark from some desolate fowlyard. In each corner of the great room was a litter of dried grass held in place by a frame of stones. These were communal beds, and Tessa, bringing her thoughts back to her own condition, realised she was lying in a smaller version assembled perhaps by Finn.

Finn. Where was he? Apart from a few old men, heads together in deep discussion, and some children playing, there was no one . . . But, yes! A young woman was stirring broth in a huge cooking pot on the fire. That curtain of long, black, straight hair could only belong to one person: Kate, the chief's daughter who had married Martin Jarvey!

'So, you've slept it off, Tessa Riley.' Kate, having turned round, smiled at her friend. 'And God love you, sure I've never seen anyone out for so long!'

The next few moments were charged with the pleasure of renewed friendship, followed by the laughing reassurance 'And don't be worrying about himself, sure he's out working with Martin and they'll be back now the day's darkening – and Tessa, the two of yous are welcome to stay as long as you want.' Eyes as brown as the softest peat suddenly became soulful. 'I'm sorry about the valley . . . Finn told us about it, and Martin's da and his uncle, God rest 'em. And your da, too. Ach, Tessa, what words can I say? We were all shocked. Holy Mother, when I think of the times we've had at Ennan Fair. And now it's gone – blotted out as though it never was. And here am I full o' the talk and yourself just dying for a cup of tay.' She turned to the big iron kettle and called over her shoulder. 'And your friend? The flighty one with the ringlets, and her flirting with all the men?'

'Marie Jane O'Malley? Oh, thank God, she and her family left for Rohira a few weeks before. She's gone into service, but I'll write and tell her we're safe when we . . .' she hesitated, suddenly realising how uncertain the future really was. 'Well, I'll be writing anyways.'

'When you've finished your tay, now, sure we'll go to the van.' Kate frowned at the children who had become quarrelsome. 'I can scarce hear meself think, still less talk with all of their racket! That's if you're steady on your feet.'

Tessa stood to prove that she was. 'Kate, these are not my clothes! God save us, the skirt must have cost a fortune.'

'Well, your own was tattered, and so stained with the peat and all, that Martin said you'd pass out again with mortification to see yourself in such a state! Although the grey's a bit short it hangs nicely, and the lavender blouse suits you. And you're not to bother yourself about the cost – sure wasn't it borrowed in the first place!' Well acquainted with the tinker's euphemism of borrowing for stealing, Tessa smiled. 'C'mon, then, I'll show you our van,' said Kate, her voice ringing with pride.

The tinker children stopped quarrelling and the old men stopped their talking to watch the two young women cross the hall. Pulling a tarpaulin which covered the crumbling doorway to one side, Tessa saw the two barrel-shaped caravans which she had thought a mirage of their starving imaginations, standing in the courtyard, aloof from an assortment of rigs and shelters. The shafts from which the horses had been removed stuck out like rigid limbs and the box on which the driver sat had been let down to make a step.

'And isn't it grand?' said Kate. 'This is ours – the newest! But come on in before the others get back. When me ma and da, and the little sisters, not to mention Finn, get at you, all chances of a chinwag will have gone to the four winds!'

For a moment the two stood admiring the gaily painted van, red and yellows overflowing and mingling with dark and light greens in a riot of colour. Flustered with pride Kate opened the door to let her friend through. 'Oh, isn't it lovely,' breathed Tessa. 'And how proud you must be. It's much nicer than your da's, only don't tell him I said so! Cushions too, begod!'

'Sit on 'em, that's what they're there for!'

'Since when,' teased Tessa, 'did tinkers go in for such refinements?'

'Since I married Martin Jarvey!'

Crimson curtains vied with white crochet work; burnished horse brasses on leather straps decorated the walls on either side of the door; and a lamp was softly lit against the darkening afternoon. A gentle warmth radiated from a tiny iron stove which had been polished until it shone like jet. On the end wall, opposite the door, was a set of three shelves where blue and white plates gleamed, and cups were still swinging gently from the vibration of their entry.

The sight of it to Tessa was a cruel reminder of the dresser which had been her father's pride. They, too, had stood plates on it, the bottom shelf being reserved for her hairbrushes and her father's jar of poteen. The present scene of cosy domesticity made Tessa realise more than ever that she was homeless. There was no place where by right she could lay her head. No place on God's earth which exuded the familiarity of home. The comfort of her father's croft filled her mind; the regularity of labour; an ordered way of life – it's all gone, she thought dully, wiped out as though it had never been.

'I can imagine what's going through your mind,' said Kate softly. 'And it's awful sorry I am.' Then she added, to ease her friend's memory away from painful thoughts, 'I still have the little goat you gave me, and would you believe, I remembered how to make cheese! And me breathing, as God is my judge, has never troubled me since I took to the goat's milk.' She paused and touched her friend's arm. 'I am greatly and for ever in your debt. And you are welcome – indeed, did me da not say the same to Finn? – you are welcome to Spider Murphy's hospitality for as long as you like.'

And so they settled comfortably on the cushions to talk

7

of how Martin had adapted to the tinker way of life and was much respected by her father and the other chiefs, until the coming of the men set them in a flurry.

Finn's pleasure at seeing his love almost back to her normal self was tinged with dismay at there being no immediate privacy in which he could tell her of this pleasure. Tessa knew what he was thinking. Their eyes met and all the warmth of his love was there for her to behold. Her face reddened. Her heart began to beat faster. With a desperate effort she looked about for a diversion.

'And you've not changed at all, Martin Jarvey,' she teased. 'Still wearing that hideous houndstooth jacket!' He brushed back the floppy hair from his forehead and grinned an acknowledgement which told her that, despite his air of bland insolence with which no one could quarrel, he sympathised with their predicament.

After Spider and Mrs Murphy, who remained by the door due to lack of space, had expressed their sorrow at the disaster which had taken her father, they all filed out solemnly, the elders first. Finn reached for Tessa's hand, and squeezed it reassuringly; she looked up at him and he returned the look with a conspiratorial wink. We are safe, it seemed to convey; safe and warm, and together. Having reached the long room of the ruined house, Tessa was quite overwhelmed to see the number of tinkers now assembled to share the communal cooking pot. The air was filled with their own, unintelligible language of Shelta, interspersed with shrieks of laughter and heated argument. Her father used to say that the only good tinker was a dead one. But, she comforted herself, Spider Murphy and his wife are good people. Kate is wonderful and Martin is one of us. Although, glancing at the chief, he looked fiercer than she ever remembered.

He was tall and thin, with long, gangling limbs; his hair was twisted into a pigtail, and his eyes were permanently narrowed and alert. As if all this were not enough to demand immediate respect, he was afflicted with a facial twitch which would set his gold earring ajig.

The tinkers having obtained their share of the pot sat and ate together in groups, the dogs lying watchful. Tessa and Finn, still with much to talk about, stayed with their friends.

8

As the evening wore on, the youngest of the riotous children stumbled, tired, dirty and fully clad, into their couches of dried grass to sleep. The elders sat about drinking and talking. Someone was playing a sad tune on an old fiddle, and a woman crooned a lullaby in an attempt to soothe a fretful child.

Tessa and Finn, wanting to be alone but not daring to make the effort, contented themselves with a series of sly little love looks. Occasionally Finn would rake the ashes with a stick, turning the clump of turf nearest to him to expose the red-hot surface. Now that Tessa was recovered, Finn's spirits were so high he felt he could go forward and conquer the world. He was better fed than ever before; earning money to jingle in his pocket; and was fairly certain of his place in the camp. He wanted to throw down the stick and reach out to Tessa, to pull her up from where she was drying out rushes and to swing her round, to dance with sheer exhilaration at their amazing good luck.

As though reading his mind, Mrs Murphy walked toward them. The lurid glare of the exposed curves illuminated the furrows which ran from eye to lip in her long face, giving her a sinister expression. She was swarthy, like her husband, and also tall and thin. Gold teeth in the cavern of her mouth gleamed as brightly as the golden hoops through her ears.

Nodding toward Tessa, and then jerking her head in Finn's direction, she said in a loud voice, 'He says you want to be married.'

Finn stopped the raking. 'We do so, Mrs Murphy.'

'I was talking to herself.'

The great room instantly became quiet. All eyes were on Mrs Murphy. Kate and Martin, who had moved further away to allow their friends time to talk, now hurried back to their support.

'Sure, and don't I know very well what you want, Finn Collins,' continued Mrs Murphy. 'But is it what she wants? Will you speak up now, Tessa Riley?'

'Yes –' replied Tessa, feeling slightly intimidated by Mrs Murphy's presence.

'You don't sound so sure?'

Finn's idea of being married over the brush had seemed wonderful at the time; it had been part of the euphoria of

imminent rescue. But now, surrounded by the strange faces
of the tinkers, rough and gruff with their alien language, and
the chief's wife making a spectacle of it – not to mention the
suddenness – she played for time.

'Broomstick weddings . . . ' she stammered. 'Sure, they're
not legal – '

'Ach,' pounced Mrs Murphy. 'So, that's the way of
it – a broomstick wedding isn't good enough for ye!'

'No! No!' cried Tessa. 'I didn't say that at all.'

'What are you saying, then? Such weddings have been
good enough for us since time began. What does it matter
whether you stand before a priest or Spider Murphy?' She
looked about her, black eyes daring anyone to answer. No
one did. The furrows on her face grew deeper. Her nostrils
flared on an intake of breath. 'Attend me closely now, the
pair of yous. Have you money? Sure, are ye well heeled
enough to pay for a priest? Matrimony in the Holy Mother
church doesn't come free, y'know.' Holding their gaze like a
stoat with a rabbit, she called on their imaginations. 'If you're
wanting to stand in a dark and draughty church, paying for
the services of a priest you don't know, saying words you
don't understand – and with a stranger dragged in off the
streets as a witness – '

'God love you, Tessa!' exclaimed Martin. 'It'll be more like
a funeral than a wedding!' With a glance toward Mrs Murphy
to make certain she did not object to his interruption, he
continued. 'Listen, this marvellous idea has just leapt into
me head. Why don't you get married over the brush with us,
and later with a priest?' He then added with his swaggering
smile, 'A tinker wedding was good enough for me. Sure, I
took no harm, did I now? And it would make Kate and me
very happy to attend y'both.'

Finn did not need to ponder on any of this. He thought
it the ideal solution and immediately put all his powers of
persuasion into the acceptance of the idea. 'Mrs Murphy's
right about the money, Tess. We'll need every penny for the
fare across.'

Tessa caught his look of eager anticipation. He was
willing her to agree. Her heart lifted, recalling what he
had said when they had sighted the caravans: 'Let's make
sure our little 'un has got a proper name and a da. Besides,'

he had added with a wink, 'there's no harm in me making sure of you, is there?' And so her hesitation was overcome.

If Finn had expected to be married at once he was disappointed. 'Marry in haste, repent at leisure,' Mrs Murphy said. Besides, she warned, it was unlucky to wed without decent money behind you, and a man had to show he could work and be a good provider.

Having agreed to a tinker wedding, Mrs Murphy there and then consulted with Rosie, who had raised fourteen children on the crystal, as to an auspicious date. Finn and Tessa had to place their hands on the crystal, and after some moments of gazing into it, Rosie announced that Fate indicated a spring wedding.

'Spring?' echoed Finn in dismay. He had hoped to be married and across the sea to England by then.

'Early spring,' replied Rosie, and added with a flourish, 'the seventeenth of March, St Patrick's Day.'

Murmurs of approval rose and flared into a burst of communal anticipation. Finn's crestfallen expression gradually lifted.

Although Tessa too had hoped to be married sooner, she was also carried along with the general excitement, for a St Patrick's Day wedding seemed to elevate their standing immediately. It was also the time that Murphy got itchy feet and took to the roads.

Kate embraced Tessa in a whirl of happiness, and then standing on tiptoe she kissed Finn gravely. Her dark eyes surveyed the scarf about his sinewy throat and immediately her thin fingers began to unfasten it.

'You and Tessa are engaged now, Finn,' she said busily. 'Did Martin not tell you it's our custom that you give her your scarf to wear as a sign that you've given her your love?'

Startled at being the centre of attention, Finn now realised why Martin had given him a new neckerchief.

'Ah, he did so, and did it not slip me mind with talk of the wedding and all!' He took the scarf from his throat and stood for a moment, uncertain what to do with it.

'Go on, give it to her, or she'll think you've changed your mind!' Kate stood, hands behind her back, watching indulgently as the scarf changed hands. Tessa tied it about her hair in the manner of the other tinker women.

11

'How do I look?' she asked, laughing.

'Just as a bride-to-be should look – radiant,' enthused Kate.

'Go on,' cut in Martin giving Finn a nudge. 'You're allowed to seal the bargain with a kiss.'

Finn was not at all sure he wanted to while surrounded by so attentive an audience. But, just in case it was the only opportunity, he decided to take advantage, and with a smile stepped toward Tessa. The pleasure of the unexpected embrace sent their hearts racing and emotions whirling. They held each other as though they would never let go, ever again, and the peremptory symbolic kiss had already kindled to warmth when Mrs Murphy's stern voice intervened.

'Being spoken for doesn't mean you're married. And until you are, Tessa will continue to sleep in the van with our Kate, and Finn under the rigs with Martin.' Although well aware of Tessa's pregnancy, the chief's wife added the maxim for which she was noted and often mimicked. 'Spider Murphy's camp, you will remember is a good one. There's no lying, cheating or stealing – and,' her eyes scanned the two young people, 'no fornicating.' The gold teeth gleamed. 'Got it?' They both nodded solemnly.

When Mrs Murphy had gone and the tinkers had resumed their previous diversions, Tessa turned to Kate with a worried frown.

'We . . . Finn and me,' she began earnestly, 'we can't possibly come between Martin and you like this . . . What the divil's your ma thinking of?'

'Will you not worry, now. You're not coming between us, Martin will see to that! But you'd better not let her catch the two of yous together! She doesn't care what you got up to before – just so long as there's none of it in her camp!'

'Oh, I wouldn't dream of crossing her,' said Tessa. 'Your ma's been very good to us, so it's the least we can do to respect what she says.' This was not entirely the truth of the matter. Tinkers were notorious for laying curses, and although not afraid for herself, she was not for anything befalling the baby; and so she played for safety.

Finn nodded in agreement and made an exaggerated gesture of hopelessness to Martin, who laughed uproariously until Finn playfully got him into a wrestling stranglehold and told him to laugh his way out of that!

Chapter Two

Finn Collins was the kind of young man who always functioned better when he had a goal to aim for, and having a time limit was a marvellous incentive to be earning as much money as possible for a 'real stylish wedding'. The occasion, according to Martin Jarvey, would be as much a social celebration for the tinkers as a personal celebration for Finn and Tessa, especially with the date being the seventeenth of March.

From now on, Martin was to be his mentor, and Martin did things with flair. New clothes would be needed. And for the wedding feast, a fine salmon perhaps, or half an ox to be roasted? And the drink! 'Ach, God love you, Finn, you'll have to fetch it up in barrels!' Martin smiled to himself. He would not put it past Rosie, the crafty old biddy, to have influenced the crystal to come up with that date so that the St Patrick's day celebrations would be at Finn's expense!

Martin was in the way of donkey trade, hiring, buying and selling. He loaned Finn a donkey and cart free of charge to play for hire in the surrounding area. Eager to earn, Finn was in the nearest town before the shop shutters were up, and being strong to lift and load, gained employment over those of lesser strength or with only a handcart to their credit.

He liked the feel of coins in his pocket. It gave him pleasure to hear them jingling together and to add up at the end of the day how much he had earned. Not that he returned to Spider Murphy's winter quarters every night. If there was a promise of early work, he slept in some unsuspecting farmer's hayloft, stable or outbuilding.

When he had saved sufficient money the first thing Finn bought was a Connemara shawl to keep Tessa warm. After seeing her shivering with cold when they were lost and wandering in the mountains, he had sworn to himself that she would never, ever, be cold again. He had dreamed of standing behind his love, folding the warmth of it about her shoulders, watching her face light up with surprised pleasure; and now he was thrilled to have realised his dream.

Tessa and Kate exchanged amused and indulgent glances as Finn boasted of his prowess in the commercial world.

'He's getting to sound more like your Martin every day!'

'God forbid!' came Kate's reply.

Finn related the wonders of civilised life, but to Kate fell the pleasure of revelation. With her hair fastened up in Finn's scarf, and warmly wrapped in the new shawl, Tessa went with Kate to sell pegs, charms, baskets and decorative rushware. They did not travel as far as the town but visited the villages and small communities.

Tessa had never set foot out of her native Ennan in all her eighteen years, and these encounters introduced her to a different way of life. Her previous experience of collective living had been primitive in the extreme, and life with the tinkers was not a lot different. But nothing she had heard prepared her for the surprise of stone-built cottages laid out neatly on either side of a street, each with a rick of turf at the side and colourful curtains declaring pride of ownership.

The little shops were another source of delightful bewilderment. Tessa stared at the goods displayed: the jars and boxes; the huge squares of white, glistening lard, and great slabs of yellow cheese. She was pleased to recognise words and read them out to Kate, from Lipton's treacle to Friar's Balsam. As for the owners of these establishments, surely they couldn't be mortal!

There was not a lot of time to stand and ponder, for Kate adhered to a strict principle of not returning to camp until all the wares were sold. The urge to sell up became more acute as the winds began to bite or the rain to fall more heavily.

The actual doorstep selling was another source of amazement to Tessa, for Kate's general attitude underwent a complete change when confronted with the woman of the house. Servile, humble, shoulders huddled and head bowed, she began to wheeze as though still afflicted with the asthma.

'Sure, it's easy, Tessa,' she laughed. 'Especially when you've been at it as long as I have. You can tell as soon as they open the door what kind of approach to make.'

'God Almighty, Kate. I couldn't be doing all o' that.'

'Could not?' Her eyebrows shot up. 'Did I not hear when we were at Ennan Fair that you got up to all kinds of schemes?'

Tessa laughed and felt her face go hot, despite the cold wind. 'I did so,' she admitted. 'But never having wheezed I wouldn't know how to start!' She pulled the shawl closer and glanced across at the shop. 'Kate, I've just got this marvellous idea . . . Instead of going on the doors and chancing your luck as to whether they'll buy or not, why not ask the people in the shop to take the pegs at, say, three halfpence a dozen. They might have the rushware, too, with Christmas coming, and all.'

Kate frowned in consideration, and after a few moments said, 'That's all very well as an idea, but I'd be losing a halfpenny on each dozen.'

'You'd be able to sell more, though, and you could provide them with a regular supply until you leave in the spring.'

Kate was impressed, and after a few more moments of reflection nodded agreement. 'Will you set it up for us? You being one of them, like. As you know, they don't trust tinkers and gypsies. And really, Tessa, you look as honest and pure as a beautiful nun with your shawl over your head and tucked beneath your chin – they'll fall for anything you tell 'em!'

'I'm only telling them the truth,' persisted Tessa, slightly alarmed. 'I live in mortal fear of trouble with the police and all . . . ' With an uncertain glance at her friend, she walked toward the shop. It was as Kate had said. Mrs Doonan the shopkeeper had never seen so honest a face in years, and yes, to be sure she would take as many pegs, good quality, mind, as they were able to produce. 'But I'll only trade with yourself. I don't want any o' them scurvy, light-fingered tinkers in my shop!' She shook her head slowly, clearly unable to fathom Tessa's involvement, and before further observations were offered, Tessa took her leave. Kate was awaiting the result some halfway down the street, and to celebrate the new trading agreement, introduced her friend to froth-edged glasses of Guinness in a public house warm with fires and bright with talk. Indeed, thought Tessa, stretching her legs beneath the marble-topped table, the world is a marvellous fine place!

As the new year of 1899 settled in, and its progress lengthened the days and made the winds less sharp, Tessa and Finn began to plan their wedding in all earnestness. The event made Tessa especially a popular figure, and in order to repay the tinkers in some small way for their hospitality, she taught those who were interested to understand numbers and add up simple amounts.

'Will you tell us now,' said Tessa when Martin and Kate were discussing aspects of the ceremony, 'why it's your custom to jump over a broomstick? Why jump over anything?'

'Tradition,' replied Kate. 'Sure, there's as much tradition attached to our ceremonies as yours. The broomstick represents a line; you're leaving the single life and crossing to the married. The broomstick itself is full of meanings. It's a sign of industry, and it has to be made of gorse or some other flowering thorn – the flowers are for fertility.'

'And you can guess what the thorns are for!' cut in Martin.

Kate cast him a sobering glance and continued primly. 'Thorns are the troubles of life which you'll face together. And of course there are lots of superstitions, warnings and omens.'

'You'll be sparing us those!' laughed Tessa. 'Finn's terrible superstitious – and I'll be nervous enough as it is!'

Following discussions with Martin, Finn aspired to wedding clothes for himself and his bride. The source of fulfilment for these aspirations was a bearded pedlar who wore a tall hat and carried his wares in a bundle.

Having bought a pair of black-and-white checked trousers, Finn was soon talked into buying 'a wrap for your lady's shoulders – of the finest cotton, eh? See how delicate the ivory colouring is – what better for a spring bride? And the fringe, eh? Just look at the fringe. Finger it. Doesn't every

16

young woman of taste like a wrap with a silken fringe? All the fine shoulders at all the country garden parties will be draped in ivory cotton like this. Come now, my fine young man, what do you say to so great a bargain?'

At last, the day which Tessa and Finn had looked forward to for so long dawned. It was still early, the sky flushed with pink and the larks on their first song, when Spider Murphy and the families travelling with him took to the road, heading toward the lucky site of the Hill of Achnochell. 'It's a glorious place,' whispered Kate. 'For didn't Martin and me marry there!'

There was a great feeling of release, of buoyant spirits, as the tinkers left the ruins of the big house. It felt, even to Tessa and Finn, like a resurrection, an emergence from the tomb; from darkness into light.

The bridal pair travelled with the Jarveys, Tessa on the box of the caravan with Kate, and Finn walking with Martin at the head of the long-tailed pony. Tessa wore a gown of summer green, begged unashamedly by Kate from the public house where they drank Guinness. She then crocheted a tiara-like cap which complemented the long fringed wrap. Never had a bride looked so winsomely happy.

The St Patrick's day weather was just as Rosie had said it would be, dry and fine, with shafts of sun and shifting cloud. By late afternoon the new camp had been reached and set up more quickly than ever Spider Murphy remembered.

The huge fire was kindled, and while the tinkers were busy with the camp, Martin and Finn unloaded barrels of ale and great jars of poteen from the carts. Tessa, Kate and her sisters had gathered shamrock and were now distributing it for every man to wear in his hat and every woman on her dress, sash or apron – first having made a posy for Tessa to be married with.

Some of the women, wearing greasy aprons from having previously roasted half an ox, were engaged in cutting and slicing. Others prepared to make griddle bread when the fire reddened, and all around children frisked and dogs barked their pleasure at being on the road again.

While all this was taking place Finn began to erect a tarpaulin shelter for himself and Tessa. He spread armfuls of sweet-smelling rushes to make a soft couch and grinned at Martin.

17

'I can't believe it! Just think, tonight I'll be sharing a rig with Tess! Can't say as I'll be missing you, boyo!'

'How the devil d'you think I feel?' came the good-natured reply. 'Barred from me own bed, in me own van, for three bloody months . . . ' He looked about to be sure he was not overheard and mimicked his mother-in-law: 'And all because "Murphy's camp is a good one. There's no cheating, stealing – or fornicating. Got it!" By all the saints, Finn, it'll seem like my wedding night all over again, never mind yours!'

At last all the preparations were finished, the shamrock distributed, and excitement was running high. The site behind the hill of Achnochell was a hollow of soft, springy earth, sheltered by a great circle of early flowering gorse bushes.

Nothing could have been brighter, more natural or spring-like. Tessa and Finn conceded it was well worth waiting for. There was a magic in the atmosphere, a magic older than the hills. An intangible force of good will, as though the very ground was hallowed by a thousand years of joyful celebration.

Kate observed Tessa's thoughts and squeezed her hand. 'I shall pray to St Teresa herself that you'll both be as happy and content as Martin and me.'

Tessa, overwhelmed by emotion, could only nod her thanks; and that was all she had time for, because the fiddle and flute had struck up; Finn was by her side; someone thrust the shamrock posy into her hand; and with the other tucked in Finn's arm, and Martin and Kate walking behind, they led the raggle-taggle bridal procession round the great circle of gorse three times for good luck. Tessa walked, head held high, with all the pride of conscious beauty and admiration; and Finn swaggered with the certainty of attainment.

'There's our rig,' he teased as they promenaded. 'Wouldn't put it past Mrs Murphy to think up some something else to keep us apart!'

'Just let her try!'

'And are we not the grand pair, now?' It had been on his tongue to add that her father would have been proud, but on reflection and recalling the old man's dislike of tinkers, her da would not have been pleased. He had not been called Proud Riley for nothing.

'We are so,' she answered. 'Especially yourself.' Never had she seen him look so handsome. The cut of the coat and check trousers set off his figure, his curls were gleaming with the blue-black sheen of a raven's wing. Preening and flaunting, he was every inch the bridegroom. And in all of this, neither had given a thought to Holy Mother church.

'And doesn't the big fella look a real boyo?' said Murphy, his body jingling with chains and bracelets. 'He doesn't know that I borrowed the white shirt from a clothesline way back. Spider, I said to meself, every goy dreams of getting married in a white shirt and so shall the big fella – and doesn't the coat fit him well?'

'It does so,' answered Mrs Murphy, who, dressed in purple, looked more sepulchral then ever. 'But I'm sure it'd fit the fella that owned it much better!'

And so the procession continued. It featured every style and every colour of clothing, and the strangest assortment of footwear – the latter providing Finn's only regret. The pedlar's stock had not included shoes, so he was getting married in the old split boots he had once considered joining the army to replace.

As the third and last circuit was completed the tinkers spread into a circle. Tessa and Finn stood before the tinker chief who, in an embroidered waistcoat and frilled shirt, looked less fierce than usual. He even smiled before beginning to speak, and was so amiable that Tessa, who had been a little nervous of doing anything out of order, felt more at ease.

'By the power vested in me,' he began, 'from time immemorial, I perform this marriage ceremony which has been handed down by word of mouth since the days our fathers travelled in Egypt.' His dark glance encompassed everyone. 'We are all gathered on this sacred ground to witness the bonding together of Tessa Riley and Finn Collins, according to the ancient rite of our people.'

He inclined his head to Martin Jarvey who, grinning broadly, and mightily pleased to be attending his friend, reached for Finn's right hand and bound it to Tessa's left with a white cord. He tied three knots, which Spider explained were symbols of fidelity, fertility and long life.

As the bridal pair promised to cherish and be faithful

to one another until death, the clouds parted like a curtain and the sun momentarily blazed. If it had been the blessing of heaven no one could have been more impressed. Even the babies hushed their grizzling and the dogs stopped their yelping. Larks sang, a distant lamb bleated, and then Kate stepped forward, the ceremonial broomstick resting on her outstretched hands.

The actual broom was a yellow glory of flowering gorse twigs tied onto a gnarled stick which had been in the Murphy family for generations. It had been decorated by Kate's younger sisters with brightly coloured ribbons which they had dyed and twisted themselves.

Martin placed his hands over Kate's and together they extended the broomstick a few inches above the ground. With hands still bound together, Tessa and Finn now had to jump over it to complete the ceremony. Clearly this was the most popular part, for the tinkers crowded closer, making jokes.

'You need a drink to steady your step!'

'Don't do it – back off while there's time!'

And warnings. 'Don't be stumbling, or sure to God you'll part!'

Then encouragement. ''Tis St Patrick's Day, boyo, you can't go wrong!'

The older children were pushed to the front of the circle and the smaller ones hoisted onto shoulders to obtain a better view.

'This is it, girleen,' said Finn, trying to disguise his anxiety with a wink. 'The last hurdle! We've got to clear it now. You heard what they said!'

'Ach, away with your superstitions!' She diffused his anxiety by gathering all her love into the glance which met his. With Tessa holding her skirts with her free hand, they jumped over the broomstick, clearing it completely. No catching of clothes, no drawing of blood on the thorns – nothing, thought Tessa thankfully, to indicate anything other than a wonderful, wonderful life with the man she adored. Then, as the tinkers cheered, Spider Murphy cut the cord which had bound their hands.

The bride and groom, not wanting to seem too eager, shyly embraced while Martin and Kate showered them with

20

gorse petals, and beneath the golden cascade their pact was sealed with a long kiss.

As they released each other the concertina started up the Bridal Reel. Finn grabbed Tessa's hand and led the dance while the tinkers roared out their wedding song in Shelta but the chorus was easily understood and Tessa and Finn joined in it heartily.

Dirram day doo a day
Dirram doo a da dee O,
Dirram day doo a day,
Cheers for the tinkers' wedding.

Then most of the women and all of the children headed toward the ox for the best cuts, whilst the others having their priorities in a different order took to the drink. They toasted the bride and groom in the 'best true water this side o' the Connemara mountains!'

'And the Saint himself bless you! Let's drink to St Patrick of Ireland!'

'St Patrick! Tessa and Finn!'

'An' the shamrock! The dear little shamrock of Ireland!'

'Ah, the blessed flower. To the shamrock then, and St Patrick, and Tessa and Finn!'

Kate laid her hand on Tessa's arm. 'God bless you both and may you want for nothing.'

As the afternoon passed into evening and sunlight gave place to firelight, the celebration was uproariously high. A couple of miles away the villagers, hearing the noise on the still night air, thanked God for the safety of locked doors and turned snugly in their beds.

Men were swinging their partners in reels and jigs, arming it and footing it with great gusts of laughter and screams of enjoyment. Spider Murphy, not renowned for his levity, made jokes. Rosie's husband, who could drink two bottles of whisky and still walk a straight line, challenged all comers.

Tessa and Finn were impatient to be on their own and wanted nothing more than to crawl under their rig, but still the dancing continued. Spider and Mrs Murphy had already retired when Martin and Kate announced they were turning

21

in. 'By all the saints, Finn,' complimented Martin, 'that was the grandest hooley . . . ' And then hesitantly, and jerking his head toward their rig, 'Are you not for the rushes yourselves? Begod, I thought you'd be the first away.'

'Not much choice,' explained Finn, glancing at the merry-makers. 'This lot will turn awful bawdy if they see us going off and, well, Tess would be embarrassed. As you know, her da was terrible strict, and anyways, life was not as free and easy at Ennan.'

Martin's pleasant face split into a grin and he playfully punched Finn's shoulder. 'Ah, the path of true love was never smooth!' And off he went, swaying happily towards his caravan.

It seemed hours later when Finn eventually took his wife's hand and made for the tarpaulin. The huge fire was banked up, the drink had already stopped flowing, and only a few were left on their feet. He crawled inside and held the entrance open until she joined him. Once inside, she peered through the gap where the flaps of tarpaulin met.

'Finn?' she said hoarsely.

'What is it?'

'Two of them have just dropped to the ground right out-side, stretched out like corpses they are . . . Surely,' dismay seeped into her voice, 'surely they're not going to stay there all night?'

'If you don't want 'em to, I'll go and drag the devils away to the fire. It'll be a mercy I'm doing them, for the poteen was terrible strong and some were mixing it with ale – they say it takes all the heat out of your body and you wake up cold to the bone. Oh, they've had a skinful all right – drunk as lords . . . ' His words had taken him outside, and now he was back, panting with the exertion. 'Are you easier now?' he teased.

'Not much . . . Drunk as lords, you say. I've heard drunken lords get up to all kinds of things.'

'Just let 'em try,' came the grim comment as they reached out to each other. 'Oh, Tess, it's been the devil of a time since we were together like this . . . '

'But it isn't the same as before, when we used to meet in our special cave. No one knew of it and we were certain no one would bother us – '.

'This is our wedding night,' he said patiently. 'The date we've looked forward to for what seems a lifetime. Our wedding night, and here we are talking low like a pair of horse thieves – and all I want is to love you. Oh, Tess, I can't believe that we're married at last. That you're me wife – what are you still spying out for? Surely you're still not bothered about the boyos outside?'

'I am so . . . Sure, I can't help being apprehensive.'

'But they're legless!'

'That's just what I mean. They could stagger, with their cups, to the nearest rig – and no tinker's going to set eyes on me, well, undressed.'

'We don't have to be undressed,' he assured. 'Do we now?' The siren call of his voice, coming at her in the darkness, took her into his arms. They held each other tightly. Like people who had been parted for many years.

After a little while the fierceness relaxed, and Tessa became aware of the beat of her heart echoing from her breast to her ears. She felt weak with need of him and yet strong in the knowledge that he was hers. The muscles of his upper arm flexed at the touch of her hand and then rippled across his shoulders. Her fingers twined about the black curls, urging his head forward as their lips met in what Tessa considered their first 'legal' kiss.

Mrs Murphy no longer had any hold over them. The release, the emotional relief, scattered all thoughts of intruders. Nothing mattered now but herself and Finn. Oh, merciful heaven! She moaned softly, not realising that caresses through clothes could be so rapturously sensuous. There was also the tempting, the tantalising promise of further delights should the impediments be removed. Her hands strayed from his neck to his throat, opening the buttons of his shirt, exploring the smooth undulations, spreading over the breadth of his chest, feeling his warm flesh.

Her body smouldered beneath the summer-green gown, her skin ached for the touch of his rough hands. The need to be closer, to feel her heart beating against his became paramount. Her fingers grappled with the bodice of her gown, and beneath it, her chemise. As though her young life depended on it she shrugged the fabric off her shoulders and pressed herself against him with a sigh of great achievement.

23

'Oh, Tess, Tess,' he murmured against her hair. 'This rig could well be heaven . . .'

'It is . . . It's paradise itself . . .'

And there beneath the confines of the tarpaulin shelter, they offered to each other their love; offered, took, and gave with all the wild ardour and eagerness of youth.

'We'll not always sleep in rigs,' he murmured later. 'Sure, we're going to have real beds, with a mattress and four legs, one in each corner. D'you know, love,' he said sleepily, 'Martin Jarvey showed me one in town, but it was propped up with bricks because one of the legs was broken . . .'

But Tessa was already asleep.

Chapter Three

When everyone had recovered from the wedding and the families were travelling again, Finn grandly announced that it was time he and Tess were moving on toward Dublin. 'To England,' he added, though they could scarcely have forgotten, for he was often talking about it.

'Move on?' echoed Mrs Murphy. It took a moment or so for her astonishment to fade, and then her mouth formed a persuasive smile. 'Sure, it's only the heathen would have their first child born on foreign soil! 'Tis surprised I am at the pair of yous!' Before either could answer she went on guardedly, 'Besides, you don't want to be frightened by any o' them sights of civilisation do you now?'

Tessa was about to say that no sight could be more frightening than the migrating bog which had destroyed Ennan, but Mrs Murphy pushed her long, narrow face nearer to tell of a boy child who had been born with the face of a pig because his mother had been chased by one on the loose.

'Not that it did 'em any harm – travelling the fairs with him they are, making a fortune out of misfortune. Y'see, Tessa, you can't be too careful while you're carrying. Will you not stay until the birth, eh? An Irish child should be born on Irish soil.' She then addressed herself to Finn. 'Surely, you understand that much, you big gobeen!'

Mrs Murphy in such a state was not to be argued with, and Martin warned him off with a quick frown.

'Irish soil!' he exploded a little later, when he was walking at the head of one of the donkeys with Tessa. 'What's so special about Irish soil?' He struck the earth viciously with his boot. 'Have I not seen enough of it? Have I not dug it, coaxed it, pleaded with it? And what happens? The spuds are blighted, even the peat fails, and the rain! Dear God, the rain!' He choked to a frustrated silence, and then launched out again.

'I'll tell you this, Tess. No child of ours is going to spend its life sleeping on rushes under rigs, and roaming about the country with a half-wild bunch of knacker's kids!' He ran a hand through his curls, realising with something of shock that he had voiced his fear. He had been afraid of Tessa becoming too settled. If anyone had told him he would have been months with the tinkers instead of only a few days, he would never have believed them. 'I want better things, not only for the child, but for you, girleen. Mrs Murphy doesn't seem to understand that we must leave – and soon! Martin said if we continue much further on the tinker's route, we'll be miles out of our way for Dublin. Can't you see, we must go soon – *now*,' he corrected himself, 'while I've still some money left in me pocket from the wedding. What does she think I've worked me fingers to the bloody bone for? Listen, love, if we don't move off on our own now, I can't see there'll be any chance of us leaving this bog-ridden country ever again.'

He turned, wondering at her silence. 'You do want to go, Tess?' His recently acknowledged fears became one major doubt, and struck him like a blow.

Her large eyes, usually a summer blue, were almost as grey as the clouds overhead. Her glance was wide and honest. Finn saw hesitation and knew what people meant when they talked of their hearts sinking.

Tessa lowered her gaze from the disappointment in his. It wasn't that she didn't want to go, just that at present familiarity was all. She would miss being with Kate and the Murphy girls – especially after the sense of isolation that had followed the disaster. She supposed it was her condition, too, which had taken the edge off her original enthusiasm. And the fanciful idea of perhaps Kate becoming pregnant, and them comparing babies and all . . . she reflected briefly on the ways of God – to be sure, they were past all her understanding. There were Kate and Martin, settled and eager to produce, yet still waiting! It didn't seem fair of the Almighty at all. She sighed. Of course Finn had always been talking of going across, and in her heart she had known that a decision would have to be made, but now, it seemed, the time had arrived.

She felt his hand warm on her shoulder. Heard his voice earnest and soft against her ear. 'Tess, we're croft people. We're settlers, not travellers. This is an opportunity to better ourselves. Do you want to repeat the pattern of life in Ennan?'

He had struck the right chord. She remembered the babies that never survived; the outbreaks of croup and cholera; the hand-to-mouth existence; unknown fevers that took pigs and people overnight.

'Besides,' he coaxed, 'we really can't stay with the knackers for ever. They're a shifty race, not counting Kate, of course, but Spider's the chief, and I don't fancy having to answer to him for the rest of me life. We've got the baby to think of, and there'll be others, Tess.' There was an upsurge of pride in his voice as he referred to himself as a family man. 'The little divil won't be one on its own like you and me. Listen to me now,' he urged, playing his last card, forcing her eyes by the tone of his voice to meet his. 'Your da wanted better things for you.' In the silence that followed he seemed to be holding his breath.

Tessa regarded him solemnly. He was certainly right on that score: her da had assumed she wanted better things, and of course she had, but in her own time. She had felt then as she did now a kind of helplessness, a rankling of the spirit, of being suddenly swept away, carried along on the tide of someone else's assumptions. Not for the world would she hurt Finn, but her emotions were struggling with the need to assert some part of her individuality.

'Everything you say is so, but you've not taken me into account.'

He was clearly puzzled. 'Ach, you're having me on, Tess.'

'I was never more serious. Will you tell me now what happens if I want to stay here with Kate, until I've had the baby? What if I, like Mrs Murphy, am of the opinion the child should be born on Irish soil? That's what I mean.'

Even then, Tessa realised, it was not herself who made

an impression, but all the mysteries surrounding birth. They crowded upon him, eroding like nothing else could his certainty of purpose. Powerless before such a barrage, he quickly surrendered his last resolve on the altar of motherhood.

'To be sure, Tess,' he said, deflated. 'If that's what you want, we'll stay until after it's born.'

'Even though,' she added, 'by then we'll be miles out of the way of Dublin, you'll have gone through all your money, and we may never get a chance to leave this bog-ridden land again?'

Having stemmed the tide of his presumptions and derived some small satisfaction, she put out a hand to stroke the donkey's ear. Her hair was not fastened in the scarf, tinker style, but blowing where the wind would take it. She walked with that lilt to her skirts, and the confident uplift of head. Once again, in Finn's eyes, she was the Celtic goddess who, with shawl across her shoulders and crook in hand, had led the herd of goats across the mountainy outcrops of Ennan.

He took so long in answering, she wondered if he had heard. 'Yes, even with all that . . . ' He felt both puzzled and fascinated. 'I can't make you out, Tess. Are you for teasing me, now?'

A tiny smile tugged at the corners of her mouth, hinting at mischievous thoughts. She stretched her hand along the length of the donkey's neck, and looked up at Finn.

'As if I would! And I couldn't be more serious in saying that we ought to make the break soon – as soon as we can.'

'But what about the Irish soil, and all?' he asked on a marvellously incredulous breath.

'What about it!' They both thought of Mrs Murphy and broke into laughter.

'You've made me a very happy fella, Tess. If it wasn't for the donkeys running off, I'd kneel and kiss your feet.'

'Ach, away with your blather,' she blushed, and pushed him away playfully.

'It's all settled then?'

She nodded. 'It is so.'

'Tomorrow then . . . ?'

'So soon?'

'Oh, God give me patience, Tess! Did y'not say the sooner

the better!' His note of frustration lightened. 'Honest, you're as big a tease as Marie Jane O'Malley used to be!'

Despite the exaggeration Tessa was pleased, for she had always admired Marie Jane. But Finn was on with his plans again. 'Tomorrow we'll spill the last of the "true water" and be on our way! We're going places, girleen!'

According to protocol Spider Murphy was the first to be notified, but word quickly reached the others. Martin had enlightened Finn about the tinker's route being off course for Dublin because he knew all the talk about Tessa's baby being born on Irish soil was merely a ploy to hang on a little longer to two willing workers with honest faces and good ideas. Oh, and weren't they impressed by the hooley, the ox and the ale! Martin and Kate, although not averse to a little exploitation, were not for having their friends used in this way.

Kate's supportive and positive attitude did much to bolster Tessa's confidence in the face of Mrs Murphy's second bout of persuasive oratory. Spider's face twitched in agreement with their departure: he was satisfied that Tessa had been repaid for having saved Kate's life, and once again he could boast that Spider Murphy owed no one.

In the hope of another St Patrick's day excess, the tinkers agreed to bid the goys farewell with a traditional well-wishing, but Finn had been warned by Martin not to foot the bill. 'If you put your hand in your pocket now, boyo, y'can say goodbye to your boat fare. I don't need to tell you the knackers are as crafty as a cart load of monkeys! The well-wishing was their idea; let 'em find their own drink.' He pushed back his floppy hair and grinned. 'Have your last hooley on them!'

The fire was stacked high, providing light and warmth and investing the clutter of carts and tarpaulins with a rakish glow to last until the first streak of dawn. The tinkers, who never let a setback stand in the way of a good time, danced and drank and kept the night alive with their shouts and songs.

Tessa and Finn, anxious to make this last occasion a memorable one, indulged in everything on offer. Tessa sang the old favourite songs, 'The Rambling Candy Man', 'Danny, We've Missed Ye' and, for Finn, 'The Lovely Lad of My Dreams'.

'D'you think the people across,' she asked, perching on an upturned barrel, 'will know any of these songs?'

'There'll be new ones,' teased Finn, and putting an arm about her shoulders, winked at Kate. 'In a few weeks from now, I'll have me arm about you, just like this, and will I not say to you, "Tess," I'll say, "sing me a new song"? And would you know, even the birds on the trees will stop to listen – '

'Will you stop your blathering!' she laughed, and pushing him away, called out to Martin. 'Come and dance with me for the last time. Sure, it can't be far off the dawn?'

The new things would come soon enough, but for the moment Tessa wanted to dwell happily on the familiar. Eventually, as the night wound down, she found herself becoming more intense, paying exaggerated attention to gathering their few belongings together; savouring her last drop of poteen, for whatever else was across, there'd be no 'true water' the likes of this! Then reminiscing with Kate on the intrigues of Ennan Fair, talking long and earnestly, with the volubility of those about to say goodbye for the last time.

All too soon, the first streak of dawn split the sky. Haste was now paramount, for in order to reap the luck of a well-wishing, the travellers had to be on their way before daylight.

'Time to be gone!' yelled Spider. He pointed towards the sliver of dawn. 'And the good luck go wid ye!'

The others took up the cry, making the hills echo, 'The good luck go wid ye!'

Finn, who wanted all the good luck he could get, had no intention of lingering. He grabbed the sack which contained their possessions, shook hands with Spider gravely, hugged Martin, and swung Kate off her feet. He nodded to Mrs Murphy and, with a glance at the sky, called for Tessa to hurry.

Kate hastily looped her ivory rosary beads over her friend's neck. 'For the baby to cut its teeth on . . . And take these . . . ' She pushed a bundle of little coats and leggings into Tessa's bag. 'There'll be plenty of time for me to knit some more, the way things are going!' A quick kiss, a strong embrace, and Tessa joined Finn to hurry away, turning to wave until the yells and well wishes faded.

For a little while they walked the track over the hill in

silence, each needing time, a breathing space to catch up with themselves, to adjust from the communal life to the solitary. And it was with the optimism of youth that they recalled not the sad times but the happy ones.

The moorland stretching east from Achnochell was green and firm, with clusters of trees dotted in hollows. Occasionally, a black grouse coughed, and sheep grazing with their lambs scurried away at the sight of the two intruders.

The spring morning being fair and warm, Tessa slipped the Connemara shawl from her shoulders and threaded it through the handles of the hessian bag. She rolled her sleeves to the elbow and squinted up at Finn, eyes narrowed against the sun, and was almost startled to find his gaze already settled on her. His mouth was curving into a grin of sheer pleasure which communicated itself at once. He gave the sack a further hitch onto his shoulder, and they both began to talk at the same time and with such a rush of words that they ended up not in conversation but in torrents of laughter. The next attempt settled into a steady flow of observations.

Distance was measured against what they knew. 'Think of it as going down to Rohira ten times,' Martin had said, 'only the road to Dublin is not half so rough. I should say you've the best part of eighty miles, easily.'

And so they strode along confidently, the joy of discovery making light of the distance. They found generous hospitality, for strangers on foot were an unusual occurrence.

Their bearing and honest faces denied any stamp of the vagabond, yet curiosity informed many a glance. Eyes went straightaway to Finn, in his corduroys, boots and shirt sleeves rolled to the elbow, to dwell on his physique and reckon there was a good deal of strength in those forearms. They eyed the sack, and then looked at the young woman who, despite her travel-stained skirt, collarless man's shirt, and the hessian bag dragging on her shoulder, was an attractive young creature. Every now and then she tied back the cloud of dark hair, as though to attempt some kind of control over it. The air and exercise had enriched the colour and texture of her skin, outlining the curves of her high cheekbones. And such eyes, they thought, blue as a summer's day, and what lashes. God love 'em, someone whispered, they're runaways! They've eloped, the young buggers! Sure, and would it not be the

31

colleen's father they concluded, who did not approve of the big fella!

'Good luck! And may you want for nothing!'

'Hope the weather keeps up!'

The spontaneity of the comments made Tessa feel special, and Finn proud to be at her side. The curious then began to make up stories to misdirect the irate parent whom they expected to be in hot pursuit at any moment.

Looking back on the journey Tessa saw a vivid kaleidoscope of fresh fields, narrow ways and ancient hedges; of old gardens and gnarled trees where yellow primroses eyed them from niches in the grass. There was the green-black secrecy of woods, and graveyards crooked with tombstones; quiet moon-silvered churches, and the brown gloom of wayside inns; springs where dainty ferns waved delicate fingers.

The kaleidoscope effect faded with the weather. 'Would you just know the weather's turned!' exclaimed Tess, fastening her shawl together with a large pin. 'Those last people said we were over halfway there.'

'Every step takes us nearer. Every step means we're that much further on. So, before the rain comes we've got to keep going until we drop.'

'Got it?' she countered, mimicking Mrs Murphy, but Finn had not heard. Hitching up the sack, he was off. She glanced after him, puzzled. Was it an edge of desperation she had detected?

Having left the hollows, the hillocks and the black-faced sheep, the country opened out and took on a more desolate look, even to the signpost at the crossroads, which with its outstretched arms looked like a crucifix.

The sun appearing in hot fitful shafts gave up the struggle at noon, and the wind took over, imperiously driving huge chariots of cloud across the landscape. They tramped on in silence, heads down. No one else was afoot, no friendly faces in doorways – not a doorway in sight, thought Tessa.

'April showers!' she observed, as the first drops fell.

'April bloody downpour! Begod, Tess, the two things I shall always remember about my native land are the peat and the rain. Oh, Holy Mother, why could it not have kept off?'

Hoping food would soften his mood, she shouted above the wind, 'Will you not stop to eat?'

32

'We'll eat on the hoof, girleen.' He slowed his pace and took a heel of the loaf and a wedge of cheese. In silence and bowed against the rain, they walked most of the day, not passing a shelter or dwelling of any kind. In vain she looked for telltale signs of chimney smoke, and strained her ears for the lowing of cattle, neighing of a horse, or even the bark of a dog.

Weary and soaked to the skin they huddled by a ruined wall, bedded down on last year's growth of valerian and brambles, and fell into an exhausted sleep.

The only remedy for warmth, when waking stiff and cold, Finn said, was to start walking. Tessa's shawl being wet was twice as heavy, her shoes squelched, and the leather had stretched so they were now too big and only kept on with difficulty.

And still it rained. But on this second day, a spiral of smoke drew them thankfully to the grandly named Donlan's Bar, which was in actuality a house licensed to sell beer and spirits. They sank onto a settle in the front room by the fire, drank poteen and watched the steam rise from their clothes. Finn slept, but Tessa talked to the few who had assembled and made herself agreeable, in the hope of being allowed to stay the night.

'God love you,' said Donlan, who was old and tattered. 'It's welcome you are, sure I wouldn't put a dog out in this.'

Finn lay on the hearth and Tessa on the settle. Her clothes had dried, and as she listened to the rain gurgling in the troughs and down into the water barrel, she could understand why Finn hated it.

The following morning Finn was awake at half-light. 'C'mon Tess,' he urged, shaking her shoulder. 'Time to be on our way.'

'Would you leave this warm hearth, already?' She gazed blearily at the sight of him hitching the sack onto his shoulder. 'Mother of God,' she breathed, 'you would!'

And so they were out, the wind fresh again, and Tessa yelling impatiently after him, 'Will you not stop to eat?' His only answer was to hitch the sack further and beckon her on. 'What's all the hurry?' she shouted through cupped hands. 'They'll not run out of boats!' And still he did not

33

look back. 'Oh, God give me patience,' she cried to herself and then after him. 'Don't bother waiting for me when you get there!' Exasperated, she sat down by a low wall and rummaged in the hessian bag, pulling out some soda bread, her white teeth sinking into the chunk of brawn left over from supper.

Having eaten, she stuffed the last of the bread in her pocket, pulled up her knees, and clasping them with her hands, pondered on Finn's obsession. Ever since Marie Jane's father, Mr O'Malley, had extolled the virtue of 'having an aim in life' Finn had never been happy unless he had just that. She recalled the pleasure it had given him – and the standing – to talk of 'going across'. The tinkers and people on the way had obviously considered him a 'boyo', and he wasn't really. He was trying too hard to be like Martin Jarvey. This mad dash, for example, was taking things to extremes ... It wasn't entirely the mad dash which rankled, but the fact of him charging on ahead without her. Martin would never have left Kate.

Tessa did not know how long she had slept. Curled up against the wall, she put out a hand to touch Finn and remembered. Christ, she thought, his first stop will be Dublin! Pulling on her shoes, stiff from having dried out too quickly by Donlan's fire, she took up the hessian bag, and feeling greatly refreshed set off. Travelling alone came as a shock, for although of late Finn hadn't said much, she missed the sight of his broad back, and had no stride by which to measure her own. There was no big, rough hand to slip her own into, and any observations, such as the whinnying of a distant goat, were made to herself.

After a couple of hours' steady pacing, the sight of Finn's inert body on the road ahead struck fear into her heart, and gave speed to her feet. He was lying stretched out, just as the earth had received him, the sack rolled to one side.

'Finn? Finn?' She dropped to her knees beside him, calling his name breathlessly, desperately, and at the same time pushing and shoving him onto his back. She saw with a blaze of gratitude that he was breathing, and then her heart plummeted. He was ill. Finn ill? He who had never ailed a day? She could feel the heat of the fever, see the colour of it crimson on his face. His parched lips moved. ' ... must get on . . . the road . . . ' His eyes, diamond-bright, opened to stare unseeingly and closed again.

She had heard that people with fevers raved and suffered delusions, and felt relieved that the 'mad dash' must have been part of it. She had also heard that people with fevers have to be kept warm. Yes, that was it. Warmth. Oh, God save him! And then in a fervent agony she repeated the words as a prayer. Quickly removing her shawl she covered him up and pushed the hessian bag beneath his head as a pillow. What, she thought in sudden panic, what will happen when the chill of night comes? What if it rains again? What if . . . ? She heard the sound of the distant goat again, steering her memory away from Ennan churchyard.

'Finn? Darling Finn, can you hear me now?' She stared down at the fixed features, the closed eyes. What would she not give to catch that conspiratorial wink, to hear his infectious laugh, and share his enthusiasm for all things new.

'I'm going to find the owner of the goat. I've got to get someone help me move you to a shelter.' She looked into the distance. They had not passed a living soul since leaving Donlan's Bar, so it was unlikely anyone would pass this way tonight. She bent to smother the heat of his face with her cool lips. 'And am I not always telling you 'tis the darlin' man y'are!' Straightening up, she gathered her skirts, and wincing at the stiffness of the shoes ran along the curve of the road.

'There must be a dwelling,' she told herself. 'There can't be all this distance with not a blessed soul in it.' The sound of the goat drew her attention to the sloping land on the far side of the road. Her heart lifted; there were voices, too.

She attempted to run faster, but the extra weight of pregnancy gave her a stitch beneath the ribs. She clutched her side and listened. The voices were now more distinct, low and mumbling, and then suddenly raised in anger. Sweet Jesus, she thought, a sob restricting her throat, they were already in a bad humour and would look upon her intrusion as something they could well do without. Although not lacking in courage, especially on Finn's account, she approached cautiously, a hand to her throat to steady her breathlessness.

The cause of their fury was a small goat which was

bordering on frenzy and almost up to its shoulders in a bog hole. For all her cautious approach, the three men, like puppets on a string, turned.

'Be off with ye,' snarled the youngest who was tall and narrow, and sported the widest moustache Tessa had ever seen. 'Can't you see we've got trouble enough? If this devil takes fright because of you we'll never get it out.'

Summing up the situation Tessa replied, 'And if you keep swearing and shouting, and whipping the poor creature, it's likely to go further in and take you with it!'

'And what do you know about goats?' demanded the eldest, whom Tessa judged to be the father of the other two.

'I know this much, that if a creature gets into a bog hole you tug it out by the tail, not the neck. Me da kept goats,' she went on with growing confidence. 'I could do anything with 'em.'

The younger men glanced at their father. A silent message seemed to pass between them. Then the great concession. 'I wish to God, you'd do something with this devil then.'

'Will you do me a favour in return?'

'Hold on now,' said the eldest brother, who always wore a cap and was given to caution.

'It's me – my husband. He's ill, up there, on the road. I want help – he's a big fella, y'see – to get him to a shelter – anything to keep the weather off. In exchange,' she prompted, 'for saving the creature.' She looked up at the scudding clouds, drawing their attention to the passage of time.

The men faced each other. She intercepted their looks and took the initiative. 'Will you give me the rope, then, and stand well back, all of yous?'

Flustered, the youngest thrust the rope to which the goat was tethered into her hands and tramped obediently after his father and brother.

Tessa noticed the flicker of interest in the brown-flecked eyes of the goat. Its gaze followed the retreating men then settled on herself. She spoke softly, trying to keep the edge of panic off her voice, trying not to think of Finn laid out on the road like a corpse. Curbing her impatience and mindful of the three men watching, she remembered the bread in her pocket, and held some of it out.

The animal slowly gained confidence, and after what seemed an age to Tessa, began to co-operate by moving itself forward with each gentle tug of the rope to receive the bread. Finding a foothold on solid ground, it emerged covered in odorous slime, and began nibbling at the loaf.

'Name's Downey,' said the old man by way of acknowledging his gratitude. 'You're not from round about?'

'We're going to Dublin, when himself is right again. Will you come and help me with him?' She saw the cautious one regarding the others. 'We made a bargain,' she said sharply. 'And I got your bloody goat out, so you come and help me with my fella!'

The old man, dishevelled and toothless, nodded and beckoned his sons to fall in step. They ascended the incline like a cortege, Tessa bringing up the rear with the goat. Silently, as though it were something they did every day, the Downey brothers lifted Finn by the shoulders and feet and carried him to a ramshackle barn where, disturbing a clutch of dusty hens, they laid him reverently on some sheaves of dried grass. They would have left without a word if Tessa had not stopped them.

'See,' she said. 'If I work for you – '

The cautious one, who, being bald, always wore a cap – not for reasons of vanity, but in the belief that it kept his brains warm – shook his head. 'Begod, woman, it takes us all our time to scratch a livin'. We've got no money to pay – '

'I don't want payment,' put in Tessa firmly. 'And I don't want anything for nothing. I'll work on your stock in exchange for shelter in this barn – just until he's well enough to move on. Sure to God, you can see how taken he is?'

The brothers exchanged looks and waited for the old man's nod before registering agreement and following him out. Tessa shut the door. Anxiously feeling Finn's forehead, she found nothing to solace her there. As well as the hot dryness of his skin which had so alarmed her, he was now also shivering with cold.

*

The Downeys lived alone in a squat, stone farmhouse which had seen more prosperous times. They were dour and never smiled, but were kindly enough. Tessa, knowing her place, never crossed the threshold. They brought her scraps of food and sometimes a jug of cold tea, in exchange for which she tended the goats, the donkey and other run-down livestock. Within a week the dusty hens perked up and began to lay, and the milk yield increased to allow the making of cheese.

As most of the work was done in the barn, Tessa was able to watch and care for Finn, gathering herbs and brewing them with water boiled on a fire made tinker style outside; pressing the potion through his lips with a battered spoon.

In the hours of darkness, when fears are exaggerated and fantasies heightened, when mice scurry and bats squeak, Tessa knew he was tormented by the curse his aunt had laid on him. Not that he admitted it even in his ravings, but the guarded look that shadowed his eyes, and the anxious frown was proof enough.

At first, she was overwhelmed with a sense of despair, recalling the fate of others the aunt had cursed. But, she reasoned, if the curse was going to be effective, surely he would have drowned like the rest of his community, or perished instead of being rescued by the Murphys?

Outrage took over from despair. She recalled the only time she had seen the aunt, and how scared she had been at the sight of the tall, gaunt figure with gimlet eyes and grey hair hanging like tassels from either side of a flannel cap. The old woman had not got the better of her then, and she certainly wasn't going to get the better of her now!

'You can sod off!' shouted Tessa. 'Back to hell where I hope you burn for ever!' She rummaged about in her memory for suitable liturgical phrases and finding none, brandished her crucifix over Finn's body, claiming protection in the name of the Holy Trinity, and adding for good measure the Blessed Virgin and Saint Teresa herself.

Was it her imagination or was Finn breathing more restfully? She curled up beside him on the dried grass, her arm over his chest, and for safety's sake, the crucifix clutched in her fingers.

So used had she been to his consciousness ebbing and

flowing with the degree of fever, she was happily surprised to find him resting more easily. His lips had ceased their endless movement and he no longer tossed his head from side to side. Touching his skin, she knew the fever had broken, and there he was watching, waiting to catch her glance and close one eye in a mischievous wink.

From that moment Finn recovered quickly, and the Downeys, appreciating unpaid labour, urged Finn to stay a few weeks longer, to take advantage of the mild weather and build up his strength for the last leg of their journey. This Finn did willingly, giving Tessa more time to rest. The Downeys, with rough-edged kindness, told her to take as much dairy produce as they needed.

It was not until after the cutting and gathering in of the sparse grasses that old Downey, when alone with Finn, nodded toward the barn which Tessa had entered. 'You'd better be on your way, boyo. This is no place for her to be giving birth, an' it's a fair step yet to Dublin.'

Tessa received the reported suggestion with relief, and began at once to gather their things. 'Yes, I've been thinking that way meself.' She patted the mound of her stomach. 'To have our child born among the Downeys' goats is even worse than in a tinker's camp!'

That afternoon they were ready for the road. The Downeys stood to watch them go, still together, still puppet-like, waiting for their father's signal before raising their hands in a gesture of farewell and goodwill.

Chapter Four

Captain O'Shea, leaning forward from his lofty position on the box of the army wagon, speculated idly on the figures ahead. What were they? Tinkers, rogues, vagabonds, thieves? Not that it mattered; he was feeling generous with the world this morning and if pushed would even give the devil himself the benefit of a doubt. He reined in the horses.

'Would you care to take the weight off your feet now?' he called.

'We would so!' answered Finn. Tessa, seeing the uniform, hesitated. 'Sure, it's all right, Tess,' he whispered. 'It's not the police, he's from the army.'

'It's a long road to Dublin,' persuaded the good-natured voice. 'Looks a lot better from the wagon.'

That settled the matter for Finn. 'C'mon, Tess,' he prompted, putting an arm about her waist. 'Up you go.'

'Here, give me your kit.' The Captain leaned down. Lord, he thought, eyeing Finn's height and breadth of shoulder, I would not like to get on the wrong side of him! He lifted the sack and Tessa's hessian bag, and was surprised to find them so light. Poor devils, he thought, is this all they've got? They clambered on board, clumsy in their haste, and Finn, standing behind Tessa, half pushed and half lifted her up the steep side of the wagon.

'I'm always glad of company,' remarked the Captain, amused at their eagerness. 'Shortens the miles, y'know.' He put out a slim, long-fingered hand to haul her on to the box. Her grasp, he noticed, was as firm as his own. He liked a strong hand; limp fingers and a flaccid grasp turned his stomach. He inclined his head in welcome. Tessa, not used to meeting strangers who represented some kind of authority, was not sure how to react. But a swift appraisal of the longish features and amber-flecked eyes told her there was nothing to fear. A tremulous smile of acknowledgement touched her mouth and was gone. Somehow that brief smile knocked him off balance, so that Finn, already on the box beside him, had to address his opening remarks twice before they reached his consciousness. Even then he could not recall what the words were, for he felt certain the wide-eyed glance of the young woman was at this very moment riveted on him. He flicked the reins to start the horses and squared his shoulders – no slouching, no leaning forward with elbows on knees. He felt strangely elated that his back was in receipt of so wondrous a scrutiny.

His certainty was not misplaced. Tessa, having settled herself as best she could among the tackle in the wagon, stared not so much at his back as at the military clothes which covered it. Somehow, the tunic and Sam Browne seemed at variance with the nonchalant way his peaked cap was tipped back on his ruffled hair. If he had been a wandering minstrel with a fiddle under his arm and a song on his lips she could have come to terms, albeit briefly, with his personality, but the severity of the uniform overrode everything, and filled her with the kind of awe reserved for priests and gentry.

Finn felt a similar sentiment, except his was tinged with an exultant thrill. Sitting on the box of an army wagon reminded him of the time he had wanted to enlist to get the money to be married, but Tess had been against it. He glanced admiringly at the Captain's highly polished knee boots – one thing about the army, he thought, they gave you a decent pair of boots. He gazed ruefully at the split in his own and hoped it would not be noticed.

'Been travelling long?' asked the Captain.

'We're not travellers, sir,' Finn pointed out quickly. 'We're not travelling people, I mean – but yes, we've been on the road too long. We're going across,' he said, with something of a flourish, 'on the midnight boat from Dublin – to England.'

'Are you, now?' smiled O'Shea. 'I'll be boarding it

41

meself – got to look after a consignment of horses.' He glanced at Finn curiously and wondered why he was leaving the country. Could he be on the run? It didn't seem likely. There was no guile or guilt in that honest, open face. Hard times drove people to extremes; he should know.

'Are you cavalry, sir?' Finn asked with deference in his voice.

'Ach, c'mon now, I'll not have you addressing me in those terms –' Then noticing the startled expression on the young man's face, he continued, 'Captain Cormac O'Shea,' and added with simple candour, 'Me name is Cormac.'

'But . . . ' Finn stammered, 'you're an officer.'

'I am so, but –'

'I'd feel easier calling you Captain O'Shea,' said Finn, liking the way the words rolled off his lips.

'Just as you like. Although I've rank, it's nothin' great,' he grinned. 'A courtesy title because I'm a veterinary.' He caught Finn's puzzled expression again. 'Just another word for a horse doctor.'

'Ah, and now you're having me on!'

'And why would I be doing that? Sure, the army has a lot of horses, and they go down with this and that, and have to be dosed and doctored just the same as ourselves.'

Finn was silent for a moment, and then, convinced the captain was in earnest, asked, 'And have you been at it long?'

'I was born into it, you might say.'

'Now I know you're having me on!' laughed Finn.

'It's no joke, I can tell you!' Cormac O'Shea was both amused at and touched by the young man's simplicity. Speaking with the assurance of one who had come from a long line of talkers, he began to explain, 'Y'see, my father was an army man with the Dublin Fusiliers when he met and married my mother, and she, God rest her soul, became that most unenviable of creatures – an army wife living in barracks. And will I tell you now, that I was the only one she raised out of ten or more of us. If it wasn't the cholera that took 'em, it was the croup. The squalor and filth of the army barracks in those days had to be seen to be believed. But, if life was rough then, it was a damn sight rougher for us when me da was drummed out.'

'Drummed out!'

The Captain half-turned to include Tessa. 'Haven't you heard of fellas being drummed out?'

There was a silence. Tessa had not heard of the drumming out process but was not sure whether to admit it.

'Is it a . . . bad thing?' ventured Finn.

'Bad! It's worse. Like being excommunicated! I remember standing by the big gates of the barrack square with the mammy and just as much kit as you've got. Oh, and the rain! Sure, the rain of God was pouring down on our heads like I've never seen since. Me da was overfond of the drink, y'see, and that's no good for army discipline. Drinking and talking were the only two things he did really well. God, he could talk the hind leg off a donkey! Anyways, there we were, the mammy and meself, two forlorn figures by the gates – and the size of the gates! You'd think they were the gates of paradise, so big they were.

'The commanding officer was a Captain Clare; we heard him read out some solemn words . . . Terrible solemn they seemed on that awful day. Then he reaches out and tears me father's tunic – that's a sign of the ultimate disgrace, and a signal for the drums to start up. I can see my da now, stumbling across the parade ground. Louder and louder came the roll of the drums behind him, the gates opened, and he was outside. Thrown out. Disgraced – and the army the only thing he knew.'

There was a short silence, interrupted only by the jingle of the harness and the creak of the wagon, while the appreciative audience assimilated the ingredients of the story. So quiet were they that Cormac, thinking he had put them to sleep, glanced at Finn and, satisfied that he at least was still awake, turned round to ascertain Tessa's state of consciousness. And she, startled at the sudden attention, asked a little breathlessly, 'What happened to the mammy and your da, then?'

At the sound of her voice he straightened his shoulders again and was happy to continue. 'I must have been about seven on the night they went into the public house. I was left outside soaked to the skin and cold as a corpse. Anyways, when they'd spent the last of their money, out they came, reeling with the drink – and the point of the story,'

43

he continued in a matter-of-fact tone, 'is that they did for each other.'

'You mean,' Tessa's voice echoed from the wagon, 'that they killed each other?'

'I do so. Not that I knew anything about it at the time. Y'see they used to fight like turkey cocks after the drink. Up and down the lane, screaming and yelling; and as you can imagine, I wasn't at all happy at this turn of events for it meant another night with an empty belly. So, do I not start up wailing meself out of the sheer misery – and then me da felled me to the ground with the back of his hand. And there I laid till daylight. They found me da in the churchyard. He'd tripped on a gravestone and split his skull; and the mammy, wandering off for help perhaps, stumbled into the river and was drowned. Captain Clare, being friendly with the Resident Magistrate, got to know about the case and set me on as a stable lad and, God be thanked, I've not looked back since. Mrs Clare taught me to read and write, oh, regular keen on the poetry they were, and at seventeen they sent me to the army veterinary school – and that's what I mean by being born into the army.'

Finn was silent for a while, assessing all this new information. The talk then turned to more general topics and after a while, having heard no comment from Tessa, Cormac glanced behind to see her asleep. 'Is she your wife?'

'She is so; am I not the lucky fella?'

'Indeed you are – I envy you your uncomplicated life.'

'What's complicated about getting married? Is it not the natural thing for a young fella to want to marry his sweetheart?'

An air of confidentiality overtook the conversation. Finn's black curls and the peaked cap moved closer together on the box.

'You not married, Captain O'Shea?'

'No. I nearly was. To begin with, I didn't think I was cut out for this one man and woman together for ever and ever, amen. Oh, I've had me share of sweethearts, but I've stopped short of the altar. Not that I'm a deceiver; no, as God is my witness, I've made it clear that I'm not the marrying kind, but it only seems to make 'em keener! Then a couple of years ago I met a woman I could have settled with. Oh,

God, sure the chemistry and all of that was there. But fate was getting back at me.'

'Y'mean she was not the marrying kind?' asked Finn, enjoying the role of confidant.

'Not at first, but I wore her down. Oh, she was the great girl, witty and winsome, the kind people write songs about. Eventually she agreed to marry me at the regimental chapel. We had a fine little house to live in – ' he paused and smiled wryly at Finn ' – me having rank and all! But she shied off at the last minute. Left me at the altar in full ceremonials; my superior officer with the ring in his pocket; the bridesmaids at the door; the padre tapping his fingers on a great tasselled prayer book – and me as cold as death.'

Finn nodded sympathetically. It all sounded very grand and far beyond his comprehension; therefore, he concluded, it must have all been very serious indeed.

'And have you not seen her since?'

'Not a glimpse, and even her mother does not know, or more to the point, will not tell me where she is. Not that it matters any more. Broken hearts are healed by time and space. But it unsettled me, d'you know. She's part of the old life, the old country, and in order to survive I've got to get out. So, I applied for a transfer and have an appointment across. I tell you, my friend, if I was a drinking man I would have been legless for weeks!'

'You mean you don't take even a drop?'

Cormac O'Shea shook his head.

Finn, who had been brought up on poteen to keep out the cold, stared in an uncomprehending manner. 'God save you,' he murmured soberly. 'You're the first fella I've ever met who doesn't liquefy his gullet!'

After a further silence during which Finn mulled over this serious matter, Cormac leaned forward over the reins. 'Y'know, I've not been able to talk about it until now. Thanks for listening.'

'And you looking as though you'd not a care in your heart!'

'It don't do to look back,' came the cheerful reply. 'And it doesn't do to look on the black side.' He drew Finn's attention to Phoenix Park and the broadening of the streets. 'We're not far from the barracks now. I have to report there, get my orders and all, but I'll direct you to the boats. And if you're going for the new life, new dances, new songs, give it all you've got!' Then on a fractured sigh, he added, 'Ah, being jilted knocks the stuffing out of you. Taught me a lesson it has. No altars for me in future. I should have stood by my previous inclination and kept clear of 'em! To be sure, you're a lucky fella to have it all sewn up at so early an age . . . '

Finn did not know what to say. Such intricacies of character were beyond him; and not caring for the silence which followed, even though it was an easy one, he plied Cormac with every imaginable question about the Dublin thoroughfares.

Tessa, waking up, was proud to hear Finn talking in so friendly a manner. Since leaving the tinkers they had not spoken at length to anyone, and the present volubility was pleasant, reassuring and cheerful.

Cormac brought the horses and wagon to a halt across from the barracks, and leapt lightly down to release the tailboard and so save Tessa from clambering down from the box. He had not noticed her condition in the confusion of getting aboard, and was now strangely moved at their spirit. Although they had little, he had not heard a word of complaint.

He was going to touch her arm and wish her luck, but forbore lest she think him impertinent. Somehow he wanted these two to think well of him; to take a good memory with them. He watched while Finn placed his big hands where her waist used to be and lifted her to the ground.

'You look rested, Tess – the sleep has been good for you.'

'I am rested – oh, and I can't believe we're really here, in Dublin!' She glanced awkwardly at Cormac, and not knowing what to say, said nothing.

'Thanks, Captain O'Shea.' Finn rolled the title round his tongue for the last time, and hoisting the sack onto his shoulder, moved off.

'Good luck!' shouted Cormac. 'And God go with the two of yous!' He watched them, knowing they would not turn, knowing they had already put him to the back of their minds in the discovery of a new world.

'I was beginning to think we'd never get here!' exclaimed Tessa. 'I can scarcely believe it; it seems a lifetime since we left Spider Murphy's!' Tessa was so excited, her first instinct was to seize Finn's hand and pull him in whatever direction took her fancy, but the sight of solid citizens going about their affairs soberly caused her to be more decorous.

If the citizens were intimidating, the architecture was even more so. When selling 'on the doors' with Kate, Tessa had been impressed by her first sight of stone-built cottages with ricks of turf at the side and coloured curtains. And on their travels, she had set eyes on some great houses, a marvellous rectory or modest country villa. But those were in isolation. Nothing could ever have prepared either herself or Finn for the quantity, the density and the complexity of city life.

Tessa, being able to read, soon felt more at ease. The boardings and billboards became a source of pleasurable bewilderment. Like children let loose in toyland, they tried to see everything at once and when they came across the same statue or shop twice, or even three times, they burst out laughing at their own ineptitude.

There was too much happening on this summer afternoon for either Tessa or Finn to give any thought to their appearance. Her pregnancy was hidden by the Connemara shawl, but her skirt, ragged at the hem, trailed on the ground. Finn's boots had split even further, his hair grown even longer, and a neckerchief about his sinewy throat made him look every inch a tinker. Nor were they aware of the suspicious glances of the bowler-hatted clerks, or the nervous looks from fashionably dressed women. The greasy sack over Finn's shoulder added little by way of assurance.

They stood before the shop windows, gazing with amazement at the displays of furniture; the life-sized figures modelling clothes; the bassinets and draped cradles. Ah, surely, she thought, almost beside herself with rapture, ah, surely to God I've seen it all! Were I to die on the spot, I've glimpsed paradise already!

It was early evening when Finn stopped to contemplate the stained-glass window of Kavanagh's public house. The lettering was fading and the red paint peeling.

'Are we not going in?' Tessa prompted.

Finn, having lately noticed the looks of passers-by, pursed his lips and looked ruefully down at his clothes.

'Our money's as good as anyone else's,' she declared. 'C'mon in, I'm starvin' on me feet.'

She lifted the latch and felt the warm stench of stale beer waft through the door as it opened. An old man in heated debate with a hawker looked up.

'Ah, a fine day it is.'

'It is so,' replied Finn. After which the old man resumed his argument.

Two women in black shawls, each silently staring into a glass of ale, looked up, eyes sharp and chins at the ready for at least an hour's speculation. They reminded Tessa a little of Finn's aunt, and not wanting such a reminder, she crossed the sanded floor and chose a bench with its back to them.

Kavanagh himself, in a dirty white apron, more than made up for his uncommunicative clientele. 'Guinness!' he roared, bringing them their order. 'Two of the best! And God love you, sir, bread and cheese? Who the devil wants bread and cheese when Kavanagh's got the best eels in Dublin! Stewed eels, then? Money? God love you, sir, it'll cost you not a penny more.'

After leaving the public house with directions from Kavanagh, they walked by the river. The wind was brisk enough to keep the Union Jack almost horizontal and the masts of the ships by the Customs House continually on the tilt.

Tessa linked her arm through Finn's. She was feeling miserable; an attack of the mulligrubs, as they said. Not so much miserable as cheated. It was like the souls in hell catching a glimpse of heaven to see the gates close, leaving them to the unknown. Had she been transported straight from Ennan to England it would not have been so bad, but to have set eyes on the wonders of Dublin and then be whisked off seemed unfair. And not to be able to find work or make a living here seemed more unfair. There was no use saying anything to Finn; they had been over the same ground time and again, and she knew well he would shake his head and say, 'No, there's no work here for the likes o' me. Plenty, no doubt for the gentlemen in white collars and cuffs, but not for a fella that can't read or write. Everyone knows there's work across for labourers – mills, factories, foundries . . . '

he would sigh with anticipatory pleasure. 'England's the place for us, girleen, and we've got to get there before our money runs out, and before the little spalpeen comes.'

They peered over the river wall at the great iron rings, at the long fingers of seaweed reaching down to the creamy, stout-like foam of the Liffey.

'Well then?' A stern voice brought Finn round on his heel. 'Tinkers in the city at this hour aren't after fresh air. Or is it the scenery you're enjoying?'

A policeman every inch as tall as Finn stood before them. Tessa instinctively tightened her shawl.

The policeman eyed Finn. 'Open the sack.'

Finn did as he was told, explaining the reason for their visit. 'England's a land flowing with milk and honey,' he said, trying to sound knowledgeable.

'So, they told you that, did they?' sniffed the constable.

'They did so, sir.'

'If you believe that you're a bigger gobeen than I took you for!' Finn did not answer, and the policemen, relenting of his briskness, directed them to the quay and offered further advice. 'Now go right there, boyo. Sure the oddest things can happen to country people like yourselves. Get your tickets from the proper ticket office and nowhere else, d'you hear?' Finn nodded. 'And don't part with money to anyone except the clerk. Have you got that?' he asked, as though addressing a deaf person.

'We have, indeed,' said Finn pleasantly. 'And thank you for your kindness.' The tinkers had taught him always to be thankful; it could pay dividends.

They hurried from the symbol of the law to join the stream of people bent on embarkation. Jostled by porters juggling with cases, dodging cabs and avoiding puddles, they stopped to gaze in awe at the flare of gaslights, and came within sight of the boat. The height and magnitude of it sharpened their feelings to immediate alarm. To such unprepared minds it resembled a huge creature glowing with different-coloured eyes; and the noise of the engines added a dimension of terror.

Finn was the first to regain his composure, and Tessa took her mind off the awful wonders by hurrying along with the others to the ticket office. Finn waited outside while she joined the short queue and regained a degree of normality by nodding to this one and having a quick word with another. The young clerk further boosted morale by complimenting her on the colours of the Connemara shawl. He had bought one that very afternoon and hoped it would look as well on his young lady as it did on Tessa.

Midnight found them standing together on the lower deck of the *Hibernia* watching the last-minute drama of embarkation: the shouting of the shoremen who, in the glare of bright lights, dashed about with hawsers, pulling and shoving, severing the gangway from the ship as though it were a limb.

Finn put an arm along the length of her shoulder and pulled her close. To him this moment was the culmination of what seemed a lifetime's ambition; but Tessa, having previously suffered doubts, was wondering if they had done the right thing. Familiarity seemed all important and none of the reasons for emigrating seemed to make sense now.

The crowded quayside echoed with messages for those on board.

'God speed!'

'Write soon – don't forget to write!'

The waving hats and white handkerchiefs suddenly became blurred. Tessa felt cheated that she and Finn had no one waving goodbye to them. There was not a soul on the quay, not one person who cared or wished them well.

She clung to Finn's arm as a steward ushered the steerage passengers below decks, where the lowing of cattle in their pens echoed the loneliness in her heart. The ship's siren blared, the propellers thrashed, and the air throbbed with the pulses of powerful engines. There was no turning back.

Chapter Five

'Finn,' said Tessa quietly as they sat on the wooden benches below decks. 'I've got the pains –'

'You mean the child?' he turned in alarm.

'I do so.'

'It can't be born here!' He looked around desperately, first at her and then at the crowds. 'Tess, what shall I do? Oh, Holy Mother!'

'I've had 'em on and off since we left the wagon.'

'Why didn't you say?'

'What, with all those marvellous things! Sure, I scarce took notice. Thought it was the cramps from the jolting of the wagon, but they're too regular now for cramps.' She touched his arm. 'Go and see if there's a quiet place round by the pens. It'll be all right,' she reassured. 'I've seen the tinker women give birth in worse places than this – but be quick.'

'You're coming with me. C'mon, I'll carry you. I'm not leaving you here with all these kids yelling about and people on the drink.'

She gathered the shawl about her, and as though she were a child, he quickly carried her through the crowds to the far end of the deck which was partitioned into pens for livestock. As he propped her up against a bale of hay she let out a thin gasp of pain.

'Tell me what to do, Tess?' he asked hoarsely. 'Oh God, I feel so bloody helpless!' He looked up to see half a dozen people had already gathered out of curiosity.

One of the crowd, a little man with a big suitcase, nodded

to where Tessa was covered by her shawl and asked fussily, 'Is she sick or is it the drink?'

'Ach, 'tis terrible sick she is,' ventured an old woman in a tweed cape. 'Can't you see the very sweat's dripping off her – and how awful pale she is. I knew a fella with the cholera who was just like that – died, he did, in a matter of hours.'

Another man with a scarf looped like a noose began to back away. 'God save us all!' he exclaimed fervently. 'Sure, it'll go through the ship like a dose o' salts!'

'They're tinkers!' yelled a voice from the back. 'You can tell by the scarf on her head – and the state of 'em. No wonder they've got the cholera, dirty devils!'

'And the bloody cheek to bring it on board – they're not fit to be with decent folk.'

Finn could scarcely believe his ears. 'Go away!' he yelled. 'For the love of God, go and leave us in peace!' Then, recalling an old tinker ruse added, 'Or, sure as the devil's in hell I'll lay a curse on yous all!'

Those in front turned to back off, but were prevented as more people, eager for a diversion, had gathered. Tessa saw all the crowd and panic through blurred vision. The pain was so intense she didn't know which way to turn to prevent herself crying out. She writhed beneath the shawl, and the onlookers thinking she was about to get up backed away.

'I'm going to report this to someone,' said a petulant little man with a big head. 'To think we've paid good money to be cooped up with the disease – sure, you've not heard the end of this.'

'It's your own fault if you get it,' jeered Finn going along with their supposition. 'You're like ghouls, so you are! We've come here out of your way and you've followed us! I've got it meself, no doubt, through nursing her, and if you don't get off so help me God, I'll come and breathe it all over you!'

The sight of the big, wild-looking man stumbling to his feet proved too much. They withdrew in a panic of speculation. He knelt to wipe the sweat off her face.

'What can I do, Tess?' He thought of the many times he had heard of childbirth and never given it a thought, and if he'd known it would be so awful for Tess . . . He felt, as indeed he was, a complete stranger to the mysteries of it all. He knew there would be blood, and the baby to see to, and the cord to be severed. But how to deal with it? And in a public place.

He jumped to his feet. 'I'll rig a shelter, Tess,' he said in a panic. 'That'll keep the ghouls off.' Glad of something to do, he unhooked a tarpaulin from an empty stall, grabbed some staves and in no time had erected a three-sided rig over the stall where Tessa lay, the entrance to it being away from the gaze of the curious. He recalled the many times he had said that no child of theirs would be born under a bush, tinker style. Merciful heaven, even that was better than being born on a cattle boat!

No sooner was it done than the crowd had returned. 'Over there – see, he's put a shelter up. She's dead already.'

'Back off will you!' A voice of authority cut through the gabble. 'Back! Beyond the pens. C'mon now, move. Passengers are not allowed this far. Can you not read?' Cormac O'Shea clad in shirt and breeches stooped to peer under the tarpaulin. Alarm vied with instant recognition.

'Good God!' he exclaimed. 'Y'know, I was thinking about the two of yous as the ship weighed anchor. Wondering whether you'd made it or if you'd changed your minds.' He glanced from one to the other. 'The steerage officer sent me to quell the racket, and they – ' he jerked his head toward the ghouls ' – they said a woman was taken with a fever, and someone else said it as cholera. I never imagined it would be you.' His forehead creased into a frown of enquiry. 'You've not been drinking ditch-water, or something?'

Finn's face split into a quick smile of relief. Seeing the Captain again immediately restored his self-confidence. 'It was they who said it was the cholera, not me. I went along with it so they'd leave her alone. She's on with the baby, Captain O'Shea.'

Cormac whistled softly through his teeth. 'What, already? Nice bit o' timing that. If she'd gone into labour on the streets, your child would have been born either in the workhouse, or the lying-in hospital for the poor. And that's no way to come into the world.'

She wouldn't have liked that at all, thought Finn, for

wasn't she Proud Riley's daughter? But, God love us, he looked about wildly, is this any better?

'The crossing,' Cormac was saying, 'can take anything from fourteen to twenty hours, depending on wind, tide and crew – with a bit of luck you'll be a father before we reach Liverpool!'

'I'll be a father sooner than that! She's been on with the pains ever since we left your wagon.'

'Good God, man! Why didn't you say?' He cast a hurried glance at Tessa. 'There's bound to be a doctor on board. Surely, out of the hundreds of people there'll be a doctor. The steerage officer will find out –'

'We couldn't afford to pay if there was, and by the time you get him anything could have happened. Don't leave her,' he pleaded. 'Did you not say you were a horse doctor?'

'A horse doctor, yes – but there's a difference between horses and humans!'

'But surely – at least you know something about it. Oh, God love her – will you stay?' pleaded Finn. 'I'll never forgive meself if anything goes wrong.'

'Nothing's going to go wrong, man. Birth is a natural process.'

'Where we came from,' said Finn darkly, 'women died, and babies died, and sometimes both died – and what will we do if the bloody boat starts going from side to side as they're saying it will?'

'Well, in that case,' he said with a quick smile, 'you'd better fetch a couple of buckets of water while it's calm!'

Finn, anxious to be commanded and to have someone in control, was about to charge off when they saw an old woman peering round the tarpaulin. 'I came to see if I could help with the laying out.' She was thin and spare, but straight as a rod, with twinkling button eyes.

'Laying out, Ma! It's a lying-in!' grinned Cormac, suddenly happy.

'I've brought as many into the world as I've seen go out of it,' she said by way of offering her credentials.

Cormac slapped a hand on Finn's shoulder. 'This is the prospective da – as for me,' he shrugged, 'I'm a horse doctor and know damn all about women. We would be relieved if you'd stay. The atmosphere's a bit thick with the cattle, but you'll not mind that.' Then he added self-consciously, 'Will you see to her skirts, and all? I've a respect for the young woman's modesty.'

'Ah, so I will, now, the poor colleen.'

'I'm off to scrounge some things; it's a great army occupation, scrounging!'

He returned to find Tessa prepared, water supplied, and the birth imminent. Suddenly, the little igloo was filled with activity. Cormac was asking questions of Finn, of Ma, and Tessa herself. She was half lying, half sitting, eyes large with fear, yet trying to keep calm by telling ma about the baby clothes in the sack, and how they were gifts from Kate Jarvey, and how if they had a son he was to be called Patrick, because they were married on St Patrick's day. And if they had a daughter she was to be called Kate. When her face twisted with what ma referred to as the 'last pangs', Finn was beside himself with incoherent lamentations; and as rags were torn up with a great ripping sound he choked on his words.

'I'm going out, sure every groan goes right through me heart. God, to think I've brought her to this!'

'Get out man,' said Cormac kindly. 'There's scarcely enough room to scratch in here, never mind move! We'll shout if we need you. It won't be long before you're the proud and swaggerin' da!'

And in the next breath he said to Tessa, 'Hold on to me arm if it helps, and when the contraction comes dig your nails in and push. What was that, ma? There's so much noise down here, what with cattle and – Oh! Its head! D'you hear that now!' he repeated to Tessa. 'Push . . . that's the girl . . . sure you've carried it about for long enough . . . '

The next half-hour seemed never-ending to Finn. He prowled round and round the pens, warding off thoughts of the mockers by addressing prayers to St Teresa herself, and then to the Mother of God. He longed for a Guinness or a drop of poteen, and was returning to the prayers again when the thin wail of a baby's cry filtered through the throb of the engines, the lowing of cattle, and the laughter of roistering passengers.

He stopped to listen. Thrilled and at the same time

alarmed, he waited. The child was born! He was a father! But why had the captain or ma not called him? There must be something wrong. Something terrible had happened. Oh, merciful God! He made for the rigged shelter and stooping to go inside, found his way blocked by the Captain who, with sleeves rolled to the elbow, was on his way out.

'She's all right, Finn,' he grinned broadly. 'Congratulations!' He was carrying something wrapped in newspapers. 'The afterbirth came quickly,' he explained. 'Ma's sent me to get rid of it.' Finn nodded uncomprehendingly and, as he lowered himself on his haunches to see Tessa, ma pushed a bundle into his arms. He stared at the tiny face, pink and peaceful, nestling against a patterned shawl knitted by Kate. The baby's blue eyes, large in the half-light, seemed to look straight into his own.

'It's a boy, Finn. We've got a son.'

'I can't believe it, Tess!' he cried. 'Oh, God love you, I can't believe it!' She looked so vulnerable lying there, exhausted after her ordeal, and so infinitely lovely that his heart bubbled over with protective love. He had been frightened lest the experience had wrought a change in her; he could see there was a change, but a serene one. The birth seemed to have bestowed on her eighteen years a maturity not evident before. Still holding the child, he leaned forward and kissed her gently, smoothing the damp hair from her forehead, and with a finger that had not seen water for days, traced away little circles of weariness. His cheek rested against hers.

'Thank God it's over, Tess. He's the darling little fella, and 'tis the grand girl you are. Your da would have been proud of the two of yous, but he couldn't be prouder than me!' He moved away a little to marvel at the tiny being they had created. 'And would you know he's got a mop of curls just like his da!' He put out a trembling hand and rested it momentarily on the baby's head. The curls were soft as down. He stared in awe at the tiny fingers, unable to comprehend the miracle of birth.

'D'you still want him called Patrick?'

'I do so.'

He laid the bundle in her arms. 'And Patrick he shall be called.' Still on his haunches, he touched her hand. 'I'm going to find a priest to baptise him, Tess, while ma and the captain are still here to guard you!'

'Can we not wait till we get to Liverpool, Finn?' A slight tone of alarm crept into her voice. 'Besides, there's never a priest travelling steerage. And you can't for shame expect him to come here with the unfragrant cattle.'

Although Finn would not admit it, he felt the child would be safe if he were baptised straightaway. He did not want to mention any of this to Tessa, but as he left she knew he would find a priest even if he had to scour the ship from end to end.

Outside the rig Cormac O'Shea and Ma sat smoking their pipes. His was short-stemmed and black, with a silver band near the bowl; hers, too, was short, but made of clay and, once white, it was now shaded with scorch marks.

'What's it like to be a da?' joked Cormac, and in his heart thought, that's one of the joys I'll never know.

'Ah, it's the grandest thing – makes ye feel like a king; that ye could go out and conquer the world!'

'And is that where you're off to now!' But Finn had gone, his tall figure already swallowed by the crowd.

Cormac smiled at Ma, and shook his head. 'Sure, anyone'd think it had never happened in the world before!' He thanked her warmly for her assistance and pressed a sovereign into her hand. 'Will you stay with 'em, Ma, until they get to Liverpool? I've got a consignment of horses to attend.

"Tis a good thing it isn't a rough passage – she's beginning to roll now, but it won't amount to much. I've done this trip some half-dozen times and known the sea so rough you couldn't keep your feet. The animals don't like it, sensitive creatures. Thank God none of them have ever decided to give birth on board!' He stood up. 'I'll just go and see the proud mammy – d'you realise I don't even know her name?' He went inside to find Tessa looking over the baby's head, eyes wide and pensive; he could almost visualise a cloud hovering. 'Are you worried about anything?' he asked. 'Would you like me to call Ma?'

'No . . . I mean . . . ' She saw him reaching for his things. 'Are you leaving?'

'I was, but I'll stay if you like, until your husband returns.'

'Will you tell me now, Captain O'Shea,' she asked,

ignoring the offer in her anxiety. 'Will you tell me if there's likely to be a priest on board?'

'There is so,' he smiled reassuringly. 'Ireland's awash with 'em coming and going.' Then, noticing a frown, he added, 'Have I said the wrong thing? D'you not want Patrick baptised?'

'Not yet – not now.' She paused, and the words tumbled out. 'Finn and me got married with the tinkers – a broomstick wedding.' She indicated the hand holding the baby. 'Did you not see I'd no ring?'

His amber eyes widened. 'What, with the little fella coming, and the ghouls, and Finn worried to God!' Seeing her frown did not lighten, he answered the question. 'No. I didn't.'

'The priest will,' she sighed. 'They always ferret out the things you'd rather keep quiet. He'll go on about "absolving the sins of the flesh" and I don't want that kind of talk over my baby's head. Besides, Finn will brood and take it all to heart. He frets about curses and luck . . . ' She lifted her tousled head a little higher. 'We are going to get married with the priest and all,' she said earnestly. 'Just as soon as we get some money.'

'If it will make your mind easier –' He reached into his pocket, produced a tiny pouch, and brought out of it a wedding ring; the one his sweetheart had never worn. 'Wear this until he's gone.' He leaned forward, and unfurling her left hand from the sleeping form, slipped the simple circle of gold onto her third finger. She glanced up at him, unsmiling, unsure, but with eyes full of relief. 'There, that will stop the priest asking any unnecessary questions.'

'Thanks.' A tremulous smile touched the corners of her mouth, and almost immediately, her eyelids closed in sleep. If he had expected an effulgence of gratitude, he would have been disappointed. But he had not expected anything. It had been his day for feeling generous, and the loan of the ring was merely an extension of it. Cormac got off his haunches and sat on the floor, resting his arms across his knees. He watched the sleeping mother and babe and reflected that these circumstances were not much different from the barrack room in which he had been born.

He felt some kind of affinity with this child. When Ma,

having wrapped the baby, had thrust it at him while she attended to Tessa, he had instinctively held it close, trying to comfort him, trying to convey, somehow, that it wasn't such a bad life he was coming into.

Having gone outside to smoke his pipe once Ma had wandered off, he marvelled that although it had long gone midnight, the deck was still lively with people who would normally have been in their beds for hours already! The marvelling was interrupted by the sight of a triumphant Finn with a flustered priest in tow.

Cormac leapt to his feet, wanting to appraise Finn of the ring situation, but there was no time. Tessa, wide-eyed and startled at the sudden intrusion, sat up against the side of the pen. The priest, quickly putting a stole about his neck, was clearly anxious to be out of these cramped conditions and back to the supper he had left.

'You the godfather?' he asked Cormac, and before he could answer, for no such arrangement had been made, he looked at Finn reproachfully. 'Have you no more godparents?' he asked, looking about as though they had been mislaid. 'Well, never mind, never mind. We cannot go soliciting godparents from a crowd of travelling strangers.' He eyed Finn again. 'I suppose 'tis unprepared you were?'

'We were so, Father,' replied Finn fervently.

The priest opened his book and began the shortened version for a private baptism. Holy water had been produced from what looked like a brandy flask, and Finn, not really listening to the form of service, waited impatiently for the sign of the cross to be made on his son's forehead.

Tessa was very conscious of the ring, the deceit, and worst of all, discovery. What if he wanted to know the church in which they had married, the date, the name of the priest?

The only one enjoying the occasion was Cormac O'Shea. He fell in with the discipline, observed the ritual, and was very conscious of the obligations being thrust upon him – though he had not the vaguest idea how they could be fulfilled.

The drone of prayers sharpened into a command. 'Will you take the child in your arms, then?' Startled, Tessa jerked the baby up as though offering a sacrifice. Finn, alarmed at the elevation, lurched forward, but Cormac calmly took the swathed bundle and gave him to the priest.

'Name?'

'Patrick,' said Cormac firmly. All three watched intently. Water was sprinkled. The sign of the cross was made, the name pronounced and the baby handed back to his mother. The priest, mindful of the supper awaiting him, removed his stole, pocketed the flask of holy water and with a rapid blessing departed.

Finn, happy with relief, smiled broadly at Tessa. He wanted to whirl her about in a jig to dispel his exuberance of spirit, but he put it all in the smile and she received it with a blush. All her shadows and apprehension fled. They both turned to Cormac in thanks, and Tessa, taking off the ring, explained the borrowing of it to Finn, who was impressed by her strategy.

She held out the ring, but the Captain, squatting down to be on her level, took both it and her hand at the same time. Slipping the ring back onto her finger, he confronted them both. So earnest was he, that Finn knelt down too.

'Now listen,' he began, with an air of confidentiality. 'Take a word of advice from your son's godfather, who is, I might add, just a few years older than you and has seen rather more of the world. I want you to keep the ring.' Why not? he thought, it's no use to me. What's the point in hanging on to bits of the old life?

'But we can't,' said Finn. 'You've done so much for us already.'

'Nonsense. I was only too glad to be of service, and in any case, ma did most of it –' He looked suddenly bashful. 'You're a real nice couple, and it's been an honour to become the boy's godfather.' The amber-flecked eyes dwelt on Tessa. 'For Patrick's sake keep the ring until Finn can get you one. Y'see, once you've got a child people expect you to be married – and by the rites of Holy Mother Church. A wedding ring will be proof that you are. Without it, you'll not get any decent lodgings, nor any kind of work. The other women will look down on you, and it will be you, Mrs Collins, who will suffer from the gossips – not to mention the boy when he starts school.They set great store on respectability across and life with a wedding ring will run far more smoothly – it'll be a talisman or a good luck symbol.'

He began to roll down his shirtsleeves, and turned the same earnest look on Finn. 'I'm not for puttin' you off, but what you said about England being a land of milk and honey, it isn't as easy as that.' The sleeves were down. He fastened the cuffs together with links of silver. 'Just in case I don't see you when we dock, I wish you both well. Rest yourselves now, for we disembark in the afternoon, and you'll have an arduous day ahead of you.'

'I'm quite strong,' Tessa replied. 'In the valley where we lived women hadn't time to lie abed for days after giving birth.'

He straightened up and smiled. 'That's the spirit.' And with a nod of his ruffled head he was gone.

The boat docked at Liverpool. Although the voyage for most steerage passengers had been uncomfortable and claustrophobic, Tessa had not known any of this. Still a little weak, despite her previous boasting, she had sat contentedly on one of the wooden benches, conscious of the speculative glances of those who had nothing else to do while waiting to disembark. The sight of the ring had given her added confidence, and the warmth of the little body tucked beneath her shawl gave a sense of purpose to what seemed a vast undertaking.

Finn now sat solemnly by her side, the sack between his knees, the bag on his shoulder, thinking – despite the constable and the captain – of the land flowing with milk and honey. All these people seemed anxious and eager to get to it: therefore, he concluded, it must be God's own truth that it was indeed so.

When their turn came to join the queue they waited patiently, cosseted by the sound of Irish voices still about them. They laughed at the jokes, and listened avidly for scraps of information; they were at once excited and yet wary of the prospect before them.

Eventually released, and not knowing where to go, they followed the long straggling line into the dock area, eyeing the officials with the utmost apprehension. Tessa envied their fellow travellers who were met and whisked off by people they knew; indeed most of them seemed to know their destination. Only a few, like themselves, stood about in bewildered groups.

It was here that Captain O'Shea caught up with them. Does he not look the grandest fella? thought Finn. The Captain was in full uniform, all khaki and deep brown; the epaulettes made his shoulders seem wider, and the polished knee boots made his legs look longer. His hat was properly in place and his bright features full of authority; in his gloved hand he held a short cane.

His impressive presence reduced them to an awed silence. Tessa felt as though she had stepped out of a fairy tale where bogs moved as though by the devil himself; where colourful tinkers were both grim and gay; where it was no sin to be a peasant; and where a cavalry officer could be mistaken for a wandering minstrel with a fiddle. The Irish Sea had been a bridge between the fey quality of the past and the present with its pressing matters of reality.

'I was hoping I'd catch you.'; He took off the peaked cap as he addressed Tessa. Beneath it his hair was smoother, the colour reminding her of the sable flanks of the horses that had drawn the army wagon. Sensing a distance he tried again. 'If you've no objection, I'd like to keep an interest in my godson, seeing he's the only one I've got, or ever likely to have.' He waited a moment and as neither spoke, he continued. 'Will you promise to write to me at the Regent Road barracks, in Salford, near Manchester – if that means anything to you? See, I've written the address down. Let me know where you settle – we have at least the auld country in common.

'Will you do me a favour now? For tonight, or until you've got your bearings, go and stay at the Salvation Army Hostel. Tell them you've just come over and ask their advice. Some of the lodging houses,' he smiled, 'are known as "fleecing houses"! Remember now, the Salvation Army.'

Tessa took the slip of paper. Her heart was saddened and her eyes were near to tears, for O'Shea was their last link with the past.

As the paper changed hands, the Captain heard himself say with an earnestness that even the noise of the overhead cranes could not cover, 'And you don't have to get married again, either. Not if you don't want to.Not if you're happy as you are . . . I mean, look what happened to me!' He stood awkwardly, swinging the cane against his boots. The noise of the cranes lessened.

There seemed nothing else to say. The spirit of comradeship, of confidentiality, had gone with the tarpaulin screen.

'You'll not be losing my address?' His eyes dwelt on the good-looking young man with the kerchief knotted about his throat, and a mop of overgrown curls; then onto his ragged princess, a wonderful mixture of the regal and the peasant. He wished them well with so much of his heart, and felt temporarily so miserable, that the only expression he could muster as he turned was, 'And God's own luck go with the three of yous.'

'What did he mean, about what happened to himself?'

'Ah, 'tis a good thing to be off the water,' said Finn, trying to dispel the emptiness left by their friend's departure. 'Sure, I never thought the sea was so long. And the cattle, Tess, they were as unfragrant as the pigs we left behind!' He shouldered the sack and touched her arm. 'C'mon, girleen, it'll do you no good standin' about. This is the land flowing with milk and honey – never mind what Captain O'Shea says; all we've got to do is to find it.'

Finn closed one eye in a warm, conspiratorial wink which made her feel better.Hugging the baby closer beneath her shawl, Tessa fell into step beside him, pleased to leave the company of the other bewildered travellers.

Chapter Six

The industry of the dock area, the comings and goings of horse-drawn vans, the shunting of engines, the shouts of stevedores and the shrill cry of gulls, were rapidly giving way to a series of sad-looking streets. A melancholy little park seemed full of idling dogs, and a solitary swing erected by a long-dead benefactor hung on one chain. After some ten minutes, the thoroughfares of Liverpool took on a more lively aspect, and Tessa's admiration for Finn grew with every step – after all, had he not experience of towns?

Finn's pace slowed.

'What is it?' she asked.

'Y'see those fellas standing in a line outside that great building there?'

She nodded.

'I'm going across to see if they know where the Salvation Army is. You've got to have somewhere to rest, having the baby and all.' He dumped the sack at her feet.

The men in the queue observed Finn's approach suspiciously. He made his enquiries, and in the same breath asked about the likelihood of work.

'You Irish?' accused a rasping voice.

'I am so.'

'My advice to you, Paddy, is to get back on that boat and bugger off!'

'And take your Fenian tactics with you!'

Finn was confused. 'You've got me wrong,' he said in his innocence. 'I've only just come over. I'm looking for lodgings and work.'

Tessa heard some of the men laughing bitterly.

'Irish, is he?'

'He wants work, does he?'

'He can have this for his bloody nerve!'

Finn reeled backward from the unexpected blow. His head banged against the wall. He shook himself like a dog coming out of water, and the warm excitement of a punch-up tingled through his veins. The men in the line broke ranks and gathered to enjoy the spectacle. Finn, stung by the injustice of the attack, took both men on, immediately flooring one, and then grappling with the other.

Tessa watched, her face a picture of distress and fear. She crouched back against the wall, terrified.

'Police!'

She heard the rush of feet, the whistles, the shouts. Patrick began to whimper. He wanted to be fed. Her breasts were heavy and her knees weak.

'Who started this lot?' demanded the sergeant, as his constables separated the protagonists.

'The big fella! Dirty Irish slobs!'

'You can smell him from 'ere. Just off the boat, he is. They come over here as cheap labour, putting English fellas out of work! By God, let me get at him!'

'Come on, all of you,' commanded the sergeant. 'Down to the clink.'

Tessa, who had backed away, now ran forward. 'Where are you taking him? He's my husband. I must know. It wasn't his fault. They just got onto him.'

'Calm down, missus. Calm down will yer?'

'How the devil can I calm down,' she countered, 'when I'm in a strange country and I don't know where you're bloody well taking him? We've only just got off the boat!'

'Eh you, Jones,' he addressed a constable. 'Take this lass to the Sal Doss, will you?'

'Right, Sarge.' As his superior returned to the culprits, the constable turned toward Tessa.

'What've you got under the shawl?' he demanded suspiciously. Tessa pulled aside the fringes. 'Blimey, if it ain't a baby!' And being a kind man, he added, ''Ere, give us the baggage, missus, I'll carry it.'

'Where are you taking me?' Tessa wasn't for moving. 'And what'll happen to Finn?'

'He'll be out in a few weeks, but don't worry, you'll be all right where I'm taking you.'

'And where's that?' She stood her ground still, refusing to move.

'The Sal Doss. Salvation Army hostel. C'mon, missus, don't start messing about.'

'Did you say the Salvation Army hostel?'

'Yes, I did. We call it the Sal Doss, some call it the Sally Army, but yes, its proper name is the Salvation Army. Shall we go now, ma'am?' he said with a sarcasm which was lost on her. 'That is, if you are ready.'

'That's all he'd gone for!' she exclaimed indignantly. 'He'd only gone to ask directions.' But the constable was not listening.

Tessa followed. She thought of all the terrors that had befallen her young life: the shock of a totally unexpected pregnancy; the destruction of the valley where she had lived; the time when Finn was near to death with the fever; the crossing of the deep sea; the birth of her child . . . Yet all of these were nothing compared to the present terror, for then she had Finn to share them with, and now she was on her own in a strange place, with very little money, and wishing to heaven and the Holy Mother that she had never left the green of Ireland.

They had reached a flight of steps outside a grimy, red-bricked building. Reluctantly and hesitantly, Tessa followed Jones into the dimly-lit interior.

'Another Irish for you, Major!' shouted the constable, directing his voice along the wide, polished hallway of the Salvation Army Hostel for Women. 'You'll be all right here,' he whispered loudly, and after a few moments of shifting about on one foot and then the other, cupped his hands about his mouth and shouted again, 'Are you there, Major?'

A door with a frosted-glass panel opened, and a woman's voice answered. 'Yes, yes, Constable Jones. I'll be with you in a minute. I've only got one pair of hands, whatever you think to the contrary!'

He raised his eyebrows at Tessa, put his hands behind

his back and began the shifting about of his feet again. The silence of the hall, the polish on the floor, the movement of the constable, and a full-length portrait of General Booth did nothing to calm Tessa's apprehension.

'They'll not send him to prison, will they?'

'Can't say, missus; you'll have to talk to Major Mary about it. She's had a lot of experience with women in your situation. He'll be up before the magistrate first thing in the morning.'

Tessa leaned back against the wall; the policeman's casual words had brought vivid memories of severe sentences passed by the magistrates in Ireland.

Suddenly she felt a compelling hand on her arm, propelling her gently but firmly toward the office door with the frosted-glass panel. She looked about for the familiar figure of Jones, but he had gone. The office door closed. Immediately she poured out their story.

'Finn's never been in trouble before – it was those scurvy fellas who attacked him. Oh, and wasn't he set up with coming to England ever since Mr O'Malley told him it was a land flowing with milk and honey.'

Between tears and almost incoherent outbursts, she supplied Major Mary with details which were neatly entered into a ledger, and having calmed down sufficiently she found herself drinking hot, sweet tea and sitting on a shiny black horsehair sofa, facing the Major, who was now holding Patrick.

Major Mary was tall and slender and the black and crimson uniform added just enough severity to redeem her features from being pretty. In a fashionable gown, her style and manner would have been the envy of a society hostess, but as a Salvation Army officer Major Mary was fighting for the Lord.

'He's a beautiful baby,' she said, regarding the passing over of the precious bundle as a vote of confidence. 'And if you are quite sure you don't want me to contact any organisation of your own faith – '

'I'm quite sure.' The borrowed wedding ring, caught in a shaft of sunlight, winked as Tessa returned the cup to the desk.

'Good, that's settled then. You and this little fellow' –

she smiled down at Patrick, nestling in the crook of her arm
– 'will be all right here until your husband is released. Oh
dear, try not to upset yourself all over again. You've been
a very brave young woman, and you are no longer on your
own. To set your mind at rest, we'll go down to the police
station tomorrow and find out exactly what has happened.
Does that make you feel better? As for work, you must rest
for a few days.'

'But I don't want anything for nothing.'

'When I consider you've rested sufficiently, there'll be
plenty of domestic work here at the hostel. But first you
must wash yourself and attend to – what did you say
he was called? – Patrick, yes. There'll be clean clothes
and you'll feel a lot better.' The baby was handed back
and Tessa followed the Major out into the polished hallway.

Any reassurance Tessa had experienced in the office
was dashed at the sight of the ablution block. After a quick
consultation, Tessa was handed over to a little woman in a
big apron. She was flushed and flustered but had a pleasantly
youthful face.

Tessa clutched Patrick closer. Her eyes roamed over the
white-tiled walls, the rows and rows of lead pipes, and the
vat-like baths – one of which was filling with hot water that
gushed like a stream in full force. Over all this lay the caustic
aroma of carbolic soap.

The little woman's soft, persuasive voice soon had Patrick
lying in a basket to be dealt with later and Tessa taking off her
clothes to get into the vat. She flushed with embarrassment
at the mud-stained skirt, ragged of hem and dirty. It lay on
the floor like a shed skin.

'I always wore clean things at home in Ireland,' she
murmured; and with intense humility submitted her hair
to a search for lice, and her body to the long-handled back
brush and the bath.

She emerged from the experience feeling smooth,
refreshed, and thankful for having been reprieved from a
near-vagrant condition. A few moments later, dressed in a
black skirt and black-and-white check blouse, she saw herself
in the mirror. Tears threatened to blur her vision, for Finn
was not there to see the transformation. Every time he came

into her thoughts, she hoped God was as good to him as to herself.

Patrick was being taken from the basket, and she turned to watch how the little women bathed him. 'Always remember to support his head like this, or he'll slip beneath the water and we don't want that, do we?'

Tessa then set to learning about applying zinc ointment to prevent chaffing, and the complexities of nappy folding and fixing with safety pins. If this was the way the new life would be, she would do her best to be part of it. Her expression never even altered when the shed skins were bundled up for the fire. The Connemara shawl and the ivory cotton wrap with the long silk fringe had previously been designated for preservation via the washtub.

The dormitory was another source of amazement. Finn had often talked of 'proper beds'. Indeed it was one of his aims that they should eventually own one. And here they were – rows of them.

She saw the amusement on the face of the little woman, and smiled. But hers was not a smile of amusement, rather one of vindication, for the sight of the iron-framed beds had renewed her faith in Finn's judgement. Like Major Mary had said, it was going to be all right. Sharing with other women, all of whom were older, and many of whom were short-stay vagrants, presented no problems. Having been used to communal life with the tinkers, she settled at once into the hostel routine.

The following morning, Tessa accompanied the Major to the police station.

'Oh, yes, he's been before the bench. Trust the Irish to cause trouble. Straight off the boat and into a brawl.'

'But he didn't start it, Sergeant.'

'That's his story, Major. He went, bold as brass, to ask men outside a labour exchange for work – men who'd been laid off because the bosses import Irish labour, dirt cheap. Now if that isn't provocation, what is? Mark you, it's the government I blame. Shouldn't let foreigners in. Oh yes, Major, he's gone down all right.'

'For how long?'

'Thirty days for disturbing the peace.'

'Thirty days!' echoed Tessa, jumping up from her chair.

'What was he to do? Stand there and let 'em kill him? And how was he to know they were out of work?'

'If you return to the chair, Mrs Collins, perhaps the sergeant will allow me to visit your husband?'

'Of course, Major, anything for you. Jonesy,' he yelled. 'Take the Major down to the cells, will yer?'

When they had gone down, the sergeant turned a kindly eye on Tessa. Marvellous, he thought, what a drop of soap and water can do. Brought her looks up real good. Still, Irish women are always good-lookers. Striking, he concluded. Yes, she's not a young woman you'd forget easily.

'Don't look so worried, lass. Our prisons aren't like the Irish ones. He'll be on velvet, your old man.'

'Velvet?'

'I mean he'll be better off now than he's ever been. A good wash, free haircut, and a suit of prison clothes. He'll have a bunk to sleep on, two blankets and two good meals a day. He's a strong young fella so they'll set him to work in the wagon repair shop. They pay 'em, too. Not much, but it's better than nowt.'

The expression on Tessa's face was doubtful. The thought of not seeing him for a whole month seemed the worst thing that could possibly have happened. Her growing anxiety eased when the Major appeared.

'What did he say? Is he all right?' So impatient was she for news that she almost added the plea, 'For Christ's sake, tell me!' But she had been told such phrases were blasphemous and not to be used. Unable to think of as compelling an alternative her lips closed in frustration.

'I'm to tell you firstly – ' Major Mary lowered her voice from the sergeant ' – that he's making the best of it. And he loves you very much. There, does that make you feel better?'

Tessa nodded. The message was a poor substitute for Finn, but still her spirits soared on a wave of gratefulness to the Major, to the Almighty – to everything. There was now a link with Finn. The Major had seen him – and thought him a fine young man – had spoken to him, and was happy to answer, as indeed she did, any amount of questions. Tessa did not feel alone any more.

Her natural curiosity and native optimism helped her in

the week that followed to absorb a measure of social conduct. She realised there was a lot to learn about civilisation as her experience on the domestic front began to widen.

Being used to dirt floors and rush coverings, the necessity for scrubbing wooden floors and cleaning stone steps had to be explained and demonstrated. Eager to earn money, and also to keep her thoughts occupied, Tessa turned a willing hand to both the kitchen and the laundry.

The chores of the day and the welfare of Patrick prevented melancholy thoughts, but in the darkness of the dormitory and between the starchy warmth of cotton sheets, Tessa allowed herself the luxury of self-pity. The whole world stopped and unchecked tears ran down her face to dampen Patrick's dark curls. An aching numbness entered her heart; she yearned for the weight of her husband on top. She dreamed of endless hours of rapture, and woke at dawn to the sound of bedraggled women cursing at having to get up.

For a couple of hours every afternoon, Major Mary, determined to integrate her Irish protégé into the English way of life, encouraged her to go for a walk, taking Patrick in a borrowed bassinet to the park. It was there, in a shop by the church, that she saw it – a Sacred Heart. Her memory went back to the black oak dresser in her father's croft, where the Sacred Heart which had been presented to her for saying the catechism, had held pride of place.

She stood gazing at it, mesmerised. The frame was a little battered, but that did not matter. She must possess it to counter the influence of General Booth. Attendance at prayers every morning and night, and the hymn singing which accompanied these occasions, was compulsory, but they meant nothing to Tessa. In Ireland, God's name was on everyone's lips. He was called upon regularly, a hundred times a day, to witness this or that. To lend a strength to an oath, to save or condemn. If it was not God, it was Christ's name which prefixed many a statement. Mary, the Blessed Virgin and, indeed, any or all of the saints were frequently appealed to. Tessa missed this element of her religion, and the Heart appealed to her mood. She hurried inside and bought it for one shilling and sixpence.

Back at the hostel, she slipped the crude, wooden oil

71

painting under the pillow. She said her prayers over it, and beneath the starched sheets recited the rosary with Kate Jarvey's beads. This secret act of defiance, apart from being positive and assertive, also brought about a deepening of religious spirit.

At odd moments she wondered about Captain O'Shea. Little bursts of gratitude would flare up in her heart, for hadn't his kindness been like that of God? And to think Patrick had a soldier, a captain no less, for his godfather! Every now and then, these thoughts would be followed by a pleasurable pride in her own progress since riding in the wagon from Dublin, and the reflection that he probably would not recognise her as the same person. He had been right about a wedding ring being a talisman. The little gold circlet warded off many a suspicious glance, and often times she felt a kind of mischievous triumph at the deception, a thumbing of her nose to the world.

The last few days of Finn's sentence dragged with the slowness of years, and now, on the morning of his release, even the last moments seemed to crawl. She was waiting for him, not in the polished hallway, but alone in the office to which Constable Jones had first brought her.

Footsteps: shoes, not boots! And when Finn stood within the framework of the frosted-glass door, she didn't know what to say. It took her only a few seconds to assimilate the change in him. The cropping of those thick, raven-black curls had sharpened his features. The weather-tanned face was sallow. But, such clothes! Unknown to either of them, Major Mary, realising that prison charity clothes would not run to large sizes, had ransacked the Army's store and provided a pair of grey flannel trousers and a tweed jacket. He wore a clean collarless shirt, and as though loathe to completely jettison the past, his own red neckerchief knotted about his throat.

Change there was, but his eyes, as darkly blue as the butterflies on the bog asphodel, had the same smile, the same love look – but for a split second they were held in abeyance.

He had last seen her cowering against the wall, and the memory had haunted his sleep, despite the assurances of

Major Mary. Having been racked both by the injustice of the sentence and a terrible remorse, he had felt apprehensive about this moment, half expecting recriminations and tears. Instead, she was confident and at ease here in this strange building, in this grand office.

Her hair was fastened up with a pink strip of muslin, and the top three buttons of her blouse were becomingly unfastened; her sleeves were folded back from the wrist. Wearing a grey silk skirt which hung in soft folds, and a pink blouse with puffed sleeves, she was enjoying his amazement.

His smile overflowed, filling his eyes, lighting his features. 'Sure, I think I'm at the wrong place!' he joked, taking her into his arms and swinging her round so forcefully her feet left the floor. 'God, I've missed you, Tess. Ah, 'tis the lovely girleen you are.'

'And are you not the handsome fella yourself!'

She leaned against him weakly, feeling his strength and virility coming at her in waves. How she had yearned to hold him in her arms and, at last, he was here, her own dear heart, her love, her darling. They kissed, and stood apart for a minute to gaze in admiration and disbelief. And then, as if it were an anguish to be separated, they held each other tightly, the embrace punctuated with small, soft kisses.

A restless, plaintive cry from the depths of the bassinet brought them rapidly back to reality. 'And who's this then?' exclaimed Finn happily, looking at the round-eyed baby, who momentarily shelved his complaint at the sight of a new face. He leaned over to pick him up. 'C'mon little fella, d'you not remember your da?'

'Of course he does! He doesn't miss a trick, cute as a cartload of monkeys!' And more seriously, 'What d'you think of him, though? They all say he's come on marvellous here.'

'God love him, he has, Tess. And I can see he's going to be every inch as good-looking as his da!' His glance switched quickly as she moved to the door. 'Christ, don't leave me with him. What if he cries?'

'Just put him in the bassinet and rock the handle. It's easy! I'm going to get us some tea and bread. Major Mary will be back soon, and we've got to talk about our future. Oh, and Finn, for God's sake don't say "Christ". They don't

73

like it. Come to think of it, when Marie Jane O'Malley went into service, they didn't like it either.' Being halfway between the door and the hall, she glanced at the full-length portrait of General Booth, and whispered, 'They're dead against the drink, too. So don't go telling the Major you could do with one!'

Tessa, not wanting to be away from him long, hurried to the kitchen, where the little woman insisted on thick slices of beef, great wedges of bread, a chunk of butter and jam.

'God alone knows when we'll eat like this again,' declared Finn, wiping up the crumbs on the empty plate with his finger.

'That's what I wanted to tell you now. The Major will be here soon with an agent from a cotton mill in a place called Manchester. He's looking for workers.' She pursed her lips and shrugged. 'Cheap labour, like the men said in the queue. I told her we'd be interested.'

'Interested!' exclaimed Finn. 'We are so. We can't afford to be arsing about. If those fellas price themselves out of work it's their own bloody bad luck.'

Tessa winced. 'Shh. Language, Finn.' She shot a hurried look at the door. 'Anyways, the Major's putting in a good word for us. Y'see,' she indicated the hessian bag by the bassinet, 'you wouldn't be able to stay here. They have a separate hostel for men, so I said we'd go to lodgings.'

'Did you, now. I wonder why you said that!' he teased, and reached for her hands across the desk. Then, on a sudden thought, he added, 'Did you say this mill was in Manchester?'

'I did so.'

'And didn't the Captain say the Salford barracks were near Manchester?'

'I've still got the slip of paper he gave me.' The good news was confirmed. With a burst of excitement she shook his hands up and down. 'Aren't we the lucky pair!'

'And didn't I tell you it was a land flowing with the milk and honey?'

'It didn't seem like it four weeks ago,' she reminded him.

'Ah, sometimes it takes a bit of finding . . .' Footsteps sounded in the hall. Voices, Shadows at the frosted glass. Tessa and Finn sprang up from the desk. A quick tap on the glass, and Major Mary ushered the mill agent into the office.

Mr Wilkins was tall, though not Finn's height; he was well-built, and well set-up, with a gold chain across his waistcoat pockets to prove it. Placing his bowler hat on the desk, he rubbed his hands together as if he were cold.

Although the Major had previously been enthusiastic about these two, Mr Wilkins had not given her all his attention. Travelling people, vagrants, and those just released from prison – especially for 'breaching the peace' – were not high on his list. He was employed by one of the biggest cotton mills in Manchester and was renowned for the quality of cheap labour he produced. Being ambitious, he was not for running that title down.

The questions came thick and fast, and Finn answered them with the engaging deference learned from the tinkers. Although not mentioning the fever that had taken him en route, he was nevertheless painfully honest about his lack of experience, money and knowledge, and about being illiterate. Major Mary, leaned against the door, trying to keep down a tide of rising annoyance that this young man was not selling himself enough.

'But Tess can read and write,' explained Finn with pride. 'She sees to all of that. And I'm a strong and willing worker, sir.'

George Wilkins acknowledged the truth of this last statement with an incline of his head. His brown eyes settled on Tessa, who, seeing Patrick was about to cry, scooped him up against her shoulder. They're a fine-looking couple, he thought. Well matched. Obviously still very fond of each other. Obviously full of vitality and optimism. His eyes strayed to the dark-haired baby – no doubt there'd be half a dozen more in as many years.

He pulled himself up from these meanderings. He was in the cheap labour trade, on the lookout for labourers and operatives with strong arms and years of work packed into them.

'Yes,' he said decisively. 'I'll set you on, Collins. And as a token of goodwill, here's a ten-bob note for the train to Manchester. It will, of course, be docked from your first week's earnings.'

'What about lodgings?' The Major spoke sharply. Although relieved at Finn finding work, it always irked her that the only way to help homeless immigrants was through people like Wilkins who were earning commission per head. But what else was there? 'They must have suitable lodgings for the child.'

'I can do better than mere "lodgings", Major.' He rubbed his hands together and addressed Tessa. 'What would you say to a little house of your own, Mrs Collins? What would you say to that, eh?'

Unable to believe their good luck, Tessa could only stammer her thanks. Wilkins, whose air of power clung to him like a second skin, smiled in acknowledgement.

'When you get off the train,' he explained, 'find your way to the church of the Sacred Heart in Ancoats.' Tessa choked down a gasp of astonishment. The Sacred Heart! She had bought it, said prayers over it, and now the church was called by the same name! 'Give my card,' Wilkins was saying, 'to Father Quinn, who, if he likes the looks of you, will make the necessary arrangements. If you get a move on, you can be in your own house by tonight.'

Chapter Seven

Tess and Finn, along with the other third-class passengers, backed away in alarm. With a frightening flash of the firebox the huge locomotive thundered into Lime Street station, filling the air with steam and their ears with noise. They had seen trains before, but never at such close quarters. Tessa stared apprehensively as the great iron wheels, screeching in protest, came to a halt. Not that there was time to stand and be terrified, for as soon as the monster stopped doors were flung open, crashing back on their hinges. Some leapt out as though to safety; others hovered, the more nervous eyeing the gap between step and platform.

'Get a move on there!' yelled a couple of porters, herding the third-class travellers like restive sheep. 'Get a move on. Train's not got all day!'

The crowd surged obediently forward, trying to get on before the others got off and feverishly hastened by the hissing of the train. Hawkers with trays of pies, muffins and toffee shouted their wares, and into all the turmoil stepped the guard.

'All aboard!' he ordered. 'All aboard for Manchester!' Tall and red-faced, fierce whiskers bristling, he strutted along the platform slamming doors and cursing the late-comers. 'All aboard now for Manchester Victoria!' He stood for a moment flicking a green flag against his leg, impatient of lovers and loiterers still by the windows. 'Stand back,' he shouted. 'Stand back at once!' He looked up at the big clock, blew the whistle, brandished the green flag, and waited with uncharacteristic patience for the train to pass, enabling him to step nimbly into the guard's van.

Tessa and Finn, watching from the window, and being tightly packed onto a slatted wooden bench with six others, were quite unprepared for the shuddering start which almost pitched them onto the knees of the people opposite. After a few more hesitant jerks, the train finally got up steam and took off like one of Martin Jarvey's donkeys.

The exit from the Salvation Army hostel had been a hasty one. After Mr Wilkins had gone in search of more cheap labour, Major Mary had uttered a quick prayer over their uncomprehending heads, blessed Patrick, hugged Tessa warmly and told Finn, 'You've got a good lass there, Mr Collins, look after her. If you hurry you'll be in good time for the train.' And to Tessa, 'You do know where the station is, don't you? Buying a train ticket is just the same as buying a boat ticket.'

Now, uncomfortably crammed and terribly jolted, Tessa felt, as always, an overwhelming pang of regret at having forsaken the familiar for the unknown. The initial lurching forward had startled Patrick and wakened his vocal chords into action. His mother sheltered him deep within her shawl, and he, missing the gentle motion of the bassinet, absorbed the mood of his parents and wailed with muted misery.

A broken window added to the discomfort of overcrowding, and, unprepared for the darkness of the tunnels, women screamed and men swore as smoke and soot blew through in great gusts. Tessa's hair had already slipped free of the pink muslin, her eyes were stinging, and the acrid fumes hurt her throat.

The warehouses, gantries, steeples and streets soon thinned out to murky fields and flat countryside. At the intervening stations, Tessa, stiff, cramped and tired of bracing herself against stops and starts, envied those who hovered on the top step. Even the platform antics of the fierce, bewhiskered guard ceased to be of interest.

'Not far to go,' beamed a large lady opposite. 'Manchester's the next stop.' It was only possible to hear when the train was at a halt, and those of a conversational nature took advantage of it.

78

'Is this Salford?' A man who had been dozing jumped up in alarm.

'Yes. Be quick and get off or you'll end up at Victoria!'

Finn nudged Tessa. 'Did y'hear? This is Salford, where Captain O'Shea's stationed.' He peered out of the smoke-blackened window curiously.

Tessa nodded. She did know, and had read the name as they approached. The guard's whistle, the jerking and the final getaway saved her from comment and induced thought. She had purposely pushed Captain O'Shea to the back of her mind. He was a shadowy figure from the Celtic twilight, and she did not see how he would fit into their new world. The key to whether he would be given the opportunity or not lay with herself; she had the address and she was the one able to write. But, reason countered, he was Patrick's godfather, and it would be ungrateful not to – besides, the ring would need to be returned when Finn bought another for their marriage in church . . .

The train was stopping again. Finn stretched his legs, others got to their feet and struggled to keep a balance. 'You stay where y'are, love,' mouthed the large lady to Tessa. 'Till it stops proper.'

Someone eager to get off had opened the door. Steam rose from the great wheels like a sigh of achievement and, thankful to be alive, the third-class passengers, with red-rimmed eyes and spoilt clothes, stumbled onto the platform.

Following the others, Tessa, Finn and Patrick, who had exhausted his tears, passed silently through the ticket barrier and were soon outside. Hansom cabs perked up for trade and newsboys gave voice to the early edition. 'Boers prepare for war! Kruger delivers ultimatum!'

Neither knowing or caring about Queen Victoria's foreign policy, the two immigrants stood in the light August rain and looked as forlorn as they felt.

Tessa enquired the way to Ancoats, and whilst following the directions, the silence which had engulfed her since the third-class ordeal gradually gave way to curiosity, and her spirits perked up like the hansom cabs.

Corporation Street, just out from the station, was congested with every horse-drawn vehicle imaginable, from the omnibuses noted for their alarming speed of five miles an hour, to the great lumbering railway wagons and the Lyons Tea van.

The scene conveyed something of the vitality of Manchester. The Cotton Exchange had ceased trading for the day and a stream of black-coated merchants and manufacturers descended on the station, anxious to leave the muck and mills for the sea air of Southport or the green fields of Cheshire. The bustle of shops and offices, the comings and goings of white-cuffed clerks, the tall grimy buildings, and the number of brass doorplates, were indicative of a commercial enterprise that thrilled Finn. This, he thought with a sigh of pleasure, is indeed the land flowing with milk and honey.

Tessa was content to be one of the crowd, to be pushed and shoved through Shudehill market, where with expert eyes they picked out the difference between the honest trader, the shady quack, and the hoarse-voiced vagabond out to make a quick penny. And still the past lingered, for Finn, feasting his eyes on the thick-bodied eels and herrings with silver gills, drew Tessa's attention to the fine salmon. 'Sure, I'll never forget Martin Jarvey saying that salmon never tasted better than when freshly poached!'

She smiled and squeezed his arm. 'Ah, Martin was the boyo, all right.'

Big-wheeled farm wagons with even bigger horses between the shafts waited outside the public houses, heads half buried in nosebags, their long jaws munching oats.

'D'you fancy a drink?' asked Finn. 'Not a drop's passed me lips since Kavanagh's Guinness.'

'Me neither,' added Tessa, thinking of General Booth. 'And I really need somewhere to feed Patrick or he'll be crying his head off when we're at the priest's.'

The Seven Stars, a black-and-white huddle of Elizabethan timbers, was sectioned off into little snugs with high-backed settles, where Tessa, under cover of her shawl, fed her baby and exchanged love looks with his father over the rim of her glass.

On the way out, she paused to look at her reflection in the flyblown mirror. 'Just look at me hair, Finn!' she exclaimed. 'Here, hold him while I fasten it back in the muslin – not that it's pink any more after all the smoke puthering through that window – and look at our faces, it's a wonder we're not taken for sweeps!'

Spitting on the corner of the shawl she rubbed the specks of soot from her own face, and then from Finn's. 'Ach, and look at your nice clean shirt – sodding train. If I never go on one again it'll be too soon.' Nodding toward the bar, she asked, 'Did you ask the rest of the way?'

'I did so.'

'C'mon then,' she said briskly. 'Let's be going.'

Following the directions, she strode along Swan Street with more confidence. Liverpool had been a worry to her, but Manchester, which lacked the grandeur of Dublin, had an atmosphere of friendliness.

The affluent end of Swan Street now gave way to a straggling conglomeration of timberyards, small workshops, joinery establishments and bakeries, and these led into the densely packed area of Manchester called Ancoats.

Row upon row of terraced houses which had seen better days bordered the streets, which were for the most part narrow. These were littered with lampposts, tall and green, with two stumpy arms near the top. They also boasted a great variety of small shops, mainly on the corners, and a greater variety still of public houses. Stone setts lined the thoroughfares and soaring chimneys pierced the sky – not that it was always evident. On days when there was no wind, the combined smoke and fumes from mills, foundries and factories hung over the streets of Ancoats, suspended like a tinker's tarpaulin at roof level.

Tessa was the first to see the church of the Sacred Heart, and a little further along, the presbytery. It was a large red-bricked house with a handsome door and a semi-circular fanlight. Iron railings to the side protected a small garden where toffee bags, confetti and cigarette packets blown in by the wind had become entangled with the weeds, and remained like miniature gravestones, a memorial to happier times.

They mounted the four white-edged steps in silence. Finn lowered the battered Gladstone bag which Major Mary had thought a little more prepossessing than a sack, and was about to knock when Tessa touched his arm.

'Will you leave the talking to me,' she whispered. 'The

mention of a proper wedding with the priest and all, I mean.'

'I will so,' he replied pleasantly, and leaning forward kissed her quickly and lightly.

'Not on his doorstep!' she giggled.

'It was just that you looked so anxious, like. You mustn't be, Tess, we could be in the house I've always wanted for you this very night, and with God's own luck.'

'That's what I mean.'

With a conspiratorial wink he seized the bronze knocker and brought it down heavily.

'Merciful mother!' exclaimed the housekeeper opening the door cautiously. 'There's no need for that, we're not deaf.' She was a big-boned woman with a face as round as a pudding and eyes as sharp as a ferret's. Seeing they were decently dressed, she looked curiously at the big man with the heavy hand. But before she could form a judgement, Tessa quickly produced the card Mr Wilkins had given her.

'He told us to ask for Father Quinn.'

The housekeeper caught a glimpse of Patrick's head above the Connemara shawl. 'You'd better step inside then,' and as though relenting, added a cautionary, 'and wait on the mat.'

Being careful to keep to the prescribed square they raised awe-stricken eyes to a life-sized crucifix hanging on the opposite wall. 'It's like living in a church,' breathed Tessa. 'And look at all these stained-glass windows, even in there!' He followed her glance to the cloakroom, the door of which when unoccupied stood open to reveal the polished mahogany casing of a lavatory. The sanitary arrangements at Ennan and the more up-to-date ones at the hostel had always been situated to the rear of the premises. To have them in so conspicuous a place seemed very odd. 'And to think me da was looked up to because he had a dresser!' She indicated the huge vases, the velvet curtains, and expensive-looking bric-a-brac. 'Sure, if Father Quinn were a cardinal he couldn't be more rich.'

The housekeeper returned and led them to the library by way of a soft turkey-red carpet. Father Quinn, tall and wearing a cassock, moved from behind a leather-topped table and raised a hand. 'May God and Mary bless you, my children,' he said in a flat, Dublin accent.

We need it, thought Tessa; oh God, how we need it. She wondered if Finn were feeling as nervous as herself. Up to this moment their journey had been a quest; all her concentration had been centred on getting here, and now the reality of it was frightening. She was suddenly overwhelmed and overawed by the grandeur, the scholastic air of the library, by all that was at stake, and by being face to face with so young and serious a priest. Her knees felt weak. Is it the drink? she thought; but they'd only had the one glass.

'Sit down and make yourselves comfortable, Mr – ' He indicated two heavily carved chairs, and looked at the card. 'Ah, Mr and Mrs Collins, that's it, and I see you've got a little one there.'

Tessa sank gratefully onto the chair, cradling Patrick on her lap, and thankful for the ring on her finger.

'I've asked Mrs Stubbs, my housekeeper, for a tray of tea. I'm sure you could do with some.'

'Yes, Father,' agreed Finn. 'We could so, and thank you.'

'It's always a particular pleasure,' the priest resumed his seat, 'to welcome those from the auld country.'

She noticed he used the same pronunciation as Captain O'Shea with the word 'auld' instead of 'old'. His tall figure was full fleshed, and his heavy-jawed face was topped with closely cut brown hair; beneath bushy eyebrows nestled dark eyes that could pierce and twinkle with equal intensity.

Tea was brought in on a tray and placed reverently on the leather-topped table. The old Irish silver and highly decorated china looked so fragile, and the whole ceremony of serving tea so complicated, that Tessa was glad she only had to drink it. Father Quinn poured and sliced with a practised hand.

'Help yourself to muffins, and I can especially recommend Mrs Stubbs's fruitcake. Come along now, pull your chairs nearer and save all that passing of plates.' Finn received the big Rockingham cup as though it were the Communion chalice, he was so afraid of spilling, crushing, or dropping it. Father Quinn smiled. To be sure, he thought, Wilkins knows how to pick 'em: docile, eager, uncomplicated and honest.

'While we're at tea,' he said pleasantly, 'you must tell me all about yourselves. I realise you have been interviewed and taken on at Atkinson's mill, but not all their employees are provided with decent accommodation at nominal rents; oh no, not by a long chalk.' He refilled Tessa's cup. 'You're looking a lot better for that, Mrs Collins. You'd gone quite pale; I expect it's been a long day for you.'

'Yes, it has, Father . . . ' She was not going into details yet.

'As I was saying, Mr Wilkins has a letting arrangement with a local landlord, but in order to safeguard his reputation as a mill agent he has asked me to ascertain whether you are people of good character. You see, we have a respectable little community in the parish of the Sacred Heart and we want to keep it that way.'

That's done it, thought Tessa. And didn't I know it all the time? And hadn't Captain O'Shea got the measure of it all, too? She sent up a swift prayer of thanks for his advice. Respectable, the priest had said. Well, she and Finn were respectable, hard-working, honest, and didn't owe a soul. Up to this moment they had had every intention of following their broomstick wedding with a ceremony in church, but Father Quinn was not making it easy. The situation was confusing and constricting, yet she was not intimidated. Feeling calmer, she sipped her tea and made up her mind. No, she decided, I can't risk it, can't tell him yet, not until Finn's got the key to a house in his pocket. She could not bear the accusing glance of those dark, piercing eyes; or to see the cloud of disappointment spread across her man's face, especially after the prison and all, and him going on about a land flowing with milk and honey. Besides, there were other churches, other priests, and another time.

Not daring to look at Finn, she circumvented Father Quinn's questions by launching into an expurgated history of their lives. Finn listened to the flow with admiration, recalling the schemes and plots she used to devise to escape her da. 'Strategies' she used to call 'em, and begod, she hadn't lost the gift!

By the time the last crumbs were devoured, Father Quinn had the information safely docketed in his mental filing system.

'That seems quite satisfactory,' he said, getting to his

feet. 'You both seem to have had more than your share of misfortune, but I trust all that is behind you, and a blessed future ahead.'

'Thank you, Father,' said Finn piously.

Following him into the hall, they waited opposite the crucifix, and exchanged embarrassed glances when he went into the cloakroom and closed the door. After the sound of flushing water, he emerged, wearing a cloak and wide-brimmed hat.

'Just follow me,' he said, going out into the street. They did, and immediately became objects of curiosity, as indeed were the parishioners of the Sacred Heart to them. The light rain had stopped, and more people were afoot.

Mill girls off the teatime shift, straddling the pavements with linked arms, broke ranks to allow the little procession through. Some children were improvising a swing with a rope over the stumpy arms of a lamppost. Gangs of young boys loitering outside the corner shops jostled and pushed each other over cracks in the flagged pavements. Occasionally, Father Quinn addressed someone or waved a hand in greeting to another, and at one time raised his hat to a nicely dressed woman who carried an umbrella and wore button-up boots.

The priest stopped outside a dreary building where a weather-stained notice board announced 'Tobias Green-ledge. Properties to let. Rents collected.'

They filed up the three steps, startling a pale-faced clerk who clearly thought business for the day was over. 'Mr Greenledge in?' asked the priest.

The clerk nodded in obvious dismay. It was now past six o'clock; he wanted his tea. He was hungry, and any clients, especially this one, meant it would be a late finish.

The priest pushed open the door of the inner office, and Tobias Greenledge stepped down from the raised dais on which stood his desk. He was a threadbare man; everything about him was worn, from his hair to the soles of his shoes. He shook hands with the priest and exchanged a few words while taking stock of the young couple.

'Well,' he hedged. 'With your recommendation, Father Quinn, and to do Mr Wilkins a favour, I do happen to have one or two properties which might be suitable.'

85

They consulted a map on the wall. 'Loom Street,' murmured Greenledge. 'Two up and two down; or there's Ancoats Lane, a back-to-back property.' They murmured again and Father Quinn preferred Loom Street.

Greenledge turned to Finn. 'I trust you can manage a week's rent in advance, young man. There are so many round here do a moonlight that I fear it's necessary. If you haven't got the rent in advance you are wasting my time. We have a saying round here that "time is money".'

'Yes.' Finn's hand went to his pocket. 'I've got the money.'

'Will you wait a minute, now,' said Tessa, her hand staying Finn's. 'We would like to see the property first. Where we come from there is also a saying: "don't buy a pig in a poke".'

Finn's heart sank. Mother of God, he thought, she's done it now.

'Very well,' said Greenledge irritably. 'Let's get a move on, I've not got all night.' Snatching a key from a hook on the wall, he hurried his prospective tenants past the pale-faced clerk and through the door.

Out again amongst the rows and rows of densely packed houses, Tessa kept an alert eye for Loom Street, and wondered how she would ever find her way about, for they all seemed the same. She looked with open curiosity and mounting excitement. Women with babies sat on front steps watching smaller children at play; men lounged against the walls smoking pipes. Some doors were wide open, others half, but all seemed to boast a fanlight displaying on a narrow shelf the figure of a saint, of Christ, Mary the Queen of Heaven, or a few paper flowers stuck in a jam jar.

Although the whole scene looked dismal and shabby to people like the priest and the woman with the umbrella and button-up boots, to Tessa and Finn the little houses resembled mansions in heaven. And, even to the outsider, Ancoats had a spirit which almost transcended its poverty. When the lamplighter was going his rounds, or on bright days when a stiff wind lifted the pall of smoke, the sun invested the begrimed streets with a kind of dignity, as though the terraces knew in some smug, inconceivable way that the people who lived in them were indispensable, that without the labour of the thousands crammed in this small area, commerce would grind to a halt.

'Here we are, Mrs Collins,' announced Greenledge, jolting Tessa out of her observations. She stood before the small house, wide-eyed, heart thumping with excitement. The paint was peeling, the windows dusty, and the inferior brickwork was crumbling around the sills; added to which the house was 'tied' with an oaken beam to the property across the alley. But Tessa saw none of this. As though in a dream, she followed Tobias Greenledge up the three steps into the front room which smelled of damp air and stale gas. He asked if Mr Collins had a penny for the gas meter on account of it being such a dismal evening. Mr Collins had, and Father Quinn produced a box of matches, struck one and ignited the gas.

'Let it warm up a second or so, and to improve the brightness you gently tug the chain on this side of the fitting, and to lower – '

'Yes, I do know about gas lights, Father Quinn. They had them at the Salvation Army hostel.'

The priest cut short his demonstration and stood back at once. He was not used to interruptions, especially by the young. But seeing her obvious excitement he quickly repented of his annoyance.

As the light flared Greenledge became animated, dancing about like an overgrown spider. 'Now, this is the houseplace, and beneath the lino are solid flags.' He stamped his foot to prove it. 'Big cast-iron range. Oven to the right; hob to the left.' Ignoring the grey mound of ashes spilling onto a tin hearthplate, he continued, 'Crossbar to lower for cooking on, and this – ' He pranced toward the smaller room which had no door and turned abruptly. Tessa, having removed her shawl, made a nest of it by the Gladstone bag, for Patrick, and felt free to continue the exploration. 'This is the scullery,' continued Greenledge. 'No gas in 'ere. The light from the houseplace shines in.' He treated them to his threadbare smile. 'You can always light a candle.' The smile gone, he announced briskly, 'Tap. No going outside for water, Mrs Collins. Lesser properties in Ancoats have a communal tap, y'know.'

Finn approached the tap with a knowledgeable air and

tested it. Tessa ran her hand along the bottom of the brown earthenware sink, making sure it was not cracked.

Anxious to settle the letting, Greenledge drew the large bolt on the back door and pointed out to the three steps down to the yard. 'No midden sanitation in Loom Street, Mrs Collins; nothing so archaic. You share both the yard and water closet with the Coopers at Number Twenty-five.' Tessa nodded her understanding, and Father Quinn, with a smile, presumed that that piece of knowledge was also courtesy of the Salvation Army. His amusement continued. Greenledge's catalogue had not included the Coopers' eight children. He imagined their mother on the other side of the wall threatening them with hellfire if they so much as whispered while the landlord was there!

'Two bedrooms.' The terse statement accompanied the opening of a plank door at the bottom of the stairs. Finn was willing to believe that it was so, but Tessa, lifting the folds of her grey skirt, climbed the short flight to a square of landing. There was a small room to the back and a larger one to the front. The dusty floorboards creaked as she crossed to the window, and the fireplace, like the one below, was endowed with a legacy of ashes. Placing her hands on the window ledge she looked onto the cobbled street and the houses opposite; at children crying and mothers shouting. She glanced down at her hands: the wedding ring, and a dead bluebottle.

Downstairs again, she eyed the black mantelshelf and thought that its beaded edge was even grander than her da's dresser had been. Finn pulled open the door of the floor-to-ceiling cupboards and fixtures, and smiled ruefully. 'We'll never have enough stuff to fill these!'

'I shouldn't worry, Mr Collins,' remarked Greenledge dryly, first casting his sharp glance at Tessa. 'A big young fella, like you – why, you'll have those cupboards filled and the bedrooms with little 'uns in no time, won't he, Father Quinn?'

'We'll take the house,' said Tessa primly. 'The rent you said was half a crown?'

'And a week in advance makes it five shillings.'

Tessa made sure their name was on the blue-covered rent book and that the correct amount was registered, and when she looked up Greenledge had gone.

'I'm sure you're going to be very comfortable here...'
Father Quinn was talking. 'I trust you'll come to me if you
are in any difficulty, just like you would have done back home
in ... wherever you said. I am your friend, your father in
God and can do a lot to help you – any kind of problems,
personal, spiritual ...'

It was on Tessa's lips to seize the moment, to confess
and confide, to make a clean start so there'd be nothing
to hide. But, lifting her head, she saw his glance sharpen in
anticipation and drew back. He reached for his hat and said
slowly, 'You will remember?' They nodded solemnly. The
priest then asked a blessing on the house, and after imparting
the information that confession was every Friday evening and
Mass at ten, eleven and three on Sundays, went out.

Chapter Eight

No sooner had the front door closed than the back, which had not been re-bolted, slowly opened.

'D'you mind if I come in?' Without waiting for an answer, a woman stepped inside, shutting the door on the voices of children suddenly released from forced quietude.

'I was waiting for him to go,' she smiled, trying to get the measure of her new neighbours. 'Real gas-bag, he is. Talk yer socks down, he would. You're Irish, aren't you? And yer name's Collins?' She jerked her thumb toward Number Twenty-five. 'I was listening – these walls are as thin as tissue paper! It's always nice to see a young couple settling in – but you two've scarcely got the cradle marks off yer arses!'

Tessa and Finn, recovering from their astonishment at the sudden intrusion began to laugh, not particularly at what she said, but because Annie Cooper inspired laughter.

The full cheeks and dimples were cheerful relics of a pretty face which had rounded out to absorb its features, so that no one noticed the colour of her eyes, only the twinkle. Nor did they notice the double chin, only the smile. Her body was also part of the conspiracy; Annie Cooper was never referred to as being fat, only big-hearted. One aspect which did not conform to the image was her faded hair. At Tessa's age it had been her crowning glory, bright as gold, a full, gorgeous plumage. But twelve years and eight children later, it was scraped back severely into a tight round bun and stuck through with black hair pins.

Her chin almost disappeared in rapture at the sight of

Patrick. 'Come to your Auntie Annie, then.' She scooped up the nest containing Patrick. 'I saw you passing by our window, but couldn't see the baby under your shawl. Oh, what a lovely little thing.'

'It's a boy,' said Tessa, her voice echoing in the empty room. 'His name's Patrick.'

'No wonder he's a little love with a name like that. I like 'em when they're little,' she cooed. 'We're hardly ever without at our house!'

She glanced ruefully down at herself. 'But I pay for it. You've only to look at me belly to see that.' And then, wistfully, she said, 'I once had a figure as shapely as your own. You wouldn't think that now, would you?' She cuddled Patrick as though cherishing the memory. The smile returned to her dimpled cheeks. 'Come on you two, come to Number Twenty-five and have summat to eat. I've a big cow-heel stew in the oven – and you're welcome to sleep the night on our hearth rug, till you get some coal tomorrow.' She looked out of the window. 'Where's your furniture? The last people brought it with 'em on a handcart.'

'They were lucky,' replied Finn. 'We've not got any, with travellin' and all.'

Annie, still holding Patrick, led the way out through the scullery. Tessa hesitated, and Finn knew she would rather have stayed in their own house a little while to savour the experience, and to ponder with him on their amazing good luck. But the promise of stew stirred the hunger pangs, and as the fireless grate held no hope, Tessa turned down the gas and followed Annie into the yard.

The Coopers' door stood open, a fire blazed, flies buzzed and a dozen children played noisily on the steps. 'Only five of these are mine. The two big 'uns are up the street, and the little 'un is inside asleep – at least I hope to God she's asleep! I miscarried with four.' She waved away Tessa's expression of concern. 'God knows how we'd have managed if they'd lived.' And in the next breath, she was saying, 'Later on you must come to the Sugar Loaf with Cooper and me. You do take a drink?' she enquired with a worried frown.

'We do so,' came the emphatic reply.

Annie laughed. 'I might've known! Show me an Irishman that doesn't!'

'We know at least one,' said Finn, moving from the heat of the fire. 'That's Captain O'Shea, Tess.'

'D'you mean he doesn't take a drop of anything?'

Finn shook his head. 'The parents and all of that turned him against it.'

'A captain?' echoed Annie, clearly impressed.

'He's Patrick's godfather,' said Finn proudly. 'A vet – well, horse doctor at the Salford Barracks.'

'He's a lucky little lad, then,' said Annie, returning the nest and baby to Tessa so that she could haul a large, brown stew pot from the oven. 'Shouldn't be short of a bob or two with a godfather like that. I can't remember the names of half of ours, and none of 'em have two halfpennies to rub together!'

They sat at a wooden table covered with linoleum, and strewn with the debris of past meals. Some of this was brushed aside, and two basins were hurriedly rinsed. The stew tasted as good as it smelled and, when served, water was added before returning the pot to the oven. Finn, now on the right side of it, felt able to politely refuse the offer of a hearth. 'I'm going to buy a bed tonight,' he explained. 'You see with us travelling and all, we've not had a proper one, except when Tess was at the Sal Doss. I mean,' he went on expansively, 'what's the use of having two bedrooms and no bed? If we take up your kind offer of the Sugar Loaf, the money'll go in drink, and we'll never be able to afford one.'

Annie nodded her acceptance of his logic. She was pleased a young family had moved in next door, and liked the big young man with the curls, the bashful kind of smile, and long eyelashes. I'm not so sure about her, she thought. Scarce said a word since they arrived. A bit standoffish. Good-looking, though, and knows it, especially in that grey skirt and pink blouse. Not be like that for long, not round 'ere she won't.

'Tell you what,' she said returning to the subject, 'Cooper should be home soon, and when he's had his tea, he'll show you where to buy a bed for next to nothing.'

'Now that's real decent of him.'

'And I'll mind Patrick while you both go. The kids'll like another baby to play with. Yes, both of you go, find yer way around a bit.'

Annie always referred to her husband as Cooper. He arrived home shortly, and Tess and Finn saw a man several years older than Annie, thin and wiry, with stubbly hair, a quiet manner, and given to wearing a tight-fitting waistcoat.

He was pleasantly surprised to see his new neighbours with their feet beneath the table. Providing for so large a family weighed heavily on his shoulders, which were inclined to stoop, and any diversion to take his mind off the arduous task was seized upon and enjoyed to the full.

The diversion at present was to make the newcomers feel welcome. He told them about Atkinson's mill, and how he worked there as a doffer. He followed this up with a dissertation on public houses and types of beer, then touched lightly on the Boers, concluding that it was 'all summat about nothin'.' He kept up a steady flow of talk all the way through the stew, which was watered again before being returned to the oven.

Having taken his tea, he stood up. 'A bed did you say, Annie?'

'How about Sad Sam's on Ancoats Lane? They'll not do better.'

He was at once alert and on the scent. 'Come on, then, you two, get your backsides off me chairs, or Sam'll be putting the shutters up.'

Cooper moved with all the purpose and speed of a whippet, and it took Tessa and Finn all their energy to keep pace with him as he dodged horses and swung through the crowds of people on their way to markets and music halls, until they arrived breathless at Sam's.

'This is it,' announced Cooper, as they crushed into the dimly-lit shop. 'There must be at least a dozen 'ere and he'll have more in the cellar.'

'It was now dusk, and in the light of a solitary lamp, Sad Sam picked his way through a graveyard of bedheads, posts and wires. Finn, flanked on his left by musty mattresses, and on his right by two beds already assembled and intact, explained he was looking for a sound specimen. 'With four good legs. I'm not for propping one end up with bricks.'

'You won't have to prop mine up, mate!' came the indignant reply as Sam emerged from the gloom. As though soothing its feelings, he caressed the nearest bedrail. 'How about this, then? Solid brass. An' it's big. Best to have 'em big. You'll fit half a dozen in there, easy!'

Tessa blushed at yet another remark on their modesty. 'Legs it might have, but the knobs have gone,' she said sharply, eyeing the bare, brass screws sticking up like totem poles. 'And should the mattress be saggin' so much?'

'Nothin' to worry about, missus. You can tighten up the webbing beneath. And the mattress is horsehair. Let me tell you, there's no bedbugs in 'orsehair. An' why bother about a few missing knobs on such a fine bed as this?'

Finn looked at Tessa. She nodded. 'We'll have it,' he said. 'On condition you deliver it tonight.'

Sam shook his head morosely. 'I'll be losing trade if I close early to deliver.'

'Losing trade!' echoed Cooper. 'Come off it, Sam. You've been goin' downhill for years!'

'Will ye listen, now?' interrupted Finn. 'Sure, we've travelled miles and miles, and crossed the water, we have. Cooper told us you were just the fella to see, an' we arrive breathless from Loom Street only to find you'd leave us this night without anywhere to lay our heads!'

'All right, all right! Calm down, mate.' Sam raised his eyes, looked at Cooper, and sighed deeply. 'I don't suppose there'll be any more trade tonight. Not that I've had much. Bottom's fallen right out of the bed business.' He turned his mournful glance on Finn. 'You'll have to wait while I put the shutters up,' he mumbled. 'But the donkey and cart's round the back, if you want to start loading.'

Having paid for the bed and not wanting to lose sight of it, Tessa and Finn walked by the cart while Cooper, knowing they would not get lost with Sam, dodged off on his own affairs. Walking at donkey pace was much slower than Cooper pace, and it was completely dark when they arrived back at Loom Street.

'Whoah,' shouted Sam, tightening the reins. 'Whoah, there.' The donkey twitched its ears and came to a halt.

'You've got the wrong house,' said Tessa. 'There's a blind at this window and the gas is lit. Ours is empty.'

'You said Twenty-seven, and Twenty-seven it is.'

Tessa turned to Finn, dismay in her voice and anxiety at her heart. 'He's right, it is our house. Greenledge must have let it to someone else. Got a higher rent. Oh, Holy Mother of God, sure we shouldn't have gone out! We should never have left it!'

'*We* bloody well shouldn't?' said Finn grimly. 'I'll get 'em out if I have to throw 'em out with me bare hands!'

Tessa, thinking of the affray at Liverpool, and concern for Patrick sweeping over her, caught hold of his sleeve. 'Let's go to the Coopers'. They'll know what's happened.'

Sam's voice cut across their turmoil. 'It isn't the wrong number,' he said dolefully. 'They've laid on a housewarming.'

The door opened, radiating warmth and welcome. Cooper, his waistcoat unfastened and his shirtsleeves rolled up, bounded down the steps and conducted the two bewildered tenants into their house.

'See what Toby Greenledge has found for us,' he said, by way of introduction. 'The new neighbours, Tessa and Finn!'

'Sure, I can't believe it!' gasped Tessa, reeling from the extremes of emotion she had just undergone. There was furniture, and a bucket of coal by the fire which was already lit. There were sounds from the scullery of crockery and bottles, of voices and laughter. But where, oh dear God, where was Patrick? Fear curled about her heart, knotting her stomach. Had something happened? One of the Coopers' children might have dropped him or fallen with him . . .

But Annie, seeing her bewilderment, gave a reassuring smile. Following her glance, Tessa crossed to where Patrick was cosily tucked up in one of the drawers by the side of the fireplace.

She looked down at the little sleeping form, at the crown of curls. Thank God he was safe; there really had been no cause to worry, for were the Coopers not kindness itself? Yet her thankfulness was edged with resentment that these other people, none of whom she knew, seemed so much at home in her house.

A glass, the only one on the premises, was pushed into her hand. 'What's yer fancy, Tessa? Guinness? If you like Guinness, you'll like our brown stout,' said Cooper, jug at the ready, imitating the spiel of the market men. 'Ay lass, you'll like our best brown – beats all that moonshine or whatever you calls it!'

He filled the glass and they waited in silence. She liked the smooth malty taste, and her approval was the signal for explanations. 'These are a few of the neighbours,' said Annie. 'We all help each other in Loom Street. We have our differences just like everyone else, but we help each other. An' for them as got nowt, like yourselves, we start 'em off. Cooper got you these cane-bottomed chairs on the way back from Sam's. One's got a hole in it, but Finn can nail a bit of wood across. An' we fetched this dresser from Mr and Mrs Barnes's — isn't that right, Barnesy?'

Mr Barnes, who was having trouble with his first pair of false teeth, left the talking to his wife.

'Eh, it's nowt,' said the old woman fiercely. She and Barnes were given to bouts of intemperance which always ended in a domestic brawl, the frequency of which had honed her voice to a permanent sharp edge. 'It's too big for us now the family's gone.'

'An' I'm Jud Patterson, the knocker up,' announced a little man with a gnome-like face.

'Are y'now,' smiled Finn. 'And what, in the name of all that's holy, is a knocker up?'

'You'd think he'd come straight from the bogs!' said Jimmy Marr.

'I have,' Finn answered, not understanding their amusement. 'I've only just set foot in Ancoats so how am I to know what a bloody knocker up is?'

'Ours is a gent of quality,' explained Cooper. 'Besides bringing the brass fender there, Jud is the only working man in Ancoats with two clocks. For a tanner a week he'll come and wake you up, rattling on your bedroom winder with a long cane — and he'll not stop until you get out of bed, open it and tell him to bugger off. That's right, isn't it, Jud?'

'Yes,' replied the gnome staidly, and added, 'I've brought 'em an enamel chamber pot as well. It's on the stairs.' Thinking it seemly to direct his glance to Finn, he added, 'It's a long way t'privy in the middle of a freezing night, I can tell yer!'

While Finn and Tessa were admiring their furnishings and expressing their gratitude, Cooper and Sam manoeuvred the horsehair mattress in front of the fire, where propped up on its narrow end it steamed steadily before the cheerful blaze. Then, with a lot of grunting and swearing, the rest of the bed was eventually persuaded up the narrow stairs, where after much fiddling with screws and pushing in of rods, the knobless brass bed stood alone and stark on the dusty floorboards.

'Holy Mother, that was thirsty work,' said Jimmy Marr to Finn as they came down to the houseplace. He paused on the bottom step. 'How about a jar or two for the workers?' he called, and with a loud laugh added, 'Don't tell us you've supped it all!'

A dark-haired, quiet-mannered woman picked up the empty jug and hurried into the scullery to replenish it.

'Who's the big mouth?' asked Tessa, warming to the occasion.

'You mean the one with the head to match?' Annie lowered her voice against the others. 'He's known as Jimmy Marr the piper. Plays the bagpipes for the Sacred Heart band and he doesn't half fancy himself in his kilt. That dark-haired woman is his wife.'

Cooper and Mrs Marr came in from the scullery, she carrying a pitcher and he the Sacred Heart tea urn filled with ale. Cups and jam jars appeared instantly.

'Let's drink to our new neighbours!' declared Cooper. 'To Tessa and Finn!'

'And the little lad!'

'May you always have work to go to, and coal to put on your fire!'

'I've got a toast,' shouted Finn. 'To Tess! There's not a woman in the land can compare with her!'

'Finn,' she protested. 'You're making me blush!' Her cheeks flushed scarlet, but the compliment, far from causing embarrassment, made her draw herself up. There had not been time to wash or 'titivate' as her da had called brushing her hair, but she felt good, well groomed, well dressed and confident. Although only wedded by tinker custom, the ring proclaimed legality. Here she was with husband, child, and a house to live in. This was her kingdom, her domain. She had arrived.

After the toasts, Jimmy Marr began to sing, the others joining in, and as one song petered out, another started up. And I don't know even one of 'em, thought Tessa on a sigh. These were the new songs which Finn wanted, and she could not sing them. There was no lilt to the voices or the tunes – and there were no fiddles, flutes or concertinas.

Finn gave up the intricacies of 'Knees Up Mother Brown' to recall the times he had sat by camp fires wishing for better things for Tess. His heart warmed to God that his wishes had come true. He remembered Martin Jarvey saying, when on the crest of some overwhelming experience, 'I feel like a proper man'. Ach, thought Finn, downing the last of his Chester's Mild, I know just how the boyo felt.

It was past midnight when Finn bolted the scullery door behind the Coopers. The house was quiet. The tea urn, emblazoned with the Sacred Heart stood empty and abandoned, the fire was low in the grate. The mattress, pronounced 'aired' by Sam, had been pushed and pulled up the stairs to join its partner.

He entered the houseplace, kicked off his shoes, and held open his arms. 'Tess, oh Tess – ' he swung her round, elated and happy ' – I thought they'd never go!'

'Sure, they meant well, but I couldn't wait to have the house to ourselves!'

'I couldn't wait to have the loveliest girleen in the green of Ireland to meself – ' He stopped suddenly and looked at her with a puzzled frown. 'I'll have to think of somethin' else, I can scarce say "the green of Ancoats"!'

'You don't have to say anything, except that you love me.'

'I do, Tess,' he held her tightly. 'God knows I worship the very ground you walk on. I love you,' he said simply. 'You and the little fella in the drawer.'

'And I love you, Finn. Oh, 'tis the darlin' man you are.' She leaned her head on his chest, and sighed with indecision. 'I want to stay like this, nice and close, and at the same time I can't wait to get to bed! Will you remember now, the last time we slept together was in Downey's barn.'

'Merciful Mother, Tess, sure we mustn't wait a minute longer! I've made up your mind for you, we're going now!' And still they lingered, exchanging little kisses, sweet and swift. 'Will you be after taking the candle?' he said, as they finally drew apart. 'There's no mantel on the gas up there. I'll bring Patrick.'

'It's like a dream,' said Tessa as she led the way up. 'To think we're in our own house, with an upstairs – and a bed!'

'And no blind at the window either!' he added, quickly substituting a padded quilt that had been thrown in with the price of the bed.

At first, both were overwhelmed by the ocean of privacy. Their eyes met and held, glittering in the candlelight. Tessa felt the old surging weakness wash over her. The colour rose in her face and her heart began to pound. She continued to stare, hypnotised by his 'love look', and thrilled with anticipatory pleasure.

Unfastening his shirt, he took it off; his belt followed, then the grey trousers from the Salvation Army hostel and the long cotton underpants, and there he stood, marvellously naked. His clothes lay on the floor, not that he realised or cared. He was proud of his strength, knowing Tessa admired his body.

Amorously adoring his strong chest and flat belly, his hard thighs and lovely haunches, she sighed with pleasure. The bulging biceps and thickly muscled forearms reminded her of the tons of peat he must have dug, and how he had hated it; and she was suddenly thankful he would never have to dig peat again.

'Oh, you're a lovely fella,' she sighed. 'Sure Brian Boru could never have looked so fine . . . ' Still fully clothed, apart from her shoes, she stood before him.

'Will you be after undressing me?' she whispered shyly.

'I will so . . . '

She stood completely still, eyes closed, thrilling to the touch of his fingers as he unbuttoned and unfastened. His rough hands moved over her body, to set her pulses racing, and her heart beating more rapidly. He did not hurry, for fear of interruption had gone, and had they not waited long enough to be alone? Each caress travelled to the very core of her being, filling her body with an urgent need. They stood for a moment, looking at each other, their bodies ivory in the candlelight, enjoying the sensations which threatened their sanity.

Emotions previously imprisoned by the enforced celibacy of the past six weeks finally tore loose. In the grip of onrushing desire, he scooped her up and put her down on the horsehair mattress, murmuring her name, calling her his love, his girleen, his darling. Her arms went about his neck, sliding voluptuously up and down his back as he covered her body with his own. As the moment of fulfilment approached Tessa's thoughts spiralled; this was paradise, this was madness; this suffocating ecstasy could be borne no longer . . .

Passion spent, they lay comfortably in each other's arms, not really wanting to move, but needing to blow out the candle, to remove the quilt from the window to cover themselves. Finn was the first to break the spell, and being once again in the land of mortals it seemed necessary that he should reach for his long johns and she for her shift.

Before blowing out the candle they looked down at the baby asleep in the drawer. 'Didn't I tell you now, this was a land flowing with the milk and honey?' he said softly, an arm about her shoulder.

'You did so.'

'Just think how much more it'll flow for him.'

'But, he'll never know,' she said wistfully, 'how to tickle a trout, and the magic of – '

'Magic me arse, Tess! There's one thing I thank God he'll never know, and that's the terror of a bloody great bog on the move. He'll never tend ailing pigs, or squat under tarpaulin rigs – '

'Come to bed, Finn?' She did not want the shadow of the disaster over their bliss. 'Before we know it, that Jud Patterson will be rattling on the window with his canes.'

Snuggling beneath the quilt, she curled up against his side and went immediately to sleep, without a telling of the rosary. Finn focused his eyes on the glimmer of streetlighting at the window, and recalled staring out of the window of his aunt's cabin on the day he left. While in prison he had thought the mockers had caught up with him, but now, lying here, he held a different view. He now saw himself as what Father Quinn had called 'the breadwinner of a good robust Catholic home'. He drew a deep, peaceful breath. He had arrived.

Chapter Nine

Jud Patterson, the knocker up, rounded the corner into Loom Street. Early morning, especially between four and six o'clock was his 'brisk time' during which he felt more lively and alert than at any other part of the day. He was a little man, insignificant to look at, and with nothing in his character to redeem this insignificance, only his calling and two large alarm clocks, the position of which elevated him in the eyes of his neighbours.

As Cooper had said, Jud was a real gent. He was also the only one who could be sure of getting paid for his services at the weekend. The man from the insurance company, the coal merchant, the grocer, and sometimes the rent collector, either received no answer to their continual knocking, or were told it would be 'settled next week', or were confronted by the youngest child opening the door with the timeworn phrase, 'Me mam's not in'. But no one kept Jud waiting. No money, no being woken up.

Moreover, he had the welfare of his clients at heart, for if there was no response on his first round he would call a second time, shouting to those like Jimmy Marr for all the street to hear: 'It's a quarter to six. Get up, tha lazy sod, or I'll come and pull thee out of bed!'

Not that his concern was always appreciated, for those of a hasty temper often opened the window and hurled out the first thing to hand. But Jud took it all in good part and never referred to the event in public. He would then report the sick cases to the timekeeper, and call to share a jug of tea with the fireman in the boiler house.

He crossed the alley where the houses were tied with the oaken beam and remembered last night's housewarming . . . very nice, very nice, he thought primly. There be no trouble with Number Twenty-seven.

The springed wires on the end of Jud's bamboo pole rapped a smart tattoo against the window. 'God save us!' exclaimed Finn jerking upright in bed.

'It's the knocker up,' whispered Tessa, sitting up in equal alarm.

Another assault on the pane brought Finn's gradually waking memory more into focus. 'It's destroyed I am,' he groaned, struggling to assemble his thoughts.

'He'll not be going until you tell him you're up. Go on.' She gave him a push. 'Oh merciful Mother, he's started Patrick off . . . '

She leaned over to lift the baby from the drawer while Finn opened the window and put his head out. 'I'm up,' he said, trying not to shout. 'It's enough to wake the dead!'

'Mill gates close at six, lad,' came the sober response. 'It's a warm start to the day. Best get you down.'

He closed the window and reached along the spiky rail for his trousers. Mustn't be late on the first day, he thought, or I'll be locked out till the end of the shift, and Cooper said they docked your pay.

'Go back to sleep, Tess. No use you getting up till the fire's astir.' Thoughts of the aunt intruded; he used to blaze up the turves for her, but not any more. What price the mockers now, with me at the mill and earning fourteen shillings a week!

'Are y'going now?' she asked softly.

'I am so.' He stood looking down at her.

'You'll be careful, you'll take notice of Cooper?'

'As though he were the Almighty Himself!'

'Ach, away with ye then!'

Sitting up against the brass bedstead, too curious to sleep, she listened to the sounds which were to become the pattern of life. Finn moving about downstairs, raking the fire. The sound of their own front door closing and causing the windows to rattle as he left to join the tide of men heading for the mills and foundries. Then the last

102

rush of clogs pelting the cobbles, as the mill hooter blared and blasted the early autumn morning.

Tessa was relieved that Cooper had promised to 'put him right' concerning the procedures, for she dreaded above all else another misunderstanding like Liverpool. A wave of tenderness swept over her as she recalled Finn's eagerness to buy the bed he was always on about, especially to please her.

She reached out a hand to touch the place where he had lain. Thank God there'd be no more sweating and fumbling beneath a tarpaulin, never sure whether a drunken tinker would crawl into the wrong rig, or worse, a sober one lift the flap by mistake!

Getting up, she laid the sleeping baby in her place, and tucking the quilt about him sorted her clothes. The grey skirt and pink blouse were hung on the bedstead for best, and the black skirt and checked blouse would be for everyday wear. Her stockings had holes in the feet and walking on the floorboards would not improve matters, but, on this her first morning, she didn't want neighbours, baby, or even Finn to intrude on her first moments alone with the house. She took the Sacred Heart from the hessian bag and crept downstairs.

The kettle, already singing on the crossbar of the fire, was set down on the coals to boil. She quickly made tea, and sipping it, moved about with cup in hand. Her eyes looked beyond the litter on the Barnes's dresser to catch sight of herself in the mirror above it. Face rosy from sleep, and hair tousled, she couldn't help but smile at the happy bewilderment lighting her features. All this was theirs. It was wonderful, like a lovely dream! And so big a mirror, too. There had never been much time, or indeed any mirrors, to encourage self-esteem, and she suddenly saw herself objectively.

Placing the teacup on the dresser, she peered into the glass. Her great expressive eyes, now more grey than blue in the dim light, held a solemnity beyond her years. The uptilt of her head added a dignity which she presumed had always been there and which Finn called her 'regal' look. She gathered her cloud of hair, twisted it into a thick bun and thought it added maturity. And, yes, she liked the look of herself; not a beauty like her tinker friend, Kate, but what the halfpenny papers called 'stunning'.

Taking a pace backward she surveyed her figure, hands smoothing down over waist and hips. Her mother had been tall, straight and slender, and although tall herself, she knew that even when the present plumpness of pregnancy had gone, her figure would never be slight – not that she wanted it to be. Just so long as I'm nice to look at, she conceded shyly, wondering at the same time whether it was seemly for a wife and mother to want to be 'looked at'.

The survey ended, she retrieved the cup of tea from the litter on the dresser, and there, surrounded by bottles and flanked by the Sacred Heart urn, stood a plaster cast of the Madonna. It had been lying about in Sad Sam's shop for months, and appreciating Cooper's invitation to the housewarming, Sam had donated it. Tessa looked at the statuette curiously, at the softly moulded features, at the smile which continued through to the painted eyes. Mrs Barnes had said that every good Catholic home in Ancoats possessed one, that to have Her on your dresser was insurance against bad luck. Face to face with such an object was slightly unnerving; Tessa crossed herself and turned her attention to the Sacred Heart. Feeling more at ease with its familiar air of sadness, the vivid colour and battered wooden frame, she placed it in the centre of the beaded mantelshelf, and behind it, for safekeeping, the rent book.

Becoming aware of the shouts and wails of the Cooper children, she wondered with vague unease how long it would be before this house was echoing with the same noise. Marie Jane O'Malley used to say that once married you grew round-bellied every year; she hoped to God it would not be like that. What had Annie said? 'I once had a figure as shapely as your own.'

Finishing her tea, she sat down on the cane-bottomed chair and thinking about their finances, made a mental list of basic necessities: table, bucket, brush, a pan, and some pots.

Her mind raced ahead to when Patrick was weaned, for Major Mary said he would need all of a gill of milk a day when he was 'feeling his feet' or he'd go bandy-legged. And besides all this, she and Finn, being brought up on the poteen, could not face life without a drop of 'how's your father' as Annie called it. Finn's wage of fourteen shillings would not go very far – and, of course, the train fare still had to be repaid.

It would be some time, then, before money could be put by to replace the Captain's ring. Finn would soon be after her writing to him at the Salford Barracks, and wouldn't it be fine if when he stepped through that door she could say to him, 'Captain O'Shea, thank you for the borrowing and here's your ring, for hasn't Finn bought me one of my very own'? Ach, she continued her thoughts, the times I used to give out about me da saying, 'neither a lender or a borrower be', and begod, if I'm not cast in the same mould meself!

And doesn't all of that seem like another world – travelling with Martin and Kate, the Downeys, giving birth on the boat; and what a sad tale it surely was about Captain O'Shea's bride jilting him at the very altar. She stared down at her left hand. This then, was the very ring intended for his own wedding. It must be, for people don't just happen to have wedding rings in their pockets! Her concern deepened. The experience had soured him, all right, for had he not said on the quay at Liverpool 'You don't have to get married again, not if you're happy as you are'?

It took Finn some weeks to comprehend the intricacies of mill work, and the mill workers' ritual that went with it. There were many delicate balances within the fraternity of mates which had not to be upset, and having got the measure of it all, he felt secure in his new life.

Although he sometimes worked an extra shift in a bid to provide more money, there was only just enough to live on. The Coopers and others were always in debt of some kind; it was a way of life, paying one off against another, playing the game of seeing what they could get away with, but it was a game Tessa could not join in.

She had considered working in the mill, but was fiercely protective of her child. To have left him with Major Mary was one thing, but to leave him to take his chances with Annie's brood and the other half-dozen she minded, was quite another. Having scrubbed floors at the Salvation Army hostel, Tessa mentioned the possibility to Annie.

'Cleaning!' she echoed. 'There's no one within miles of Ancoats can afford a cleaner.'

'What about taking in washing?'

'There's a lot of women already onto that. Mark you, there's more money in speciality washing. Not everyone can do it.'

'Tell me about it?'

'Well, for ordinary washing you'd have to buy a tub and a dolly peg, that's a wooden stave with three legs on, which you put in the tub to stir and pound the clothes with – otherwise you'd get terrible bloody backache with bending over! Then you take 'em back to the customer wet, and that gives you backache, too!'

'An' the speciality washing?'

'You've got to be good at it, Tessa. Got to do 'em better than the laundries. The clothes have to be dried, starched, ironed and folded right. It means more outlay, too, for the irons – and then,' she inclined her head dolefully, 'p'raps hardest of all, is finding customers. You've got to be recommended for speciality washing. People in nice houses won't trust their delicate stuff to strangers.'

'A fine chance I have of being recommended, I hardly know anyone!'

'Well, if you're that taken with the idea, why not ask Jonty Johnson, y'know, the landlord of the Sugar Loaf, to ask about for you?'

As the new year of 1900 approached, Jonty Johnson still had not heard of anyone wanting speciality washing. 'But, I've got another idea, Tessa,' he said, placing her glass of Guinness on the mahogany bar. 'D'you fancy doing a turn?'

'What d'you mean, a turn?'

'Singing,' he explained. 'Up there,' he nodded in the direction of what was known as The Room. 'Regular,' he said, 'every Friday and Saturday night. D'you remember on Christmas Eve how they all stopped singing just to listen to you?'

Tessa stared at him, wondering if she had heard right, and recalling how Flowery Nolan, the street singer back home, had told her she'd never be short of a penny while she could sing. Why had she not thought of that herself!

106

Mistaking her astonished silence for hesitation, he leaned over the bar by way of encouragement. 'It'll mean free Guinness, lass. Folks in The Room at the weekend will buy you a drink to sing their favourite songs, which are easy enough to pick up. And when you've had enough to drink, just put the money in your pocket and tell 'em you'll have one later – make as much as two shillings a night, and free booze.'

'Me, singing in there?' She drew back from the bar, as if to reflect, but was already calculating what an extra four shillings a week would provide. It might run to a pegged rug for the hearth, lino for the bedroom, decent boots for Finn – and, dare she think it, a little to put by for a wedding ring. 'Sure, I can't believe it. Oh, did I ever tell you, Jonty, you're a gent of the first water!'

'Not that I can remember! But I take it that you're on?'

'Oh, I am so,' she answered, breathless with excitement. 'Wait till I tell Finn.'

'Is he not in tonight?'

'He'll be a half-hour yet. There's cheap coal at the sidings and him and Cooper are trying to borrow a handcart to fetch some.'

'Will he mind about you doing a turn?'

'Mind?' she echoed. 'Are we not scratching round for every penny? Will he hell mind!'

People who spat, swore or smoked were not allowed in The Room at the Sugar Loaf, neither were those wearing clogs or shawls. In keeping with these sartorial rules Tessa wore her grey skirt which clung softly to her hips, and the black-and-white check blouse. A neat white collar, which could be removed for washing and tacked back on, added a provocative touch of primness to her personality.

The appointment of the 'new turn' packed the Sugar Loaf at the weekend. Having left Patrick safely tucked up in a makeshift cot, and Finn to bank up the fire and have a 'good wash' before following, Tessa went early to go over some unfamiliar melodies with Titch Bradley, the pianist, who was so small his feet only just reached the pedals.

George Wilkins, on one of his occasional visits to the

Sugar Loaf, pursed his lips and nodded in the direction of The Room.

'Quite a songbird you're got there, Jonty.'

'Ay, we 'ave that, Mr Wilkins. At least she stops 'em all talking about this South African business! Haven't you heard her before?'

'No.' Wilkins shook his light-brown head. 'Been out of town. Too busy. It only needs a war to step up the demand for cotton. Set me up a glass of the best, will you?'

His glance strayed again to The Room, and having taken up his drink, pushed his way through the Saturday night crowd and stood at the threshold of the door. Thus it was that Tessa saw him, glass in one hand, and the thumb of the other hooked in his waistcoat pocket. The reflection of the gaslight on his gold watch chain drew her gaze. She recognised him at once and felt a flutter of panic at the presence of a superior. He was linked immediately with the other two influential people in their lives, Tobias Greenledge and Father Quinn. Oh, Holy Mother, she thought, and isn't the sight of him enough to put me right out of tune!

But, far from putting her off, Tessa seemed to draw the audience together in a tapping of feet and fingers, a swaying of bodies. Her pleasure at their response added a lustre to the performance, and made the rendering of 'Paddy McGinty's Goat' even more hilarious.

George Wilkins' golden-flecked eyes took all this in, and he discovered himself to be pleasantly intrigued by the thought of having seen her before. When Tessa next dared glance in his direction he had gone, and she let out an audible sigh of relief. Titch Bradley, thinking it was on account of the last song, winked up at her – his sign that it had gone down particularly well.

'Who's the songbird, then, Jonty?' asked Wilkins on his way out.

'Tessa Collins. Lives round the corner in Loom Street. That's her husband in the Vault – big Irish fella, works at Atkinson's. Set him on yerself.'

'More than likely,' he agreed, and tossing a sixpence across the bar, added, 'Send her a drink in, will you?'

'Yes, Mr Wilkins. Oh, Mr Wilkins?' he called after the

departing figure. 'I don't suppose you know anyone on Oldham Road wants washing done?'

'Now how do you expect a man in my position to know things like that?'

'Just thought you might, that's all. I'm trying to put some work in the way of Tessa Collins.'

The mill agent paused at the door, and as though coming to a considered conclusion, said, 'Leave it with me, Jonty, leave it with me.'

Chapter Ten

It was a bright May morning. A stiff breeze raced across the sky, hurrying, pushing, relieving Manchester of the fumes of industry. And in the town itself, most of the talk concerned the war, and how Lord Roberts was hurrying and pushing the expeditionary force to relieve the besieged town of Mafeking. Cormac O'Shea, hot and dusty from the stables, entered the officers' mess with his friend and colleague from a neighbouring barracks.

'The usual?' Nick Styles indicated the bar with an incline of his sandy coloured head and laughed softly. 'I don't know why I even bother to ask!'

'You live in hopes that one day I'll surprise you and ask for a double whisky!'

Nick had long since given up trying to persuade the Irishman to drink something stronger than ginger beer shandy, and had even lived down the embarrassment of ordering so mild a tipple, especially in the mess. But then O'Shea was the kind of the fellow you never minded going out of your way to please.

'Pint, then?'

'A bucketful!'

Cormac sat down, and taking several letters from the back pocket of his breeches, idly looked them over and pushed aside what were obviously a couple of bills. Oh, not another, he thought, not another invitation to a garden party! Did colonels' wives have nothing else to do? Ach, that's more like it – cricket at Old Trafford; tickets for the pavilion. He pulled a wry face. Subscription due for the *Stable* magazine;

notice of a lecture on the poetry of Dean Swift – and what was this? The handwriting was neat and carefully rounded, and he knew at once that it was from Tessa Collins.

'Interesting?'

'You've taken your time! A fella could die of thirst.'

'And you're stalling, evading my question.' Nick set the glasses down, tasted his beer and leaned forward confidentially. 'You've been staring at that letter for minutes on end. Do I detect a woman?'

'Yes. Ah, God love you, Nick, a rare young woman.'

'They're all rare, at first.'

'There speaks the cynic, and women don't like cynicism in one so young! If you're not careful it'll develop into a full-blown malady!'

'Like the stable sickness –'

'Ach, now, don't be tempting providence!'

Nick raised his glass. 'Let's drink to a speedy victory in South Africa.'

'Speedy! When the Boers have got Baden-Powell and over a thousand troops cornered at Mafeking!'

'Lord Roberts'll soon sort out the bloody Boers. They don't call him the siege-breaker for nothing.'

'I drink to it all,' said Cormac easily. 'But mostly, I raise me glass to the cavalry – and me godson.' He reached for his pipe, and tapped the notepaper with the stem. 'Didn't know I was a godfather, did you? Not set eyes on him since the day he was born. His mammy – and his da – are rare folk from the auld country. Pleasant, unspoiled, unsophisticated. Y'know the kind?'

The sandy head shook soulfully. 'I do not, thank God. Sounds extremely humdrum to me. And if the beguiling epistle isn't from one of the young ladies at the University Settlement, we'd better get on and discuss whether this outbreak is notifiable . . .'

Later on that night, Cormac sat by the open window enjoying the cooler evening air. Despite being on duty and the noise of the traffic and the shout of revellers on the road below, he felt at peace with himself.

He had often recalled the farewell scene on the quay at Liverpool with the big young man and his ragged princess beside him.

And I really thought they'd forgotten me, especially after a few weeks had passed. He stretched his legs, lit his pipe, and admitted for the first time that he had been disappointed, felt almost spurned by the lack of communication. Ridiculous, wasn't it? Strangers they were, ships that pass in the night. Had they tied the knot properly? he wondered, smiling at the memory of Tessa's panic when Finn went for the priest, and she with no wedding ring on her finger! Now, in a generous mood, he could cast aside previous despondency and look forward to renewing the acquaintance.

He was familiar with Ancoats; more smoking chimneys to the square mile than anywhere else on God's earth! 'The skies may be sulphurous,' Nick had said, 'and the area described as a "slum", but there's a grand spirit of social service.'

And sure, it's the oddest thing, thought Cormac, that Nick's sister is part of the setup at Ancoats Hall, which the map told him was not all that far from the Collins's address. He strove now to recall any snippets of information about this philanthropic work. Nick's sister, a graduate, had said 'What Oxford University is doing for Whitechapel in London, Owen's College is doing for Ancoats in Manchester.' And so he had been press-ganged, via the Styles family, into what became known as the Manchester University Settlement, or briefly, as M.U.S.

Cormac rekindled his pipe. And wasn't it the grand scheme? Culture and recreation for the uneducated. Poetry, plays, clubs for cripples, clubs for boys and girls, debating societies. And Audrey Styles even spends a couple of afternoons a week reading to the blind. He admired their outreach, but up to now his own contribution had been merely to make up a foursome with Nick and Audrey for the Saturday night dances – and for a couple of poetry readings; for hadn't Captain and Mrs Clare instilled into himself as a boy the love of poetry? They'd had a good time too, a few weeks back, when the Ancoats Hall piano, roped like the Ark of the Covenant to a milk float, had swayed its way through alleys and courts, gathering the crowds for a singsong like the Pied Piper had gathered rats.

His eyes returned to the letter, noticing the length of it as though having started she did not know where to stop. All their adventures, from the troubles at Liverpool to getting used to Manchester customs, were related. He smiled in the darkness. The event was a few weeks away, but he would not forget. *Come on July the twenty-ninth*, she had written. *It's Patrick's birthday so we will not forget.*

Finn arrived from the mill in a jubilant mood.

'You'll never guess what's happened today.'

'Sure, I'm not in a guessing mood,' Tessa had said, tending a pan perched on the crossbar of the fire.

He sat on a cane-bottomed chair and took off his boots. 'I had to go and see Mr Wilkins today.'

'God save us!' She turned in a panic. 'You've not been stopped!'

'Me stopped?' he echoed. 'And how would Atkinson's be managing without me!'

She stood still, and her voice emerging from a tightened throat did not seem like her own. 'What did he want, then?'

'He's heard that Mrs Collins was after taking in washing. "Nothing fancy," he said. "Just sheets and towels, but there could be table linen and lace, if Mrs Collins can starch nicely." '

'Finn!' Her throat expanded with relief. 'You did say yes?'

' "Mr Wilkins," I said, "sure Mrs Collins has a marvellous hand with washing of every kind, and would be only too pleased to oblige!" ' Patrick, crawling towards his father's boots, was lifted up, and held chuckling and kicking above Finn's head. 'When I've had me tea, son,' he spoke in tones of exaggerated excitement, 'I'll go to Ancoats Lane and see if Sad Sam's got a washtub for your mammy.'

'And I'll have to borrow some soap,' added Tessa, caught up in the jubilation. 'The insurance man'll have to wait for his money this week; I'll buy starch instead.'

Tessa tackled the subject of washing with the same determination as Queen Victoria regarded the relieving of the besieged garrison at Mafeking.

'We are not interested in the possibilities of defeat,' Her Majesty remarked. 'They do not exist.'

By the time Captain O'Shea received her letter, Tessa was known to be as good and hardworking a laundress as a singer. The borrowed soap had been returned, and a bargain of a mangle obtained from Turner's laundry which was being refurbished. The cast-iron frame showed no rust, and the heavy wooden rollers, only a little worn, and turned by a huge handle, crushed and squeezed every drop of water out of anything which was fed through. Being far too big for the house, it occupied a corner of the yard and was covered by an old tarpaulin.

On dry, windy days, the yard was festooned with lines of sheets and towels elevated above the grimy walls by a long prop. Another investment was an airing rack which Cooper had fixed to the ceiling above the fire, and which was lowered and raised by means of a pulley attached to the scullery doorjamb. On wet or murky days, when no breeze disturbed the puther of filth from factory chimneys, the sheets and lace-edged pillow slips steamed ferociously from the rack, making the air damp and the windows a cascade of condensation.

Speed was essential to Tessa's schedule, for she had made it clear to her clients from the start that she had no time to deliver or collect. The only drawback to the scheme was that people expected their laundry to be ready at the appointed hour.

She had a little help in this direction, for sometimes one of Annie's children would do errands, and when in the mood, the eldest turned the mangle. Although Tessa was not for actually leaving Patrick with the Cooper brood, she had no objection to their playing with him in her own house.

Despite being friendly by nature, and there being many other Irish immigrants in Ancoats, Tessa did not form any friendship the depth or quality of that previously shared with Marie Jane O'Malley or Kate Jarvey. At present she did not feel the lack of such comradeship, and still regarded Annie Cooper with a kind of wariness.

Although used to the communal life from their travelling days, now they were settled Tessa began to resent the way Annie regarded their house as an extension of her own. Yet, she was so good-natured, and nothing was ever too much trouble, that to mention the subject, even to Finn, would seem ungrateful; especially after the fixing of the drying rack.

Tessa's most illustrious client was Mr Wilkins himself.

His laundry was usually packed and waiting, especially at the month end, for then he collected in person and settled the bill. At other times it was delivered and collected by Danny, a young lad of gangling proportions, who, according to Mr Barnes, was 'a bit short'.

Today, no matter how much she hurried, Tessa knew the Wilkins wash would not be ready. The fire had almost gone out, one of the irons had spread soot, and she'd had to wash the corner of the sheet again. She cast a hurried glance at the blue-mantled Virgin on the dresser, and then at Patrick crawling under the table.

'Will you come out o' there?' she called. 'Come and let me wash your face. Mr Wilkins'll be here any minute, and you're as black as a sweep!' But the child would not come out; he liked it beneath the table, and regarded her with rounded eyes, knowing she was too big to crawl after him. Hoping to God he would stay there, she quickly placed the cool iron on the red cinders and, taking the hot one off, spat on it. The saliva bubbled across the smooth, shiny surface to vanish in a loud hiss. She turned to the table and began to iron with swift, heavy strokes. But, despite her haste, the laundry was not finished when George Wilkins tapped on the open door.

'Will you sit down, Mr Wilkins? Sure, it's nearly ready.'

'Don't bother yourself, Mrs Collins.' He smiled and rubbed his hands together. 'I realise I am a shade early, but it will be pleasant to sit and watch how perfectly you perform your task.' He lowered himself gingerly onto the chair by the dresser, then satisfied it would bear his weight, leaned back with folded arms.

'You seem to be settling in nicely,' he remarked, shuddering inwardly at the clutter of clothes in so small a room.

'We are so, Mr Wilkins.'

'I've not been to the Sugar Loaf lately. Do you still find time to sing?'

'Oh, I do, I do. Sure, it's like getting paid for a night out!' She laughed at her own comment, and suddenly felt awed, realising this was the man who, as Finn so often said, was 'like God so far as we're concerned'.

'I hope Mrs Wilkins won't mind you being late with the washing,' she commented more soberly.

There was a short silence. 'Mrs Wilkins – died.'

'Oh,' Tessa turned her large eyes toward him in immediate sympathy.

'It happened two years ago when my son was born. A very gifted woman, my wife was, clever and beautiful; too good for me . . .' There was another silence. 'I live with my unmarried sister who looks after the boy. Used to live hereabouts, y'know, but when I married, my father-in-law bought us a fine house on Oldham Road.' He tapped his white fingers against the dresser top, suddenly annoyed for revealing so much of his private life to a mere washerwoman, albeit a young one. Annoyance changed to a startled frown. It drew Tessa's gaze, and to her horror she saw Patrick crawling from beneath the table. Somehow, he had struggled free of his leggings and was moving swiftly toward the mill agent. Tessa, already flushed with haste and the heat of the irons, turned crimson, for her son, bare-bottomed and dirty-faced, smiled and held the wet leggings up for Mr Wilkins's inspection. Not knowing what to say, and terribly flustered, Tessa fumbled with the iron, and swore as the smooth black edge seared the skin of her wrist.

'Are you burned badly?' Wilkins jumped up from the chair.

'It doesn't matter,' she answered, more irritated by the way the day was going than with the pain.

Wilkins took charge. 'Here,' he said, manoeuvring his polished boots clear of Patrick. 'Over to the window.' He took the hot, reddened hand in his own cool-fingered grasp and examined the burn. 'You need some flour for it; keeps the air out, at least that's what my sister does.'

Eyeing Patrick with distaste, Wilkins stepped around him to follow Tessa to the cupboard by the side of the chimney breast. As she stretched up to the shelf his gaze followed the curve of her waist to the upreach of her bosom and extended arm. Strong arms, he thought; dimpled elbows. Immediately, he recalled her holding the baby at the Salvation Army hostel at Liverpool; how he had thought there would be half a dozen more in as many years. The association with sexual vitality struck at him sharply.

Tessa looked from him to the flour. She made a helpless gesture. 'Have I to be mixin' it with water?'

'Allow me,' he replied shakily. He sprinkled some flour on

116

his white handkerchief and applied it to her wrist, watching the movements of his fingers as though they were not part of him. Beads of sweat broke out on his forehead.

'Ach, and sure, it feels easier now.' Her lilting voice brought him back to reality. 'The sting's gone out of it.'

He glanced about to be sure he wouldn't stand on the child and resumed his seat, sitting in silence while she folded the laundry. When it was neatly packed in the Gladstone bag, he took the money out of his purse. Again, he watched, fascinated, as her capable fingers closed with amazing rapidity over the money, which was swiftly conveyed to the pocket of her skirt.

'Well,' he said, standing on the top step. 'I must get a newspaper, they say the news from Pretoria is not very good.'

Not knowing what to say, Tessa smiled briefly and nodded. When he had gone she sank down onto the vacated chair, and seeing Patrick still trailing the wet leggings, began to laugh.

'And who was a little spalpeen today?' she addressed Patrick, having related the tale to Finn after tea.

'Has he not a boy of his own?'

'You'd not think so by the look on his face!' She shot him a quizzical glance. 'And talking about looks, you've been up to something, Finn Collins!'

'Could you not fancy a change from sitting on these hard-bottomed chairs?'

'I could so.'

'Could you not fancy a black, shiny sofa like they had at the Sal Doss? Y'know, the one that had the picture of that fella above it?'

'Ach, you mean General Booth's picture. Yes, I could fancy a sofa, but we've not that kind of money yet.'

'We might have.'

'And from where might we be getting it?' Her tone was scarcely encouraging.

'Now just because I backed the wrong horse on Derby Day –'

'How much's gone down the Swanee this time?'

'Saints preserve us, Tess, nothing's down the Swanee.' He began to explain. 'Will you listen calmly now? I've laid out ten shillings – '

'Ten shillings!' she cut him short with a horrified whisper. 'That's more than half a week's pay, and you likely to lose it all!' Tessa was not given to temper or tears but today nothing had gone right. The few shillings left over from his wage lay on the table, fuelling her astonished anger. 'You're not a gambling man, and Marr the piper knows it. Knows he can take you for a ride any time!'

'Will you let me explain, Tess?'

'What is there to explain?' She dumped Patrick on the floor and got up from the chair, facing him across the table. 'If there's one thing that puts the fear of God into me – and you very well know it – 'tis the fear of getting into debt, and having to borrow to keep the roof over our heads. If we can't pay the rent Greenledge won't wait. Look how he evicted the Thompsons from the next street. Standing in the drizzle they were, their few sticks of furniture forlorn an' miserable without the support of four walls. She, God preserve her, with the kids crying into her skirts, was frightened of having to go to the workhouse; and he was racin' round like a whippet to raise a loan for a cheap cellar lodging for the night! Is that what you want for us?'

'The trouble with you, Tess, is you've got too much bloody imagination!'

'And the trouble with you is you never stop to think!' The full fury of her frustrated day rose into a crescendo. 'You never stop to think what'd happen to us, to me and Patrick, just so long as you fall in with Jimmy Marr and the other fellas!' She turned her head away, eyes bright with unshed tears.

'Tess, it isn't like that.' His voice was low, patient and warm. Casting aside the warmth she ran into the scullery. Her fingers curled hard over the rough edge of the sink. Her heart was hard, her mind a blank. She heard his chair scraping back on the flagged floor and stiffened. Merciful God, ten shillings, just like that! If he thought he could coax her out of this one, he could think again!

The front door slammed. He had gone out. Patrick was frightened and began to wail miserably.

Chapter Eleven

Tessa stood for a moment longer, then quickly stooped to lift Patrick. She cuddled him to her heart, her lips against the soft dark curls until he had stopped whimpering. 'Oh, Patrick,' she murmured miserably. 'What are we going to do now?'

She crossed to the dresser and stood with the child in her arms before the blue-mantled Virgin, looking into the chiselled features. Patrick's eyes followed his mother's, and he, too, watched the figure expectantly. When nothing interesting happened he wriggled to be set free. She put him down absent-mindedly, and sighed. How quiet it was. Even the fire had settled, the street seemed silent, and next door could have been empty. Since the disaster of Ennabrugh Tessa did not care for solitude, for into it strode giants of torment, remorse and uncertainty. They were there already, filling the silence with alarm and dread. It all seemed so final, the banging of the door and no last word of outrage. When they had quarrelled about the money he'd lost on Derby Day, it had seemed to blow up quickly and was soon over with a kiss.

'C'mon, little fella,' she addressed Patrick briskly. At least the sound of her own voice was better than the tomb-like quiet, and having something to do stopped the progress of the giants. 'Let's see if your leggings are dry, shall we?' She took them from the side of the fireguard, and Patrick, as if sensing his mother's unhappiness, put up no struggle while she sat him down and pulled them over his chubby legs.

The scullery door opened, Tessa looked up quickly,

hopefully. It was Annie Cooper. 'I heard the door bang, nearly shook the winders out! He's got some strength, that husband of yours.' She entered the houseplace and leaned against the table edge. 'First barney, is it? You're lucky, me and Cooper were fighting rings round before the wedding day was done! What's up, then?'

Tessa's eyes registered blank disappointment. Oh, if only it had been Finn. She knew Annie was being 'neighbourly', as they called it, but her emotions were still jangling, and the last thing she wanted was to go over it all again.

Annie spared her the trouble. 'Yer needn't tell me, love. I heard it all – walls as thin as tissue paper. You mustn't be hard on him, he was only taking a chance for you and the little lad.'

'But he swore he'd never go into a bookies again –'

'Bookies?'

Tessa was puzzled; Annie knew very well the meaning of the word. 'Yes,' she said impatiently. 'Betting. Horses, y'know.' In a calmer voice, she added, 'Not that you can blame him. I've seen Marr the piper shouting the odds of flies crawling down the window!'

'But you are blaming him, aren't you?' The usually cheerful tone had an edge to it. An edge which said, you ought to thank God on your bended knees for Finn Collins. If you'd gone on like that to Jimmy Marr, by God, you'd have got your eye blacked. 'There were no horses,' she said. 'And no bookies' parlour.'

'How d'you mean?'

'If you'd have given him half a chance he would have told you that Marr's taking the odds on Mafeking being relieved on the eighteenth.'

Tessa watched Patrick shuffling on his bottom toward the table, and remembered Mr Wilkins mentioning that the news from Pretoria was bad. And I took no notice. What's a war in South Africa to do with us, I thought, and now because of a wager it's on our very doorstep!

'Some says Lord Roberts won't get there till the twenty-first, others say he'll be too late to find any alive, but Finn and Jud Patterson have settled for the eighteenth – today.'

Tessa seized on Annie's every word as though it were a lifeline. Finn had not, after all, broken the promise made on Derby Day. True, it was gambling just the same, but he wouldn't realise that, especially with Jimmy the Mouth egging him on.

'Where are you going?' asked Annie, as Tessa untied the strings of her coarse apron, and then scooped Patrick up from beneath the table.

'I've developed a sudden interest in the war, and if Mafeking's going to be relieved tonight, I'm going to be with Finn when he gets his winnings!'

'Now, you're talking sense,' Annie called after her departing figure. 'And watch that Jimmy Marr – it won't be the first time he's got out of paying up!'

The light of the May evening was beginning to fade as Tessa, with Patrick astride her hip, hurried past the oaken beam, through the ginnel at the side of the house, and onto the next street.

Groups of tousled children sat on doorsteps, whips and tops idle, hoping to delay a little longer the call to bed and the need to wash their faces and dirty knees. Older boys and girls loitered by the corner, indulging in flights of fancy which were only possible in the shadowy time before the coming of the lamplighter.

Tessa saw none of this. She was intent on reaching the Sugar Loaf and fighting down the fear that he may not be there, and if he wasn't, where in heaven's name would she look?

The Sugar Loaf boasted three entrances, the doors of each bearing a stained-glass window which stated boldly and unequivocally, so that no error of judgement was possible, the words: PUBLIC BAR, JUG AND BOTTLE, VAULT.

The way to the Room where Tessa sang was through the Public Bar; and it was to the Jug and Bottle that Jimmy Marr and Cooper ran to fill the Sacred Heart tea urn with Chester's Ale; or Mrs Barnes scurried with a quart jug beneath her shawl; or children were sent for a bottle of brown stout. The Vault, with its sawdust-covered floor, wooden benches and strategically placed spitoons, was reserved for men. Here the profane could spit, swear, and swill; the harassed find refuge in a game of dominoes and a half pint; and the voluble could hold forth and the troubled sit in silence.

Tessa hesitated. Then, with Patrick still in her arms,

face flushed with hurrying, she lifted the latch and peered through the crack.

Finn, sitting morosely by himself, stood up and quickly joined her outside. 'I was comin' back, Tess,' he said gruffly. 'I shouldn't have slammed out like that, not on you –'

'And I shouldn't have been giving out before I'd heard the full story.'

They stood for a moment by the Vault door, he looking down at her over Patrick's head and she looking up, her eyes large and dark. A mutual forgiveness passed silently between them. They released their glances gently, slowly, almost reverently; it had been a hallowed moment.'

'Annie told me about it, Mafeking and all,' she said softly, by way of explanation.

'Here, give me the little spalpeen.' He stepped into the street. 'And let's go into town. I couldn't settle if we went back, anyways.'

'I didn't bring me shawl.' She looked ruefully down at her dull, black working skirt, then up at him in his shirt-sleeves, just as he'd walked out. She remembered their travelling days, standing outside Kavanagh's Bar in Dublin, and Finn's hesitation on account of them looking like tinkers. 'Our money's as good as anyone else's,' she had said.

'I'll go back for it, and I'll get me coat, if you like.'

'No.' She handed Patrick over, and linking her arm comfortably in his, they set off toward Oldham Road.

'It isn't faith in Lord Roberts that made me lay out ten bob, y'know.'

She looked up at him knowingly. 'It's because of Captain O'Shea, isn't it?'

'He's a good omen for us, Tess.'

She squeezed his arm. 'You and your superstitions!'

'You wait and see,' he laughed. 'We'll have a sofa out of Mafeking or me name's not Collins!'

For a brief moment she allowed herself the wistful indulgence of hearing him say, 'Sod the sofa, Tess. Let's go and see the wedding rings in Ikey Solomon's window.' She indulged her wistfulness still further. 'An' we'll get married, Tess, with the priest and all.'

The brief moment passed. Besides – the daydream faded on a note of practicality – we need a sofa.

'Annie said to keep an eye on Jimmy Marr –'

'I will so, Tess. He'll not do a disappearing act with my winnings.'

They reached Oldham Road, and remarked on there being more people about than usual. The mood was one of general optimism. Those heading for the music halls were counting on a 'rollicking good laugh'; Miss Horniman's patrons en route to the Gaiety Theatre expected the performance of *Hamlet* to exceed the excellent reviews. And the Halle Orchestra, which was at the Free Trade Hall for only two more days before going on tour, were fully prepared to interrupt their programme with suitable patriotic music should an announcement of Lord Roberts' victory be made during the performance.

It was not only the anticipation of exalted pastimes which filled the air with excitement, but also the simpler pleasures. Just walking the streets was a convivial experience: the flare-lit markets were abuzz with a warm-hearted cordiality; and special cheers of exuberance were raised at the sight of the high-wheeled evening papercarts, whose fast-trotting ponies were always a marvel of speed and grace.

Although affected by the magic of the May evening, Tessa and Finn exchanged anxious glances when Manchester's various clocks announced in various voices first eight o'clock, and then the quarter and the half of the hour. As the chimes and tones grew nearer to nine so Finn's anxiety mounted. Clearly, those assembled were expecting news of the besieged garrison. Talk was rife.

'Eh, don't build on it,' he heard someone say. 'I've spent the last two nights in Piccadilly and nowt's happened!'

'Don't know what's come over folk, gathering like this. Anyone'd think it were t'scholars walking at Whit Week or t'Trade Union processions!'

'I'm not grumblin',' laughed a pieman. 'Good for trade. Lord Roberts shouldn't be in too much of a hurry!'

'You wouldn't say that if you were holed up by the bloody Boers!'

As darkness closed in, a peculiar sensation swept through the city. It was like a holding of the communal breath, which suddenly was let out on a great cheer. Church bells gonged and pealed and rang. Cannons were fired in celebratory shots from every barrack ground that possessed one. Into all this went the breath of thousands, yelling wildly, madly, joyfully.

'Mafeking!'

'Mafeking's been relieved!'

'Roberts has done it!'

'Mafeking! Mafeking!'

'Three cheers for Lord Roberts!'

'Three cheers for Baden-Powell!'

Tessa and Finn, caught up in Mafeking fever, hugged each other. 'And isn't Lord Roberts the lovely man!' she shouted against the noise, thinking not of the rescued garrison, but of Finn's winnings.

Patrick, hoisted onto his father's shoulders for safety, gazed round-eyed in wonder at the flags springing up like mushrooms on a dung heap. Everyone seemed to be getting a Union Jack; Patrick held out his hand, but in his lofty position no one noticed. Never having experienced this emotion before, his bottom lip began to quiver, but at the same time he was too intrigued by the celebrations to let his yearning be known more forcefully.

Men and women in hats and coats rubbed shoulders with those in shawls and caps. Complete strangers embraced. People clung to each other with tears of joy streaming down their faces. Soldiers pouring onto the streets from the barracks stirred the public imagination even more. Cabs and trams ground to a halt as drivers deserted their vehicles.

'Mafeking! Mafeking!'

The cry was on everyone's lips, to be shouted and yelled over and over again. Doors of public houses were thrown open wide to accommodate the revelry. Gaslights flared from every possible window, and young men unable to contain their exuberance vaulted over the most unlikely obstacles, swarmed over statues and perched on pinnacles.

'How about a Union Jack for the boy!'

Patrick, attracted to the bright colours, seized it at once. The soldier who had pushed it into his hand was almost gone before Finn shouted out.

'Captain O'Shea!' he yelled. The retreating figure, with cap pushed to the back of his head, stopped and turned.

All three exchanged glances of utter astonishment. Finn

recovered first, extending his hand, which was gripped and shaken heartily. Tessa was too taken aback to follow suit, indeed she had never shaken hands with anyone in her life. The tremulous smile, which she had given him on the road to Dublin, again touched her mouth briefly and was gone before he could respond.

'Jesus, Mary and Joseph!' gasped Finn. The stark and utter amazement as the three faced each other set them off into a shy laughter.

Cormac's glance moved up to the delighted child, to the black curls tumbling onto a wide forehead, to the large eyes contemplating the flag; eyes which, he guessed, in the light of day would be blue, not a deep colour like his father's, or the grey-blue of his mother's, but something in between. He recalled the sensation of first holding the little creature . . . And now, begod, just look at him! And his da looks as though he's found his land of milk and honey after all. And his mammy? She was not the ragged princess of the quayside any more.

'I got your letter,' he articulated, as the barrel organ began grinding out 'Soldiers of the Queen'.

'Will you be comin' for his birthday day?' Finn asked anxiously.

'As if I'd miss it! Y'know, of all the people on the streets tonight, the odds of me giving a flag to my godson must be a thousand to one!' His glance strayed to Tessa's hand, and his memory to the ring . . . his ring. If it had been any time other than Mafeking night, he would have pondered the cause of his curiosity, but just now he and they were all part of the wildest celebration Manchester had ever seen.

'Cormac! Yoo hoo, Cormac!' A shrill voice took advantage of a pause in the barrel organ's repertoire. Cormac's head swivelled round and, following his gaze, Tessa saw a fashionably dressed young woman who, unable to cross Piccadilly for the crowd, was standing on the step of a deserted cab, waving a feathered hat frantically to catch his attention. He waved his own in recognition.

'That's Elfreda,' he explained cheerfully. 'We got off the tram and lost each other when the dancing started!' He waved his hat again and laughing as Patrick made a grab for it, added, 'I'll go and fetch her over – back in a minute!'

He pushed his way into the crowd, and unable to battle against one of its crazy surges was absorbed into it at once. Tessa, suddenly conscious of her own clothes against those of Elfreda, felt she could not possibly have borne the comparison, and was relieved she wouldn't have to. The almost magical appearance of Captain O'Shea had happened too quickly for her to assemble any kind of composure, or form any impression of him. It would all be different, she was sure, on Patrick's birthday.

Finn's eyes clouded with disappointment. He had been about to suggest the Captain accompany them to the Sugar Loaf. Ah, merciful Lord, he thought, imagine the look on all their faces to see himself walk in with not just a soldier, but an officer! The sudden disappearance of the feathered hat reminded Finn that his winnings were in the custody of Marr the piper, and steadying Patrick with one hand and grabbing Tessa with the other, he forcefully shouldered his way to Newton Street and from there to Ancoats. Finn need not have worried; the Mafeking money had been taken over by Jonty Johnson and was paid out readily.

The relief of Mafeking had so seized popular imagination that as far as the Sacred Heart parish was concerned the war was over, and the name itself passed into regular use as a byword for celebration and revelry.

'We've had a Mafeking good time,' people would say.

'It were like Mafeking all over again.'

Finn, determined to possess a tangible memento of the occasion, set off the following Saturday afternoon with Patrick in his arms and Tessa by his side in search of a sofa, preferably a shiny black one. The sun shone and a brisk wind kept the pall of smoke from forming over the town. Tessa referred to these rare occasions as 'good drying days' and they never ceased to lift her spirits.

Consequently, and only slightly due to the recent glimpse of the fashionably dressed Elfreda, Tessa had given more thought to the few clothes she had, and how to get the best out of them. She decided on her pink blouse, turning back the cuffs to just below the elbow, and leaving the three small buttons at the throat unfastened. This, she thought, would make up for the black working skirt. She dared not wear

126

her grey one for fear of Patrick staining it with his sticky fingers, his uncertain bladder or his suddenly deciding to be sick, events which never occurred while Finn was carrying him. With her dark hair pinned up into a thick bun, and the pleasure of the 'jaunt' radiating from her, more than a few heads turned as she passed, and some, complete strangers, smiled. But up to now their search had not been successful, and arriving at Shudehill, all hopes were pinned on Sad Sam.

He emerged from the gloom of his shop and blinked like an owl. 'Eh, look who it is.' He smiled in a melancholy manner, and on hearing their request, shook his head. 'No sofas, mate. Not had one for weeks. Tell yer what,' he leaned forward, 'I know who wants to get rid of one.'

'Go on,' prompted Tessa. 'Who?'

'I'm supposed to be going to the house to give them a price for it.'

'Ah, sure it's decent of you, isn't it, Tess, decent of him?'

'If he ever gets round to telling us where it is!'

'I'm taking the bread out of my own mouth, doing this, yer know,' he was slightly aggrieved at her levity. 'I'm only putting you in the way of it because of your house-warming. I'd not sold a thing all that day. Thought God had forsaken me, I did, an' then you turned up. You was a real gent, mate. Now,' he cast a baleful glance at Tessa, ''ere, I've written it down.'

Finn's good-natured face creased into a smile as he stood aside for Tessa to take the note. The address given was Oldham Road, and with his aim in sight, he hitched Patrick further up against his shoulder and set the pace briskly.

Having reached Oldham Road, they continued a while until Tessa paused at a house on the corner. There was no garden frontage or protection of railings, merely one handsome step from road to house. The grime had already bitten into the surface of brick, but the lace at the windows was white, and the brass knocker bright as a halo.

The door was opened by a middle-aged woman who clearly regarded them with suspicion. She looked at the big man, who wore neither collar nor cap, and at Tessa's colouring. Irish, she thought, or I'm a Dutchman. Finally she looked at Patrick, who stared back through his fringe of dark lashes.

Her judgement came down on the side of caution. 'If you'll wait here, I'll see about it.' She closed the door and they heard her shouting, 'It's the man for the sofa!'

After a few moments the door swung open again. Finn stared in disbelief. 'Mr Wilkins, sir! Sorry to be botherin' you – we must've got the wrong number.'

'We have not!' put in Tessa. 'The paper says 147 and 147 it is.'

Wilkins did not know who was more surprised, his employee or himself. His dark glance covered all three. 'No, Collins, your wife is quite correct. So, you want to buy my sofa, do you?'

'We'd be after looking at it first,' said Tessa.

'Then,' he announced, rubbing his hands together, 'you must come inside.'

They hesitated, and with the uncertain air of people attending a funeral, filed into the parlour. 'That was my sister,' he explained. 'She's always wary of strangers, but, I may add, is delighted with your laundering, Mrs Collins.'

Was he remembering Patrick and his wet leggings, she wondered? The recollection of her son's occasional incontinence and his insistence on drawing attention to it filled her with a desire to get out quickly. She glanced at Finn, already by the sofa. Her heart beat faster, more on his account than her own: it was black and shiny, just like at the Sal Doss, and just what he wanted. But there he was, prowling round it, tinker fashion. 'Showing satisfaction lessens your bargaining power,' Martin Jarvey used to say.

'What will you be wanting for it, sir?' Finn asked.

Wilkins thought for a moment and inhaled deeply. 'To you, Collins, ten shillings. My sister wants a new one, and the rogue on Shudehill would have given me next to nothing anyway.'

Finn consulted Tessa with a glance. She took the money from her pocket. Wilkins watched her approaching hand with a strange fascination. He wondered if her fingers would brush against his, and whether she would be as aware of the contact as himself. But, all too quickly, the fascination ended. Her fingers had not touched his, and the half-sovereign lay there on his palm, cold and flat. He felt he had to say something, anything.

'Don't go. Not yet, Mrs Collins. I think my sister has something to say to you.'

'Oh, merciful Lord,' murmured Tessa, when he had gone. 'I hope the washin' was all right.'

'An' why shouldn't it be? She wouldn't get it done better anywhere else.'

To calm herself, Tessa touched the sofa, pressing her hands over it, sitting on it. Then, moving nervously to where the dark green leaves of a magnificent aspidistra towered over a piano, she gave a little laugh. 'I bet Titch down at the Sugar Loaf would like to get his fingers on this.' As she lifted her head from the inspection she saw Miss Wilkins standing in the doorway.

She was as fair as her brother was dark. Pale, honey-coloured hair, thin and wispy, was pulled away from her face and tied with a broad black velvet ribbon. Her face was slightly lined about the mouth and forehead, and the straight nose and stern blue eyes gave her a look of authority, which on closer acquaintance her kindly manner and soft way of speaking denied. Tessa prayed she had not heard the reference to Titch getting his hands on the piano, but if she had, Effie Wilkins showed no sign.

'So, this is the wonderful laundress?' she smiled. 'My brother intimated you could do with a little extra work to set yourselves up?'

'No, there must be some mistake.' Tessa looked from Miss Wilkins to her brother, who had just entered the room and stood by her side, and then to Finn. 'I've no room for any more washing.'

'My brother was thinking perhaps you could manage a couple of hours twice a week to wash the floors. It would be a great help to me. You see, it's so nice to find someone trustworthy –' Her eyes switched to Patrick, who was making rapid progress from the sofa to a low shelf of Royal Doulton figures. Finn turned and whisked him up. 'What d'you say, Mrs Collins?'

'To be honest and all, I'm not sure,' stammered Tessa, overwhelmed by the offer, and at the same time distracted by Patrick who was now well into tears of frustration.

'If it's the child you're concerned about, come in the

129

evening,' suggested Wilkins. 'The Coopers would probably mind him, they seem to mind everyone else's.'

Tessa looked from one face to the other. They were all waiting for her to speak, to say yes. Patrick's howls of rage loosened her tongue.

'Patrick!' she said sharply. 'Will you stop that noise! You can't be touchin' everything you set eyes on!' But Patrick was not to be mollified, and sensing her panic, he set his tearful gaze on the Royal Doulton and wailed even louder.

'I'll take him outside, Tess.'

'No, Mr Collins, don't do that,' Miss Wilkins soothed, reaching into her pocket. 'This'll stop those tears.' She held out a twist of barley sugar, and began to unwrap it slowly. 'It never fails,' she smiled, as Patrick conveyed it to his mouth. 'There now, we can hear ourselves talk – and, what was it you said, Mrs Collins?'

'Yes,' she agreed quickly, hoping to get out before Patrick's sharp teeth nibbled their way through the barley sugar. 'But not on Friday or Saturday, because I sing at the Sugar Loaf – the public house near Loom Street,' she added, but Miss Wilkins, not used to the idea of women frequenting public houses, cast an enquiring glance at her brother.

'And believe me, Effie, she does that very well, eh Collins? Packs 'em in, so they tell me.' He rubbed his hands together briskly and moved out to the passage and the front door.

'I'll be round for the sofa later, sir, as soon as Cooper and me can get a donkey and cart.'

Wilkins nodded his agreement. They stood, slightly awed, and then filed out onto Oldham Road. Once outside, like children released from school, they hurried away, their quick Irish brogue wafting back on the wind, and filling George Wilkins' heart with a peculiar emotion . . . a kind of envy.

Chapter Twelve

The sofa, known as the 'Mafeking sofa', was positioned beneath the window, where it almost filled the wall and directly faced the scullery. With the dresser opposite the fireplace, and the square table and two cane-bottomed chairs in the centre of the room, the furnishing of Twenty-seven Loom Street was, due to lack of floorspace, complete.

'Are we not the grand folk!' exclaimed Finn, after the installation.

'We are so . . . ' Tessa cast a kindly eye on the statuette of the Virgin with whom she had cultivated a hesitant relationship. Representing as it did to her a mixture of heaven and earth, she sometimes felt the figure was sympathetic and understood the problems of mortal women. But there were also the frustrating moments when she felt like shaking it into some kind of action only to suffer immediate guilt and remorse.

'Yes, God's been good to us, Finn – and to think they called me da Proud Riley because he had a dresser and a few goats! Sure, we've done so well, I scarcely know meself!' She breathed out on a long, luxurious sigh. 'Isn't it nice, you and me with our backsides on something soft and comfortable.' She wriggled off her shoes and stretched her legs out over his knees.

'An' me with me hands on somethin' soft and comfortable!' He patted her thigh playfully. 'We can make love on the sofa, too . . . '

'What, down here?'

'An' why not? Patrick's getting big now, there's not a lot

of room in the bed, and there we are whisperin' like a pair o' horse thieves so as not to wake him.'

'No, I couldn't!' she said emphatically. 'It'd be like living with the tinkers over again, what with the walls as thin as paper, and I couldn't be sure there wasn't a gap in the blind, or a shadow – '

'No one's going to stand outside with their eye to the window!'

'Then one of the Coopers could be at the back door for something, and you'd have to open it in your underpants. Sure, I'd be mortified! Besides, it reminds me of the Sal Doss. People never made love on theirs – not under General Booth's picture! And d'you think I could enjoy tumblin' about on here, on the very place where Mr Wilkins used to take tea with his sister, sitting up straight, him in his coat and watch chains, and her in that nice gown, drinking out of dainty cups and balancing plates of fancy cakes on their knees like we did at Father Quinn's? No,' she shook her head. 'Sure, it's a fair and beautiful thing, but it's haunted by the fine manners.' She regarded him soberly. 'And I even feel when I'm sitting here that I've got to watch me language!'

While Finn often spoke of Captain O'Shea, Tessa said little, and during the days approaching the birthday wished the visit was over. She also wished she had never seen Elfreda, for the sight of her had been very unsettling, although it was not so much her as the ideas associated with her. Having had an insight into the Wilkins' way of life and household graciousness, she wondered if Elfreda lived in such a house. Most crushing of all, she had hoped Captain O'Shea would be impressed at her new refinement since her near-vagrant state on the boat, but now, after seeing his companion, she did not feel refined at all. No, she wished they had not met on Mafeking night.

As for Patrick's birthday, she would feel embarrassed at not returning the ring. Not to return it was like 'putting on good nature' as the saying went – not that Finn would ever see it that way. A week before Patrick's birthday Tessa decided that she was not going to feel under obligation any more; neither was she going to wear a borrowed ring for the rest of her life, for as she saw it they would never have enough money to buy one.

What if? Her imagination kindled, warmed to the germ of an idea. What if I were to lose it? What if it came off while washing the clothes and was emptied down the grid in the yard? At least, God forgive me in this world of sin and deceit, that's what I'd tell Finn, and Annie Cooper would spread it about. I can see no harm, she thought, for our respectability is well established, and people do lose things.

Avoiding the Virgin on the dresser, and directing her glance to the Sacred Heart with Patrick's Union Jack behind it, Tessa felt an upsurge of thanks that the facility, the gift for thinking up schemes and strategies had not gone. Since Finn left her to do all the talking anyhow, he would happily leave the explaining of the loss to her. But she would return the ring and let the Captain in on her deception. After all, it had been his idea to deceive the priest at the baptism in the first place!

It would be a relief, she thought, not to have it on me mind any more. But to be really honest with meself, and before the Almighty, sure the sight of it reminds me that Martin Jarvey would never let Kate wear a ring he had not put on her finger. And thinking that way was not fair to Finn. He works – we both work – all the hours God sends and we only just scratch by. It's just that Finn doesn't think like Martin. He thinks of sofas instead! Now, if he had asked me about it, given me a choice of either that or a wedding ring of our own, I would probably have decided on the sofa just the same, firstly because it had been one of his 'aims', and secondly because we'd never have enough money to buy one again.

As Finn says, she summed up to herself, I've got too much imagination. She came down to earth, jolted back into practicality. After all, I'm nineteen, a wife and mother with a house to run and work to do, not a sixteen-year-old with a head full of romantic ideals, and memories of other times, and other places across the sea.

Patrick's first birthday was on a Sunday. Tessa had not stipulated a time in her letter, but they presumed he would call in the afternoon. Not wanting to miss the Captain's arrival, Cooper and Finn had given up their usual jaunt to the Vault and had brought jugs of beer to the house.

The day was hot and still, the air hung thick and low and grey at rooftop level, retaining the heat which had filtered through for the past two days. There was no sun, no breeze. Every door and window was open from front to back to encourage the circulation of air.

Children played and quarrelled half-heartedly in the streets whilst their mothers sat on doorsteps or stood talking at corners. Every one of them knew about the impending visit of Captain O'Shea and they were determined not to miss it. Some even doubted the veracity of Finn's statement.

Dogs lay panting, and cats, from the safety of window ledges, stretched themselves lazily. No claxtons or sirens blasted the Sabbath air; only the whistle of the occasional train, the trams rumbling down Oldham Road, voices raised in an argument somewhere, and a distant piano through the open doors of a public house. Suddenly the street went quiet, children stopped quarrelling, women talking, and inside Number Twenty-seven Finn murmured, 'Oh, God save us, he's here!'

With a gazelle-like bound, Cormac O'Shea landed on the top step. Knowing that Finn set great store by a uniform, Cormac, who would have settled for an open-necked shirt and blazer, sweltered silently. His tallish figure in tunic, Sam Browne, and knee boots, was a rare sight in Ancoats. Although his arrival was evident, he tapped the doorjamb with a short cane. 'The Pied Piper!' he announced cheerfully, indicating a huddle of ragged boys, who, with Mafeking still in mind, had marched down the street behind him.

'Little buggers!' shouted Cooper, and at once the troops scattered, beating a retreat as fast as their spindly legs could carry them.

Finn pushed his way past Jud Patterson, Jimmy Marr, Titch Bradley, and Mr and Mrs Barnes, who were sandwiched on the sofa beside the quiet, grey-looking Mrs Marr and a florid-faced woman who had wandered in with Titch.

'So, you found us all right?' asked Finn by way of introduction, and said to the neighbours, 'This is Patrick's godfather, Captain O'Shea.'

Cooper straightened his waistcoat and rummaged among

the jars and cups until, with a flourish, he produced a glass. 'A shandy, is it, Captain?' he said in his imitation barman's voice. All eyes were turned toward Cormac, full of disbelief.

'It is so,' he said, showing square, even teeth as he smiled. 'And for the love of God, will you fill it to the brim!'

He had not known what to expect, but he had certainly not anticipated a reception committee. At first glance their presence had dismayed him, but now, as he recalled Tessa's unease when they had met on Mafeking night, he thought they might well take the initial awkwardness away from the reunion.

'Glad I'm in time to drink the little fella's health!' he exclaimed. And having got the measure of the company, he peered through the haze of ale-scented cigarette smoke to see Tessa emerging from the scullery, where she had taken a struggling Patrick to wash his chocolate-covered hands and face.

Cormac moved further into the room, laid his cane, hat and a neatly tied parcel among the debris on the table, and lifted the shandy. 'Here's to Patrick,' he said, raising the glass toward mother and child, and giving the occasion an air of grandeur. 'Here's to the birthday boy, Lord bless him!'

'Eh, Captain, we can't toast the lad,' said old Barnes. 'We've supped up!'

Cormac reached into his breeches pocket, brought out half a crown and indicated the jugs. 'No doubt they'll refill?'

Jimmy Marr took up the coin, seized a couple of jugs, and was through the door in a trice. The rest of the reception committee beamed their approval and thought Patrick a lucky boy.

'Will you not take the weight off your feet, Captain?' Finn pointed to the chair at the side of the dresser, and adjacent to the open door. It was the good cane-bottomed chair on which Mr Wilkins, Father Quinn, the rent collector and other esteemed callers sat. Cormac would have liked to remove his tunic and belt, to roll up his shirtsleeves and feel the air, however warm it was, on his arms, but he decided for Finn's sake to sweat it out a little longer.

Tessa swore softly to herself, and the flushed cheeks

were not so much to do with tending the fire necessary to boil a kettle, as at things not working out as expected. She cast a look of recrimination at the blue-mantled Virgin, and inwardly raved.

She raved at Mrs Barnes for bringing Patrick a bar of chocolate. Chocolate in weather like this! And didn't it melt all over him before he could eat it? She raved at Captain O'Shea for arriving the minute she'd put her apron on. She raved at the neighbours who had been sitting on the sofa like crows on a fence – not that there were either in Ancoats – since opening time at the Sugar Loaf. The house did not seem to be her own! And God only knew why the Captain had sent out for more drink! And what if he left before the neighbours and she didn't have a chance to put her strategy to the test? And Patrick always started grizzling when there were too many people about. And why was Annie watching her? If I was presenting him to the Pope she couldn't be watching more, she thought. Oh, if only it wasn't so hot and airless. She glanced at the Sacred Heart. What wouldn't I give for just a whiff of the winds that raced across the Great Bog of Ennabrugh; winds that had driven the copper-coloured clouds like great chariots over the mountainy outcrop . . .

A tremulous smile of welcome touched her lips as she acknowledged Cormac's presence from the doorway of the scullery. Annie Cooper and the others, Jud and Titch, did not know why they stopped talking to watch the progress of the young woman with the curly-haired child straddling her hip. Eh, thought Annie, you've got to hand it to her, she can't half swan it. Like at the Sugar Loaf, standing there with her hand on top of the piano, as to the manner born; or walking down the street in that fancy shawl like the Queen of Sheba.

'So, this is the little fella,' said Cormac. He, too, was conscious of being watched, only his observers were also passing the open door. Word had got about. 'There's a soldier at Number Twenty-seven, go and have a look!'

'Patrick, me boyo, to be sure you've grown an awful lot since I last saw you!' And to Tessa, 'Will he come to me?'

'And why not, it's his godfather y'are. And he can walk, now.' She backed to the end of the dresser to demonstrate. 'Go on, Patrick, walk to Captain O'Shea.'

The brass buttons and epaulets caught the child's interest. Wide-eyed and eager, he toddled toward the door and stood triumphantly between the polished boots. Wedging himself between Cormac's knees, his recently wiped face rosy with the excitement of exploration, he reached up to the brass buttons.

Cormac's heart warmed, as it had on the boat crossing when Ma, while attending Tessa, had thrust the little bundle into his arms. Ah, did I not tell you, son, he thought, sure and did I not tell you twelve months ago that it wasn't such a bad world you were coming into? 'I've brought something,' he explained to Tessa. 'But we'll give it to him later – I promise you it isn't chocolate!' She nodded, pleased to interpret that he was outstaying the others.

Jimmy Marr returned with the ale and a bottle of ginger beer to mix a shandy, and Finn passed his packet of Woodbines round. Cormac, to amuse Patrick, lit his pipe, and pursing his lips blew perfect circles of smoke into the haze above. After a toast to the 'birthday boy' the men talked of Mafeking, and the women alternated between the ailments of children and speculation as to whether Tessa's ring would be swept out to sea, swallowed by a fish to turn up on Shudehill market, as was reported in *The Manchester Guardian* a few years back.

Finn noticed the jugs had gone dry, and recalling how Martin Jarvey had warned himself at the wedding and at the well wishing of being over generous, hoped the Captain would not fall into the same trap. Besides, he, like Tessa, wanted time alone with their friend. He need not have worried, for the army had well equipped Cormac to detect and deal with scroungers.

But despite there being no replenishment, Tessa presumed that her neighbours would have stayed all night if Georgie Cooper had not run in, terrified. 'Mam! Mam! Our Tony's got into Mrs Barnes's house and he's striking matches!'

Jimmy Marr ran out with the Coopers and the Barneses. 'No show without Punch,' winked Jud Patterson. 'We'll be going,' he said politely, including Titch and the florid-faced woman. Cormac, with a nod to Finn, stood to see them out, and despite the heat, closed the front door.

'Fancy us all getting lost on Mafeking night,' he said,

hoping to bring a note of intimacy in what up to now had been generalities. 'Didn't stand a chance when I left you, finished up in Albert Square without me hat!'

'Make yourself at home, as they say in Ancoats,' Finn responded. 'And take your tunic off – you're sweating like a pig!'

'I will so,' he laughed, 'and indeed I am. Better hang it behind the door or Patrick'll be through me pockets and smoking me pipe! Got a nice little place here,' he complimented, rolling up his shirtsleeves.

'We've tidied up in your honour,' laughed Tessa, clearing the jars and jugs off the table and feeling more in command now the neighbours had gone. 'You can't usually move in here for washing on the rack, buckets of starch in the scullery, piles of ironing on the chairs, and Patrick's playthings on the floor!'

While Finn and Cormac helped Patrick open his present of brightly coloured wooden building blocks, Tessa's mind as she prepared tea now began to centre on the returning of the ring. She had felt terrible guilty after telling Finn of the supposed loss. 'What the devil will he say?' he had asked in a panic. 'Will you tell him, Tess? Sure to God, it's all my fault. I'd forgotten. We should've got one instead of the sofa –' She had closed his lips with her finger, put her arms round his neck and told him they could do without a ring, but not a sofa, and, yes, if he'd give her a few minutes alone with the Captain she'd do the telling. She had kissed him full on the lips. 'And what's that for?' he had teased.

'Because,' she had replied with a tightening of her throat, 'you're the darlin' man, and I love you.'

'An' what have we here?' declared Cormac in admiration, as Tessa, who had covered the bare wooden top of the table with one of the Wilkins' cloths she had in for laundering, placed on it a huge brown pot of tea and soda bread baked that morning – sure, the fires of hell, she thought, could not have been hotter than this houseplace. She had been up at the cool of dawn and would never have stoked the fire in weather like this to heat the oven to bake for any person who was not Irish. She added butter, and a plate of fancy cakes from Hewitt's corner shop, and thought the spread looked as fine as Major Mary's afternoon tea at the Sal Doss.

'I always say,' said Cormac, obviously delighted, 'it takes the Irish to appreciate a good soda bread.'

'Will you be having yours on your knee, like?' Tessa addressed Cormac, knowing how much Finn detested juggling plates. 'We have only the two chairs for the table.'

'If we pull the table toward the sofa for Finn and me,' said Cormac, 'I'll fetch a chair for you – there.'

Once at the table, the formality which Tessa had feared never materialised. They remembered Ma and hoped God had been good to her; Finn related his Liverpool experiences; and Tessa talked as she had wanted to of the 'auld country' while Finn laughingly defended the new country, the land flowing with milk and honey, where there was a roof over your head and bread in your belly. Cormac was amazed at how they had adapted to the new life, and as one subject after another was exhausted, his mind got around to wondering whether they had married in church. It was then he noticed there was no ring on her finger.

As though taking up his thought, Tessa looked at Patrick playing with his bricks under the table, and said to Finn, 'Will you take him out to the yard for a pee?' And by way of explanation to Cormac, 'If we don't remind him every couple of hours he wets himself, y'know. And Finn?' she called as he was disappearing through the scullery. 'Will you keep the back door closed?' Then to Cormac again, 'Sure the Coopers are God's own people, but they're always comin' in for something or another.' Her voice lowered to a conspiratorial tone. 'Captain O'Shea . . . '

'Can you and Finn not see your way to call me Cormac?' There was almost a plea in his lowered voice. 'After all, I am your son's godfather.' But realising she hadn't even heard, he continued with, 'Is there anything wrong?'

'No, nothing. Will you listen to me now? I'm returning the ring you so kindly lent us –' She extended her hand, and pushed it toward the slim fingers, brown against the white of the cloth. Quickly, and more concisely than she ever imagined possible, she explained the situation, and was honest about deceiving Finn and the neighbours. 'I don't like being either in debt or under obligation,' she concluded. 'It's like you are with the drink because of your parents, and I'm like this because of me da.

139

Don't look so stricken, for God's sake, Captain. Take it!'

'Regard it as a wedding present, then.'

'We . . . we didn't get married.' Relieved to be off the subject of the ring, she briefly explained about the house, and the priest's attitude to respectability within the community. 'And now things have dragged on, and it's all got so complicated.' She indicated the ring still lying on his open palm, then reached out and closed his fingers over it.

'Very well,' he hunched his shoulders in a shrug. 'If it'll please you. If that's what you want.' He slipped it into his pocket.

'Besides, you might need it yourself,' she added shyly. 'You and Elfreda walking out, and all.'

'Walking out!' he echoed as Finn brought Patrick back inside. 'Did I not tell you on the way to Dublin that I'm not the marrying kind! Sure, in England,' he explained more softly, ' "keeping company" and "walking out" don't necessarily lead to the altar. Elfreda and meself make up a foursome with my army friend Nick Styles and his sister Audrey. We like each other's company, but I'll be needing a shroud before a wedding ring!' He glanced mischievously at the two serious faces before him.

'Will one of yous be askin' me to the Sugar Loaf? It's on my way back into town, and they tell me there's a fine singer there at weekends!'

While Patrick, exhausted from his birthday celebration, slept heavily in a big dropsided cot which Cooper had rescued from the firewood yard and repaired, Finn, already sweating in the grey suit from the Salvation Army, sat proudly beside Cormac – having introduced him to Jonty Johnson – in The Room, and felt once more that he had arrived and that his luck was in. When Tessa sang 'Lovely Lad of my Dreams' and looked straight at him, he blushed and smiled like a bashful boy.

Tessa, standing by the piano, wearing the summer gown of apple green in which she had been married, looked pleasantly cool. The day had gone well, her self-imposed mission had been accomplished, and she was in fine spirits. This was echoed in her looks and her voice. There was no background chatter when Tessa sang. Sometimes the audience joined in a chorus when bidden, and often tapped their feet, or nodded their heads to a lively tune, but no one talked.

Tessa's voice struck at Cormac. Dear heaven, he thought, 'tis like Ireland itself. His throat tightened with a bittersweet sadness for what might have been if this little gold circlet in his breast pocket had been placed on the finger it was intended for.

After the applause, a second glass of Guinness was placed behind the first on the piano top. Someone requested 'The Minstrel Boy' and after that came a couple of the 'new songs', as Tessa called them, songs made famous by Marie Lloyd and other music hall artists.

Taking out his watch Cormac was amazed at how the time had fled. It had all been more enjoyable than anticipated. He would rather have stayed, or arranged for Nick to bring the girls here. Although they usually settled for the Palm Court in the Grosvenor Hotel, Ancoats was University Settlement territory, and surely any insight into or contact with the community would be valued? If he was going to stay for another song, it would be one of his own choosing. Something rollicking, something from the auld country – and not Paddy McGinty's bloody goat!

'Will ye be giving us "Cockles and Mussels"?' He threw in his request among others, but picking out his voice was not difficult.

'Where's me Guinness, Titch? I'm too thirsty and dry to sing a note!'

'Here, that'll oil yer tonsils, lass!'

Cormac, watching her neck arch gracefully as she downed half the glass in one, smiled and shook his head. There was no artifice about these Collinses; it was their naturalness which had appealed to him on that summer morning outside Dublin.

'Alive, alive O . . . ' he roared, enjoying himself.

'Cockles and mussels, alive, alive O.'

On the last chorus he made his way to the door, followed by Finn, who was not for sitting in The Room without a mate, even for Tess. Cormac approached the bar. 'Will ye send a whisky in to Mrs Collins – and Finn, have one on me. Jamieson's, of course!'

Punching Finn playfully on the shoulder, he tucked the

141

cane beneath his arm, and every head turned to watch him go out.

He was hot and sticky and could do with at least a change of shirt – no fit state for the Palm Court, where, no doubt, Nick would be the essence of coolness! He had purposely not mentioned a further visit to Finn, for having been in Salford now for over a year, he had applied for a prestigious move to the School of Equine Studies in the south of England. He might not be the successful applicant, but the paper he had written on the outbreak of 'Stable Sickness' would surely be in his favour. But distance was nothing nowadays, there were letters and trains. One thing was certain in this world of sin and deceit: not a year would pass without him seeing that fine, strapping godson on his birthday. Thinking of deceit, what about the ring Tessa had returned? Ach, God save her, she had some funny ideas.

Chapter Thirteen

Toward the end of August, after a particularly arduous day of keeping the coals red to heat the flat irons, Tessa, tired and irritable, had just flopped down onto the sofa beside Finn when they heard footsteps approaching. They looked at each other with unspoken enquiry – was it someone for them, or for next door? It was for them. A sharp tattoo of knuckles got Finn to his feet. He peered through the lace curtain which covered the lower half of the window and was already grubby through much pulling aside.

'Christ!' he exclaimed. 'It's Father Quinn. What can he be after, now?'

'You'll never find out standing there, open the door. No, wait till I get me shoes back on – '

The priest, used to waiting while his parishioners made last-minute adjustments, stood patiently on the top step until the door was opened. Brushing aside Finn's apologies, he laid his wide-brimmed hat by the statuette of the Virgin, wished it was not so hot, and smiled. 'So, this is the famous Mafeking sofa.' He knew how to flatter the vanity of his flock. Everyone, no matter how poor, possessed something they were proud of, and he used this ploy shamelessly, especially if the visit was of a delicate nature.

'Tessa's just getting the tea on, Father. You'll be takin' a cup?'

'Yes, I certainly will. It's thirsty work talking in such hot weather. Little one upstairs?'

'After a lot o' bother,' said Tessa, tersely. 'Sure, the heat and light nights don't help at all.'

The priest leaned back on the sofa and stretched out his long legs, commenting all the time on how well they had settled and what a fine home they had got together. 'Thank you, Mrs Collins, thank you.' He received his tea and sipped it. 'Very refreshing. Will y'sit down, now, for it's the both of you I want to talk to. I left it until fairly late so the child wouldn't interrupt us. I heard you singing at the Sugar Loaf last weekend, 'tis a fine and cheerful voice you've been blessed with.'

'Thanks, Father.'

'Now,' Quinn pulled his legs in and sat upright, 'your son is over twelve months –'

'Yes, but he's been christened,' intervened Tessa, uneasily. 'We told you when we came.'

'I know, I know.' He shifted uncomfortably before their apprehensive glances. 'There will be . . . another child?'

'When God wills.' Tessa frowned. 'Why d'you ask?'

'It's my duty,' he replied quietly. 'Most Catholic families – the Coopers being a fine example – would have another little life on the way by now.' He looked about the room and patted the sofa. 'You've both worked hard and gathered some nice things. But I must warn you not to let material matters come before creating life. You are not,' he quickly scanned Finn's open and surprised face, 'using any method, any device to hinder the procreation of children?'

'No, Father. May God strike me dead if I tell a word of a lie.' Finn shook his head adamantly. 'Me and Tess, sure we love each other, Father; there's bound to be others, 'tis only natural.'

The young priest drank the last of his tea. 'Yes, of course. This is part of my duty, you understand, to make sure you don't sin in ignorance against the teaching of Holy Mother Church. Come now –' getting to his feet, he tried to rally them with a light laugh ' – don't be looking so worried, the pair of you!' His usually smiling eyes were shaded with anxiety, for he was conscious of having brought a shadow into this household which would not be leaving with him. Still, it was his duty, and duties were not always pleasant. Finn leapt to open the door. The priest offered a prayer, asked a blessing then, reaching for his hat, went slowly down the three steps.

Tessa sat down stiffly on the cane-bottomed chair. 'What d'you make o' that, Finn? What the devil does he expect us to do – manufacture some, like we did the poteen?'

'Ah, the priest was only doing his duty, like he said. Sshh, don't let him upset you, girleen,' he put his arm about her shoulders. 'You've often said about God being good, an' before we know where we are there'll be a houseful of 'em, yelling and screaming like next door!'

With a mutual but silent consent, Father Quinn and the object of his visit were not mentioned again, even though they were in both their minds. Tessa had talked it over with the silent Madonna on the dresser, and had fully expected to find herself pregnant. That she was not came more in the way of a rebuff than a disappointment, for she had hoped it would not be her fate to grow round-bellied every year.

Perhaps the request had slipped the heavenly mind and the error would be rectified next month. 'Enjoy yer freedom, while yer can,' said Annie on hearing about the visit. 'Once yer start again, 'appen you'll not stop. Just look at me, a right sight, I am. Pregnant every year if Cooper's not careful, and does Father Quinn come with so much as a quarter of cheese to help feed 'em? Does he hell!'

Tessa accepted the situation philosophically, until she noticed that Finn, despite his joke about them soon having 'a houseful yelling and screaming', seemed preoccupied. Surely he hadn't taken the priest's 'warning' to heart? Then she recalled Tobias Greenledge's remark: 'A big young fella like you, why you'll have those cupboards filled, and the bedroom, with little 'uns in no time.' Sad Sam's words about beds echoed too. 'It's best to have 'em big, you'll fit half a dozen in that, easy.' And part of Finn's persuading her to emigrate had been uttered with an upsurge of pride. 'We've got the baby to think of, and there'll be others, Tess.'

His mates at the mill like Cooper had eight or nine children. And indeed fertility abounded. Never, it seemed, had the streets of Ancoats been thronged with so many large families, English, Irish and Anglo–Irish. They crowded the corner shop, clinging to the skirts of the eldest girl, and went to Mass in droves.

'Sure, to the merciful Mother,' Tessa exclaimed. 'We're

145

not on our last legs! I'm not yet twenty, and you're only twenty-four!' But his face remained unsmiling and he made no comment.

Every night, in his desire to father another child, he thrust himself against her. And she, catching the mood like the children catch the measles, thrust her prayers fervently and feverishly before the Virgin. After the second month had flown past, Tessa began to resent Finn's demands. Never did she think to hear herself whisper from the depths of the knobless brass bed, 'No . . . not again.'

'Ach,' he coaxed, leaning on his elbow and bending over her. 'C'mon love, sure you can't be serious?'

The slight abrasiveness of his touch had always made her nerve ends tingle, but now she stiffened against the contact. The rasping, grasping hands did not seem to belong to the same man. What's happening to us, she asked miserably. Only a short while ago his touch took me heart away with the pleasure of it. Sure, an' Brian Boru could not have been a better lover. Her mind dwelt lovingly on how they had enjoyed each other, teasing, laughing, loving with all the fierce ardour of their tough mountainy upbringing. All that, her thoughts plummeted to the present, and now I feel empty. I feel nothing. No, not nothing . . . but sickened.

'Finn. No!' She reached beneath the bedclothes and flung his hand off her body. 'When I said no, I meant it. You're not your old lovin' self any more. It's like a crusade – one of your "aims". And I'm not going through this every night just because of what Father bloody Quinn said! When I think of the way our Patrick was conceived, this is like a penance! You're not even enjoyin' it yourself any more. And God knows I'm not at all! It isn't me you want – it's what you can get out of me . . . ' Her voice trembled to a halt. 'I'd never have thought it of yer, Finn.'

She sensed his bewilderment as he lay back in silence. Intense helplessness radiated from him in waves, washing over Tessa and threatening to drown them both. Her voice came out of the darkness, small and bleak. 'I hate Father Quinn, I hate him.'

The days following Tessa's refusal were heavy with unadmitted regret, recrimination and remorse. Both being convivial by nature, such a strain was far outside their

146

experience. It was worse than the Derby Day and Mafeking rows rolled into one. Tessa took to staying up later, ironing or starching. Lying awake beside a restless, resentful man was nothing to look forward to. She had not realised either just how much this ordered world, bounded by convention, by obedience to a church and community, had become an essential part of his life. He wanted desperately to fit in. He wanted safe things, a good Catholic home – and family. If only I'd known he'd turn in on himself like this, she thought, I'd have put up with it. Anything would be better than this. She thumped the Wilkins' sheets about the washtub with a vehemence; scrubbed their floors violently; and at the Sugar Loaf gave preference to requests that were fiery and mettle-some.

One day, when Tessa was putting sheets through the mangle, Annie brought a jug of tea into the yard. 'Eh, hold on,' she joked. 'You'll 'ave the handle off if you turn it any harder! It's easy to see you've no news that'll cheer Father Quinn!'

'It's a good thing he's not here, I'd have him through the rollers, sharpish!' She took the tea, and sipped it gratefully. 'Thanks,' she said above the noise of the children's play. 'I've not had time to scratch, still less put the kettle on.'

'Talking about being cheerful, Tessa, Finn's about as cheerful as an undertaker.'

'He is so, Annie. And it's all because of Father Quinn. He's not just got the mulligrubs, he's sad, sad from the heart. If I could conceive tomorrow I would, anything to get him back to his old self. But life's in the hands of the Almighty and He's taking His time!'

'It's pride, luv,' said Annie with conviction. 'Fellas are all the same, they're ruled by what's in their trousers.'

In the three months since Father Quinn's visit, the Loom Street household had changed drastically. Even Patrick knew there was something wrong. It would all begin with the evening rush of clogs, when his father would stand outside the window, spit on his finger and rub it up and down the glass to make a squeak. This was the signal to climb on the sofa, thrust his curly head up beneath the lace curtain and try to imitate the noise. In no time at all his father would be up the three steps, hoisting him to shoulder height with such speed that he felt a great whoosh in the pit of his stomach. He would pretend to be a giant, and yelled with delight at being able, for this brief moment, to touch the clothes on the airing rack, and make a lunge for the chains of the gaslight, only to be borne away within inches of the goal.

Once set down, Patrick usually felt safe and happy listening to his parents discussing the affairs of the day for his father could never be in the house ten minutes before, in sheer exuberance of spirit, he was tormenting his mother: untying her apron strings; creeping up to pull out a hairpin – always the one which let it all down. Sometimes he would tease, chasing her round the table for a kiss, until Patrick laughed so much he got the hiccups. But now all this had stopped, and suddenly Patrick's little world was fragile.

As for Tessa, she welcomed the Wilkins' cleaning as a relief from a situation she could not change. Her duties consisted of brushing the first flight of stair carpet, washing the kitchen floor and paintwork, and stoning the front and back steps. On Thursday there was the dining room, passages and entrance hall, window sills and lavatory. She was thankful that the parlour with its precious Royal Doulton and handsome piano was not included; neither were any of the bedrooms.

Miss Wilkins had not intended to start a ritual of leaving a tray of tea and cherry cake for her cleaning woman, but there had been something appealing about the first sight of her standing on the threshold of the back door, apron in hand and a coloured shawl framing her smooth forehead. Soft tendrils of hair added a fey quality to her expressive face. She showed Tessa the big urn of hot water which always sizzled on the hob of the kitchen fire. 'You'll refill it, of course?'

'Yes, Miss Wilkins, to be sure,' she had replied.

Watching Tessa turn her attention to the cupboard beneath the sink, where the buckets and floor cloths were kept, Miss Wilkins wondered at her brother's totally unexpected offer of a cleaner, for he was not altruistic by nature. Whatever his motive, she was pleased to be relieved of the laborious tasks, for it gave her more time to spend with her nephew. It had crossed her mind just once that Mrs Collins might bring her little boy along as a companion for David, but the recollection of the undisciplined scene in the parlour when they had called to see the sofa banished the thought. Besides, he was a bit young, and George would never have agreed anyway.

The stern air of authority which surrounded Effie Wilkins was a by-product of her appointment as head of Every Street Board School. When her sister-in-law had died three years ago, she saw it her duty to give up her career – and pension – to move in with her brother and bring up his son. Her colleagues had advised against it. 'If he marries again,' they said, 'where will that leave you?' But George had been so cut down with grief that he had sworn on his wife's grave not to remarry. Nor was he interested in the pathetic little object that had brought about her death. He would have had David reared at the Foundling Hospital, and later sent to a boarding school. But for the first time in her life, Effie knew herself to be needed desperately, and she had given herself utterly to the child's welfare. No longer a baby, the little boy was dark like his father, with great round solemn eyes. He was dressed like a little gentleman, never seemed to cry, make a noise, or get under anyone's feet. David looked upon her as his mother and she regarded him as her own. If she had any nightmares it was always the same one, that George, despite his graveside oath, would be bowled over by some woman who would only marry him on condition he sent his sister packing.

Effie Wilkins' heart, then, was warm and soft, and capable of many affections. And when young Mrs Collins, embarrassment colouring those finely shaped cheekbones, accounted for the absence of a wedding ring, Miss Wilkins provided a substitute in the form of a solid brass curtain ring. 'And if that comes off in the wash,' she had smiled, 'there's an ample supply in my workbox!'

And young Mrs Collins, she felt sure, had hurried away from home without eating properly. This was never so, but Tessa had learned from the tinkers never to dispel such illusions, and so the ritual of the tray was appreciated.

Mr Wilkins still called at Loom Street to settle the laundry bill at the end of the month. It could, of course, have been settled on her cleaning nights, but he had got into the routine of calling. It gave him a sense of satisfaction to watch this handsome young woman handling the sheets on which he would lie, and the towels he would hold against his body. He always arrived too soon and sat stiffly on the chair by the door, drawing a sense of wellbeing from the pleasant smell of hot linen. If he did speak it was about the weather. 'It's a cold one, Mrs Collins,' he would say, rubbing his hands together; or 'My word, it's certainly a wet one, Mrs Collins.' The answer was always the same. 'It is indeed, sir.'

She had no time to speculate on the weather, only to curse when it rained on a yardful of washing which had been almost dry. She was also weary of this fixation for another child which had come upon them – and of the Virgin's stubborn refusal to co-operate. But her philosophical nature came to her rescue; there was work to be done, and money to be made doing that work. It was only when singing at the Sugar Loaf that she felt alive again. The songs, especially the old songs, rekindled her imagination; she was jolly or sad, sentimental or patriotic. And in this process Tessa began to observe the response of the audience, to realise how best to manipulate their emotions, to make the evening more of an experience than just a singsong. Titch Bradley, having accompanied a variety of voices in his time, recognised the evolution of something different, and subjugated his own style to hers.

One Wednesday cleaning night, Tessa drank her tea and ate the cake with a sigh of gratefulness. She had relished the crumbly texture, the eggy taste and the sweet softness of the cherries, especially today, for she had taken on extra washing and it had been particularly arduous.

She overfilled the zinc bucket with water, and in lifting it staggered a little. She swore beneath her breath, and, suddenly, George Wilkins was there.

'Oh!' She bit back an oath.

'Allow me, Mrs Collins,' he said breathlessly, and before she could answer, his hand had covered hers on the handle. His words conjured up a vivid memory of Kate's good-for-nothing brother, Mick Murphy, and her flustered voice asking 'What will your own women think of you fetching water for a goy?'

'Oh, no, sir,' she answered quickly. 'It isn't a task for gentlemen.'

'Well it didn't look as though you were getting very far with it. And seeing I'm paying you by the hour, it's in my interest to get both you and the bucket to the front door as soon as possible.'

He released his hold and stood for a moment looking down at the reflection of her face, the little wisps of hair dancing disjointedly on the surface of the water. He straightened up, and she, not wanting him to think her frail, or worse, drunk, quickly explained about overfilling it, and ended with, 'I'm all right, sir. I'm a strong woman.'

His eyes roamed over her arms, muscular and yet dimpled. 'I can see you are,' he answered. And without another word, he took the bucket to the front door, set it down and with a quick nod hurried away. He hurried because he was discomfited by the incident. She was right. Gentlemen do not carry buckets for any woman, still less one that cleaned the steps of his house. Effie was upstairs occupied with the boy. He hoped she had not seen him.

He closed the parlour door and leaned against it, trying to define his behaviour. It defied all logic. He who had never touched a damn bucket in his life! And worse, Tessa Collins obviously thought he had acted stupidly.

'This is asking for trouble,' he muttered to himself. 'Some of these Irish women are born schemers . . . ' Yes, he thought, she could read anything into the incident. No doubt it would be the talk of Loom Street tomorrow. 'Just fancy,' they would say, 'Wilkins carrying the bucket to the front door! Better look out. He doesn't do owt for nowt.' He took a cigarette from a silver box and lit it. He was being unfair to Mrs Collins. He knew instinctively that she was not that kind of woman, so why was he sitting here in the semi-darkness trying to discredit her?

Chapter Fourteen

Having stayed up late to finish ironing some cloths which were needed for a funeral tea the following day, Tessa turned the gas down and undressed by the banked-up glow of the fire. Miss Wilkins had given her a cast-off flannelette nightgown to be torn up for floor cloths, but never having possessed one and having always slept in her petticoat, Tessa decided it was far too good for so terrible a fate. She pulled it on with a sigh of pleasure, not noticing that it was wearing thin or the little sprigs of pink and green flowers had faded. She, too, like Elfreda, Audrey Styles and Miss Wilkins, was in possession of a nightgown.

She had also stayed up late to pray before the Virgin, feeling that perhaps she had not impressed the Holy Mother strongly enough of their need for a child. Yet what more could be done? Smoothing the nightgown over her hips, she turned and searched the chiselled features of the faintly smiling face, and then dropped her hairpins in a little heap beside it.

She heard the groan of the bedsprings above, the creaking of bare floorboards, and the stairs taking up the cry as Finn slowly burdened them with his weight. He unlatched the stair door and peered into the glow-light. His chest and feet were bare, and his close-fitting long underpants held together with a large safety pin.

She received his admiring glance and said softly, 'It belonged to Miss Wilkins.'

'Ah, sure it never looked so good on her ...' He wanted to go down on his knees and clasp to his lips each bare foot peeping from beneath the hem, but it would give her the wrong impression. Instead he leaned across the table, turned the gas up a little and ruffled a distracted hand through his hair. 'I don't know why I came down, Tess. Can't seem to sleep if you aren't there. I wondered when you were comin' up.'

'So you can poke yourself at me again!' In the flare of the half-light she saw the stubble glistening in the bristly cleft of his chin; his eyes were bright and uneasy. 'I'm sorry,' she murmured. 'I shouldn't have said that.'

'You've every right, Tess. I'm comin' it too often.'

She looked at him with a quizzical sadness. 'We used to have such marvellous good times . . . I wonder if it'll ever be the same again.'

'Christ!' His voice rose in alarm. 'Don't say that, Tess, don't even think it.' He sank slowly down into the chair.

She grabbed the other chair from the side of the dresser and sat opposite him.

'Is it ill, y'are?'

He shook his head and stared beyond her. The dull red glow of the banked-up fire made him think of the peat fires of Ennan, and in particular, the one on which his aunt had burned his best clothes.

'What is it? You must tell me?' She reached out and touched his hand. 'Is it something I've done?'

'No,' he muttered thickly. ''Tis the woman regal born y'are to be puttin' up with the likes of me . . . ' His voice trailed away helplessly. a muscle at the side of his strong jaw twitched. Their shadows beneath the gaslight seemed to grow larger and heavier against the wall, and Tessa, recalling his fever in Downey's barn, knew he was haunted by the curse of the old aunt. His eyes, which wore that same guarded look, and the anxiety etched on his brow, were evidence enough.

Tessa crushed her hands together in an upsurge of despairing anger against something she could neither understand nor do anything about. She believed in luck and God, angels and the devil, and all the customs and fetishes which sprang from these beliefs; but none of them held a grip on her as they did on Finn. She wanted to get up and set the kettle for morning; to let the rack down and see if the clothes were dry —

anything except sit beneath this crushing sense of failure and futility. With sudden passion, her voice, low and insistent, cut the silence and scattered the shadows. 'She's dead, Finn. The Aunt Hanratty is dead. Her body is buried beneath the Great Bog of Ennebrugh – and the curse, with her soul, is burning in hell.' She searched for words of conviction; for an antidote, something to calm and quell, something to banish. 'Will you listen to me now? Will you count your blessings, as they used to say at the Sal Doss? You've had the marvellous good luck. You survived the disaster, fever, the crossin' of all that water, being in jug. There's Patrick; a roof over our heads; a fire on the hearth; work to go to; money in your pocket for a jar and a smoke, decent mates to share 'em with . . .'

'And only one child to our name.'

'For God's sake, Finn, he's only eighteen months old –'

'The mockers are crafty,' his voice was quiet, devoid of emotion. 'Can you wonder we've no more. Wasn't it a cursed tongue that talked you into a broomstick weddin' against yer judgement? An' didn't I ferret about for a priest to baptise the boyo – driving yerself into deceiving him? Sure, if it hadn't been for Captain O'Shea telling us of the Sal Doss and lending us a ring, there'd be none o'those blessings you're on about. He's good for us, Tess, but then you go and lose the bloody ring!'

'I found it again,' she lied swiftly, to humour him.

'You never said.'

'You never noticed.'

'And why did Father Quinn come asking all those questions? He knows there's something up.' His voice quickened and took on a lighter note. 'Remember what he said?' Eager to explore this new avenue of escape Finn rushed on: 'If we're in trouble, he's our friend, our Father in God. We'll tell him everything and see if he'll marry us, proper like.'

'We'll do no such thing, Finn Collins,' said Tessa on a swift intake of breath. 'When we first came here I thought of nothing else – that, and hoping you would at least look in Ikey Solomon's window for a wedding ring of our own. But seein' everything was going right, you never bothered. But now you want to use me as an easy way out to dodge the mockers!' She glanced at the Coopers' wall and lowered

154

her indignant voice. 'You want to get married not because of me, but because you think that's the reason I've not become pregnant. I am not,' she leaned forward to tell him, 'I'm not going to lose what bit of well-earned respectability we've got. We can't get married in Holy Mother Church and keep it quiet – there are banns to be read, and priests to see, and in no time we'll be the talk of Ancoats. Just think what Jimmy Marr would make of that in the Vault!'

'So,' he gasped wildly, 'we're going to stay like this, living in mortal sin? Drawing a curse on our heads!'

'We're going to stay like this,' she said with a grim calmness. 'To prove we are *not* going to draw a curse on our heads.'

He was silent, and after a little while looked up at her. She let out a thankful sigh that, for the present anyway, the shadows had fled. The guarded look had gone from his eyes, the anxious creases from his brow. He scratched his bare chest, and stirred by her practical approach, pushed back the chair. 'I wish I'd your strength of mind, girleen. I can take half a dozen on in a punch-up, but when it comes to anything like this . . . C'mon,' he stretched out to turn off the gas. 'We'll have Patterson rattling at the windows before we've even gone to bed!' He felt less haunted for having shared his fears, but not knowing how to express the emotion, he said with a smile, 'I was never a match for the old aunt, but you, Tess, you're match enough for anyone!'

'Yes,' she replied, giving him a playful nudge. 'And don't you be forgettin' it.'

For a while after he had gone to sleep, she kept guard as she had done in Downey's barn, warding off the mockers, defending him with the will of countless forebears, who in their time had grappled with the spirits of wild mountains and desolate valleys.

She also realised more clearly than ever the importance of another child. It was not the 'pride of his trousers' that had driven him to excess, as Annie had said, but the aunt's curse playing on his mind. Isn't it just the natural contrariness of nature, she thought; when I didn't want a baby and scarcely knew what I was doing, I got landed with Patrick!

Tessa stepped up her campaign of prayer. She now sought the assistance of the Virgin every morning before starting the boiler, and for as long as she was able at night before her eyes closed in sleep. Working also on the assumption that prayers in church might carry more weight, she called at the Sacred Heart on the way to the Wilkins' house.

The atmosphere inside the church was rosy with incense and imbued with hope, candles were burning, people praying, kneeling here and there in untidy heaps. Tessa, pressing Kate Jarvey's rosary beads to her forehead until it hurt, struck at the gates of heaven and tore at the garments of the Mother of God.

The anguish of prayer ended, she opened her eyes to the blaze of glory that was the altar; and into the monotonous ebb and flow of ceaseless mutterings, a question from past confessionals flashed across her mind. 'Had she any previous sin remaining unconfessed?' She had always answered that she had not. But now Finn's words echoed starkly. 'Are we going to stay like this,' he had asked, 'living in sin?' She had not thought of their relationship in that light, or because of 'respectability' had not wanted to. It wasn't as if they had just 'shacked up' together, like some of the shiftless back home. Besides, as Spider Murphy had pointed out, the ceremonies of the travelling people had been in existence long before that of Holy Mother church. The more she pondered on these things the more uneasy she felt. It was as though the ground for petition was being cut from under her feet. She got up off her knees, genuflected, and hurried out to work.

Reaching the red-brick house, she quickly slipped into the kitchen by the side door, and flinging off her shawl, set the kettle to boil for tea. Rolling her sleeves to the elbow, she gathered together the bucket, scrubbing brush, floorcloth and a bar of carbolic soap. She had just finished her cake when George Wilkins, stirred partly by curiosity and partly by the compulsion which made him seek her presence, entered the room.

'Good evenin', sir.' She carried the tray to the sink.

'Hmm . . . it's a cold one, eh, Mrs Collins?' He walked toward the fire rubbing his hands together. 'You're a little late tonight. Not that I mind,' he added, as she began a flustered excuse. 'I only mentioned it because you've missed my sister. She's taken the boy to see the parcel post escorted down Market Street – the soldiers, you know. But I can look after you, Mrs Collins, and if there's anything you need, just mention it.'

'Sure, I've everything.' Her voice rose above the clanking of the bucket, and the slosh of water over the floor. He stood looking down at her, fascinated by a hole in her stocking, and the creamy skin beneath. The soles of her shoes needed repairing too, not to mention the worn-down heels. He felt piqued that she had not made an effort so smarten up for her work. His glance travelled along the sweep of her back, from thigh to shoulder, and the sight of her body as it worked rhythmically backward and forward was not, he decided, without attraction.

George returned to the parlour, trying to analyse his thoughts and motives. Since his wife Sylvia had died, he had concentrated all his thoughts to advancing his position with the mill-owning fraternity. The memory of Sylvia had always remained with him and he liked it that way, but now, in the semidarkness of the parlour, he tried to hold on to the glimpses of the wife he had adored . . .

And then he wondered what gave Mrs Collins pleasure. Surely singing was not the ultimate? He sighed. She was happy indeed if such simple pleasures sufficed. Did Collins take her out? Probably not, working too hard and too long, poor devil. What would Mrs Collins think of Belle Vue Gardens, the big shops of Deansgate, tea with the orchestra playing, Blackpool Tower even? He stirred uncomfortably, knowing there was no philanthropy in such musings. Until he had seen Mrs Collins singing in the Sugar Loaf, every thought of the opposite sex had featured only the memory of his beloved Sylvia. But now another image trespassed on the sanctuary of his mind: that of a washerwoman, Effie's cleaning woman, the wife of a 'paddy', a 'potato-head'. And what, he questioned, was he going to do about it?

As the weeks passed, Tessa watched the shadows gathering again about her husband. And to her own dismay she sometimes found herself wondering whether they were being punished for what the Church considered 'unconfessed previous sins'.

One afternoon at the Wilkins' house, Tessa, intent on quelling these thoughts, realised that she had gone to clean the dining-room floor, and had forgotten to bring a taper to light the gas. As she turned to fetch one, George Wilkins loomed in the doorway like a genie from a bottle.

'God Almighty!' he gasped. 'Oh, beggin' your pardon, sir.'

'These were on the kitchen table.'

She took the matches and crossed to the lights which were positioned on the walls. As each one flickered under its beaded shade, her face softened with delight.

'I suppose,' he said, in a measured tone, 'many men have told you, Mrs Collins, what an attractive young woman you are.'

She turned a startled look on him. 'No, sir, only me husband.'

'I think you are very attractive.' He noticed she had tidied her hair and no wisps had yet escaped, but the strictness only made her look more vivid.

She turned at once, partly to cover her confusion, but also to adjust the flow of gas to the lights. George Wilkins moved swiftly from the door to stand close behind her. She felt the predatory pressure of his hands, pressing, searching out the curve of her breasts, and then sliding down to her waist. He turned her toward him. She did not look at him; if she did, there was no sight in it. Her head swam. Reality was suspended, and the only thing which registered life was her madly beating heart. She stood stiffly, like the statues on Piccadilly. He gazed at her with passionate intentness. The sheer animal warmth of her captured his senses, and to hold a woman again in his arms sent the blood pounding through his veins.

Before Tessa could bring any judgement to bear he began covering her face with soft, quick, agonised kisses. He released her and stood back, his dark eyes devouring her face. The gas hissed softly.

'Have I to apologise?' he asked. 'Well, I'm not going to. I've waited weeks to do that.'

Tessa had moved further away, and the movement unlocked her tongue. 'Mr Wilkins, will you please remember that I'm a respectable woman. You shouldn't be thinking those things, still less doing 'em, and being proud of yourself . . . ' Her fingers plucked at the sack apron as she backed to the door, listening to the small shocked voice which was but an echo of the shrieking protest held down by fear and subservience.

'Please . . . please don't go yet, Mrs Collins. I swear I'll not touch you again. But you must listen to me.' His words halted her progress. Sighing with relief, and occasionally fingering the gold watch chain across his waistcoat pockets, he continued. 'You'll never know how much you have occupied my thoughts, after seeing you in the Sugar Loaf, and more often since I saw you all hot and harassed when you burned your arm. You'll also never know what it means to have you under the same roof even for a few hours a week. It's as though you kind of . . . sanctify it with your honesty, your candour, your simplicity.'

Tessa having now lost the drift of his words, eyed him with the tolerance she reserved for Danny who was 'a bit short' and brought his laundry. 'If it's all the same to you, sir, I'll go to the kitchen and hot me water up.'

His jaw sagged and eyebrows rose in sheer unbelief. He wanted to go after her, to shake her, and demand something by way of comment. What had she felt? What did she think? Was she not even shocked, angry, prudish? There was bound to be some emotion behind the 'respectable woman' statement. How could she just dismiss the incident out of hand?

The clanking of bucket and kettle brought his thoughts to action, and he fled to the parlour. The room was lit by a street lamp and it suited his mood. Taking a cigarette, he considered himself no further forward. Like a lovesick youth he had made advances, revealed his heart and still had not got the measure of her. At least he had held her in his arms, kissed her; not that he could recall the sensation now. He had been too overwhelmed by the suddenness of the incident. He had, of course, anticipated such a situation many times, but closing in on impulse had rather fragmented the enjoyment. All the thoughts which had surrounded the memory of his wife were now transferred to Tessa. He no longer felt cheated by fate. 'Faint heart,' he told himself in a jovial mood, 'never won fair lady, and I intend to win this one.' Even though the 'lady' was wearing an old serge skirt, had holes in her stockings, and was given to rolling her sleeves up.

Chapter Fifteen

Tessa, her face burning from chin to hairline, hurried along Oldham Road. Loosening the shawl from her head, she welcomed the cold dash of the east wind about her neck, her ears. But its icy touch did nothing to dampen the smouldering fires of outrage and frustration. She lessened her pace, not wanting to arrive home in turmoil. Perhaps Wilkins had been at the drink? Yes, that was it – and yet her memory told her there had been no hint of it on his breath. Memory, having been nudged, took her back to Ennan where that scurvy tinker, Mick Murphy, made the mistake of thinking goy women were fair game. And, if Mr Wilkins thinks I'm going to stand there like Dooley's ghost so he can run his white hands all over me body, and say all those fancy things, he's got another think coming!

Perhaps I'm reading too much into the incident... There was often gossip about the overlookers at the mill taking liberties. But then she thought better of it. With God's own luck he might not be there next Thursday, he might have come to his senses. One thing was certain, Finn must never, ever know, for mill agent or not, he'd go for Wilkins and end up, Oh God save him, in Strangeways prison. The sombre vision of the evicted Thompsons came into her mind... Standing in the drizzle, children crying into her skirts, and him racing round like a whippet to raise a loan for a cheap cellar lodging for the night. Oh, why can't fellas keep their hands to themselves? God preserve me, she sighed, from thinking about the whole bloody shebang!

She pulled the shawl about her head, and approached

Loom Street. The only man I've ever wanted is the one I've got, she thought warmly, and all he needs is a brother or sister for Patrick to lift him from the mulligrubs. She was glad their house was the end of the row, and had three steps leading up to the door. Sure, the good luck was with them, and poor Finn couldn't see it.

Wouldn't it be the marvellous thing, she thought wistfully – and one of these days it will happen – that I'll go in and find him returned to his old lovely self: boasting about our connection with Captain O'Shea; teasing the life out of me and the boy; and breaking into a jig when the mood takes him. With a quickening of the heart, a lightness of step, and wanting it so much to be right because of Mr Wilkins, she pushed open the door. But the shadow was still there. The brooding mists of Ennabrugh had followed them to Ancoats.

Because of her refusal to speculate on the situation at the Wilkins' house, the arrival of 'cleaning nights' came as something of a shock. Wednesday was easy to cope with, for George was never home, and Miss Wilkins, as always, was most affable.

Thursday was a different matter. Tessa woke with a hollow feeling. She felt empty. Neglected. Standing before the Virgin, she had hoped to receive comfort or assurance, but had received nothing. Now, reaching for her shawl, she told Patrick to be a good boy for his da, and that birthday bricks were for building not throwing. With a reminder to keep a good fire going for the rackful of clothes above, she smiled at Finn, and gathering her shawl against the cold, went slowly out.

She let herself into the Wilkins' kitchen through the side door; not wanting to draw attention to her arrival, the inclination was to creep about and be as quiet as possible. But, she thought, surely it was better to act normally, pretend last Thursday never happened. Taking off her shawl, she turned up the gas. 'Merciful Lord,' she muttered. 'There's shadows enough, without the gas burning at half-cock!' She set the kettle to boil for her tea, and after taking the cloths and bucket from beneath the sink, she ate part of the cake and wrapped up the rest for Patrick, listening all the time for footsteps. Had he gone out after all? Was he really embarrassed and ashamed?

She washed the kitchen floor, and while waiting for more water to heat, went to prepare the dining room. With a sinking heart, she observed a sliver of light beneath the door. So, he'd been there all the time. Why, she wondered, had he not come to the kitchen to pass the time of day, as usual? Dismissal. The word echoed about her head. She was going to lose the cleaning and, worse, the laundry . . .

The door opened, startling Tessa into mumbling hurriedly, 'If you're busy, Mr Wilkins, I'll be doing the stairs and – '

'Come in, Mrs Collins, I want to talk to you.'

She followed him into the room, a tiny frown plucking at her brow, her questioning eyes heavy with anxiety.

'Sit down.'

She looked at the embroidered covers and then at her shabby serge skirt. Rubbing her hands on the sackcloth apron, she gingerly obeyed. Wilkins sat in a winged chair by the fire. Reaching into a silver cigarette box he extricated one with trembling fingers, and lit it. Their eyes met. He saw the confusion on her face, and his heart seemed to shift. He wanted his body to move toward her, to take her in his arms, to lie her back on the sofa and kiss all the puzzlement from her face. He was appalled by the sudden desire.

Tessa sat very still, hands tightly together on her aproned lap. He had not yet spoken, his face looked strange, and the cigarette, untasted, was burning in his fingers. 'What is it, Mr Wilkins, are you ill?'

He heard her voice as through a fog. 'No,' came the curt answer. 'I'm not ill.'

'I can't be doing with a lot of shilly-shallying, sir. Are you dismissin' me?'

'Good God, woman, no! What would Miss Wilkins do without you?'

'I'll be going then, sir, to do the stairs.'

'Going?' The word echoed through the fog again. Dear heaven, he thought, I love her. I want this adorable peasant more than I've ever wanted any woman, even Sylvia. 'Wait,' he called as she turned to the door. 'I said I wanted to talk to you.' He stood up, his hand gripping the ornate edge of

162

the mantelshelf. Mustn't frighten her off. Mustn't have an outraged Mrs Collins running from the room just as Effie was coming home! There must be no scenes, no embarrassment. She must be at ease. 'Mrs Collins,' he began. 'Do you . . . like being here, working for me?' He spoke without eagerness, yet with a morose excitement.

'Oh, yes, sir,' she answered readily. 'Miss Wilkins is the spirit o' kindness, what with the laundry, and you setting Finn on – '

'Yes, yes,' he interrupted, annoyed at the reference to Finn and laundry. God, did this woman think of anything else? 'I'm pleased about that, because I happen to like you, very much.' She moved nearer the door. 'Hear me out,' he said civilly, as though addressing a clerk. She paused. 'I want you to make . . . ah, let me see, now? Yes, an assignation with me.'

Tessa, not having come across the word before, frowned. 'What d'you mean, Mr Wilkins?'

He sighed. It would have been much easier if she had comprehended. 'Next week my sister will be taking the boy to Blackpool for a few days . . . ' He thought of all the effort he had put into persuading Effie to go, and hoped it would not be in vain. He began to feel like a common seducer. 'I wondered if you'd come, not to clean floors, but to keep me company . . . ' He closed his eyes before her astonished glance, and felt another twinge of shame. 'You're a grown woman . . . ' He swallowed hard. 'I want to make love to you. Now don't go getting alarmed. I know you have no feelings toward me. And I must say at once,' he added hastily, almost regretting his outburst, 'that I will not force myself upon you. And I'll understand if you refuse.'

'I am refusing. I'm not that kind of woman!'

'I know you're not, Tessa.'

Startled at the familiarity, she clamped down on him at once. 'I'd rather be called by my married name, sir.'

'Very well,' he replied impatiently. 'Very well, but only if you stop calling me sir. Can you do that?'

'Yes, Mr Wilkins.'

He sighed again. Well, it was a beginning. 'As I said before, I'm not going to force myself on you. I shall be here in this room next week, waiting for you to come of your own free will.'

'I'll not be coming!' she was aghast. 'I can't. I won't!'

'Think carefully, Mrs Collins.'

'You said I could please meself!'

'You can.'

The underlying threat drained the colour from Tessa's face. He immediately felt mean and low, but with Tessa in the room, only a few feet away, he would stoop to anything.

'Will you listen, now,' she gasped with some ferocity. 'I'm not being your "fancy woman" – for that's what you want, isn't it?'

'No, not at all,' he answered vaguely. 'Sit down, Mrs Collins, you looked for a minute as if you were going to faint.'

She remained standing. 'I'm surprised I didn't drop down dead, the things you were saying, and me a respectable woman.'

'I know you're bloody well respectable! I wouldn't have asked you otherwise. And I am asking, Mrs Collins.'

'Ye keep saying that – '

'You'll not understand this,' he said, suddenly elated with a line of reasoning that mitigated, to some extent, his own behaviour, and would give her respectable Catholic conscience leeway. 'I need you to banish a ghost. To exorcise an image, to break the hold my dead wife has on me. An assignation with you will set me free. Free! D'you understand?'

'You mean,' she asked in a small voice, 'just the once?'

He did not answer. His face switched suddenly from hers to the direction of the front door. The sound of Effie's voice reminded Tessa of the stairs and dining room not even touched.

'Don't panic, Mrs Collins. It will be all right,' he said hastily. 'You can go now. I'll explain to my sister.'

Out on Oldham Road again, this time not noticing the icy wind, Tessa was at first shocked that a man in his position should suggest such a thing. So mortal a sin. How often had she, from the safety of her own doorstep, heard about employers wielding power over their female servants: it was the theme of the halfpenny books; the subject of melodrama; but in actuality – oh, dear God, it didn't bear thinking about! One thing was for sure, wild horses wouldn't drag her into that dining room next week.

While the first shock wave was ebbing, the second came in with full force, filling her with shame and a kind of horror at failing to anticipate the situation. If only she had faced up to reality instead of hoping he would have thought better of it, or that he'd be away, or that heaven would somehow intervene. Of course, she could always tell Wilkins to sod off, and keep his jobs . . .

Pulling the shawl about her head and feeling comfort in the soft woolliness of it, she threaded her way through streets which looked as weary as she felt; houses with paint peeling off the woodwork, and grimy fanlights awash with vases, Virgins and Sacred Hearts.

Tessa, passing the church, paused, then retracing her steps, slowly went inside. She hovered in the porch, considering . . . She had had enough on her plate coping and humouring Finn without being burdened with 'confessional phrases'. Her regard for Father Quinn had also diminished. She laid the blame for Finn's despondency squarely at his door, and consequently she avoided him. It was a measure of her helplessness, then, that she now stood in the semidarkness of the church. She stood hesitantly at the back. A tram lumbering up the road illuminated the east window, and between the pillars lights of adoration flickered, blue for the Queen of Heaven and red for St Joseph. A few people, anonymous in their adoration, crouched low or knelt upright. As the lumbering of the tram faded, reverential whispers spilled into the silence and rosaries clicked as they touched the pew.

I too have knelt there, she thought, and in the desperate language of the heart I've sought guidance. What should I do? What should I not do? Tell me, show me, give me a sign. How I have yearned and longed for consolation, confirmation. I too have knelt there and adored. She turned. But not any more.

She hurried home, past the ginnel where the oaken beam spanned the two houses, up the steps, and entered to the delighted yells of her son clamouring for his slice of cake.

'Just brewed the tea, Tess,' said Finn, pouring some into a saucer to make it cool for Patrick. 'Come and sit by the fire, girleen, and drink your tea while it's hot. Begod, Tess!' he exclaimed, as she came under the light. 'You look banjaxed.' Concern edged his voice. 'What's up, love? Where's your smile an' song, then?'

She eyed him warily. 'Same place as yours, Finn.'

Chapter Sixteen

Tessa did not kneel by the blue-mantled Virgin during the next few days. Her solace and encouragement came from the battered Sacred Heart on the mantelshelf. It was her old companion in trouble, and had seen her through the lonely time in Liverpool with its compassion and reassurance. A symbol of tears and suffering, it appealed to her mood. There was a sense, to, of familiarity, for a Sacred Heart on her father's dresser, and not a blue-mantled Virgin, had been part of her growing up.

Over the weekend Tessa wearied herself with physical labour. She lived in a state of exhaustion and muddle, flopping in and out of it like a creature in a bog. Singing at the Sugar Loaf was her salvation. Titch Bradley thought she had never been on such form. She experienced all the despair of exile; the sorrows of loneliness; and the poignancy of disillusionment. Women dabbed their eyes with handkerchiefs, and men, sniffing audibly, sent another Guinness to the piano.

'Here's a whisky, lass,' said Titch. 'Someone's enjoyed your performance – Irish whisky an' all.'

There was only one person who had ever bought her whisky. 'It'll be Captain O'Shea! God, Finn'll be pigsick he's missed him.' She looked toward the door. 'Play 'em a medley until I get back.'

The suddenness of the occasion gave her no time to build up apprehension about her appearance, or about figures of authority. Cormac, having seen her in fine spirit on Patrick's birthday night, wondered at the change of mood, and hoped nothing was wrong. He had been awarded a place at the School of Equine Studies in Sussex, and somehow, ridiculous as it might seem, he did not want to leave Manchester if all wasn't well with Finn and Tessa.

'Thanks for the drink,' she said, her features warming into something more than the usual tremulous smile of acknowledgement. There had not been much to smile about lately, but this familiar face from the 'auld country' with its longish features, amber-flecked eyes, and ruffled hair – sent, she was sure, by those Celtic gods the schoolmaster used to tell them about – began immediately to lighten the anxiety which had threatened to take her apart. Then the smile changed into a startled awareness of his companion.

'I'm Audrey Styles,' she said, thrusting out her hand. 'Glad to meet you, Mrs Collins. Cormac's told us so much about his godson, I feel I know you already. If we wait for him to introduce us,' she cast a roguish look at Cormac, 'We'll be here all night!' Tessa, conscious of the knot of people watching from the bar, shook the gloved hand and found it as firm and strong as her own.

'Will you listen to her giving out,' he countered. 'If it wasn't for me, sure you wouldn't be here at all!'

'It's a mercy that either of us are. There we were on our way to the theatre,' she appealed to Tessa, 'going up Oldham Road on the tram – the guard had already rang the starting bell, mark you – when he,' another roguish look at Cormac, 'suddenly jumped up from his seat, shouted "It's Friday night at the Sugar Loaf!" and dragged me off the tram with him – while it was moving!'

Under cover of the ensuing laughter, Tessa, not wanting to appear rude by staring – not that it bothered anyone else, including Jonty Johnson – saw an auburn-haired young woman in a dark green felt hat, a fashionable, long-jacketed costume, and a knitted scarf, thrown nonchalantly about her throat.

'I hope it was worth it, Miss Styles.'

'It certainly was – and you must call me Audrey. Miss Styles sounds terribly stuffy. As Cormac said, "a voice not to be missed". I'm not an authority on singing,' she laughed, 'but you have a distinctive tone, a rare quality, and, more important – I know what it is!' she exclaimed to Cormac. 'She's an entertainer, don't you think?'

They talked briefly about how it was too early for Finn to be at the Sugar Loaf, him having to wait until Patrick was asleep; and then how they had better be off or they would be well and truly late for the theatre. Cormac, as a final gesture, indicated her fingers curled about the glass, and said with a twinkle in his eyes, 'I see you found your ring . . . '

'Captain O'Shea,' she said on impulse, 'do you believe miracles can still happen?'

'We make our own miracles happen,' he answered softly.

On Monday morning, when Finn had gone to work and Patrick was not yet awake, Tessa sat by the hearth sipping her first cup of tea before firing the boiler. Three days till Thursday, she thought, only three days. If I don't go to the Wilkins' house we could risk losing all this. But the very thought of the alternative covered her body with a burning blush . . . and as though committing a mortal sin was not bad enough, what if she were to become pregnant as a result, for it was the fertile time of the month? Fertile . . . Oh, God, she put down the cup and stared into the flames with a fast-beating heart. 'God forgive me, oh merciful God forgive me!' An awful strategy was forming . . . building up slowly, like the clouds over Ennabrugh.

Thursday dawned and no miracle had occurred. Tessa was not surprised; perhaps she had lacked faith. It did not matter now. She had decided to answer her own prayers, and since making the decision a wonderful sense of ease had taken her over, a strange buoyancy of spirit. She, Teresa Collins, was going to shape their lives and create her own miracle, like Captain O'Shea had said. And when apprehension began to creep upon her, she had only to look at Finn in the fiendish grip of his dead aunt's mumbo jumbo, and the apprehension disappeared.

George Wilkins had said, 'I need you to banish a ghost.'

'And I,' she murmured, while ironing his sheets. 'I'm going to use you, to banish not a ghost, but a curse.'

The thought of his white fumbling hands made her stomach lurch, and her heart hammer with dread. She had said wild horses would not drag her to that parlour, but she had reckoned without her love for Finn. He was being destroyed by a curse, and she was going to save him, as surely as he had saved her from the terrible disaster at Ennan.

When he came home, smelling of oil and with fluffs of cotton adhering to his curls, Tessa made a special fuss of him.

'An' what have I done to deserve this?' he whispered to Patrick, as she took his tea from the oven. 'Your mammy's got me favourite colcannon –' he raised an enquiring brow – and five Woodbines, begod!'

'Will you be telling your da,' she leaned forward to the delighted child, 'it's because he's a lovely fella!'

'In this case,' he added, 'we'll go for a gill when you get back.

She nodded, and not trusting herself to look at him, pulled the shawl about her head and went out.

The evening was black, cheerless and bitterly cold, there was no one about and her footsteps echoed against the closed doors and windows of the silent streets. 'When you get back' Finn had said. Ah, when she got back she would be a different woman. A woman who had known another man's advances. Mrs Murphy would have called it fornication, the priest adultery. Some would call it love, others a crime. I call it a miracle. Oh, God forgive me, it's got to be a miracle. Christ alone knows how much I have prayed for a child. The Blessed Mother has seen more tears these past months than I've shed in all me life before, and still she wouldn't help us. 'I've done with praying and crying and beseeching,' she told the soft folds of her shawl. 'If yer want 'owt done,' she mimicked Annie Cooper, 'yer must do it yersel.' That's just what she was doing, answering her own prayers, making life right again for herself and Finn.

As for Mr Wilkins, he would be there, waiting, wondering if she was going to turn up; perhaps even planning revenge if she didn't, for it would be a blow to his pride. 'Come of your own free will,' he had said. She sighed and wished he had just taken her unawares. That would have absolved her from any decision. But he knew she would have fought like a tiger. 'Oh, it's the crafty sod he is. But, I'm telling ye, George

170

Wilkins, there's one here just as crafty. I've not lived with the tinkers for nothing!'

She turned briskly on to Oldham Road, head unbowed before the cold, each step strengthening her resolve. Then, suddenly, the house came into view, and her resolve almost crumbled. The side door stood ajar as usual. She stood looking at it, hesitating. How many times had she pushed it open without thinking, and hurried in? Now, her body felt leaden, the door stiffer.

Inside, little noises greeted her, all struggling for a hearing, clamouring for attention, eager to impress their views. The tick of the wall clock was loud and full of portent, the drip of water from the kitchen tap sounded hollow, and the fire hissed slyly.

With an air of resignation she took off her shawl and stood pressing her hands together. The attitude reminded her of Wilkins and focused her attention on the evening ahead. Her eyes strayed to the cupboard where the bucket and cloths were kept . . . the money was on the table . . . the tea tray set . . . he had set it. Bravery and purpose were all very well outside, but here and now, the magnitude of what she was about to do made her feel sick.

George Wilkins paced to and fro, past the shelf of Royal Doulton figures, round the new sofa, and back to the winged chair. His eyes were rounded in a state of astonishment. To think that he, a man in his position, was standing here on his own hearth, totally subject to the whim of an Irish washer-woman!

He glanced at the ashtray piled high with half-smoked cigarettes. Effie didn't allow smoking in here. No doubt the place smelled like a taproom, but that wouldn't worry Mrs Collins. What the devil was she doing in the kitchen all this time? He always knew when she had entered the house. Hoping to heaven she had not taken out the bucket and cloths, George fingered the gold watch chain bridging his waistcoat pockets and fought down a desire to go and see. If she came, it must be of her own volition. There was a sound in the passage, footsteps, slow and heavy. God in heaven, was she carrying that bloody bucket after all? The door handle moved. She was not carrying a bucket.

Tessa closed the door and stood with her back against

it. She was wearing her shabby cleaning skirt and a faded flowered blouse, over which, because of the cold, she had drawn a long knitted cardigan, her hands thrust deep into its pockets. Out of a pale face blazed the eyes of a zealot.

Hell, he thought, this will never do. He rubbed his hands together, 'I'm glad you came, Mrs Collins. It's a cold one tonight, come and sit by the fire?' As though walking in her sleep, she obeyed. He poured some wine into two glasses. 'Here, drink this.' Before he could raise his glass to pledge the evening, she had downed it in one gulp. Taken aback, he decided against the pledge.

'The glasses are only little,' she explained, feeling warmer. 'Can I have some more – in a bigger glass. Y'see, I usually drink Guinness . . . ' And if I drink enough, she thought . . .

If I get some wine inside her, Wilkins thought, she'll thaw out a bit more. 'I can scarcely believe you're here,' he said happily.

'No,' she replied. 'Neither can I.'

He moved over from the table and, enjoying the role of seducer, sat by her on the sofa. Not close, it would not do to frighten her off. 'You're not very talkative, Mrs Collins.'

'Sure, you'll have to forgive me, sir. I mean, Mr Wilkins. Y'see, I'm not used to this . . . I don't usually talk to gentlemen.'

'Not even in the Sugar Loaf?'

Tessa, watching him refill her glass, did not answer. While passing it to her, their hands accidentally touched, and although hers were cold they scorched his fingers. He replaced the decanter, feeling a flush creep up his neck and over the stiff white collar. His heart began to pound beneath the facade of his waistcoat and he felt stifled. Fighting down an urge to fling off the waistcoat, he said in a controlled, affable tone, 'Your hands are cold. Here, let me warm them.'

He took her free hand, for the other held the glass to which she clung as though it were a lifeline. Her eyes widened, and the utter vulnerability of her glance made him feel ashamed of his exploitation, and at the same time excited.

She looked about, above him, past him, anywhere but at him, and finally at the Royal Doulton, and remembered how Patrick had wanted them. Oh, if only . . .

His fingers were fumbling at her wrist, seeking to unfasten

the button on her cuff. There was no button, and he became flustered to find himself struggling with a safety pin. She watched the cuff flap untidily open, and suddenly felt afraid of the naked desire which was flooding his face; of the sudden sensuality of his wide-lipped mouth; his rapid breathing. He raised her hand to his lips, and closed his eyes.

Tessa sat completely still, observing the adoration of George Wilkins with a sudden air of detachment. She felt a certain tolerance, a kind of indulgence, for this was her miracle.

'Warmer now?

'Yes.'

'Your thoughts were miles away, Mrs Collins?'

'No, Mr Wilkins. I was thinking about . . . us.'

'Were you, by Jove!' His brows arched in delight. 'I've thought of nothing else for weeks.' The sweat glistened on his forehead. 'It's devilish hot . . . '

He placed his gold watch and chain on the mantelshelf with an air of deliberation. And, as though suddenly arriving at a decision, he struggled out of his black coat and fought feverishly with the buttons of his waistcoat to emerge free of the restrictions of years. For here, with Tessa Collins, he felt younger, nonchalant and daring.

Tessa reached for her glass. She did not need to down the entire contents now, but sipped it slowly. Over the rim she watched his tall, well-built figure cross to the door. Her heart soared. Was he going out? Had he decided not to bother? With a twinge of dismay she saw him lock the door. Then, holding up the key, he removed the glass from her fingers and placed the key beside it on the table.

Returning to the sofa he pushed her gently back and sat on the edge – leering, she thought, and something inside her yelled it isn't me, it isn't me! This is happening to someone else. Oh, please, Holy Mother, St Teresa, let it not happen? His smooth, white hands about her face and neck told her it was happening. Through the flowered cotton of the blouse she felt the weight of his hands lingering over the curves of her breasts, trying to centre on her nipples. Her eyes flew open wide in alarm. Uttering a stifled cry of protest, she tried to edge away.

'Hush, hush,' he said softly, continuing to fondle and

caress. Tessa lay still, her heart pounding in her ears. A choking sensation filled her throat as he began to unfasten the opening of her bodice. She thrust aside her head, crushing down the impulse to push him away, trying to drown her fear by reminding herself of the miracle. He seemed not to mind that she said nothing, that her eyes were closed and her head turned. The touch of his fingers against her flesh told her he was unfastening the ribbons which held her camisole together. She felt the release and almost fainted with the shame of lying there with the upper part of her body exposed to his avid gaze.

Abruptly he pulled away from her and tore off his white winged collar. She watched it flutter to the floor where it lay as stiff and helpless as herself. Collar studs and cuff links followed, rattling away to clink against the skirting boards. He had stripped to his long snow-white underpants, his well-fleshed body bulged at the waist, as though there was not enough muscle to hold it all in. His face was congested, his brown eyes gloating, and his pink body throbbed. No longer able to restrain himself, his hands were fumbling about her skirts and petticoat. Stretching out, he had almost rolled on top of her when she warded him off.

'I can't! I can't!' she cried.

'Tessa,' he whispered hoarsely. 'You can't hold back now. You'll never know how much I need you.'

Even miracles have their price, she thought. And fighting down her last scruple, gazed at her arms. Not wanting to touch him they were outstretched almost to crucifixion level. The thrust of his body compelled her to lower them onto his pale shoulders, to brace herself to receive him, offering her empty womb. For beyond her physical confusion, her shame and despair, there was compulsion; she was urged on by the vital need for a child. Any child, so long as she gave birth to it. This child of Wilkins would break the mockers' hold on Finn. He would think it was his, and he would never, ever know any different.

Wilkins was still, at last. Thank God, oh, thank God and the blessed angels it was over. His grasp of her weakened. She inhaled on a great sigh of infinite relief, and felt tears of humiliation gathering in the corner of her eyes.

Pleased and pleasured, George dressed, and Tessa, embarrassed, turned away from him to fasten up her clothes and straighten her hair. When she turned again, he was holding out a glass of wine. 'It wasn't all that bad, was it?' He smiled shyly, feeling like a boy revelling in his first conquest. 'I think you were most co-operative, Mrs Collins, most co-operative.'

She tipped back her glass and drained the last of the wine. 'I'm glad you think so, Mr Wilkins, but if it's all the same to you, I'll be after going now. Finn will be worried if I'm late.'

Unlocking the door and following her to the kitchen, he indicated the untouched tray. 'You'll take the cake for your son?' What beauty of form, he thought, to be hidden by so shapeless a cardigan. And to think only a few moments ago I held that vital body in my arms, and now she's going back to her illiterate Irishman. She had wrapped the cake, scooped the money from the table, and thrusting it deep into her pocket reached for her shawl.

'You will come again?' He was annoyed at the anxiety in his voice.

'Only to clean the floors, Mr Wilkins.' She turned her back abruptly, holding on to the edge of the table.

He stood quite still, staring at the tousled pile of dark brown hair. It was as though she had struck him. He put out a hand to touch her sleeve. Without turning she moved further along the table, wishing he had not followed her.

'Tessa?' Her shoulders stiffened and he amended the familiarity. 'Mrs Collins?' Tessa began to turn slowly, and he thought she somehow looked different. She was different. She lifted her head to face her employer, her seducer, the father of her child. The miracle had happened. She knew, she just knew.

Her face wore an air of grim strength. Her wide mouth was set in a positive mode and her large eyes were almost narrowed into determined rectangles. 'You gave me to understand it would only be the once.'

He rubbed his hands together uncertainly, his mind bordering on confusion. He was seeing a different woman, and felt he was standing in the presence of someone superior. He pursed his lips and looked at the floor. If he had found the other Tessa interesting, this new one was even more so. He could not let her go now.

'I know this evening has been a shock to you. Perhaps you need time to get used to me. For us to get used to each other. What you're really saying to me, Mrs Collins, is that we should wait a little longer before we meet again. That's it, isn't it?'

'No,' she answered with brutal frankness. 'It isn't.'

'I'll ask you again, when you've had time –'

'The answer will be the same,' she insisted in a frantic tone. 'Y'see, I'm going to have a baby, and it wouldn't be right.'

'You didn't tell me this before?' he accused.

'I'm tellin' you now, sir. That's why I'm only coming to do the floors. I came tonight because I was afraid I'd lose me place, and the washin', and Finn his job –'

'And what makes you think you still won't?' he demanded in a harsh whisper. 'What makes you think anything has changed?'

'I've changed,' she said simply, and continued with bland innocence. 'I came because of what you said about your wife, about banishing a ghost, and being free and all of that. You and Miss Wilkins have been good to me. I wanted to help you, that's all.'

For a second George felt it was beyond his comprehension. He no longer seemed to be in command of a situation he had created.

He reached out clumsily, as if to take her arm, to embrace her. She drew back swiftly and took up her shawl, pulling it over her shoulders and head, holding it together beneath her chin. His lower jaw fell, for the shawl, pressed so tightly around her face, had transformed her appearance dramatically to that of a nun. Her brightness, her strength and beauty which a few moments ago had gilded the kitchen, were now withdrawn into a veiled, forbidden figure. They faced each other in silence for a moment, then Tessa turned and walked out.

On Oldham Road her pace quickened. She walked with a swing to her shabby skirts, and a confident lift of the head. She was once more the Celtic goddess of Finn's imagination, who, with crook in hand, strode over the mountainy outcrops of Ennan.

Just fancy, she thought, I came this way a couple of hours ago thinking I'd be a different woman, prepared to feel all kinds of terrible remorse, and I don't at all. Neither am I afraid of George Wilkins. Sure, it would be kind of awkward when he came to settle his laundry, but if it wasn't for himself Finn would be in the clutches of the mockers until it rained whisky!

She felt calm. The decision to commit mortal sin had been her own. She had answered her own prayers, performed her own miracle by seizing the opportunity presented by fate. Finn knew it was her favourable time of the month for conception, and tonight, after their gill at the Sugar Loaf, Finn would look at her and say with hope in his voice, 'Shall we try again, Tess?' And she would reply, 'Yes, my darling, darling Finn.' And their love would be charmed, as it used to be before Father Quinn covered it with his shadow. She had the power to make it so, to make it a night Finn would remember. If the old aunt was watching from the shades of hell itself, she'd know the mockers had no hold over Finn any more, for Proud Riley's daughter had seen to it.

Behind the blinds of the parlour, George Wilkins reached the winged chair and shrank into it like a disturbed spider. Curiously enough, it was not the memory of Tessa Collins on the sofa which botherd him so much as Tessa Collins in the kitchen. He could see now that he had underestimated her, stupidly considered her to be devoid of reasoning power. What had gone wrong? Was she playing hard to get? No, she was incapable of ruse when it came to sexual matters; all these respectably married Catholic women were tarred with the same brush. No, there were no veiled mysteries in the depth of those long-lashed eyes. She was merely exercising the terrible right of the heart – she did not want him. Of course he hadn't expected her to swoon in rapture, but neither had he expected such an unlooked-for and dramatic end to the evening. Perhaps when she came next week . . . Dear heaven, I wish she'd told me about the child in the first place, he thought irritably. And hunching himself further into the chair he acknowledged that he was not being teased, or even asked to wait. He was being rejected. But in the goodness of her heart, and despite her already carrying, she had been concerned enough to help him exorcise Sylvia's ghost. He clung to the warming thought, wrapping it about him like a muffler. She had understood about his banishing of a ghost, and had been prepared to help him to the extent of allowing him to love her. Looking back, he could hear the sincerity behind the attractive Irish brogue. 'Sure, and I hope to God, your wife's now at rest, and yerself free.'

Oh yes, he was no longer haunted by the memory of Sylvia; he was haunted now by Tessa Collins.

Chapter Seventeen

When Tessa told Finn he was to become a father for the second time, it was as though she had waved a magic wand. He became a young man again. The mists of Ennabrugh cleared from his eyes; happy triumph covered his face; the wide shoulders squared; and Patrick giggled until he got the hiccups to see his mother swung around by the waist as far as the restricted space allowed.

His whole being glowed with pride and pleasure, and the sight took her back to Ennan, to when she had met him outside the chapel and he had stood free of his aunt, his own man, and the knowledge had conveyed a touch of princeliness upon him.

The news was related with pride to Cormac O'Shea when he came from Sussex for Patrick's birthday in the heat of July. Doors and windows being open to catch even the slightest current of air, he bounded up the steps, tapped the doorjamb with his cane, and stepped inside. The first thing he noticed was the absence of neighbourly crows inside — they were perched on doorsteps instead, and had received due acknowledgement.

Finn mixed him a pint of shandy, and while Patrick played with his present of a large wooden jigsaw puzzle in the shape of a spotty dog, they drank to the new baby.

On previous occasions Tessa had been too flustered, overawed or unprepared to take stock of Cormac, beyond the 'wandering minstrel' image which she thought had suited him admirably – even now, she had to look twice to be sure it was a short cane he carried, and not a fiddle.

Although not as handsome and well built as Finn, Tessa thought his quality of spirit more than made up the deficiency. He could be twinkling and quick, serious and soulful, and somehow, when he was about, things seemed different. The houseplace had been as hot as hell while she baked the soda bread, Finn had grumbled about the jug of beer going flat, there was Patrick's white blouse to keep clean, and they'd both been on tenterhooks perchance Marr the Piper called to swirl his kilt. None of that mattered now. The beer tasted delicious, the heat went unnoticed, Patrick looked like a cherub, and if Jimmy Marr did intrude they were sure Captain O'Shea would know just how to send him off.

As he sat on the cane-bottomed chair, the skirt of his tunic flaring onto the lean thighs, she thought of Finn's nice dancing legs and how they had not danced at all since arriving in Manchester – and would they ever dance again?

He told them a little of the School of Equine Studies, and how London was already going crazy with preparations to mark the coronation of King Edward and Queen Alexandra the following June. That Nick was still at the Regent Road Barracks, and what a fine fella he was, and how he missed him and Audrey and Elfreda, and the 'whole shebang up north'. But in another couple of years he would have his extra qualification. 'I've often fancied meself as being in with one of the big breeding stables, like Doyles in Cork, y'know.'

They didn't know, but the way he had of talking, even mucking out a stable would have a fascinating side. The evening concluded at the Sugar Loaf where Cormac was as much an attraction as Tessa's voice. He recalled the melancholy aspect of his flying visit with Audrey, and before leaving, chose his opportunity to enquire, with a twinkle in his eyes, 'How about the miracle – did you make it happen?'

She nodded. 'I did so.'

And after putting in his request for 'Cockles and Mussels', he hurried off to catch his train to London. Tessa treasured their little 'asides' with a sense of conspiracy. Somehow they had been partners in intrigue since Patrick's baptism; it seemed part of the 'auld country' and appealed to her nature. But she hoped to God there'd be no more intrigue, for the last terrible one had almost taken her apart.

The baby was due about Christmastime, and Tessa hoped it would arrive early. For the past six weeks there had been no money from the Sugar Loaf, for to appear at a public venue in an advanced state of pregnancy was immodest in the extreme. But an early birth, she thought, would allow her to take advantage of the seasonal generosity of those in the Room to make up the loss.

Although able to carry on laundering until the last pangs dragged her down, she had been unable to cope with her cleaning engagement. Wilkins, out of pique, wanted to take the temporary cessation as an excuse to dispose of her services altogether. But he had reckoned without his sister, who, never having gone against him before, had insisted he kept the position open. To have pressed the matter would have set her thinking he had an ulterior motive.

Tessa's indifference astounded and infuriated him. It was as though nothing at all had taken place between them, and such an attitude made it both impossible and humiliating for him to even try to reopen negotiations. Sometimes George longed for her, at others he hated her, so to avoid torturing himself had given up calling at Loom Street, leaving the settling of the laundry bill to Effie on a cleaning night.

Tessa, being short of money, with all the worry that that entailed, and also being denied the escape of singing, resented these last weeks of pregnancy. That Finn was patience and helpfulness rolled into one only served to remind her that so he ought to be. Gone were the aspirations of being his saviour, of having performed a miracle – and to think she had schemed to get like this! Captain O'Shea had a lot to answer for, too; him and his bloody miracles. 'We make our own,' he had said. She regretted her strategy and vowed never, ever to become pregnant again – not for Finn, priest or the Pope himself!

And she had so looked forward to a better Christmas this year, with a pudding and custard sauce. Patrick was to have had one of those teddy bears which hung in shop windows, and Finn some extra Woodbines.

They would have had to make do with an end of bacon

if Miss Wilkins had not, when calling to settle the laundry bill, left a cockerel along with a rich fruit cake. There had sprung up between Tessa and Miss Wilkins a friendly understanding, a kind of teacher-pupil relationship, which began when Tessa mentioned Captain O'Shea's connection with the Manchester University Settlement.

'Well, that is interesting, you see, my sister, Sylvia . . .'

Suddenly Tessa's mind was filled with . . . Sylvia. Miss Wilkins' sister . . . David's mother . . . George Wilkins' wife . . . Sylvia, the ghost.

'Are you all right?'

'Yes . . . it was just – oh, nothing . . . Go on, Miss Wilkins.'

'David's mother, you know, had been closely associated with the Settlement since its inauguration – its beginning,' she amended. 'Started a children's theatre at Ancoats Hall, oh, yes,' she said, warming to the subject, 'there's as many as six hundred children waiting to get in on Friday night. And it's still going strong. I shall take David when he's old enough. As for the Styles family! My dear, I know the parents well from my days with the Board of Education. Audrey is one of the resident staff. A very attractive young woman, and so clever, what with tutoring pupil-teachers, running the Penny Bank, throwing herself into the campaign to abolish child labour – and, of course, Women's Suffrage. Not only the vote, but women's welfare. I'm sure an enquiring mind like yours will find the books and lantern slides and magazines of interest.'

Always eager to learn, and more so in her present condition, Tessa was delighted with outdated copies of *The Manchester Guardian*, especially the reviews of theatre and music hall.

Annie Cooper did not know what to make of such fraternisation. In her world you knew your place. You were either one of the bosses or one of the workers. But all this rubbing shoulders with people off Oldham Road, well, she didn't hold with it.

Christmas dragged into the New Year of 1902, and on a murky day of yellowing fog, Tessa, with the pains already advanced, hauled up a rack of wet clothes to dry, while Finn banged on the wall to summon Annie Cooper. The fire which had been lit in the front bedroom gave out little heat, the chimney smoked, and the gaslight flickered uncertainly. At the last stage of labour Annie lumbered up and down the stairs for water, or whatever else the stern-faced doctor wanted. Finn had insisted on a doctor, an insurance against the curse, Tessa thought, but the five-shilling fee for delivery would further decrease their income. She swore at the curse, the dead aunt, and bitterly resented the five shillings – wasted it was. The tinker women never had a doctor, the people in Ennan never had a doctor. Birth was a natural thing, a bit of help from a neighbour was all you needed.

She recalled Patrick's birth, the shelter that Finn had rigged; she smelled the hay, the cattle, saw the lantern swinging; and nursed the memories of Ma, God bless her, wherever she was . . . and Captain O'Shea, extending a lean, sun-browned arm. 'Hold onto me hand' he had urged. 'And when the contractions come, push.' And Finn? But Finn, having farmed Patrick out to the Coopers, was walking the streets as he had walked the decks. There was no firm hand to hold on to, nothing.

Even before Annie put the tiny bundle in her arms, the doctor was rolling down his shirtsleeves. 'I've done my job, Mrs Collins,' he said. 'And I would now like to be paid for it.' She told Annie to take the five shillings from beneath the Virgin on the dresser as she saw the doctor out.

Looking down into the elfin face, she touched the layer of straight, dark hair with her forefinger, and sighed contentedly that Finn had a daughter. She pulled the shawl up closer over the baby's head to keep out the draught and wondered what they would call her. Then she rememberd telling Ma that a boy would be called Patrick and a girl Kathleen, after Kate Jarvey.

'Kathleen . . . ' She smiled, and murmured the name again. Yes, she liked it. Would they call her Kate for short? No, she decided, it was a reflection of the past, the old life, and her children would sing the new songs their father had intended for them. People wouldn't refer to her as a colleen, or girleen – except perhaps her da – they'd call her 'lass'. Ach, sure, she thought, there's no music in the word at all – just fancy, Proud Riley's granddaughter a 'lass'!

'Anyways, Kathleen Collins,' she smiled on a sweet sigh of achievement, 'your da will be the proudest fella in Atkinson's mill tomorrow!'

Tessa did not regard Wilkins as the child's father, indeed, she did not regard Wilkins at all. There was no room for regrets and remorse. Neither was there patience with Annie and Mrs Barnes, who urged her to stay in bed for ten days at least 'so that everything went back, proper like.' She was up the next night for the 'wetting of the baby's head' and the congratulations of the gathered neighbours, including Sad Sam, who happened to be in the Sugar Loaf when Cooper had ran to the Jug and Bottle department with the tea urn borrowed from the Sacred Heart. The following morning she was up to heat the irons, and at the weekend she entered The Room to an enthusiastic cheer.

'Ee, if it wasn't for the colour of her eyes, she'd be a right little Collins,' remarked Annie Cooper a few months later when Kathleen's features were more defined. 'An' it isn't fair,' she addressed the baby in exaggerated tones, 'that yer big brother's got all the curls!'

'She doesn't need curls,' said Finn, who was not willing to hear even a whisper of criticism. 'With the looks of her mammy, she'll knock all the lads for six! 'Eyes as dark brown as the turf your da used to dig – and wouldn't he have been the proud granda!'

Not if he knew the truth, thought Tessa recalling that Wilkins' eyes were also brown, but then, only the very brave can bear the awfulness of truth.

Kathleen's birth went some way to reassuring Father Quinn that the young 'come overs' were not going astray, but the child's baptism was another matter. Was there nothing straightforward about these Collinses? The choice of god-parents was not good. Miss Styles from the Settlement was not a young woman he approved of – not that he approved of the Settlement itself. Much of their educational, philan-thropic, and political outlook, not to mention their ideas for social reform and the bolstering up of trade unions, was not in line with Holy Mother Church. He regarded it as a hive of freethinkers and advocates of birth control, and most of his parishioners, knowing of his disapproval, did not become involved.

If the choice of godparents surprised Father Quinn, it astonished Tessa. Audrey Styles had called at Loom Street just before Christmas with a nursery book for Patrick from Cormac, who had drawn the short straw for Christmas duty and would not be up north. Tessa, opening the door had felt mortified, painfully conscious of her condition, of Patrick with a treacly face, the ashes not cleared from the hearth, and the house filled with steam from the boiler – and there on the doorstep was Miss Styles, looking elegant and slim in a long dove-grey coat.

But Audrey, as Tessa now called her, did not seem to notice any of this. She was of the breed who could be equally at ease among the potted palms of the Midland Hotel or the flagged floors and sawdust of the Sugar Loaf, an attitude which endeared her to Cormac O'Shea.

Seeing the steaming rack of clothes and the overworked young mother, she slung her lovely coat on the back of the Mafeking sofa, and touching Tessa's arm in a friendly gesture said, 'Shall I set the kettle to boil? You look as though you could do with a cup of tea – no, Tessa, don't stop anything on my account, everything's convenient ... tea, milk.' She waved a braceleted hand over the strewn table, and immediately went into a game of 'peep' with Patrick beneath it.

While Tessa finished filling the rack and Audrey waited for the kettle to boil, she took the unresisting Patrick, who was delighted at this attractive source of attention, into the scullery for a wipe over with the flannel, all the time talking about the giant's house they were going to build with the wooden blocks.

Somehow, Audrey succeeded in keeping Patrick amused, while over the tea Tessa enquired whether she and Cormac had reached the theatre from the Sugar Loaf in time for the performance. After discussing the review of Harry Houdini's latest exploit, Tessa confessed to never having had the time to go to the music hall.

'And I'll have even less when the baby comes!'

'Talking about babies, you'll go a long way to find a godfather for the new arrival as conscientious as Cormac. Do all Irish folk take their religious obligations so seriously?'

'Ah, sure they don't at all – not the ones I know. Patrick is a bit special I suppose, him being at the birth and all.'

'At the birth?'

'Has he not told you about the boat?'

After Tessa had related the event, Audrey heard herself saying she'd be thrilled if they would consider her as a godmother for the new baby. And although the request was sincere and spontaneous, her heart beat a little faster to realise the godparenting would be shared with Cormac.

When Finn returned from the mill and heard that Tessa had accepted Audrey's offer, he would not be satisfied until Audrey had asked her brother, the much talked about Nick, to be the godfather.

Father Quinn, when they had gone to see him about the arrangements for the baptism, pointed out that it was usual to have two godmothers for a female child.

'Patrick's only got one godparent,' came the firm reply. 'And he's all right.'

The priest thrust his hands deep into his cassock pockets. 'Would it not be wiser, then,' he suggested, 'to choose godparents from your own locality – the Coopers for example?'

'What use would it be, Father?' asked Tessa. 'If Finn and me, God forbid, were run down by one of those horseless trams, sure, the Coopers haven't enough to keep their own, what with her expecting again.' God save her, she thought, always boasting about Cooper being 'careful' – but not this time, and the poor soul's nearly wrecked herself with purges and pills in an attempt to abort, but in the end God's will has prevailed.

'And there's the spiritual aspect to consider.'

'Sure, Miss Styles and her brother, now, are well able to take care of Kathleen Teresa's religious and physical welfare, otherwise,' Tessa added, with barbed simplicity, 'we wouldn't have chosen them.'

Nick, at first, had tried to impress upon his sister that his frivolous nature could not possible bear the responsibility of godparenting. He, unlike Cormac, had no desire to cultivate friendships with 'unspoiled and unsophisticated' people from the 'auld country'.

'You ought to be flattered they bothered to ask you. And

186

it's the least you can do to support a brother officer who is at the far-flung corner of the country! As for responsibility, if the worst did happen – '

'And it will! Just my luck for the parents to die in the next influenza epidemic – '

'I,' said Audrey, 'would relieve you of any obligation. But it won't happen. The Collinses are survivors. No one is going to die, and you, Nick Styles, are being stuffy, rude, arrogant, snobbish – in fact, I often wonder what Elfreda sees in you!'

'All right! All right, old girl. Peace. Peace. I will agree to take unto myself a godchild, for better or worse, so help me!'

On Patrick's third birthday Tessa found herself pregnant again. She was devastated and could not, at first, bring herself to tell Finn. Kathleen was only six months old and still being breast fed. 'Keep 'em at the breast for as long as you can,' Annie had said. 'Stop yer from conceivin'. I fed our Tony till he was two.'

Tessa was not the only one suffering acute dismay. Audrey Styles had hoped to accompany Cormac to Loom Street on what they referred to as 'the birthday visit', not particularly to see her goddaughter, for she often called when in the vicinity, but in the hope of furthering her friendship with Cormac. Audrey now admitted to herself that she wanted more than friendship, and their relationship was not developing along the lines expected – it wasn't developing at all! 'Give it time,' Elfreda had said. 'He'll need to finish his studies before thinking of the future with certainty.' It wasn't so much the future that gave Audrey need for concern as the past. The Collinses were part of his past, and there were reservations on his part she did not understand. Why, for example, had he never told her about attending Patrick's birth? And why did she feel unable to talk to him about it, or even just mention it in passing conversation?

Having travelled overnight from Sussex, Cormac had taken a cab to Ancoats Hall, where he was to join the female staff – and Nick, if his duties permitted – for lunch. Ancoats Hall stood on an ancient site, a spacious, two-storeyed country house with grounds sloping down to the River Medlock. It had been the seat of the Mosley family, who were lords of the manor of Manchester until 1845 when the manorial rights were sold and the borough was incorporated. By that time the reigning Mosley, daunted by the strides of commerce and industry, had sold up. The purchaser was James Murray, a fine-cotton spinner to whom industry presented no threat. The fumes which bit into the stone and begrimed the walls, that killed off all the bluebells, and depressed the environs, also put money into his pocket. With the demise of James Murray, the hall remained unoccupied until Thomas Horsfall installed an art museum in the South Wing, and invited the University Settlement to make their home in the North Wing.

The cab, not willing to negotiate the curving drive, stopped at the entrance on Every Street. Cormac, walking slowly up to the Hall, pondered on the graciousness of the past – the pursuits of which had brought squalor and decay to thousands. Before entering the Settlement offices in the North Wing, he looked across the grimy slope, once the terraced gardens of the Mosleys, to the mean rooftops of Beswick on the far side of the River Medlock, and among them a forest of smoking chimneys. The rhododendron bushes, like most of the inhabitants of Ancoats, were struggling to survive; the blades of grass were as sparse as money, and even the weeds looked consumptive. He thought of Sussex and fresh, sweet air, and country children with rosy cheeks, and swore at the unfairness of life. Thank God for people like the Styles, and Elfreda, and Alice Crompton the Warden, and old Horsfall there – Ancoats would be a damn sight worse without 'em. Who in their right mind would choose to be in Manchester in midsummer?

After a plain but pleasant lunch in the long dining room, at which Nick had not been present, the members of staff went about their duties, and Audrey, looking cool in a cream linen costume, intimated her intention of accompanying him to Loom Street. She was at once aware of a change in their immediate atmosphere, a change which seemed to be a pattern of their relationship. There was something about Cormac she could not fathom, for always, at the very moment when she hoped to get through to him, he would throw up a barrier which caused her to retreat.

Perhaps it was this indefinable quality which attracted her to him. She knew he was not short of female company in Sussex, and she had other men in her life, kind, handsome creatures who openly adored her. Her mother reckoned she was wasting her time on this charming Irishman, but Cormac O'Shea, the indefinable, was different. You never knew what to expect – and that was the rub as far as she was concerned. Somehow, to have gone to Loom Street with him on this annual pilgrimage would have meant a sharing of something precious. And he had shied away from a sharing, he wanted to go alone. So be it. Oh, to be a fly on the wall, to see him at home, at ease with his compatriots. It was strange, too, that Tessa never talked intimately about him, and that they never referred to him by his Christian name.

'Ah, soda bread,' breathed Cormac, as Tessa brought it to the table. 'Lord bless you, it's like a taste of the auld country!' And after the fancy cakes and strong tea, he, noticing her lack of sparkle, took advantage of Finn's preoccupation with Patrick's present of coloured crayons and picture book, to ask, 'Having trouble with your miracle?'

She shook her head and gathered the plates.

'Whatever it is, there's always an answer if you look far enough . . . '

As she took the plates into the scullery he wished for the hundredth time she could bring herself to call him by his first name. He knew that Finn, enmeshed in the admiration of all things military, liked to say the word 'Captain', but Tessa – there, he thought of her as Tessa, and when talking about them to the Styles referred to her in the same manner. Yet she and Audrey were on first name terms . . .

'I'd better be saying a word to Kathleen,' he smiled, 'or Audrey'll never forgive me!' He crossed to where she was propped up in one of the big drawers. 'Oh, you could've done better,' he teased, as the solemn brown eyes regarded the unfamiliar face, 'than to saddle yerself with a godfather the likes of Nick!'

That evening they went to the Sugar Loaf, where the clientele no longer stared at his uniform, and would shout a greeting, or pass a brief word of welcome. He stood on the threshold of The Room waiting for Finn to arrive before

189

going to sit by the piano. Hearing someone ordering a drink to be sent in to Mrs Collins, he turned to see Jonty Jackson raise his hand and say, 'Certainly, Mr Wilkins.'

'No need to tell her who it's from.'

'Very well, Mr Wilkins.'

Cormac raised an arched eyebrow. So, that was Wilkins, the mill agent. Could he be the cause of Tessa's lost sparkle? Later, with Finn, he shouted for the now obligatory 'Cockles and Mussels' and felt like the male counterpart of Cinderella when, at the stroke of ten, he had to fasten his tunic, put on his cap, reach for his cane and hope there was a cab on Oldham Road to get him to his train on time.

Audrey was at Loom Street when Annie Cooper's eldest ran up the yard steps in a panic. 'I'm going for Mrs Barnes,' he yelled. 'Me mam's having the baby!'

It was made plain that Tessa was too young and inexperienced to attend a lying-in. 'I mean, what would you do if it was the wrong way up, or if it's face turned blue, eh?' Tessa had acknowledged her ignorance.

'I only found out the other week,' she said to Audrey, when Mrs Barnes had gone up to Annie, 'that apart from a saint which women pray to for a child, there's a saint which women pray to who want to be spared the privilege. Only,' she lowered her voice, 'I don't pray any more.' She conveyed the knowledge of her unexpected pregnancy in a look so helpless that Audrey was overwhelmed with pity.

'You don't have to rely on prayer,' she said, softly. 'That poor woman need never have gone through nine births and endless miscarriages if Cooper had taken proper precautions.'

'But, they don't work! Look at Cooper, supposed to have managed the art of "being careful". And look at me, with Kathleen still at the breast!'

'I don't mean being careful, I mean a proper preventative. Enlightened and responsible men adopt these methods now.' She paused and added with a wry smile, 'But I can see the men in Ancoats don't fall into that category. Not after Father Quinn has threatened us all with hellfire.' Audrey lowered her voice. 'Listen, Tessa, there is a birth-control device for women, and volunteers are needed to be fitted with it. Would you be interested?'

'Interested!' she exclaimed. 'I would so.' Her excitement faded. 'But himself would never agree.'

'With a bit of luck, Finn may never know. Listen, after your confinement, come to the Welfare afternoon at the Settlement and talk to Doctor Louise Harris about it.'

'And would it really stop me having any more?'

'That's the idea, but you mustn't breathe a word to anyone. Any publicity at this stage could put the trials in jeopardy.'

Round-bellied every year, thought Tessa dismally, after Audrey had gone. Yes, she added, as Captain O'Shea said, there is an answer. And, yes, I shall go to see Doctor Louise, but I will not talk it over with Finn.

Knowing she had at least a chance of not being 'round-bellied' every year gave Tessa a philosophical approach to the pregnancy; in her mind, she regarded this as her last, and the idea of having some control over her life gave a boost to her morale.

When Joseph was born Effie Wilkins was quietly pleased when Tessa asked if she would be his godmother, and Titch Bradley was delighted with the honour. Miss Wilkins had also, in Finn's presence, outlined the benefits of attending the Welfare afternoon, once a month at the Settlement, with Kathleen and Joseph. This provided a perfect cover to see Doctor Louise Harris, who impressed upon Tessa that her husband would never know she was wearing the device. No one would know, only herself and God, but that of course was up to individual conscience, and Tessa's had long ceased to be troubled on that score. It was at this time – in order that he would think he was controlling their affairs – that Tessa impressed upon Finn the importance of following Cooper's example of 'being careful'. They now had three children to clothe and feed, and were only just keeping, by dint of her earnings, out of debt.

Tessa, having seen how the birth of a ninth child changed Annie Cooper's full cheeks and cheerful dimples into a pale and flaccid mass, was even more convinced that she was doing the right thing in taking part in the trials. Although Tessa had not liked her neighbour's intrusive habits, the fact of her not bouncing into the scullery at all was disturbing.

The wetting of the baby's head had been more like a wake than a celebratory gathering, and Cooper wore a surliness that did not suit his whippet-like figure. The older children, wary of yet another responsibility, flocked to the streetcorner where sympathy was readily dispensed. The younger ones gazed in silent resentment at the weakly little brother who wailed and whimpered as though already doing penance for having been born. Tessa could need no more conviction than this; for already, at twenty-two, she had three children under five, and at that rate, in ten years, God forbid, she could well be in Annie's position!

At first, she thought the black rubber device, although uncomfortable, too good to be true, and worried lest Finn would somehow notice a difference. But as the weeks went by, she became less anxious, and with a diminishing fear of unwanted pregnancies, rediscovered a pleasure in their love-making which had been absent for some time. Finn, sensing her satisfaction, reckoned it was due to his management of the art of 'being careful' and was equally pleased.

Tessa began to feel like the 'modern woman' or the 'new woman' as featured in the magazines Miss Wilkins and Audrey passed on, and this positive attitude gave her renewed energy for everything she tackled.

Effie Wilkins had been right in her surmise that Tessa would find a wealth of interest at the Settlement. Her one afternoon at the Welfare every month was put to good use. Apart from talks on nutrition, hygiene, baby problems, and a cheap assortment of second-hand clothes and toys available, there was the painless administering of the Socialist gospel. Then, over cups of tea and a biscuit, there were questions or discussions about the new Education Act, a housing survey, and the fact of women as well as men having certain rights in the community.

Sometimes, while the children were playing with brightly coloured buckets and spades in a sandpit, Tessa, who had no experience of museums, allowed her curiosity to take her to the South Wing. Often the only visitor, she walked along the gallery, marvelling at the solitude, and listening to the echo of deep-throated clocks. She gazed in wonder at the Pre-Raphaelite pictures on the wall, the artefacts under glass domes, the huge Chinese vases, and then at the cordoned-off rooms. She wondered if Father Quinn slept in such an impressive four-poster bed, and how the devil they would wash such embroidered draperies! There was a drawing room with sofas covered in striped satin, and delicate tables which she'd be afraid to put anything on. And a dining room elegant with Sheraton, Hepplewhite, and a magnificent Japanese lacquer firescreen.

Unable to attend any evening events or lectures at the Settlement because of the cleaning, laundering and singing, Tessa joined the Free Library, and became an object of interest, walking down the street with her shawl somehow secured fetchingly about the shoulders, two books under one arm, Joseph in the other, Kathleen at her skirts, and Patrick running on ahead.

On cleaning nights George Wilkins watched her arrival from the window, and was insanely jealous of the immediate buzz of conversation between her and his sister which emanated from the kitchen. The indifference with which she treated him was awful to bear – he wondered sometimes whether the entire episode on the sofa was a figment of his imagination. He had even taken to sidling into the Sugar Loaf at weekends, to discover the 'song bird' was so much in demand that other publicans had offered as much as ten shillings a night if she would sing for their customers. Her loyalty to Jonty Johnson was not the only consideration which prevented her accepting these offers. Her decision was coloured by the proximity of the Sugar Loaf to Loom Street, and her good working relationship with Titch Bradley, to whom the offers did not apply. Jonty Johnson, taking advantage of her situation, pressed five shillings into her hand every now and again, reckoning he could always meet these other offers if it came to the crunch.

And another thing, thought George Wilkins, when in a vengeful mood, according to Effie she was friendly with Audrey Styles! God in heaven, that Settlement had a lot to answer for, giving the labouring classes ideas above their station in life. What a set up! God knows why that Irish officer should keep turning up every year for the boy's birthday. He recalled the bare-bottomed, dirty-faced little creature holding up a pair of wet leggings, and shuddered.

And then they'd the cheek to rope in the Styles brother and sister! And as if that didn't stretch credulity enough, his own sister had, without consulting him, agreed to do the same for the latest! 'But she's your cleaning woman,' he had argued. 'An Irish, bog-trotting washer-woman!'

'Yes,' she'd replied, with an odd inflection in her voice. 'If you had not set her on when they came to buy the sofa after Mafeking, I would not have had the privilege.'

It wouldn't have been so bad if the godfather had been Nick Styles, but no, she was sharing the 'privilege' with a stunted piano player!

Heaven only knows what would have happened to the Collinses if I hadn't have rescued them, he thought peevishly. It was me who brought them from Liverpool; me who set him on at Atkinson's; started her on with the laundry – and set 'em up with Toby Greenledge; and now she treats me as if I were nothing. Well, I can wait, Mrs Collins, by God, I can!

Chapter Eighteen

By the year of Patrick's seventh birthday there had been a General Election landslide for the Liberals, with Campbell-Bannerman pledging 'no tax on the people's food', a pledge the poor of Ancoats hoped he would keep. And Elfreda had married Nick on Cormac's last leave before he returned to Salford for good. Tessa, concerned that Joseph's speech was not as advanced as it ought to be for a three-year-old, was waiting to see Doctor Louise at the Settlement when she met Audrey and heard about Elfreda's ivory gown, the pageboys dressed like soldiers, the guard of honour from the barracks, and how the reception was held in the recently opened Midland Hotel. Oh, the dancing, the flowers and feathers, the sashes and uniforms . . .

Then, as though saving the best until the last, Audrey's creamy skin flushed like a rose. 'Oh, you should have seen Cormac, Tessa. He struck such a good figure in his dress uniform. With his hair brushed and glossed instead of being ruffled, he looked different. He was positively glowing – with a kind of pride I suppose – he's qualified now as a veterinary surgeon, y'know, and will be returning to Salford soon. But Tessa, all the women were after him!' She paused as Joseph scrambled down from his mother's knee and on to hers. 'I really can't believe, can you, that he's not the marrying kind? I mean, why does he bother if he's not going to settle down? I know he takes other women out to dances, and he's had one – Moira something or other – on the go down south. A man that has so much to offer can't stay single all his life . . .'

Tessa did not quite know what to say; it was clear

that the Captain had not told Audrey of the time he was jilted at the altar. And, of course, she and Finn would never dream of discussing the Captain's past. But surely he must know Audrey was very fond of him? But, rack her brains as she might, Tessa could not recall any sign that he regarded Audrey with more affection than that of a friend. Further, Tessa was amazed Audrey could wait for what must be all of six years since Mafeking night! She couldn't understand it at all, for she and Finn had suffered terrible heartache when kept apart. Not that she'd have the nerve or confidence to talk about affairs of the heart to anyone as sophisticated as Audrey!

Tessa, being of an enquiring mind, absorbed every particle of what she saw and heard in the Settlement, particularly an incident about marriages being solemnised, not in church, but legally at the District Registrar's Office in Jackson's Row, off Deansgate.

On the Welfare afternoon, although pressed for time, she left the children in the sandpit and hurried to enquire the amount of publicity in the way of banns such a ceremony involved. The young clerk, being used to dealing with embarrassed people, showed her a list displayed inside the porch, of those intending to marry. 'Nothing like the local publicity of the traditional church banns,' he said. 'And, if this isn't discreet enough, it's quite in order to be married in an office on the other side of town.' Tessa fled.

And so she outlined her plan to Finn after his favourite tea of cabbage, onion and potato, baked in the oven. He looked up in astonishment. 'Are we not all right as we are? Why bother now? Besides, this . . . Registrar's office sounds like Spider Murphy over again.'

'And have I not told you twice already, that unlike a broomstick wedding, a Registrar wedding is legal?'

'Not in Father Quinn's book it isn't.'

'But it's the law of the land. What's he to do with it?'

'Sure, y'know the Church's arguments, Tessa.' He pushed the dish in which the colcannon had been baked to and fro. 'I thought we were settled,' he sighed. 'You reckoned you were content to live in sin, and now, just because *you* fancy the idea, you expect me to fall in – and it'll cost, y'know. You forgot to

ask about that, didn't you? Listen, girleen, listen to me now.'
With a glance toward the Cooper's wall he lowered his voice.
'I was after getting married, thinking that if we put things
right, it would break the run of bad luck we were having.
But now everything's right, thank God. We've got a family,
and we're not up to the ears in debt. An' you're happy enough
with your singin' and the Settlement, like. Why disturb things
now? Leave well alone. Let sleeping dogs lie. It doesn't do
to disturb affairs that are going right.' He pushed back his
chair from the table. 'You're only thinkin' this way,' he said
with his bashful smile, 'because Elfreda and Captain Styles
got married.'

'It's no such thing, Finn Collins! It's the kids. You
know what us not being married makes 'em, don't you?'

'You weren't bothered when we just had the boyo. Sure,
you didn't trouble yourself that he'd be called a bastard. And
you were hard, Tess, to me. It would've eased my mind to
have gone to Father Quinn and got him to marry us.'

'Is that ye last word then?'

'It is so,' he replied gravely.

'Very well.' She spoke so briskly that he looked up
from lighting a cigarette in alarm, but she began clearing
the table and mixed her starch with terrible concentration.

Tessa's worries about the children continued with a
brush with authority, and the shadow of Father Quinn. The
Settlement people had more than once showed surprise that
Patrick was not at school. Of course they understood the
economics of Patrick being at home to turn the mangle and
collect and deliver the laundry, but, they asked, would the
Attendance Officer?

Miss Wilkins also realised Patrick's value at home, but
contributed to the persuasion by relating David's progress.
He had gone to the Sacred Heart because it was near and
she could take milk and toast to the school gates at morning
playtime.

Tessa, however, thought school from six to fourteen was
far too long. She had learned all that was necessary at Pat
Feeney's school in less than two years, and saw no reason
to get her son off so quickly.

The decision was taken out of her hands when Patrick,

returning from having delivered a clean bundle of laundry, heard a voice say, 'Not at school, sonny?'

Patrick, with a lurch of the stomach, realised this was the Attendance Officer, still referred to by the old appendage as the 'School Board'.

'Let me see, now . . . ' The man, keeping an expert grip on the boy's braces, opened a large black book. 'Collins, Patrick. Number Twenty-seven, Loom Street?'

'No use taking me home,' he replied, fearing to get his mother into trouble. 'No one's there.'

'You know what happens to children who stay away from school?'

'No,' gasped Patrick. 'I want to go home . . . '

I'll give this one the fright of his life, thought the Officer, marching him off at a brisk pace. A small boy on his own had been easy to spot, especially when trying to pop a tar bubble with the toe of his clog! Mid afternoon was the quietest hour of the day, except for the rag-and-bone man, who stopped pushing his handcart to remark with a good-natured shout, 'Pick on someone your own size!' The older children were at school, the little ones asleep, and the wage earners sweating among the combing and carding machines. Dogs lay panting, their long, pink tongues lolling to one side; and cats sat on brown-stoned window sills waiting with feline patience for the cool of the evening.

Patrick, who thought he was destined for the police station, about which his mother had warned him many times, stared at the presbytery door in joyful disbelief. A hefty knock shattered the silence of the afternoon and brought Mrs Stubbs in a flurry of annoyance. 'Five minutes . . . ' she muttered. 'I put me feet up for only five minutes, and someone has to call!'

The study was cool, and the calmness of it soothed the boy's fears. He was with Father Quinn; everything would be all right now, nothing awful would happen, and his mother would not get into trouble. Patrick had been before with his father to settle the formalities of Joseph's baptism, and he remembered the smell of the room, leather and tobacco, with a waft of incense clinging to the priest's cassock.

Father Quinn turned to Mrs Stubbs asking for a tray of tea; she nodded ungraciously. Tea! The word shrieked in her head. Why, she'd only just cleared the luncheon! For that nice Canon Sullivan, or Father Flynn, it would be a pleasure, but for the 'School Board' and a truant!

'It's Patrick, isn't it, from Loom Street?' He recognised the family resemblance, and was about to put out a hand to ruffle the curly head and set the lad at ease, but the stern look of the Attendance Officer prevented it. 'I see you've brought a friend?'

'He's the "School Board", Father.'

'And what are you doing with the School Board, Patrick?'

The boy, seeing where the question was leading, lowered his eyes. He remained standing, eyes downcast, but through the fringe of his dark lashes watched the two men shake hands. The priest moved to sit behind his desk and the Attendance Officer drew a chair in front of it. They began talking and looking through the black book. Patrick was wishing he had made a run for it when Mrs Stubbs brought the tea.

'Sit down, Patrick,' said the priest, presuming the boy had been sufficiently chastened, 'and tuck into the cake.' He leaned forward confidentially. 'If you leave so much as a crumb, Mrs Stubbs will crown you!' Not realising he had been so hungry, Patrick cleared the tray. Mrs Stubbs couldn't grumble now, he thought, as Father Quinn poured him his third cup of tea.

'These people are very hard put to –' the priest was saying.

'Yes, yes, I know! But their private affairs are not my concern. The Education Act of 1902 says the boy should've had a year's schooling already, and if he's not in school tomorrow –'

'You may leave the matter safely in my hands,' interrupted the priest, getting up from behind the desk. 'I think I know what line to take.' And still talking, he conducted the Officer to the front door, where he went in search of other prey.

For the next twenty minutes Father Quinn told Patrick about school and the wonderful world that would open to him once he learned to read. He tried to stimulate a desire for knowledge with books, pictures and odd little treasures exhumed from coffin-like drawers. Naturally quick, Patrick listened attentively to the soft musical voice, and was fascinated by the expression of the bushy eyebrows. The mellow chime of a French ormolu clock, on which Cardinal Richelieu sat with pen poised, brought Father Quinn to a halt. 'My goodness, the teatime shift will be on the streets soon. Time I took you home.'

Patrick felt very proud as his fingers curled into those of the priest, and as they walked, men off the shift would shout:

'Cooler now, isn't it, Father?'

'Evenin', Father!'

'What's the nipper been up to now, eh!'

They were past the ginnel with the beam across, and Father Quinn, letting go of the boy's hand, sent him to scamper up the steps. 'Mammy, Mammy!' he heard. 'I've been caught by the School Board, and Father Quinn's given me tea and brought me home!'

Teatime, five o'clock shift time, was always Tessa's ironing time. Caught by the School Board! She closed her eyes and her heart panicked. For some reason, she glanced at the blue-mantled Virgin before replacing the iron on the red embers. And then the second part of his statement registered. She had not met the priest alone since he had called about their lack of family, and now, having been 'fitted' she was uneasy, despite Doctor Louise's assurance that their records were confidential. Someone had once told her that priests were trained to winkle out the innermost secrets of the soul, and having so many secrets made her feel vulnerable.

The priest was enjoying his self-imposed role of avenging angel. It gave him satisfaction to bring Mrs Collins to book. He had known from the very first time they entered this house and he had tried to explain about the gas, he knew then she would be one of his difficult parishioners. In his ignorance, he had thought to have moulded her to his ways, but seven years later she was no nearer being moulded, and with that interfering Audrey Styles wasn't likely to be. Still, her husband was pliable, and he had made a start with Patrick. He could not, of course, swear to it, but he suspected a sailing close to the wind somewhere.

'But,' he ended his homily, 'if the boy does not attend school – tomorrow, Mrs Collins. Tomorrow, you understand – your husband will find himself up before the magistrate.'

The busy eyebrows rose in challenge. Tessa bowed her

head before the oppressive strength, and took up the iron. 'Yes, Father. He'll be there.'

'Be minding your manners, now, Patrick,' said Tessa on the following morning. 'And don't get into any fights . . .' She paused from cutting bread for her youngest to groom her eldest. 'Be still, will you, now! If you brushed your hair proper, yourself, there wouldn't be so many tangles. Oh,' she tried to cheer the downcast face, 'it isn't as if you don't know the other scholars. There's Tony from next door.'

'I don't like him, and he's upstairs in the juniors, anyway.'

Kathleen and Joseph, still in their nightshirts, sat on the Mafeking sofa watching this major event in their brother's life with rounded eyes.

'Look out for David Wilkins, then. He's been going since he was five –'

'He'll be upstairs as well, and I've not seen him for a long time.'

'Neither of them will be upstairs at playtime! Remember not to be after talking in lessons. And be good for Miss Donovan, or you'll get the strap, and that won't be nice on your first day.'

'None of it will be nice.'

'You didn't say that yesterday when Father Quinn was givin' out . . . there,' she planted a kiss on top of his curls and thought how like his da he was. 'You look real smart.'

'That was yesterday. Do I have to go, mam?' Every now and then he used the word mam instead of mammy, and Finn had graduated to dad, despite her referring to him as 'da'. Another thing she had become aware of was that none of her children spoke with the Irish brogue they had been brought up on. Somehow, almost imperceptibly, they had become anglicised.

'You do so,' she returned sharply. 'You heard what the Father said about your da being summoned, and dear God, Patrick –' She found no words to convey her terror, and ended lamely, 'We don't want that.'

She heard the Cooper's door open and propelled her son out on to the street. With a look of sheer envy at Kathleen and Joseph standing on the top step, Patrick tagged along with the Coopers, not daring to look back, or to wave, for fear Tony would call him a baby.

When the school bell clanged for midday dinner, Patrick was one of the first through the door. He arrived home, panting and hot, kicked off his clogs, and rushed into the scullery to drink several cups of water and then put his head under the tap. Through the window, he waved to his mother, who was turning the mangle while Kathleen fed some sheets through it and Joseph sat underneath, chuckling as the water dripped on him.

'Will you be cutting some bread for these while you're at it?' she called, and remembering the lecture on hygiene at the Settlement, added, 'And be sure your hands are clean!'

Having filled the line in the yard, Tessa brought the excess sheets inside, and letting down the rack, glanced at the three standing about the table, stuffing their mouths with bread and cheese, or in Joseph's case, treacle. 'Keep his fingers out of the basin, Kathleen, he'll have it everywhere!' Her lips twitched into a smile as she turned to the rack. Patrick would not tell them about school until he was ready, and he wouldn't be ready until he had the full attention of his audience, which, with a bit of luck, could be spun out to beyond schooltime. Not if she had anything to do with it!

Pulling up the rack, she sat firmly down on the Mafeking sofa, while, with hands thrust deep into his trousers pockets, Patrick related how the brick walls of the classroom were painted dark green, and there were notices hung on nails, and a picture of St Francis over the teacher's desk. Miss Donovan was always shouting, and the strap hung on the wall by the blackboard. Father Quinn had mentioned his name in assembly.

'What for?'

'Me being new. Everyone turned to look at me –' And yes, he told his audience, he had kept out of Tony Cooper's way, and he had met up with David Wilkins at playtime.

Tessa sighed with relief. 'Did I not tell you it'd be all right? And yes, Patrick Collins, you have to go back. And hurry or you'll be late and get a black mark.'

What Patrick had felt unable to tell his audience was how he had come to meet David Wilkins. At playtime, he had rushed into the yard like the others, yelling 'Hooray!'

at the top of his voice. After the second 'Hooray!' he realised everyone had found a friend for a wild fifteen minutes. Standing on his own by the gate, and feeling utterly miserable, he saw Miss Wilkins approach.

'Patrick!' she had exclaimed. 'So, you've started school?'

'My first day, miss.'

'It takes a bit of getting used to – but I'm glad you're here. D'you think you could find David for me? He's usually waiting.'

'We all had to go to the lavatories,' he explained, proud of his use of the word and his grip on procedure. 'He might've had to wait until the last – the big lads push in first. I'll find him.'

'Quickly, now, or the bell will be going.'

Glad of something to do, some excuse to run through the playground, he dashed through games of marbles, tag and football, shouting, 'David Wilkins! David Wilkins! Yer aunt wants you at the gate!'

Suddenly David was running with him, and both laughing, they raced to the railings, not having exchanged a word. Aunt Effie, smiling at the panting boys, removed a cloth from a basket and produced milk and buttered toast, which was shared with Patrick.

'I can see I'll have to bring enough for two in future,' she said, still smiling. Those nearby looked on in envy, but had to be content with water from the iron cup chained to the cloakroom sink.

In a few weeks the schools closed down for the long summer holiday, and Patrick, now of an age to appreciate such a godfather, looked forward to introducing Captain O'Shea to David. He talked of nothing else, and God help her, he had Finn to encourage this hero worship! Still, Tessa thought, I'd rather him be struck with the Captain than Father Quinn, although he gets his share of it! She wished it hadn't been the priest who had got Patrick into school, for it had given him the opportunity to infiltrate their household again. Already both he and David attended mass and confession regularly, and were to be confirmed for Easter. Tessa, too, was more aware than Finn that the neighbours, and the Coopers in particular, were suspicious of her success at the Sugar Loaf, their connections with the Wilkins, the Settlement, and now Patrick with Father Quinn. Jud Patterson, always a fair-minded man, had hinted that it all stemmed from her neighbours being jealous, and that she should watch out for herself.

Annie by this time had purged herself into another abortion, for the last baby, the whimpering little brother whom they had named Ronnie, was what the doctor had called a mongol. Just before the school holidays, Tessa, hearing Annie bang urgently on the wall, realised Cooper was at work, and hurrying in was moved to the heart by so much self-induced pain. Not knowing what to do, she obeyed Annie's instructions, until the bleeding was staunched, and she was lying back on the bed with her feet raised.

Differences were overlooked in extremes, and Tessa wanted to put her arm around the plump shoulders, and tell her to bugger the priest and see Doctor Louise about being fitted – so she'd never be in this terrible state again. But, while she made some tea and cleaned up, common sense prevailed, for since Ronnie's birth, Annie could not be trusted.

Ronnie had been the last straw, and family life was now set on a downhill course. The elder Cooper children, in receipt of playground taunts, were ashamed of the little creature who at twelve months couldn't sit or hold his head up. The youngest child was frightened of him, the elders couldn't be trusted with him. To get any kind of peace from his grizzling and crying, Annie got into the habit of sending to the druggist for a pennyworth of a soothing mixture known as 'goody', until it had become part of his diet.

The burden of providing for so large a family had always weighed heavily on Cooper. Now beaten and cowed by circumstances, by the impossible task, he took refuge in the surliness which had accompanied Ronnie's birth. The doctor had warned against any further family. Another child could be, if not mongoloid, deficient in some way, and that Annie could well do without. Marr the piper had offered in jocular mood, to fix him up with a fancy woman, but on reflection, Marr considered she'd be hard up to fancy Cooper!

The Coopers, it seemed, were destined for celibacy, but with the disintegration of family relationships it would not, it appeared, be a problem. But Annie could not bear the comparison of her life to Tessa's. She was now so far removed from the dimpled brightness with which she had scooped Patrick up from his nest in the Connemara shawl as to be unrecognisable.

Round-bellied every year . . . The phrase struck fear in Tessa's heart. Oh, thank God for the University Settlement; for sensible women who thought beyond the Church. Audrey had said that Cormac was a good Catholic, and he, too, was in favour of anything that reduced poverty. Tessa realised she had thought of him for the first time as 'Cormac', not that it was surprising, for the kids were always on about 'Uncle Cormac'. Now he was back in Salford they would probably be seeing him more often.

Chapter Nineteen

There was no longer any formality about or great preparations for the Captain's birthday visit. The children, especially now that David and Patrick were inseparable, saw to that, keeping watch as to when he would round the corner, racing each other to meet him, wanting to know, with the avid curiosity of the young, details of equine surgery: was the 'gas' administered to the horses with a mask, like at the dental clinic? And did they really use a block and tackle to move their inert bodies?

The parcel in his gloved hand was never handed over without three guesses each as to the contents, and unable to bear the sight of Kathleen and Joseph, with eyes as large as saucers, envying Patrick's anticipation, he had them searching his pockets until with squeals of delight their little fingers closed on a packet of toffee cigarettes each, or chocolate cigars, or sugar pipes. This year the 'birthday boy's' gift was a leather football – a real bladder and case – with his name engraved around the middle.

'Christ, Captain,' laughed Finn, indicating the scullery where the washing of hands was extended by arguments as to the placing of makeshift goal posts. 'They'll have it through someone's window in no time!'

'If they don't have us flooded out first!' Tessa looked up from slicing the soda bread. 'Will you hurry now, the two of yous,' and pausing to wink added, 'Sure, the Captain's starving on his feet . . . Finn, will you set the chairs? The kids'll sit on the sofa. Kathleen, see if you can find Joseph a clean bib – and if you wet the tay, Captain, we're nearly set.'

'D'you realise, Patrick,' said Cormac when they were seated, 'that on your seventh birthday there are seven of us about the table?' His smile included David, who thought Uncle Cormac was everything and more than he had expected. They were allowed to wear his hat and strut about with the short cane, and he even played football with them in the ginnel at the side of the house.

Cormac looked at each of them, from Patrick's sturdy figure, shirtsleeves wet at the wrist, curls freckled with droplets of water, to David, with a shock of hair so brown as to make his face seem pale. So, this was the Wilkins boy whose father sent anonymous drinks to Tessa? He didn't look much like his da, at least not from the glimpse I got, he thought. The lad's a different kettle of fish, lonely, scarcely strong enough for the rough-and-tumble world of the emerging century. He and Patrick would be after making good pals.

Next to David was Nick's goddaughter, barely four and looking like a little waif in her grey-and-white check pinafore. Dark solemn eyes peered from under a straight-cut fringe, and her gaze alternated between looking up at David and down on her little brother, safely anchored on his mother's knee.

Although looking at Joseph, Cormac's amber eyes, did not dwell on Tessa. She sat erect, 'like a woman regal born' Finn would say, and with her thick hair coiled on top of her head, and those vivid features, the glance would linger to marvel at the change over the years, and he would not embarrass her for the world.

Joseph was an innocent-looking infant. His face was round, his ready smile sweet, and when he drooped silky lids seductively over blue eyes, even the most terrible outrage was charmed. Pity he's a bit slow with the talk, thought Cormac, who had to ask Kathleen to interpret.

They've done well, he mused, to bring 'em all up, and make the place so comfortable on nineteen shillings, or was it now twenty a week? Not that they'd have managed without Tessa's jobs – three on the go. And there was old Finn, he thought fondly, every inch the family man! If things had worked out right seven years ago, he, too, could have had a family like this. Still, it wasn't too late. Nick was thirty-five, three years older than himself. Elfreda was thirty-one. Best

207

to take the plunge later than sooner, maturity must count for something. But his heart shied away, refusing to travel another inch in that direction. Yes, these were his family, they were growing apace, but God, sure it made a fella feel old!

After tea, he told them a little about his appointment as Chief Veterinary Officer, and that he would be on the move here and there, but still quartered in Regent Road.

'Ach, yes,' teased Tessa, 'we get to know what you're up to!'

'You do?' His brow cleared. 'Oh, you mean through Audrey!'

'Now that you're back,' said Finn, 'will you not come with her? We'd all like you to come more often than on Patrick's birthday. Just be droppin' in, any time.'

'No, not "anytime"!' put in Tessa briskly. 'I run what amounts to a laundry, and now I've lost the help of Patrick, sure there's no time to scratch, still less to stop and chinwag! Audrey knows the best times, so if you come with her, you'll oblige me greatly.'

'So speaks the lady of the house,' answered Cormac, raising his eyebrows at Finn, and with an incline of his head, he laughingly told Tessa, 'Madame, your slightest wish is my command!'

Then, as sounds of disruption came through the adjoining wall, the elder children were sent out to play, while they talked of the tragic change in the Cooper household brought about by Ronnie.

Later, when the younger children were asleep, Cormac, who seemed to have been deliberating on something, stretched out his legs from the Mafeking sofa. 'Seeing there's no singing at the Sugar Loaf midweek, how about me treating you both to a music hall? We can just make it to the second house.'

Had he suddenly grown two heads they could not have stared more. Finn, never keen to go beyond the Sugar Loaf, hesitated. 'Can we not just have a few jars with Jonty?'

'What, on the boyo's birthday?'

'It's like this, Captain. Y'see, we've never been to a music hall before.'

'Time you did.'

'He's right. It is so, Finn!' declared Tessa. And then,

in a more wistful tone, 'I really would like to go, just once. Y'know, when they ask me to sing music hall songs at the Sugar Loaf, I sometime pretend, only to meself, like, that I'm doing a turn at the Osborne!'

'You never said, Tess.'

'It's only a daydream. D'you remember Marie Jane O'Malley and her daydreams?' Momentarily she was back in Ennan, marvelling at the high-flown ideas of her friend wanting to get into service at the Big House – and, by all the saints, she had! Tessa came down to earth quickly. 'You've got to be really good to tread the boards.'

'Boards?'

'That's what they call the floor of the stage.'

Cormac looked from one to the other, from Finn's uncertainty to Tessa's eagerness. 'C'mon, Finn,' he appealed. 'For God's sake – it's my treat!'

'We couldn't be in your debt again, Captain . . . '

Her eyes widened. How could he say such a thing! This curtain ring on her finger, so far as Finn was concerned, was the Captain's gold wedding ring, a debt he'd been prepared to ignore for years – and now he was kicking up rough about a paltry fourpence in the gallery or ninepence in the stalls! Why was Finn being like this? She hoped to God he wouldn't be stubborn, it was a chance in a thousand. 'Finn . . . please?'

And so, leaving Patrick in charge and with instructions to be in bed himself by nine o'clock, they set off to the tram stop. It was not yet dark, and the trio were a source of great curiosity. Curtains twitched or heads turned to catch sight of Finn wearing a check jacket he had bought from Ikey Solomon's. He'd always fancied one ever since Martin Jarvey sported a houndstooth affair way back at Ennan. The check jacket and grey flannel trousers gave him assurance. Tess always said he cut a fine figure, but a fella had to feel right – not that he felt right at all, about this music hall shindig.

Cormac swinging along easily was pleased at his strategy. Tessa was having a night out, a night off, where all she had to do was sit back and enjoy herself. A chance remark of Elfreda's had set him thinking. 'Tessa's an entertainer, a natural.' She was good, too good to be stuck at the Sugar Loaf. She just needs her ambition kindling, he thought, like those tinker's fires she talks about.

Tessa, her arm in Finn's, strode along – she could not moderate her gait to the shorter steps of other women. She, too, wore new clothes. The occasional five shillings which Jonty pushed into Tessa's hand every now and then had been saved in the Penny Bank run by the Settlement. The money was to buy new clothes for the children so they could join in the Whitsuntide processions. But, as Audrey pointed out, Whit week was a long way off and in the meantime Tessa needed a new outfit. 'No,' Audrey had insisted. 'Not from Ikey Solomon's pawnshop, but from Lewis's Arcade in Market Street.' What an adventure it had been, one that could not possibly have been undertaken without Audrey. To be treated with deference from 'Madame' in Gowns, and to try on different things before purchasing was an experience never to be forgotten.

And so Tessa strode along with Finn, in her full-skirted gown of forest green, the dark material relieved by a detachable Puritan collar of white lace. Being on the tall side, she wore the outfit well. Excitement gurgled up within her, sparkling in her eyes, colouring the contours of her high cheek-bones. They were 'going out', like the Captain and Audrey, Nick and Elfreda, and all the thousands she had noticed on her cleaning and singing nights – people going 'somewhere'.

As though layed on for the special event, the huge giant of a tram which glided to a halt was horseless.

'Upstairs?' questioned Cormac. 'Better view.'

'No, oh God, no!' She had seen these vehicles carving their way imperiously through Piccadilly. A sinister sight at first, with their huge iron wheels grating and sparking on the rails. The upstairs to which Cormac referred seemed a long way from the ground and was not for her.

'Inside now,' said the guard. 'Move along please, move along there!'

Tessa grabbed the back of the wooden seat. 'They're as bad as Jarvey's donkeys,' she laughed, flopping down. Cormac, sitting behind, bought the tickets and handed them to Finn. 'Give these to Patrick; it's a new collecting craze with the kids.'

As they got off the tram, the Osborne rose up like a cliff from the sea of commerce that surrounded it. They passed the queue for the gallery and entered the foyer, en route for the shilling seats, the best in the stalls. The opiate air from the first house rolled like a welcoming fog. Tessa and Finn gazed at the Moorish decor, just as they had gazed at Father Quinn's hall on that first day, years ago. The gallery with all its gilt and glamour, the vaulted ceiling and huge elephant heads topping the pillars, was a source of fascination. And when the great coronet of lights above their heads began to fade to a velvet gloom, Tessa swore the age of miracles had not passed at all.

Cormac, an inveterate theatre-goer, had sampled the character of every music hall in Manchester, from the Ardwick Empire, to the Metropole, Openshaw. Each hall had it's own following, for the same turns went the circuit. The Osborne was commonplace but intimate; it lent itself easily to establishing a rapport between artists and audience.

There were some twenty or so turns before old George Formby, and Cormac settled back in his chair; for him, until the top of the bill, the main pleasure of the evening would be the casual observance of his guests.

Pinpoints of light appeared in the orchestra pit as the Zampa Overture set an exciting pace and the drums began to roll. The illuminated red number signs changed in their frames on either side of the stage to number one. Although it was too dark in the auditorium to read the handbill, Tessa remembered the first act was the Gibson Trapeze Artistes. And so the entertainment started, vivid, brash and gay; from the cheerful knockabout humour of the tramp and the swell to the Vampire Dance. Then came the great Cinquevalli, juggling with cannon balls from the Crimean War, keeping a hypnotising stream of them weaving through the air. There was not a stir or a movement. That these relics of warfare should continue in an unbroken circuit was of grave concern to all, and as they were brought deftly to a halt, feet thundered appreciation.

The stage side numbers changed again. Tessa laughed as she never had before, at the waiter, staggering onto the stage with a great pile of dinner plates, trying to keep them in position with his chin. He swayed dangerously this way, and then leaned too far the other; the audience gasped, the nervous shrieked, and the doggish young men in the gallery threw peanut shells. When he dropped the lot everyone screamed! Next, to spread an air of calm, two young ladies played 'The Honeysuckle and the Bee' with radiant virtuosity on a harmonium and clarinet. The audience began to sing, swaying in their seats.

> You are my honey, honeysuckle,
> I am the bee,
> I'd like to sip the honey sweet from those red lips, you see.
> I love you dearly, dearly, and I want you to love me
> You are my honey, honeysuckle, I am the bee.

This was one of the many requests at the Sugar Loaf and Tessa joined in, revelling at the familiarity. It was followed by Pollocks Performing Dogs and then came poirot in bell-bottomed trousers and a French stovepipe hat; and a dozen more, all of whom were a tremendous warm-up for the top of the bill: George Formby, 'The Lad from Wigan'.

The audience began to clap slowly, excitement rising in a swell. 'We want George. We want George!' The orchestra started to play George's tune. The number in the illuminated frame changed. A bell rang. Cormac sat forward in his chair. Tessa and Finn, not knowing what to expect, looked at each other, and the Osborne held its breath. Suddenly, the curtain swung up, and the lights focused on a scarecrow of a man with a pale face, battered billycock hat and check muffler. His jacket, fastened tightly about the middle on one button, was too small, his boots too big. He shambled on into a gale of laughter, studiously pulling down a sleeve of his coat, his face undergoing excruciating contortions of amazement and frustration when both sleeves would not cover his bony wrists at the same time! Each movement was precisely engineered, nothing was wasted, nothing left to chance. The audience were in paroxysms of laughter and he hadn't started yet. Even waiting until the last titter faded was an amusement in itself, and when silence eventually prevailed the working lad from Wigan received their homage – with a cough. Not that it was hard to manufacture, for the poverty of George Formby's youth had undermined his strength, and all the apparent foolery echoed experience. Looking about as though bewildered, he was startled into the first words of his act by the sight of the conductor standing with baton raised. 'Good evenin', Alf,' he said, and leaning forward with an air of confidentiality, added, 'Ah'm a bit tight on me chest toneet, but ah think I can mannidge!'

The audience loved every moment of his gormless character and straight-faced humour. He sang 'Looking for Mugs in the Strand', and they roared; and when he tried to dance in his big boots, falling over himself, feigning buckled knees, dizzy spells, and bouts of coughing, they were beside themselves.

Tessa walked out of the Osborne still in a dream. Finn and Cormac were going over the jokes and stunts, but she didn't want to talk yet, didn't want to dispel what had been a magical evening. And then, on the tram, she turned to Finn. 'Sure it's the finest thing,' she sighed. 'this side o' the Connemara mountains! We're going to have to take the kids. It's only fourpence in the gallery, half-price for them, and Joseph'll be on me knee.'

They fell to discussing which turn they had liked most, and then onto the singing, and when Tessa laughingly told them she could have done better herself, Cormac reflected they had made a start.

By 'we' he meant himself, Audrey and Elfreda, along with a few folk from the Settlement who had been dragged into the Sugar Loaf to give their opinion. But, as Nick – who accused them of meddling with peoples' lives – had pointed out, if she were indeed a second Marie Lloyd, not that there ever could be, but if she were, who was going to give her a chance? There was no shortage of bottom of the bill material, and that's where they all started. Further, could she be persuaded to take a chance? Would she want to? Would Finn let her? Was it fair to put unsettling ideas into her head?

213

Chapter Twenty

And so, when money and time could be afforded, the music hall became a feature of family life at Number Twenty-seven Loom Street. Money was not always available, and when it came to a choice between a pint and a packet of Woodbines, and a fourpenny seat in the gallery, Finn's choice was a foregone conclusion.

But when funds were available, the Saturday matinee was the cheapest, and Tessa and the children – as a reward for helping get the laundry out – would walk to the Osborne, Tessa and Patrick taking turns to carry the chubby Joseph. After queuing outside, and being jostled at the 'Tickets', they climbed into the highest part of the auditorium, known as the 'gods'. The seats were a series of stone steps rising sharply from a cage-like safety barrier. Patrons took their own cushions, or sat, like Tessa, on a shawl or on folded coats.

David Wilkins often went along, and for days after the house on Oldham Road echoed to treble strains of Lottie Collins's 'Ta-ra-ra-boom-de-ay', at which his aunt smiled and his father frowned.

'I've told you before, Effie,' he said darkly. 'All this is no good for the boy. You'll see where it'll lead, what with music-hall matinees, this children' theatre thing and Ancoats Hall, and now confirmation classes and Mass – you know I don't hold with church.'

'And because of that he's had to wait until he's nine to be confirmed! I should have put my foot down before. As for the Settlement, Sylvia would have approved. Were she here today, both she and David would be totally involved.'

'It makes 'em soft, effeminate, all this art and poetry rubbish.'

'You wouldn't have him grow up into a streetcorner lout, would you, with an empty head? Really, George, when you have not, in all these years, taken any interest in him, you must permit me to know what's best.'

'And you think mixing with the Collinses is best, do you? He spends more time there than he does here! His mother's your cleaning woman. She does the laundry. Sings in a public house – in Ancoats of all places! Apart from influence, you never know what he'll pick up there.'

'You are being unreasonable again,' she said calmly, 'as you always are in these periodic outbursts. May I remind you that the Collinses are hard-working, clean and honest – a bit careless in some things, but she especially could make something of herself, given half the chance.'

'And that sounds very much like Miss Styles – God,' he appealed to heaven, 'what a set up. Old man Styles is a banker in Cheshire, daughter's a bluestocking, son's an army officer, and they're all attached to that ... peasant family, through a jumped-up Irishman, swinging his cane and wagging his chin as though he's been vaccinated with a gramophone needle!'

'You're getting to sound very much that way yourself. And, as I keep reminding you, it was you who set Mrs Collins on in the first place.'

Wilkins avoided his sister's eyes. Did he detect an undertone in her voice? An awful thought shot through his mind. Had Tessa Collins told Effie? His winged collar suddenly seemed several sizes too small.

Cormac need not have been concerned at 'putting ideas' into Tessa's head. They were there already, and had been planted way back in Ennan, when Flowery Nolan, the street singer, had said she'd never be short of a penny while she could sing. 'Singin' on the streets' Finn had echoed. 'Proud Riley's daughter singin' on the streets! I'd rather starve.'

'You can do as you please, Finn,' she had replied. 'But, I'm not for starving.'

Not that they were starving, but if she became good

enough to tread the boards there would be money to get Patrick some decent clothes for his First Communion. Extra money . . . just a little more would ease the anxiety of their tight budget. It would be tighter still, were it not for the second-hand clothes sometimes available at the Settlement.

Trying to improve their standard of living, though modest in the extreme, stretched resources to the limit. The back bedroom was now in receipt of another of Sad Sam's double beds, in which the three children slept. There was a warm feather eiderdown, a big chest of drawers, hooks on the wall for clothes, and a strip of turkey carpet to stifle the creak of the stairs. Downstairs, Finn had applied whitewash to the yellowing ceiling, and cream distemper to the top half of the houseplace. For the lower half, he used a lead-based paint of dark green against which dirty fingermarks would not show, and on the line of demarcation, Tessa pasted a narrow order of pink roses. Green and cream linoleum covered the floor, a pegged rug lay before the hearth, and the square table was now covered with a checked cloth, although for special occasions, Tessa was still not above borrowing a white one in for laundering.

'These material things', as Father Quinn had called them, thought Tessa, eyeing the Madonna thoughtfully, would not have been possible if they'd had more children to provide for. She fully acknowledged to herself that she was not on speaking terms with the Virgin any more, and her beads were not overworked either. In fact, she would have returned the Virgin to Sad Sam, but Finn, like old Mrs Barnes, regarded her presence on the dresser as a kind of good luck symbol.

Opinion in Hewitt's corner shop echoed Annie Cooper's sour conviction that Number Twenty-seven had 'come up in the world'. 'I always knew,' said Annie, with a knowing nod. 'I knew right from the start that there was summat funny about Tessa Collins. She was always a bit above herself. But yer know the old proverb, 'Pride goes before a fall.' Now he's as nice a fella as you'd wish to meet. Lets her have too much of her own way, he does.'

'Not like poor Mrs Marr,' said Mrs Hewitt, carefully weighing a pound of sugar into a blue bag. 'Marr went home drunk on Saturday night and threw her out of bed, he did, to make room for his fancy woman. Not only out of bed, but down

216

the stairs. Jud Patterson and his missus took her to Ancoats Dispensary. If they'd gone to the police station, Jud said he'd have been done for grievous bodily harm, what with the state of her, but she wouldn't go. Everyone knows it happens, and I can't see why Father Quinn doesn't do something about it! And on Sunday morning, there was Marr, large as life, leading up the Sacred Heart band, swaggerin' and flauntin' hisself. You hypocrite, I thought, you bleedin' bloody hypocrite!'

Whatever else of importance happened in the year 1908 – such as the Suffragette campaign turning militant, Lloyd George's scheme of an old age pension, and the limiting of work in the coal mines to eight hours a day – to Tessa and Finn, 1908 was referred to as Patrick's confirmation year.

It pleased Finn that he and David began to attend confirmation classes and Mass with enthusiasm and regularity. It made him feel good to see his first-born taking pride in his appearance, not for school or going to tea with Miss Wilkins, but for church; putting a shine on his clogs and, entirely without coercion, washing his hands and face and brushing his unruly curls until they shone. He was also as proud of his son's friendship with the well-mannered Wilkins boy as he was of his own with Cormac O'Shea. It was better than Patrick making a pal of that ruffian Tony next door, who, on his father's admission, had been pilfering from market stalls. Cooper had taken his belt to him the first few times, but now Ronnie had sapped his initiative for correction.

Although Father Quinn constantly said there was no need for families to go into debt or pawn their goods to buy new 'First Communion Clothes', most parents did. Tessa, determined not to become caught up in the spiral of debt, saved all her 'drink money' from the Sugar Loaf, and made one Guinness last all night. Cabbage and ribs, the recent delicacy, gave way to crubeen, a cheaper dish of pigs' feet, and cow heel stew was progressively watered down in the Cooper manner. Sad Sam, when they'd gone to buy the children's bed, had told her how to make 'pobs'. 'Ee, lass, I were brought up on pobs, sticks to yer ribs it does. Just cut a thick slice o'bread, put it in a basin, pour some tea on it, with sugar and condensed milk, and churn it up to a paste. Dose 'em up with that; give 'em a basin apiece, Mrs Collins, and that'll fill their young bellies.' Despite these economies, when Tessa saw the price of a new suit and shoes it became evident that there'd be no money left over for a celebratory tea.

'Ach, it isn't at all like the auld country,' she remarked wistfully. 'Back in Enna, there wasn't half the money, not a quarter of what's comin' in now, but we didn't seem to need money for a hooley, and we had 'em at a drop of a hat, as Titch Bradley says. I remember the hooley after my First Communion. Me da couldn't even get to his feet, so we had to stay the night at the O'Malley's.' She glanced at the mantelshelf. 'Did I ever show you the Sacred Heart that used to be on me da's dresser? I got that for reciting the catechism. Mr O'Malley bought me a veil for the Communion.'

'Sure, it'll be nice though, Tess,' Finn offerd uncertainly. 'They'll all be in church with us: Captain O'Shea and Audrey; Captain Styles and Elfreda; Miss Wilkins because of David –'

'Ach,' she lamented. 'It isn't like coming back to tea and all. It's as though he's not finished off properly. You can't bring 'em all to the house with nothin' to eat and drink – and no, Finn Collins,' her eyes flashed a warning, 'don't you even think of gettin' ale on the slate at Jonty's!'

Eyebrows were raised and curtains twitched when, a week after Tessa's lament, the postman made one of his rare visits to Loom Street. Finn, home to his midday dinner, and recognising the black ink and the bold, swift strokes of a broad-nibbed pen, handed it to Tessa.

'What's up with the Captain? I hope to God, he's not after being abroad for the Communion. Patrick'll be rare disappointed.'

Tessa opened the envelope and read the brief letter. 'Holy Mother,' she gasped. 'Look, this ... paper ... is worth ten pounds! To be cashed at the Settlement Penny Bank, he says!' Finn was at her side in a trice, looking as wonderingly as she at the cheque. '"A completely new rig of Communion clothes for his godson," he says, "and if there's any money left, use it for extras."'

'Christ! He's the generosity of God Himself.'

'But Finn,' she gasped, 'we can't take it. There's ten weeks' wages from Atkinsons' here!'

'We can so,' he replied, determined to accept the salvation. 'If the Captain wants his godson to look a swell, the least we can do is make sure he does! And were you not saying about a hooley an' all? C'mon now Tess, 'tis the Captain you'll be doin' proud as well as Patrick. Write an' give him thanks, an' get down to the bloody Settlement while the going's good!'

There was a great flurry of excitement on Easter Sunday, despite Father Quinn's constant reminders that it was the occasion that mattered, not the quality of outfits or the fact of a special visit by the bishop, who arrived in an episcopal cab drawn by a white horse. Both events drew crowds to the church gates, whilst at the presbytery, Mrs Stubbs, despite Father Quinn's constant reminder to 'keep it all plain', had prepared a fine lunch to impress the bishop, his chaplain, and visiting clergy.

Tessa, in view of her visitors, had made Number Twenty-seven as free of laundry as possible. Not a bowl of starch or an iron was in sight. There had been money left over from Patrick's outfit, and Tessa had purchased a dozen glasses and blue-rimmed tea cups, saucers and plates. Extra fancy cakes were ordered from Hewitt's, and Patrick had gone for a large jug of fresh milk and a basin of butter to the dairy on Ancoats Lane. After baking lots of soda bread, Tessa called a halt and hurried to the municipal baths. For the past few years this had been her Sunday morning equivalent of Mass. At the ticket office, for tuppence, she obtained a chunk of carbolic soap and a large red-bordered towel. Pushing through the turnstile and aiming for the door marked 'Female' she was relieved not to have to wait. Immediately shown into a steamy cubicle, Tessa undressed and sank into the large vat-like bath of hot water, which reminded her of the ablutions of the Sal Doss. The weekly visit to the Public Baths was a treasured time – the only time she was ever really alone, and from which she emerged feeling sleek and new.

The Day itself was dry, although a weak sun, having poked and picked at the pall of smoke over Ancoats, gave up altogether and disappeared. Finn, wearing his checked jacket and flannels, had not been able to pass up the opportunity of being seen at the Sugar Loaf with not one officer, but two, and was relieved when he, Cormac and Nick had been sent to the Sugar Loaf out of the way while the three women organised the dressing of the children and prepared tea for after the Communion. Tessa had invited Miss Wilkins and David, and was going to make the shortage of space an excuse for not including George but, to her relief, Effie had already begun making excuses on his behalf.

Nick, having been dragooned into attending by both wife and sister, had been given strict orders. 'If you're beastly, or patronising,' Elfreda had said while pinning on a large-brimmed hat, 'I shall never forgive you.'

'All right, darling, all right! I shall be all things to all men – and women, including the species called neighbours.'

'And don't be funny, either.'

'I shall regard the event as training for my goddaughter's turn . . . '

'Talking about turns, I like Cormac's idea for a Communion treat on Easter Monday. The kids'll love the Ardwick Empire, and Tessa's dying to hear Eugene Stratton singing "Lily of Laguna".'

In a pleasant baritone voice, Nick began to sing softly, 'She's my lady love . . . ' Crossing the room, he slipped his arms about Elfreda's waist . . . 'she is my dove, my baby dove . . . ' and eyeing their reflection in the mirror he continued, 'She's no gal for sittin' down to dream . . . ' He paused, and said, 'Hate to tell you this, old girl, but Tessa won't be hearing "Lily of Laguna".'

'Why ever not?' Elfreda, disengaged his arms and turned to face him.

'The Empire's closed. The Variety Artists' Federation has advised all its members to withdraw their labour – they're on strike.'

'Oh, damn! I recall something now . . . Marie Lloyd joining the pickets, sticking it out for those who earn thirty bob a week. But the strike's only in London, surely?'

'It's spreading, and with Easter Monday being a heavy box office, they're kicking where it hurts. No, my love, you'll have to settle for the Sugar Loaf, so best get used to the idea!'

Before going to the Sugar Loaf with Nick and Cormac, Finn had brought some bottles of Guinness and lemonade for Tessa, Audrey and Elfreda. The latter looked at the lack of assortment, then at each other and spluttered into laughter. 'It's no laughing matter,' said Elfreda. 'All I drink is gin and it!'

'Well,' said Audrey, 'who's for a shandy!'

'No thanks! We had a name for that at college, which I will not repeat in front of the children!'

As Tessa poured her Guinness into one of the new glasses Elfreda reached for the lemonade. 'I'll drink with the children, it's safer!' She handed the glasses to eager hands. 'Careful, now, Joseph,' she supervised his drinking. 'If the bubbles get up your nose, you'll sneeze all over that nice blouse, and your mother'll crown you!'

'It's amazin' how you have a way with kids,' said Tessa. 'Just think, this time next year, you could have one of your own.'

'Good Lord, don't say that! I prefer other people's! Nick isn't the family type of man, either.'

'D'you mean you'll never have any, at all?' Tessa asked in amazement.

'None.' The reply was so immediate and cheerful, they collapsed into the giggles again.

Tessa glanced at Sad Sam's clock. 'Holy Mother, just look at the time. Elfreda, will you take Joseph into the yard for a pee, or he'll never last the service. Kathleen, you go to the lavatory, too –'

'Yes, mam,' volunteered Patrick, who did not like being reminded and was sure Miss Wilkins never said things like that to David. But, he conceded, his mam was much more beautiful than Miss Wilkins. She was wearing a purple skirt and a mauve blouse with a purple ribbon round the collar, like a narrow necktie. She'd got a long purple jacket to match the skirt, and because she never wore a hat, would take a black lace veil to cover her head in church. None of the other lads had a mother so young, and who could sing –

'The yard, Patrick, the yard!'

Annie Cooper, having no child of confirmation age and having left Ronnie at home, dosed with a pennyworth of 'goody', was one of those clustered outside the church to nod, frown and gossip, not so much about the children in their Communion finery, as about the relatives and parents accompanying them.

'Wait for it,' whispered Annie. 'Here comes the Queen of Sheba.'

'Ee,' replied Mrs Barnes, 'give credit where it's due.'

'When she moved into Number Twenty-seven, they had nowt,' came the acerbic reply. 'Not a stick to their name – and now look at 'em!'

'That's what I mean. They've worked hard for what they've got – '

'And here comes the army – God, why should England tremble!'

'We allus said Patrick was lucky to have a captain for a godfather.'

'An' Kathleen's got Captain Styles, and Joseph's got Miss Wilkins. What's the matter with any of us, eh, Mrs Barnes? Well, I'll tell yer – we don't wear big hats! As for "Uncle Cormac", there's more to that than meets the eye, you wait and see.'

And so the children in their finery, and the parents in their pride, and the relatives in a state of sentimental euphoria, passed beyond their critical audience into the kindly embrace of Holy Mother Church.

Inside, to Tessa's dismay, Miss Wilkins, after arranging for David and Patrick to sit together with the other candidates, came with her brother to share their pew. Oh, God be thanked that she'd entered first! Joseph and Kathleen were perched between herself and Finn, next came Miss Wilkins, with her brother at the other end. The length of pew seated six adults, so Cormac and the others sat behind.

During the first hymn, Finn, head and shoulders above the rest and more noticeable in his check jacket, proudly nodded an acknowledgement to Mr Wilkins, who, had also been looking round. He had not wanted to come, had known he would be miserable, but the sight of Tessa bucked him up. She of the clanking buckets, he thought; would to God I were a floor!

Tessa gazed at the glory of the high altar, the blaze of candles, Father Quinn wearing gorgeous Easter vestments, swinging the thurible, causing the incense to rise like a prayer. She gazed at the visiting clergy moving slowly into different positions, and at the bishop, magnificent in a great cape, as if it were a dream, a pageant, an enactment of some strange ethereal play instead of her son's First Communion.

Apart from the baptisms, she had not been inside the church since kneeling at the altar, listening to beads click against the pews and seeking an answer to her predicament. And here, between herself and Finn, was the answer: Kathleen. A quick glance showed Kathleen to have sidled her way beyond her father to Miss Wilkins. Tessa suddenly felt breathless, and was glad when they were bidden to sit down. At home the relationship between Effie and Kathleen had never occurred to her, but now it struck her forcibly. Her eyes strayed further, to George Wilkins sharing the pew with a daughter he didn't know he had. Kathleen was Finn's daughter, her heart cried out, Finn's! Finn's! Fiercely protective of husband and child, Tessa cast any other thoughts to the back of her mind, where they belonged, where they had stayed – until now.

Lowering her head submissively, the fear of God beat down, crushing, stifling. Or was it fear of Father Quinn, fear of discovery, of scandal, of being ostracised, of losing her jobs? Some wouldn't even send their laundry to her if they knew. 'Let us not,' Father Quinn had once said, 'treat the matter of respectability lightly.' But most of all she feared to lose Finn, and the dreadful effect the deception would have on him. But, she argued with herself, there was no choice. Did I not pray to the Virgin, to the saints, and in this very church to the Almighty Himself? I was driven, she thought desperately, to save Finn from that bloody curse of his aunt; driven to save my husband's sanity by the only means possible; driven to make a miracle. The inability to father another child had all been in his mind. Look at him, she thought fondly, standing there like Brian Boru, proud of himself and the family whose size he thought he was controlling. Oh, God forgive her, that was another thing!

But Joseph? Where was Joseph? He was not in the pew. Someone touched her shoulder. Startled, she turned to see him smiling sweetly at Audrey. Bored with his mother's serious mood, his father's survey of the congregation for work mates and his sister moving sideways, Joseph had decided to go one better and had crawled under the pew. Sitting next to Audrey, Cormac, who had spent a lifetime sensing and interpreting the mood of restless, nervous creatures, now held Tessa's gaze momentarily with his own. He saw the cloud in her eyes slowly pass, and then let go with a nod to where the candidates were now standing. Yes, thought Tessa, this is Patrick's day – not to be spoilt with twinges of remorse and thoughts of Wilkins. Amen.

Patrick and David stood out from among the others, for apart from the quality of their charcoal-grey suits, white shirts and black neckties, Patrick was a handsome child with a ready smile and pleasing manner. He was neither shy nor precocious, but he and David had spent hours practising their responses, and what movements they had to make, and to where. Whilst the others had been giggling during instruction, they had drunk in every word.

David, more slightly built, with his shock of dark hair and solemn brown eyes, carried himself with a dignity beyond his years. Patrick was his first friend, and for that Effie Wilkins was grateful, for otherwise, she had thought, he would have been an old man before his time. The rough and tumble of family life at the Collinses was good for him, and she had repaid the debt by including Patrick in David's Settlement activities like the Boy's Club football team, the swimming baths and Friday-night theatricals at Ancoats Hall. With all that, and the Confirmation classes, they had both learned the discipline of attendance.

Finn had taken Kathleen in his arms when they stood up, so she could see the boys at the front, and the little girls in their white frocks and veils. The organ played softly . . . the children moved softly . . . the bishop spoke softly . . . And Tessa shed tears of happiness and thankfulness, knowing that her da would have been proud, knowing that this was what Finn had wanted when she all along, had been shillyshallying about leaving Murphy's camp.

Once back in Loom Street, where the fire burned brightly against the dull afternoon, coats were hung on the hooks behind the door, and under the influence of warmth, tea and soda bread, even Nick's truculence disappeared. Seeing the Coopers had been at Patrick's first birthday, Tessa, despite the coolness that had sprung up, had invited them – so long as they brought a couple of stools – to tea.

Merciful Lord, thought Cormac, as they entered through the scullery, Tessa had not exaggerated. They looked ready for the knacker's yard! She was no longer big, bright and bouncy, but fat, slovenly and slow. As for Cooper, where was all that master of ceremonies touch; the dash and verve; the tight waistcoats?

Elfreda, helping herself to a third slice of soda bread, wistfully regarded the netted frill of a doily on which the bread was displayed. 'Wish I could get my doilies like this.'

Tessa, knowing it was borrowed from the laundry, said quickly, 'You just starch 'em, and while they're still damp, pull the edges away from under a hot iron.'

Mrs Knowall, thought Annie, taking another slice. If they keep on like that, she'll have a bigger head still!

'This soda bread is delicious,' put in Effie. 'You must let me have the recipe.'

'No one can make it like the Irish,' said Cormac, and added in a darker voice, 'Your attempts are doomed to failure, Miss Wilkins, unless you change your nationality!'

Tessa was the only one moving about; her strong, fine hands serving, pouring, passing; every movement indicative of a strong kind of gracefulness. Every now and then Finn would catch her attention with his slow, shy smile, which Tessa received brightly as she dispensed cups of tea to their rightful owners.

'Come on,' urged Annie. 'Get on yer feet, Finn, and say a few words, or the Captain'll beat you to it.' But Finn was not one for taking the initiative. It was as though having taken the big decision to come to England, he had run out of aims and the initiative to fuel them.

'Cormac?' Audrey gave him a dig in the ribs. 'Say something to mark the First Communion of your godson before he runs off to play.'

'There'll be no playing,' warned Tessa, 'till he moves himself out of that suit.'

Cormac pushed back the cane-bottomed chair. He had removed his tunic, loosened his tie, and turned back the cuffs of his khaki shirt. His hair was ruffled and the amber eyes aglow with a real and intense, if not

225

emotional, pleasure. He would have liked to have said this house had been like a home to him; every year on Patrick's birthday it had been like going home, and he'd looked forward immensely to being with him, his parents and now his sister and brother. But he couldn't say any of that, not with the Coopers present, not with Audrey by his side and Nick handy with his cynicism. So, he uttered the usual phrases and cut them short: ' . . . for the children have been good for far too long. Just to thank their mammy and their da for a lovely Communion tea and,' he paused to wink at Kathleen, 'I hope Kathleen remembers to ask me to hers.'

'I'm asking you now, Uncle Cormac,' she replied, and was startled when they all laughed.

'And I, Miss Collins,' he announced gravely, with a bow, 'accept your invitation with pleasure!'

'You've been very good,' said Elfreda to Nick on the way to the Sugar Loaf. 'So far, that is.'

'There's always alcohol,' he quipped, 'to quell the inane chatter of the proletariat.'

'Inane chatter, I may remind you, Nick Styles, is not the prerogative of the proletariat!'

'Good Lord!' exclaimed Nick on entering the Sugar Loaf. 'What a crowd – are they giving it away?'

'The Osborne's closed – on strike,' shouted Jonty happily. 'It's an ill wind, as they say!'

Tessa sang to a packed Room. She was still wearing the purple costume, but the outfit was softened by Elfreda's hat. 'Try it,' she had said, pinning it in place. 'It'll make you feel more theatrical – see if it doesn't.'

From the very first song, Tessa knew it to be true. The female singers at the music halls always wore hats. I could boost this act, she thought, by wearing different hats for different songs and moods. I must keep an eye on what Ikey Solomon has to offer.

Tessa felt jaunty this evening: the day had gone well, and the Captain, the Styleses and Finn occupied a table near the piano. Nick was leaning back, balancing the chair on two legs, his freckled features bearing all the signs of resignation. Oftentimes, Tessa would focus her attention on a particularly difficult person, and concentrate on winning them over. Sure, I'll sort him out, she thought now, and launched into 'How'd you Like to Spoon With Me?' Nick was amazed by the sheer artistry of the performance: the movement of hands and eyes; the control, the perfect gestures; the intonation of certain words. She gathered her audience, and even Nick was hers to do with as she pleased. Elfreda was right, he thought, she is a 'natural'.

Later, back at Loom Street, Finn, after making a pot of tea, announced his intention of going to bed. 'The day went well, love.'

'It did so, thank God.'

'D'you know, Tess, I heard the lads talking about becoming altar boys. Just think, David and our Patrick.'

'Once Father Quinn's got 'em, Finn, I wouldn't be surprised at anything –' But she doubted if he'd heard. The stairs creaked – more subdued since the carpet – and the floorboards took up the cry in the room above. The bed groaned as he sat on it. One shoe was dropped on the floor, she waited for the other. Then there was silence.

She took down the Sacred Heart from its place on the mantelshelf and kissed it, holding it to her, folding her arms about it. Finn was right, the day, apart from that moment in church with Wilkins, had gone well. For her especially, it had gone marvellously well. Time had been called, the towels thrown over the pumps, Finn had gone to the tram stop with the Captain and the Styleses, and Tessa had found the Room empty save for herself and Titch. He had closed the lid of the piano and squinted up at her. 'How about you and me, lass, doing a turn on the boards? There, I thought that'd make those big eyes boggle! Listen, lass,' he continued, 'the managers are not kowtowing to the Variety Artists' Federation. People want to be entertained, theatres have to be filled. They're even dragging old hands back from retirement, scraping around for anything, and giving new talent an opportunity. Oh, there's a great shortage of artistes to fill the bills. I went to see Mr Broadhead, the gent what owns the Osborne, the Ardwick Empire, oh, a whole string of 'em, he's got. He's auditioning next Monday at the Metropole. What d'you say? You an' me do well together.' Her reply must have been positive for they had arranged to

227

meet at the tram stop. 'I know you must tell Finn,' he added as they left. 'But keep it quiet, eh? If we don't succeed, the fewer that know about it the better.'

She replaced the Heart and knelt by the fire, holding her hands above the glowing ashes. She wasn't going to tell Finn until he came home from work tomorrow. She wanted to keep the dreams to herself for just a little while longer.

Chapter Twenty-One

'Scared?' asked Titch as they boarded the tram to Openshaw from the bottom of Every Street.

She nodded. 'I keep telling meself it's only like being at the Sugar Loaf.'

''Course it is.' He caught hold of the back of the wooden seat as the tram lurched, and stood aside for Tessa to sit down before joining her. 'They're going to pay us, y'know – a guinea apiece.'

'I didn't know they paid you for auditions.'

'Well, I didn't tell you before, but it's not so much an audition as the real thing.'

'You mean a full-blown audience?'

'Like at the Sugar Loaf,' he winked, 'only bigger. Didn't want you worrying.'

'Worrying! It's bloody exciting, Titch.'

'Spoken like a trouper!' His tone became serious. 'What does the trouper's husband think about his wife treading the boards?'

'He didn't say much, except to watch out for pickets.'

'We'll be all right, lass, they only picket at weekends.'

'I asked him not to mention anything to the Coopers or Marr the piper, for they'll be bound to ask where I was, and if anyone saw us at the tram stop they'll be doubly curious. Anyways, Finn thought we were crazy but wished us luck. Fancy, a guinea apiece, sure we'll hardly know ourselves!'

'Mark you, we'll earn it, lass. Monday and Tuesday nights are not the best, and if the gallery give us the bird we're finished. But, whatever happens –'

'Fares please.'

'Two tuppennies.' He looked up at the guard, and added with a grin, 'And no cracks about half fare!'

'You beat me to it!' he laughed, and clipping the tickets, continued up the aisle. 'Any more fares, please. Any more fares?'

'Don't throw those away, Titch, they'll do for Patrick's collection. He hasn't got any red ones.'

Titch passed them to her and continued, 'Don't be put off by . . . well, you've seen acts yelled off the stage at the Osborne, haven't you? But if the artiste would only persevere or, like Marie Lloyd once did, tell 'em to sod off, they'd admire your courage and oftentimes give you a big hand. We're there to do our act, and by God, Tessa we go straight through that routine even if they throw eggs! I'll warm 'em up a bit first and we'll launch straight into "Paddy McGinty's Goat". You brought yer shawl? Good lass. Just take your cue from me.'

'You sound as though you've done this before?'

'It were twenty years ago, and in those days not every artiste could afford their own accompaniment, so I used to work the circuit playing the piano for 'em. But then the halls got their own orchestras and work was hard to come by, so I set up as a piano tuner, and took to playing in public houses. From the minute Jonty set you on, I knew you were a natural. I could see you put your heart and soul into yer act.'

'"Tis a dark horse you are, Titch Bradley; sure you never said a word of this before!'

'Nothing worse than a 'has-been' living on memories –'

The guard clanged the bell. 'Metropole!' he shouted, and cupping his hands round his mouth, yelled again up the winding stairs to the top. Instantly, a scuffle of feet brought people hurrying down to crowd the platform, where gasps of alarm and shouts of 'Bloody fools!' filled the air, as a couple of daredevil young men jumped off before the tram glided to a halt.

The Metropole, like the Osborne, was one of sixteen theatres created by Alderman William Broadhead – called Billy Bighead by local folk – to cater for the large numbers of Mancunians who had by the 1890s moved from the city centre into the outlying areas. The Alderman and his family aimed to provide entertainment locally for the tram fare added on to the cost of a theatre seat, even in the gallery, was prohibitive to those on low wages.

The Metropole, which stood on Ashton Old Road, filled just such a need. Already, despite the absence of big names from the bill, a jostling, good-natured queue was forming. Not wanting to attract attention, and the discrepancy in their heights certainly would, Titch hurried Tessa to the artistes' entrance, and while he presented his letter from Mr Broadhead to the stage doorkeeper, Tessa stood in the passage, her heart racing at the overcharged atmosphere.

People ran about in seeming confusion, shouting and swearing; stagehands, musicians, artistes were dashing out for a second house in Ashton, whilst others dashed in for their last hall. Some were still in their make-up, some in stage clothes.

Titch approached with a harrowed-looking man in a dark suit, crimson cravat and a pale face. 'This is the manager,' he said, beckoning Tessa to follow.

The manager acknowledged Tessa with a curt nod. 'This strike'll kill me ... ' he sighed. 'I've got to keep the hall going with the usual two performances and matinees three times a week. "Business as usual," says Mr Broadhead. "Give new talent a chance," says Mr Broadhead. He doesn't know how unpredictable new talent is!' He led them to where the wings opened out into a much larger space. 'There's a notice pinned to the wall with the evening's acts in numerical order. The front-of-house man is on strike so we have no frames with the corresponding number for the audience. You're down here as "Titch and Tessa".' He paused. 'Same name as Little Titch?'

'But two inches taller – and no, I don't sing or dance in big boots.'

'Pity,' he sniffed. 'Thought I was on to something good. Right. You're after the acrobats.' He glared at Tessa. 'Make-up, woman!' he snapped. 'God, to think we've come to this.'

'Give us a chance,' said Titch. 'We've only just got in!'

'Get a move on, then. If any of the preceding acts get the bird they'll be off sharpish, and you'll have to go on sooner than you expect. Good luck,' he added with a wan smile. 'Ask the doorkeeper to show you to my office when you're through. If you're any good I'll need details for Mr Broadhead, but in any case you'll want your money.'

Tessa peered into the grubby make-up box with its garish colours and then at the painted faces of those coming and going.

'We have to colour our faces because of the limelights,' explained Titch. ''Ere, let me practise on meself, then I'll have a go at you. "Titch and Tessa",' he mimicked. 'Sounds like a double act from a kids' pantomime! We've got to think of a catchy name for you . . . and quick. What d'you think of "Tessa Collins from Killarney"?'

'Killarney, I don't even know where it is.' Tessa watched him anxiously, dabbing and rubbing and blacking his eyebrows.

'Where d'you come from, then?'

'Ennan.'

'That's no use. Don't they have counties over there, like Lancashire and Yorkshire?'

'They used to say our poteen was the best this side of Connemara.'

'That's it!' he announced, flourishing a dusty powder puff. '"Tessa Collins from Connemara"!'

'But what about yourself?'

'You heard the manager – the name raises expectations, and we don't want any clouded issues, as they'd say at the Settlement. I can't tell yer what it means to me to be on the boards again, and to have this . . . this God-sent opportunity to launch a reet good act. Now, how do I look?' He turned from the flyblown mirror.

'Same as those,' she indicated the others, 'so it must be right.'

'When we're further up the bill,' he said, deftly rouging her cheeks, 'we'll be able to go into the dressing room and have someone do it for us.'

'If we don't get the bird! Honest to God, Titch, I swear I'll never yell at another bad turn so long as I live!'

'You'll not get the bird, Tessa. Just do a repeat of the Sugar Loaf, only project your voice a bit more up t' gallery. Wonder what the old Joanna's like and what compensation I'll have to make for your songs? Listen,

I'll go on first, warm 'em up a bit with a tune or two.'

She nodded, and so they waited in the wings, alert and curious, anxious to get on, eager to try their skill at winning the audience over by sheer force of personality. She touched his arm. 'It's all been so rushed, I've not had time to say that you're lookin' quite the part in your blazer and boater, and whatever happens, thanks for fixing it up and all. I'm going to make the most of it – just in case . . .'

'Thanks, Tess. I tell you what,' he looked round. 'I could do with a pee.'

'No you couldn't,' she said firmly. 'The minute you go out the back, the acrobats will decide to come off and I'm not going on that stage alone!'

As though on cue, the acrobats hurtled off the stage, cartwheeling into the wings, followed by cheers and shouts of appreciation. 'There's no one to announce you,' panted a harlequinned acrobat. 'He's supporting the strike – get on,' he gave Titch a push. 'Get on and announce yerself before they start stamping their feet!'

Tessa's heart beat faster as the diminutive figure strode into the limelight. Without a word of announcement he went straight to the piano and began to play a medley of popular tunes, first sitting, then standing, and finally with his back to the piano. The gallery loved it and yelled for more, only to be told coyly, 'I'll do it again – if you're good!' As the laughter settled, Tessa heard him listing the names of famous Irish female performers. 'Maggie Duggan, Nellie Gannon, Kate Carney . . . but the latest talent to wing it's way from the Emerald Isle will make you laugh, make you cry,' Titch pulled the words from the air and used them with full dramatic effect. 'She can make you want, and make you sigh! Ladies and gentlemen, it is my pleasure to present to you . . . The Colleen from Connemara, Tessa Collins!'

The warmth of the Connemara shawl, engagingly draped about her for the song added to the comic intensity of 'Paddy McGinty's Goat'. Tessa eyed the house with a conspiratorial relish. With comic movements, vocal inflections, and every now and again, swivelling a fearful eye at the supposed antics of the goat, she invited them all to join in the fun. It had worked at the Sugar Loaf, and it worked even better at the Metropole.

Then, having jettisoned the shawl at the quick-change booth in the wings, and uninhibited by the constraints of the Sugar Loaf, she changed the mood to that of superlative tenderness, and sang as one who understood to the full the pathos of 'A Broken Heart'.

Having got through the repertoire, the house wanted more. Eyes shining, and heart bursting with achievement, she acknowledged Titch, and launched into the old Boer War favourite, 'Goodbye Dolly Gray'.

'You're on,' said the manager, when they called to collect their money. 'I was at the back of the house and saw you. The audience lapped it up. So, you're on. It's fixed or it will be when Mr Broadhead draws up a contract – not that there'll be any drawn till the strike's ended, just in case you happen to join the Variety Artists' Federation! You are free, I suppose, to go on the circuit?'

'Oh, yes,' replied Titch.

'No . . . not every night,' stammered Tessa.

'Oh, other engagements? Miss Horniman perhaps? The Palace? Have I to bargain for the honour of billing you?' His eyebrows rose higher with every question until they almost disappeared in his hairline.

'Give us a minute to sort it out will you?' said Titch. Taking Tessa by the arm and moving over to the window, he looked up at her, his large, good-natured face puzzled. 'What's up, lass?'

'Every night!' she echoed. 'How can I sing every night when I've got the Wilkins' cleaning Wednesday and Thursday?'

'A chance of a lifetime and she talks of the Wilkins' cleaning! Let 'em get someone else, or do it in the afternoon.'

She thought for a moment. 'Yes, but not on the weekend, Titch.'

'We get more money for the weekend.'

'And that may be so, but I'm not taking any chances where my livelihood's at stake. I don't want to queer the Sugar Loaf pitch, for if this falls through, Jonty's not likely to take me on again. Listen, until this is more definite – I mean, when the strike's over we could be out on our ears – I'll do every

234

night except Friday and Saturday.' She smiled ruefully. 'It's all very well for a bachelor fella like yerself, but Finn and me have a family to clothe and feed.' And so it was finally settled.

'Four nights a week,' she told Finn excitedly, 'and a Saturday matinee. Would you ever believe it, me on the boards – the music hall – and they liked me! thirty-five shillings a week,' she declared. 'And if the Variety Artists' Federation gets its way, there'll be extra money for the matinee. Sure, I scarce know meself, Finn. Are you not pleased for me?'

'I am so, girleen, but it takes a bit of gettin' used to,' he replied with a shy smile. 'What will they all be thinking, y'know, the fellas at Atkinsons's. The Coopers? The neighbours are a bit funny already.'

'Neighbours? Workmates?' she echoed as the exultation shrank. 'Haven't you forgotten Father Quinn!'

Clearly he had. Tessa, still standing by the table, looked down at him on the sofa. He was so innocent and uncomplicated of heart that all he wanted out of life was to be accepted into a community, to have his place in the order of things like at Ennan, and anything that disturbed this acceptance he could not, or would not understand. Having come from the adulation of a paying audience, the regard of a commercial manager and the excited discussion with Titch, Tessa now fully recognised this inability and regarded it as a kind of tyranny. For all her love and understanding, his lack of interest – he hadn't even asked what she had sang – cast a long shadow over her triumph.

She knew Miss Wilkins, Audrey and Cormac would be thrilled at her news. 'Well done,' Miss Wilkins would say, as though to a promising pupil passing an exam.

'Congrats, oh, a thousand congrats!' Audrey would say, giving her a big hug.

And Cormac would say, with eyes atwinkle, 'Ach, and did we not know it all the time!' or something like he'd said on the Dublin Road. 'Whatever you're going for, give it all you've got.'

And Nick would come out with some crack like 'Marie Lloyd had better watch out.' Already, she could feel their warmth and pleasure – and all her husband could think of was the effect on the bloody neighbours!

Finn, a firm believer in not disturbing things that were doing well, thought Tessa was crazy to curtail the intake of laundry now that she had established a good reputation for it. But, time being in short supply, something had to be dispensed with, and space in so small a house being at a premium, Tessa reduced the laundry to that of the Wilkins, the undertakers, and the table linen from the Settlement. She cleaned for the Wilkins in the afternoon as Titch had suggested, and although work was hard, the anticipation of a place on the bill at the second house made light of it.

'Celebrations are in order,' declared Audrey to Jonty Johnson. 'Tessa and Titch are at the Osborne, and for their first appearance on home ground it would be nice to get everyone who knows them to the performance. Come on,' she chivvied. 'Get one of your publican friends to manage the bar – it's only for one night. And besides, you need to see what a treasure you have.' And to Cormac she sent a note: *Don't you dare be out of town next Monday. We're all going to wish Titch and Tessa well.*

Elfreda and Nick guaranteed their presence, as did Miss Wilkins, who was taking David. 'But dear me,' Audrey told Miss Wilkins, 'the bother I had to get Finn to attend. It was one damned excuse after another. First, he had no money, and when I told him it was my treat, he said he'd have to look to the kids, and when he knew they were coming he invented some tale of having promised to help Cooper with the coal. But of course the Coopers, despite Annie's attitude, couldn't refuse a free night out. I was so exasperated I said to him "Finn, I can't understand you, she's your wife, and if we're all there and you're not, it'll be worse than no one being there. In fact, Finn, I'm telling you straight, I'll cancel it, Cormac and all, if you don't come!"'

Finn in his best clothes, sitting in the stalls with friends and family, shifted uncomfortably as Tessa's number appeared in the frame. Cormac had pointed out that at number ten she had progressed already, and that second-house audiences were more discerning than first-house ones. Finn nodded. He was not dull or slow-witted, and Tessa doing a turn at the Sugar Loaf was familiar and predictable territory. But he felt out of his depth with all this talk of bills, boards and warm-ups.

The lights dimmed to pick out Tessa. 'That's mammy,' whispered Kathleen to Joseph.

'W . . . w . . . where?' he stammered. 'W . . . w . . . where?' Although now able to talk, he did so haltingly and became easily exasperated when he couldn't get the words out.

'There on the stage. That's our mam, and that's Titch at the piano. You've got to be quiet, except when we clap.'

They were applauding already. Applause before she began boosted confidence, especially with the Osborne being their local hall.

'They'll probably give us the bird,' Titch had joked. 'Local audiences want blood.'

'And they'll bloody well get it!'

Her smile was radiant as she acknowledged their welcome, casting an arch look up to the gallery, giving a mischievous wink, an intimate nod, a wave of the hand. Acknowledgements over, she launched into her act. On the halls there was more scope than at the Sugar Loaf. A large receptive crowd always reached depths hitherto unknown. She could let herself go.

Most of the popular music-hall song sheets bore the copyright warning, 'This song may be sung in public without fear or license, except on music halls.' Tessa, having none written for her, performed only those without the clause, but into these undistinguished songs she infused her own brand of Celtic humour, pathos and innuendo. Her range was broadening every week and tonight Titch had, 'in honour of the occasion', written a comic song especially for her called 'The Lass What Does Our Laundry'. The audience was convulsed with laughter as she coyly produced a pair of stiffly starched drawers, a shrunken vest, and other accidents of laundry with perfect rhyme and studied timing. A pause being enough at first, then longer for the innuendo to sink in.

'If they take to us on home ground,' Titch had said. 'We're made.' The audience roared. They were made.

Tessa had not been aware of the familiar faces. She did not see faces, but expressions: the cynical, the bored, the yawn. These were an affront to the act she and Titch had put together and were worked upon until won over.

A final chorus, the last ruthless descent of the curtain, the mighty round of applause – and a different illuminated number in the frame. Not staying for the rest of the bill, the Ancoats contingent, their curiosity satisfied, pushed their way to the bar to await Tessa and Titch, all except for Miss Wilkins, Audrey and Elfreda, who took the children home.

'Here are the worthy troupers,' grinned Nick. 'Flushed with the wine of success!'

'Don't you believe it, that's with having to get out of the dressing room sharpish!'

To show his appreciation Jonty suggested they all return to the Sugar Loaf for drinks on the house, and Annie, having first called back at home to be sure Ronnie was asleep, waived her disapproval still further and followed Cooper for the free drinks.

Finn was not sure what to make of the congratulatory remarks directed to him.

'Bet you're proud of her, eh?'

'Turned out to be a real stunner, your missus. Who'd have thowt it.'

'Going up in the world,' they joked. 'Soon be at the Palace, playing to the toffs. Real plush, none of Billy Bighead's cheapskate stuff there.'

'You'll still talk to us, when she's famous?' grinned Jud Patterson. 'Be getting your own alarm clock next!'

'Anyways,' Cormac raised his voice, 'before we all forget what we came for, raise your glasses ladies and gentlemen, to the success of . . . Tessa and Titch!'

Tessa, not used to adulation at close quarters, blushed and bloomed with embarrassment.

'Will you ever remember the first time we went to the Osborne,' Cormac laughed, 'and how magical you thought it all?'

'I still do,' replied Tessa. 'And it's all because of Titch.'

'And the music-hall strike!' cried Titch, adding piously, 'God be thanked for the strivings of unsatisfied souls!'

'Oh, and that song "The Lass What Does Our Laundry" was enough to make a pig laugh! I nearly choked on me pipe!'

*

Back at home, in the early hours, Finn tossed restlessly. He wasn't looking forward to going to work. No one had a wife who was a music-hall artiste; some had wives who earned a bit more than they did as doffers or winders, but that was in the mill, and accepted. One fella's wife was in service, and they were always taking the micky. They would know Tessa was earning double their wages because of figures in the papers explaining the reason for the strike and monetary advancement seemed to set people at odds. Hadn't Jud already hinted about the alarm clock? And sure it was churlish of him to resent her earning power, but he couldn't help it. She'd been on about their kids having never joined the Sacred Heart scholars procession on Whit Friday because they had no new clothes. This year they were all excited about taking part. The trouble with Tess was she wouldn't buy anything on the slate. People always did it, he mused, and managed to get back on an even keel again. It was all right for Tess, she had been brought up with the distinction of being Proud Riley's daughter, she was used to being 'different'. How had it all come about, he wondered? It seemed like a great snowball rolling on and getting bigger. Where would it end?

Chapter Twenty-Two

Not wanting any interference from Father Quinn, or to arouse the ire of the Education Authority, Tessa made sure that Kathleen started school in the September after her sixth birthday, along with Joseph who at five was to go into the nursery class. Because they were so much younger and not as able to take care of themselves as Patrick had been, Tessa accompanied them on the first day.

While the other scholars were playing noisily in the yard, a young nun, Sister Madeleine, allowed her to give the newcomers an introduction to the cloakroom. It was great and lofty, with dark green pegs on which to hang coats, each identified by a picture. Kathleen's was a tram, and Joseph's a dog. School pinafores, also dark green, were to be put on as coats were taken off, and then the bewildering journey through an echoing corridor to an airy classroom, with long windows. Both children held her hand tightly while surveying the frieze of St Francis surrounded by animals and apprehensive glances were cast at the tables, benches, slates, chalks and rows of folded canvas beds on which they were to rest in the afternoon. The bareness of the room was redeemed by a cheerful fire burning brightly in the grate, cordoned off by a large brass fireguard; crouching beside it was a huge black coal scuttle.

The school bell clanged and cut short the survey. Merciful mother, thought Tessa; they were so small and helpless, lost in so large a place. Joseph looked at her reproachfully, his bottom lip trembling, and Kathleen's glance was hard with anxiety. Tessa thought she was too thin. Somehow Kathleen had never been a bonny baby, in fact, now she came to think of it, she had never been a baby in the sense that Joseph was. Perhaps being made responsible for her little brother had made her seem older.

'I'll look after Joseph, mam,' she said, 'and just for today we'll wait and come home with Patrick for dinner.'

'I'll have something nice in the oven,' Tessa promised, touching her daughter's sleek, dark hair. Having kissed the upturned faces, she hurried out of the grim building.

Going home to an empty house seemed strange at first, Ronnie's demanding but inarticulate cries drifted through the walls more clearly without the background noise of her own. What will they do with him? she wondered. Annie couldn't keep him on goody forever. They had propped him up once on the step, hoping it would be a diversion, but the strange noises he made set the dogs barking frantically, and invited the taunts of older boys.

When the helplessness of it all made Tessa's heart heavy, she glanced at the Sacred Heart, crossed herself, and thanked God her three were normal. Although Joseph's speech would always be halting, he was perfect in every other respect.

Despite, or perhaps because of, his speech problem, Joseph was a clever child, quick to perceive a situation and exploit it. The discovery that he could be sick almost at will, and especially when separated from his interpreter, earned him a place in Kathleen's class instead of the nursery, and because of his good looks and pleasant manner, he was popular with the teaching staff. Not wanting her brother to be thought a dunce, or to become frustrated, Kathleen went over the letters and numbers they had learned at home, and when out delivering laundry or doing errands made a great play of counting change and reading door numbers.

'Wangling favours again,' Annie Cooper told those assembled in Hewitt's corner shop. 'If that was one of mine, he'd just have to keep being sick, but oh no, not hers! She's pushing him, that's what she's doing, hoping he'll be clever for being a year ahead, like the Wilkins boy, to make up for his stuttering and stammering.'

Life, Tessa reflected, came in patches, with long lengths of tranquillity to prepare you for the upheavals. Such a year of upheaval was 1910. Piccadilly had a look of Stonehenge on this fine April morning. The last remaining pillars of the Old Infirmary, which had overshadowed Piccadilly for more than a hundred and fifty years, were about to be demolished. Things, people said, would never be the same again.

David and Patrick were among the crowds. The clocks struck eleven. In view of all, four white calico banners bearing the words 'Votes for Women' were hoisted, for wherever there was an assembly, it was suffragette policy to hoist banners. The foreman's whistle rose above the whine of electric trams and the clip-clop of horses' hoofs. Crash! The mighty Ionic pillars hurtled to the ground, one after the other, lying awkwardly, like broken bodies.

People gasped at the clear, uninterrupted view of Piccadilly: telegraph boys leaving the Post Office in Spring Gardens on their bikes; the Venetian Gothic-style warehouses of Portland Street; the ornate Queen's Hotel; the conglomeration of shops, eating places, and public houses interspersed with ginnels; and the streets with strange names.

'Wonder what they'll put there.'

'Nowt that'll be any use.'

'Some say it'll be a library.'

'Nay, I heard it were to be gardens.'

'Let's go,' said David, pulling his friend away. 'I'm glad it's down, we've had nothing but the Infirmary at school for weeks.' He raised his eyes despairingly. 'Got to write a blinkin' essay for Chinny on how it came down.'

David, on leaving the Sacred Heart school, had wanted to go to St Gregory's, where all Catholic boys in the area were destined to go, but his father, who had given up being a mill agent and accepted a place on the board of Atkinson's, had insisted the boy sat the entrance examination for Manchester Grammar School and to Effie's delight he had passed. At first he had not liked standing at the tram stop in a uniform and brand-new satchel on his shoulder, but the friendly Mr Chinhaworth, his form master, had helped the new intake to settle down. He was referred to by the boys as Chinny.

'Well, what did Chinny say about the Infirmary?'

'Used to be a lunatic asylum in the early days, and people injured in the Peterloo Riots and the Chartist uprisings were taken there.'

'There'll be no railings now for the suffragettes to chain themselves to! Remember last time how Miss Gore Booth blushed when the wind ruffled her skirts!'

'And didn't Miss Pankhurst give it to 'em good, and d'you remember when Miss Crompton was arrested?'

The Women's Suffrage meetings had drawn David and Patrick because they formed a liking for one of its stars, the beautiful Alice Crompton who sometimes gave a hand with the children's theatre on Friday nights, but who was mainly concerned with the Suffrage Movement. She was also a friend of Aunt Effie.

Father Quinn had been horrified to see his protégées carrying one of the dreaded calico banners and walking behind Miss Crompton, who carried Ancoats' own flag at the head of the big suffrage procession.

He neither rebuked nor upbraided. 'We must,' he said softly, 'offer up a prayer for those unfortunate and misguided women.'

Miss Crompton had sympathised with the boys, particularly as David's father had threatened that any connection with the Settlement would be severed if his son was caught hanging about with suffragettes again. Miss Crompton had encouraged David to continue with his piano lessons, and admired his drawings. Patrick badly wanted to be praised for something, but she just ruffled his curls and he blushed and was happy.

Then came the dreadful day when Miss Crompton was leaving Manchester for London. 'Friday night won't be the same, miss. Are you getting married?' David had asked.

'Good heavens.' She threw back her head and laughed. 'Whatever gave you that idea? No, I'm going down with the Movement. Parliament is there and we need to impress the government.'

'Will you come back, miss?'

'I don't know, Patrick, but if I do, you will be big boys or young men even.'

'We'll light a candle for you and say a prayer, miss. Won't we Patrick?'

'But we'll not let Father Quinn know.'

She had stood in the doorway and waved goodbye, hoping life would keep their minds open, and smiling at the idea of them risking Father Quinn's displeasure. And even now, as the dust was settling on Piccadilly, Alice Crompton, being forcibly fed in prison, found the memory of two boys lighting a candle for her in Ancoats, very sweet and strangely comforting.

Tessa, who never passed the Infirmary without giving a brief thought to Mafeking night, hoped its destruction would not be an omen. She pulled herself up with a smile. Omens – I'm getting as bad as Finn! Then King Edward died in May, and as soon as he was buried, municipal preparations were started for the Coronation of George V and Queen Mary. Every child of school age was to receive a commemorative mug, streets were to be decorated and parties held, and for Titch and Tessa, the Coronation theme had to be worked into their act, for topicality was paramount.

The months passed into October and it was still dark when Patrick heard Jud Patterson's canes rattling against the front window. He was about to curl up against Joseph, a comfortable bolster between himself and Kathleen, when he remembered he and David were serving at the nuns' early-morning Mass. This was a special one, David's last, because he'd not been getting to school on time.

He tumbled out of bed, dressed hurriedly in the dark and, opening the door, met his father on the square at the top of the stairs. Not saying a word they descended. At first, Finn had not liked his early-morning solitude splattered with questions and schoolboy chatter, but after all, the Sacred Heart was only called upon to administer the early-morning Mass four times a year. Fancy our Patrick being a server, he often thought. And me at his age knew of nothing but peat and pigs. This was what he had come to England for, a land of milk and honey for his children. Patrick abstained from food and drink because of his coming Communion, and as they walked out into the street together, he thought, I'm dead lucky to have such a big strong father – no one pushed him around. Joining men in caps and clogs and women in shawls, they dodged overnight puddles and his father's mates would tease, 'Going to work, eh, nipper?' Or 'So you've got him on part time, eh?'

'It's the nuns' early-morning Mass,' he would exclaim before dashing off through a ginnel.

Father Quinn and David were already at the convent door, and with a nod of the head, they entered. No pleasantries were exchanged before the Mass and the boys preferred it that way. Their footsteps fell softly on the polished floor and Patrick would be forever grateful for the pair of sanctuary slippers his mother had bought him with her music-hall money. Sure, he'd be mortified, she'd said, to have to leave his clogs at the door like a Mohammedan!

Reaching the vestry, Patrick pushed open the heavy oak door, allowing the priest and David to enter first. These gallant little gestures were what Father Quinn liked to see. He had trained his boys well, to bow and genuflect gracefully instead of bobbing up and down like corks on a rough sea. Hanging up their coats, Patrick put on a black cassock and lace-edged surplice. Once gowned, the difference between a white shirt and grammar school tie and a well-darned gansey were hidden. It was Patrick's turn to dress Father Quinn, while David, head high, went to light the candles, and a special one for Miss Crompton. David liked arranging the Communion vessels, lingering over the silver and lace-edged altar cloths. The ceremonial dressing appealed to Patrick's nature. Just as he liked to see Uncle Cormac in uniform, and Jimmy Marr leading the pipers, he liked laying out the priestly garments. Each item was put on with a prayer, there was a last-minute arrangement of the stole, and then, at David's appearance, they processed, walking with dignity, heads bowed, hands joined in a prayerful attitude before their faces, to the nuns' chapel.

That was another thing they liked about Father Quinn; he was always dignified and deliberately careful, not like Father McGrath who rustled about, fumbled everything and was always apologising and gabbling. Patrick would glance at David, expecting divine wrath to descend, but the Almighty was more tolerant, for Father McGrath was spared to deputise every absence at the Sacred Heart.

A bonus of the nuns' early mass was breakfast at the presbytery. It was, they thought, like eating with God. Mrs Stubbs brought eggs and bacon on a silver salver, from which Father Quinn served. David, very conscious of having consumed the Sacrament, regretted having to mix it with earthly food and would have gone to school on an empty stomach, but he conceded that breakfast there was possibly holier than breakfast at home.

Patrick, to whom eggs and bacon were something very special, could hardly wait until grace was said before starting. At home, the savoury smell of fried eggs and bacon had only become familiar since his mother went on the stage. 'What's the matter with the old dishes, like crubeen and colcannon?' Dad had grumbled.

'Oh, so it's the old things now,' his mother had replied briskly. 'And who wanted new things, new country, new songs?' Dad had continued wiping the fat from his plate with bread and had not answered.

But David's mind was on higher things. 'What does it feel like, Father, to elevate the Host?'

'It makes you feel very humble, David, very frail and very conscious of unworthiness within.' It was the perfect answer.

'Time you were on your way to school,' he said, after the last slice of toast had been devoured. 'But I want to take the opportunity of putting into your minds the thought of one day entering the priesthood.' He looked at the astonished faces and smiled. 'Yes, it's the greatest and noblest thing for a young man to be a priest of the Catholic Church. Did you not feel something of that this morning?'

It had never occurred to either of them that priests must have once been small boys, and Patrick, looking at the stern face opposite, felt sure Father Quinn had never kicked a rusty tin through the butcher's shop window, or knocked on doors and run away, but noticing the twinkle in his eyes, he found he wasn't so sure.

Tessa would never forget the Friday following Patrick's early Mass. As soon as Finn came in off the shift with cotton clinging to his curls and grease smudges on his arms, she knew something was wrong. His face wore that self-harrowing expression she had hoped never to see again. He walked slowly, dumped his brew can on the table, and sank on to the Mafeking sofa.

'I've been stopped.'

She saw the white of his upturned eyes, heard the despair in his voice. 'Jesus, Finn, what did you do?'

'Do? What did I do? Worked me fingers to the bloody bone for Atkinson's. Touched the forelock, yes sir, no sir, three bags full sir! Didn't put a foot wrong, a word out of place. Never a minute late or a day off ill – and I'm one of the first to go, not even on short time.'

'But, I was reading in the *Guardian* this new expeditionary force of Mr Haldane's means uniform production will be stepped up.'

'But uniforms aren't cotton. Manchester's bloody cotton!'

'Who else has been laid off – not Cooper?'

'Oh no, not Cooper. 'We've reduced the manpower,' said young Mr Atkinson, "on a humane basis".'

'What did he mean?'

'He meant, Tess,' came the heavy reply, 'that fellas with working wives were the first to go. Wilkins knows you're onto the laundry, cleaning, the Sugar Loaf, and everyone knows you're on the bloody music hall.'

'Finn, 'tis a terrible thing altogether, but you'll get something else, and until you do, we can manage easily on what I earn.'

'What *you* earn!' he said bitterly. 'New clothes, new this, new that, eggs and bacon, fresh milk for the kids, talkin' lessons for Joseph – and there's still to be some left for the Penny Bank!'

Still standing by the table, she stared down at him. 'I can't believe this. I can't believe me ears. What you're saying is that if we were still on your wage, up to the eyes in debt and living like paupers . . .'

He cut her words swiftly. 'Wasn't I knowing you'd overreach yourself, Tess, and you have. I've often wondered where it would all end, and now we know. Oh yes, you're on the up and up, but I'm down.'

Outside they heard David and Patrick laughing as they pushed each other off the three steps before coming in. The door burst open. Their laughter stopped. Happy faces dimmed. Patrick placed a florin on the table, for they had just delivered the Settlement table linen. Finn stared at it, then he said to the boys, 'will you go now, and tell Jud Patterson yer da won't need a knocker up any more.'

247

One thing's certain, thought Finn; when the boyo gets up for his next early mass, he won't be going out onto the streets with his da.

For George Wilkins the end of October brought a feeling of satisfaction. An old score was settled and Tessa Collins, he hoped, would recognise it as such. He had always promised himself that Collins would be the first to go if ever short time came. Yes, that would set the ball rolling. Young Mr Atkinson had said they would all get good references, but Collins had done 'time' in Liverpool, a minor charge, of 'disorderly conduct'. No one wanted troublemakers. And of course his inability to read or write was no help; and the fact of having reached thirty-three and done nothing to remedy to the situation showed a lack of initiative. He had looked forward to seeing Tessa, to smirk perhaps . . . What he had not been prepared for was his sister's news that Mrs Collins had left, suddenly, without notice.

Everyone else's comment – Cormac, Audrey and Titch, those at the Settlement – was the same. 'Well at least you can hold the fort until he gets something else.'

'Will you call? she asked Cormac, her eyes grey with anxiety.

'I will so.'

'Just for a talk. Call when I'm at the Sugar Loaf, for he's taken it bad, and I'm afraid for him.'

'Sure, a fine figure of a man like yerself can turn a hand to anything at all,' said Cormac as they sat at the square table, shandy and a bottle of Chester's ale between them.

'Not when you can't read or write – it comes into everything, receipts, delivery notes. Y'know, I've been to every soddin' mill in Manchester – an' yet they're still taking on school kids, half-timers.'

'Oh c'mon, Finn,' said Cormac, half an hour later. 'We've gone through six or seven possibilities already. And what's the matter with working at the Settlement? Just because Father Quinn doesn't approve, it doesn't mean you've got to stay out of work! Besides, what can he offer, for God's sake? Tessa says there's enough money in the Penny Bank to get your own hand-cart, or even a donkey and cart, like you used to have with . . . who was it . . . Martin Jarvey? But you don't fancy that either.'

'It's Tess's money, Captain, she earned it for the kids and the house and all. I'd be worried sick lest there wasn't enough trade. With my run of bad luck, sure, anything could happen. Besides, there's more competition than there was with Martin. He was a boyo, was Martin Jarvey – did I ever tell you now . . . '

Christmas came and went, and the children's pleasure rose above their father's anxiety. They went to the Settlement party, and came home with balloons, tin whistles, and excited tales about a man who pulled a rabbit out of his hat. The school put on a jelly tea and potted meat sandwiches the day they broke up for the Christmas holiday, and Tessa took her own three and David to the Osborne, to see their first pantomime. She followed the routines carefully, for she had been offered a part and turned it down because of Finn's attitude. With loss of job went loss of pride in all he had achieved about the house. He wouldn't even clean a window or turn the mangle.

Her heart was sore for him. She knew with a chilling awareness that he was dwelling again on the curse of the Aunt Hanratty. Only this time, he recognised her awareness, and it only added to their predicament.

She often reached out to touch him, to hold him, or lifted her head for a kiss, but there was no life in his response. Not that she could call it a response when it was more a withdrawal. He seemed to think that everything she did was offered out of pity. And he didn't want anyone's pity.

Unwilling to accept even a packet of cigarettes, he took himself out of the house and down to the markets, 'beggin' as he called it, 'like a cripple to a cross' for casual labour and enough to buy Woodbines and pay his corner at the Sugar Loaf.

He spent more time in the Vault, making a pint last twice as long, playing dominoes, or looking into an empty glass. At first drink made him feel better, more able to step back and think it wasn't so bad after all. But as the glass got emptier he began to wonder what would happen to him in the end, and the fear of failure and death crept upon him like the mist on Ennabrugh. The glass, finally empty, reflected his life. He felt as useless as Ronnie, and that whatever happened to him would be bad.

'I remember Dad being like this when I was little,' said Patrick, rubbing dubbin into his football boots. 'He will go right again, Mam?'

'Please God,' she answered, eyeing the blue-mantled Madonna on the dresser. No use looking or even applying to her.

'What happened to bring him out of it last time?'

'A miracle,' came the reply. 'Kathleen – your sister.'

But this time there was no miracle, at least, none she could perform. She gave up. Finn, she thought, dear darling Finn, you're going to have to do this on your own.

But this time, the mist of Ennabrugh cleared from Loom Street as quickly as it had come. Having done the Saturday matinee at the Metropole, Tessa brought Titch back to talk to Finn and cheer him up, and when they arrived, there he was with the kettle on the boil, putting out the cups while Kathleen sliced bread and Joseph knelt by the fire with the three-pronged toasting fork.

'You couldn't have timed it better,' declared Finn. 'Y'know, Titch, I swear she can hear the kettle being filled from the tram stop!'

'Finn?' She put down the suitcase in which she transported her 'effects'. 'What's happened?'

'Ee, you're lookin' great, lad,' put in Titch. 'Hast tha got a place, then?'

'I have so. You see before you Private F. Collins of the Lancashire Fusiliers!'

Chapter Twenty-Three

Tessa was furious, then tearfully furious, first with Finn, and then with Cormac when he called the following Saturday to wish Finn well.

'He'll be back soon, he's gone with Cooper to fetch a couple of bassinets to fasten together for Ronnie. Oh yes, Finn's the great one now, the boyo. And you, like the others, have called to wish him well! Sure, in all me born days, I never thought when I asked you to come and talk with him, that you of all people'd talk him into the stupid, bloody army! He's admired you for years, Captain O'Shea, but I never thought he'd be daft enough to follow your example!'

'Hold on! Hold on a minute. As God is my judge, I didn't influence him at all. The army's a thing a fella has to make his own mind up about. I know he's always fancied himself in a uniform, so have lots of fellas. But they don't just up and join without a blind word – he should've told you. But there again, if he had, you wouldn't have agreed.'

'Ach, 'tis right y'are. I'm sorry for givin' out, and you being such a good friend and all. It's just that things have been so difficult lately. Take your coat off. You must wait, or Finn and the kids'll be terrible disappointed.'

'What you've got to consider,' he said, struggling out of his greatcoat, 'is what alternative did he have? Was he to sink beneath that crazy aunt's curse? He's done something positive, Tessa. Solved his own problem. And after all, the army's a great life . . . ' Turning from hanging his coat on the hook behind the door, he realised he had used her Christian name, actually called her Tessa – and she'd noticed. He'd seen that startled uplift of the head. 'Not that I'd have advised him to join in October anyways. God, I've sneezed me way through some draughty barracks!' Then, seriously, 'You're working too hard, Tessa –'

She caught the sharp glance of his amber eyes again. 'I wonder,' she said softly, 'why you've never used my name in all these years?'

'I could say that of yerself. Uncle Cormac I am, the Captain I am, but never just plain and simple Cormac – not from you, anyways. Now tell me, how's the show going?'

That's what she liked about these Settlement folk. They were interested in your life, how things went. They thought about you. Not once had Finn ever asked that question. Not once had he expressed any pride in her achievement.

'Sit you down and tell me while I wet the tea.' He slung the tired-looking dishcloth over his shoulder and assumed the stance of a waiter. 'I can juggle plates, too!'

'Not mine, you don't!' She leaned back on the sofa laughing. 'Oh, 'tis crazy y'are! Really mad for a Chief Veterinary Officer! The army's done you no harm.'

And so Finn returned, having inspired Cooper with his positive attitude to do something useful for Ronnie. The bassinets were to be joined together, head to tail, to make a gondola kind of equipage, for due to a spinal abnormality Ronnie would never walk. Finn was on form again, he was the man she loved, teasing her and the kids. His good humour made the weekend in the Sugar Loaf neighbourly and convivial, and back home again they made love happily for the first time in months.

The weeks following, Finn reported to Ladysmith Barracks in Ashton to be kitted out and undergo initial training. After that there would be a week's leave before joining the regiment on manoeuvres in Aldershot.

When he first walked down Loom Street, resplendent in khaki, with his bulging kitbag, big boots and puttees about his lower legs, the neighbours gathered round. Soldiers of any kind were a rarity and commanded much attention. Having got used to Captain O'Shea, they now turned out in droves to welcome one of their own.

'Eh, but you do look a swell,' said the older women.

'All the nice girls love a soldier ...' chanted the young.

'So, you're off to see the world, lad, at the King's expense?' said the old men.

'Where's yer rifle?' said the young.

When he finally escaped their admiration and entered the houseplace, all Tessa could say was, 'Oh, Finn ...' Her head rested against the rough khaki coat and her thoughts continued miserably. What have you done, oh, my dear heart, what have you done? But the face she lifted up was as bright as when she sang 'How'd You Like to Spoon With Me?'

'The children crowded about him, thrilled to have a father who was a soldier.

'Will you go to foreign lands,' asked Kathleen, 'and bring us back a parrot and a monkey?'

'That's what sailors do. Soldiers fight,' said Patrick with scorn.

'Uncle Cormac doesn't fight, clever clogs! Just because you go to St Gregory's you think you know everything.'

'Uncle Cormac's a vet, he fettles wounded horses.'

'What wounded horses?'

'Eh, cut it out you two,' admonished Finn. 'No arguing. Store it up till I'm gone!'

The last week went all too quickly. Tessa had hoped he would come to see her and Titch at the Osborne, but he didn't. Audrey Styles took his photograph with Cormac, and then with Tessa, and then another with Tessa and the children. 'All the fellas have photographs,' he grinned.

'But Finn, you will get someone to write for you,' she said before he left. 'Your mate perhaps, that one you call Nobby Clark? You must let me know how you are and what you're doing?' She burst into a flood of tears. They had never spent a night apart since leaving Liverpool and she didn't know if she could bear it.

'There are no wars,' he said gruffly. 'No one's going to shoot me. And sure, I'd never believe to see my Tess in tears ...'

The children, holding on to his hands, walked with him to the tram stop. Tessa stayed home and waved goodbye from the doorstep, until their figures were blurred by tears.

To stand at a tram stop crying would only make the kids unhappy, and spoil their pride in having a soldier dad. She worried about his literacy, but Cormac assured her the ranks were sprinkled with men in a similar position and provisions were made.

The first night without Finn was wearisome. She tossed and turned and missed his broad back against hers, the firm male hips on which to rest her hand. Recalling the Sal Doss at Liverpool, she crept downstairs, took the Sacred Heart from the mantelpiece, snatched Kate Jarvey's beads from the foot of the Madonna and scrambled back to the acres of empty bed. She kissed the Heart, hugged it and placed it tenderly beneath the pillow. Her dear Sacred Heart . . . battered and bruised, 'a very present comfort in the time of trouble'. Then thinking of her faraway lover and murmuring her beads she sank into an uneasy sleep.

The children were not as upset about their da's absence as they might have been, for while the mist of Ennabrugh had clung to him he had not been communicative, and they had slowly adjusted to his withdrawn attitude. Nevertheless, Tessa thought it wise to organise the family straightaway before the household arrangements drifted into chaos.

'Patrick, you'll continue to take the laundry, clean the windows and turn the mangle for me,' she announced over their favourite tea of meat and potato pies from Cunliffe's cook shop. 'A great strapping lad like yerself, what else would you be doing?' Whilst waiting for David to finish his piano lessons and essays for school, he could be mixing with undesirables, or be drafted into one of the local gangs terrifying the elderly, tormenting the young, and mocking the afflicted. He could be, but not if she had anything to do with it.

'Kathleen,' she continued, 'will clear the table, wash the pots and clean the steps. And Joseph will go errands – with a note – and polish all the clogs and shoes.'

'Why have we to do all this?' asked Kathleen.

'Because I'm rehearsing for a pantomime,' came the brisk answer. 'I'm also after going to a sewing class at the Settlement, and that's between the laundry, the Sugar Loaf, travelling to and from the music halls, and cooking and washing for three young scallywags!'

Having hand-sewn her own clothes at Ennan, she now asked Sad Sam to look out for a sewing machine on which she could 'run up' clothes for the children and make her own theatrical costumes. Every minute of every day was filled, her mind occupied and busy – until she got into a cold, silent bed and the night yawned.

It was three weeks before Christmas when the first letter arrived. Tessa looked at the strange handwriting and wished for the hundredth time that Finn had learned to write:

> *Dear Mrs Collins and children*, it began. *We will be home for a week's leave in the New Year before going abroad. Finn is looking forward to it and sends his love. Yours truly, Nobby Clark.*

She stared at the short letter with disbelief. Abroad? He'd not been in five minutes and they were sending him abroad. She wanted to grab the pen and ink and write off straightaway to ask why? Why? *Dear Mrs Collins and children*. What can you write in answer to so short and impersonal a note? What could you write that mattered when it would be read out by Nobby Clark. And what kind of name was that anyways? One thing was certain, Finn wouldn't want to know about her singing part in 'Aladdin and his Wonderful Lamp' or Titch's latest idea. Not that she had gone along with that at first.

'You're sitting on a winner with "Lovely Lad of my Dreams", Tessa. You can't fail. Give it the same treatment as Marie Lloyd gives "The Boy I Love is Up in the Gallery" and it'll be the rage. Yes, I know you only sing it for Finn, but he's never at the halls to hear you. Just imagine him sitting up there, and give it all you've got.' So she had, and Cormac and Audrey agreed he had been right.

Because of Finn being away, Effie Wilkins invited Tessa and the children to spend Christmas day with her. Then, somehow, Elfreda and Nick were coming, and as Audrey had been occupied at the Settlement and unable to stay with her parents in Cheshire, she came too and brought Cormac.

George, taken aback at these arrangements, at his sister's

'high-handedness', declared he wasn't having his house filled
with strangers 'guzzling and drinking'. 'Furthermore,' he
fumed, 'if they come, I go to the club.'

'Very well, dear,' Effie had said mildly. 'They usually
do an excellent goose at the club, and you'll enjoy the
solitude.'

Because of Finn's absence Tessa made it a good Christmas.
Their first Christmas tree and the decorating of it caused
great excitement, and for each child there was a present
made mysterious by being wrapped in fancy paper. After
the eleven-o'clock Mass, they enjoyed the day and dinner
with Effie. Tessa's heart still shrank when they adjourned
to the parlour, and during games of 'Musical Chairs' she
avoided the sofa with something like real panic.

Tessa was annoyed at the vague reference to Finn's leave.
Not knowing actually when meant they could neither meet
him off the train nor arrange a welcome. And then, one day
when she opened the door in a hurry to catch the tram for
the matinee, he was there, greatcoat collar up to his ears,
kitbag on the step.

Oh, the sight of him was lovely. The height, the breadth
of chest: her Finn, her Brian Boru. She flung herself into his
arms, crushing her coat, knocking her hat askew. 'Oh, Finn,'
she moaned against his lips, cold with the keen wind. 'Your
letter never said when you were coming . . .'

His first warm appraisal had hardened when he noticed
the case, her clothes. 'Oh, not the bloody music hall
again.'

She pulled him inside. 'See, the kettle's set.' She glanced
at the ebony-cased clock. 'Oh, I don't want to leave you, but
there's a matinee – '

'Where's the kids?'

'I can't leave them alone. The minute my back's turned
they push the table to the dresser to make a space for the
latest craze, all-in wrestling. David and Kathleen, too. No
holds barred, serious stuff. And they've got to watch Joseph,
who's experimenting with matches – '

'So, where are they?'

'At the Settlement. Children's activities. Whoever's in
charge brings 'em home and stays till I get here, it's never

more than ten or fifteen minutes. They're all helping me out, Finn.'

'You'd better get off, then.' He stood in front of the fire, blanking it out, still in his greatcoat. Hard he looked, face set as rock.

'Right, I will!' She grabbed the case, rammed her hat back in place and hurried out. 'Fate . . . ' her breath caught on a sob as she ran to the tram stop ' . . . Sodding fate, that he should come now. And dear God, it's his last leave before going off to a heathen country.' There was tonight's performance as well. Her throat tightened. He wouldn't like it, and God, could you blame him? But the panto had to go on. She was already being awkward in not working Friday and Saturday night because of Jonty; Billy Bighead did not like being messed about.

While on the tram she thought of Audrey and Cormac. If they had been in that situation, Cormac would have thrown his pack into the house, grabbed her case and took her by the arm to the tram. He'd have found a seat in the stalls, killed himself laughing at Widow Twanky, had drinks lined up for the interval and whisked her off after the matinee for a fish tea. But she wasn't Audrey and Finn wasn't Cormac.

Being in panto was not like being on the bill, she reflected, for being involved in the story you were in the house all night or all afternoon. On the bill, you just buggered off after your turn. It was going to seem a long matinee.

On the way home she rehearsed speeches and devised strategies to smooth Finn's humour, but before opening the door, she knew he wasn't there. The children were not yet home either. He'd be in the Vault of course – and she wasn't going looking for him.

His absence gave her time to gather herself. She was not going to argue or make his leave in any way unpleasant. But, she had a job to do, a public to entertain. She could tell him that as yet she'd had no money from the army, and if she had not got this lucky break, he'd be spending his leave visiting wife and children in the workhouse! She could say it was his crazy idea to join the army, and someone had to hold the family together – if he'd wanted the world to stop, he should have given it notice. All of this she could say, but wouldn't.

When the children arrived, Patrick and David wanted Cunliffe's meat and potato pies for tea. 'Wish my aunt would get these,' said David, who stayed to eat whenever he could. 'Can we take a basin for peas, Mrs Collins?'

'You can so. But here, you'll need more money.'

'And a jug of gravy?'

'Yes, anything, everything!' she replied with a laugh.

Over tea she told them Finn was home but he'd had to go out and would be back later. If he wasn't back by the time she went out, David and Patrick would be responsible for keeping the peace.

The ice was well and truly broken when Tessa returned from the Osborne. 'Sounds like a real shindig in there!' she exclaimed to Titch. The door opened and they were pulled into the warmth. Guinness was poured and a glass pushed into Tessa's hand.

'What is it for you, Titch?' asked Cooper in his best barman's voice. They had all followed Finn out of the Sugar Loaf, pockets stuffed with bottles.

'Give us a song, Tessa,' shouted Marr the Piper, and sweeping the table clear lifted her onto it. 'And Titch, give us a bit of the old soft-shoe shuffle.'

'Here's to Tess!' Finn raised his glass, and murmured, ''Tis the woman regal born y'are.'

'I'll be your sweetheart,' sang Tessa, 'if you will be mine . . . '

Relieved to see Finn his old self, Tessa sang and got them to join in the choruses, and Titch had them in fits of laughter at his comical attempt to do a soft-shoe shuffle, until Annie yelled through the wall, 'You're not at the Osborne now. Give it a rest will yer!'

'It'll be our Ronnie,' explained Cooper, in the silence that followed. 'Noise makes him fretful – and she's not herself any more.'

Lying in Finn's arms later that night, Tessa, realising how much she had already missed him and how much more she would when he was away in some heathen place, also realised she must not make him feel sorry to have enlisted. Love was the thing. Her love would go with him, protect him. They would light candles for him; she would insist the children said the rosary. 'And when your term of service abroad is over' – they had heard these phrases from Cormac and Nick – 'you can put in a request for a posting nearer to us. Yes, when you're home again, we'll–'

'If you're not engaged at the bloody music hall!' he cut across her whispers with a chuckle. 'You know, the fellas don't believe me when I tell 'em you're on the halls . . . '

That's a little progress, she thought. He must be a bit proud of me to tell 'em. 'I'll give you some bills, and the photographs that Titch took. But it's work, Finn. It's what I do best and you must accept it, just as I accepted you going for a soldier.'

'Anyways,' he murmured into the night, 'you needn't bother about the kids, love, I'll look to 'em this week.'

Tears rolled silently down her cheeks.

No week ever passed as quickly, and on the Sunday morning after Mass Tessa and the children accompanied Finn to Victoria station. She stared at the crisscross of girders, at a couple of pigeons, at the train steaming, anxious to be off, anxious to take all these men away from their families. The children had been kissed and told to be good, to attend Mass, and to look after their mammy. Tessa reached for Finn and pulled him to her. 'Be careful and don't get into any fisticuffs . . . ' Her voice trailed, her lips trembled.

'You've been grand, Tess,' he said in a last embrace. 'You're the only woman I've ever loved.'

'So you just be sure to come back to me.'

'Don't I keep telling you there's no wars, no battles?'

The huge wheels turned, groaning with the effort, hissing with short impatient puffs. A sergeant barked orders. The guard ran along the platform waving a green flat. 'Keep back there!' The train moved slowly, taking its time, building up steam. Each window was filled with cheerful faces, waving, shouting, whistling. Tessa's smile was courageous to the last, disguising the prickle of tears. She had not known the human heart could feel so empty, so desolate.

The panto season ended, and the snows of winter melted into the warmth of spring. Children played with whip and top on the flags, and the great ark of a bassinet, a monument to Finn's positive mood, stood outside the Cooper's house bearing its grotesque child.

Kathleen sometimes tried to interpret his noises, and she and Joseph would be drawn into play with the younger Coopers. Tessa tried to steer them off this course for she had heard Annie plying the child with questions.

'Did Captain O'Shea come to the house often?'

'Did he always have his young lady with him?'

'What does yer mam do at the Settlement?'

'D'you think she's one o'them suffragettes?'

And there were queries about the music hall and money. Tessa felt like barging in, but decided Annie had enough to cope with. Instead, she collared Kathleen. 'If Annie, or anyone else asks questions about me, or any of us, just say you don't know and they'll have to ask me. D'you hear me, Kathleen? Annie Cooper is a gossip of the first water.'

The stifling heat of a sulphurous summer was upon them when a badly spelt letter from Private Tatty Entwistle arrived bearing a Gibraltar postmark. Finn was well, the weather was hot, and there wre apes as big as dogs. What, she wondered miserably, happened to Nobby Clark?

Patrick, in his last year at St Gregory's, yawned over the pros and cons of Asquith's Home Rule Bill for Ireland. David at the Manchester Grammar School followed Captain Scott's route to the South Pole, but the news which grabbed public attention was the sinking of the world's greatest ship, the *Titanic*.

Tessa and Titch had advanced on the Broadhead circuit. Their ties with the Sugar Loaf had been severed for it was regarded as competition. But despite their popularity, Tessa could not bring herself to jettison the safety net of the laundry, for on the boards you were only as good as your last performance.

Audrey and Cormac had got into the habit of going away for the weekend, or even an entire week. 'Not to Ireland,' she told Tessa in one of their intimate little talks. 'I'd love to go and see his old haunts, but I realise that's in a different compartment.'

'Does this mean wedding bells at last?'

'Not for him it doesn't! It means sharing the same room . . . the same bed.'

'No strings,' Cormac had whispered in Audrey Styles'

ear. 'You're a grand girl and I'm very, very fond of you. If this is how you want it, if this will make you happy, we'll make love and have fun. I'm more than capable of taking your body, but not your heart.'

Too late, she had thought; you've had my heart for years. I'm settling for second best, and for that, my dear Cormac, I am grateful.

'I hope,' teased Tessa, 'that you've taken . . . precautions?' Since Finn had gone away, Tessa, not needing it had had her 'device' removed. Her relationship with Audrey had become that of old friends. The children were becoming more self-sufficient, burdens were lightened, and Audrey's long-lived passion for Cormac formed at least some part of their conversation.

'Not the kind you had,' answered Audrey. 'He wears, and I see that he damn well does, what they wickedly call "French letters". You're not shocked,' her eyebrows rose on an enquiring note, 'about us having, what do they say? "Relations outside marriage"? Mortal sin and all?'

Holy Mary, thought Tessa, if only she knew the half! Who am I to sit in judgement?

Although still finding fulfilment and escape in her work, Tessa worried about the lack of news from Finn, and from time to time experienced anxious moments about the growing up of her children. Getting a job for Patrick had been of the greatest importance. He did not want to go into the mill, nor the iron foundries, or even try for an apprenticeship in trade. It was Cormac who suggested the Railway Stables on Midland Street. He even took Patrick to be interviewed, and while they were there, looked over the horses in the sickbay. The stable manager was impressed and thought Patrick would make an excellent groom. Term could not end quickly enough.

There was going to be one hell of a shindig, thought Tessa, when Kathleen came to leave the Sacred Heart for her senior school. She and Joseph would be separated for the first time. This was not too bad, for he was settled and had a system mapped out at the Sacred Heart, but the crunch would come when he was eleven and had to attend St Gregory's. Patrick would have left, and his stammer would make him fair game for bullies. He was still the most beautiful of her children; his chubbiness had evened out, and he was on the brink between little boy and big boy. He was a free child. His speech defect had kept him out of Father Quinn's hands; there was no potential in the church for a chorister or an altar boy who could not respond immediately and clearly. He was free in that he lived happily with himself, within the shelter of his imagination; free, in that he owed allegiance to no one, except Kathleen. Still, Tessa would console herself, anything could happen in a year.

And then the postman called at Number Twenty-seven Loom Street with a letter not from Private Tatty Entwistle, but the War Office. Finn's term of service abroad was over. He was coming home – an invalid.

Chapter Twenty-Four

All Ancoats was abuzz with the news. Finn could have won the VC, the fuss everyone made. No claxons or mill sirens shattered the tranquillity of Bank Holiday Monday in August 1913. Outings to Heaton Park, Daisy Nook and Belle Vue Gardens were cancelled in favour of the Sugar Loaf in order to welcome him home. Patrick draped bunting about the doorway, and 'Welcome Home' posters hurriedly painted by David were stuck in the windows.

As the summer afternoon wore on, all Loom Street kept watch for the military ambulance. Father Quinn was there, waiting to bless; Marr the Piper was there to give a swirl on the pipes; the Pattersons and Barneses were on their step; the Hewitts at their shop window; and assortments of Coopers were everywhere. Tony, now a drummer in the Sacred Heart band, was supposed to be on the lookout but was larking about with Kathleen instead.

Tessa wished Cormac and Audrey had not been making an illicit long weekend out of the Bank Holiday. If they had known, they would have been there, and she valued their support for herself and for Finn. Cormac would have known what to do.

George Wilkins, having heard the news from David, happened to be passing the end of Loom Street, and lingered. He had caught sight of her looking – elegant, he conceded, but subconsciously so. And to think she'd once cleaned his floors, lain on his sofa. Of course, he could ruin her, bring her to heel with just a snap of his fingers – a word here and there, to this person and that. All this he thought when the agony was upon him. True, the distance between bouts of desire for sweet revenge and ardent longing were becoming greater. But he couldn't keep away from music halls; wherever she was billed he was there, unnoticed and insignificant in the full house. Sometimes he sent a drink backstage, anonymous, of course. Another time he had sent flowers and slinking in the shadows outside, had waited for her and Titch – ridiculous little man – to leave, waited to see his flowers in the crook of her arm. But when they came out, his were not the only flowers. Her arms were full of them and had overflowed to Titch. Best never to have sent any than be one of many. He did not repeat such foolishness.

The sound of a whistle interrupted his reverie. Joseph, on the opposite corner, was the first to see the ambulance as it lumberd over the cobbles up Every Street. He ran, blowing on his whistle as a signal. Wilkins moved closer. Marr played on his pipes, walking up and down the street, his kilt aswirl. Cheers greeted the ambulance, heralding its approach, welcoming home Loom Street's only soldier. As the vehicle slowed, the pipes faded, and as it halted, they stopped. In complete silence, an orderly in a white coat jumped down from the driving seat, opened the rear doors, and let down the step. The hush deepened as Finn appeared and was helped down. David and Patrick rushed forward to meet him, but found no words to say. What had happened to their dad, the big man they had waved goodbye to at the station, massive in army greatcoat? Walking slowly, breathing laboriously, Finn, his curls heavily streaked with grey, face gaunt, figure bone thin, wept at the familiar sight, the dear faces. God be thanked, he was home at last.

The houseplace had been kept cool from the sultry heat. There was no longer any need to keep a fire burning all the time, for Tessa had had a gas stove with three burners and an oven installed in the scullery. The room was bright with flowers; the dresser and mantelpiece were polished; the kids had been told to tidy their things away; and the pegged rug had graduated to a full-sized carpet square, crimson with a floral background.

'Sure, and it's a treat to be home – or am I in heaven?' he said, acknowledging the changes. He balanced himself by the dresser as Kathleen hurtled forward to hug him with a strangling vigour. 'I must be in heaven,' he teased, 'for our Kathleen's given her old da a kiss!'

Over Kathleen's head, firmly planted against his chest, the faded blue eyes sought Tessa's. Fear, pity, and disbelief were twisting her heart, wrenching it. Her Brian Boru, the Lovely Lad of Her Dreams, so ill and racked beyond all belief. How dare they do this to him? She locked and unlocked her hands. Five years working her way up on the boards had schooled her to smile, to laugh, even though the tears pricked and the heart was low. Kathleen stood aside, and heard her mother thanking God he was back.

'Finn,' she said, her lips against his hair, her strong body against his frailty. 'It's all over now, there's no going back. You're here with me and the kids.' She changed her voice, to include all those gathered at the step. 'This isn't the army, Finn Collins, we don't stand on ceremony – will you be sittin' down!'

The ice was broken, she led him to the sofa, and while neighbours, priest, and Jonty Johnson filed past to shake his hand and tell him what a fine fella he was, she hurried out to the medical orderly. 'How did he get like this?' she demanded. 'What can you tell me? You must know.'

'According to his papers, ma'am,' he said in a clipped accent, 'he developed a chest complaint and didn't report sick, but continued doing his duties – better than most. The conditions of service, the toughening-up process, often meant days and nights in wet or damp clothes which didn't help. It was a miracle he kept going so long. It was only after his collapse that the MO discovered he'd been coughing and spitting blood for weeks. Despite being a big man, he had no reserves of strength to call on – probably half starved when he was young – consequently his decline was rapid.'

'How long will it take him to recover?'

The orderly shook his head sadly.

'You mean . . . ?'

'You mustn't live in hope, ma'am, there is none. Just a matter of time. There'll be a pension, so don't worry on that account.'

At least, she thought miserably as the ambulance lurched away, followed by clustering children, at least I've got him here, if he's going to die at all. Better like this than a name on one of those Rolls of Honour which had sprung up after the Boer War. It did not occur to her that their names were sprinkled with glory; that the Rolls were evidence of their sacrifice. Finn was cheated of that. Posterity would remember him no more than it had his parents, who died ignominiously in a remote Irish bog. The memory of the Aunt Hanratty rose unbidden; Tessa turned and swept into the house.

The presence of neighbours, old mates from Atkinson's and drinking pals from the Vault gave her and the children time to readjust. Time ... Thank God it was a Bank Holiday and there was no performance to attend; at least she wouldn't have to leave Finn on his first night home. Her heart felt heavy at the malignity of Fate, and then she hated herself, because in his terrible state, she had experienced a pang of pity for her own aspirations. But now, more than ever, she needed to forge ahead with her career – this was Audrey's word, and it sounded good. No expense would be spared. Finn would need special food, good things to build him up, delicate things to tickle his palate, medicines to make him well. But, in his present state, would he understand all this?

In the scullery, while making the tea, she told Titch that the pantomime was out of the question for this year. 'I couldn't leave him. He never approved it when he was well.' She shook her head. 'Every afternoon, and every evening from seven till half-past ten. Impossible!'

'Contracts are up for renewal at the beginning of October, on account of the rehearsals for the panto. But you must work till October. If you break your contract before, we're finished with Broadhead's.'

'No, I wasn't for breaking anything, Titch,' she said desperately. 'I'm going to need every penny I can get for himself. But will you be able to get anything ... I know the boards mean more to you ... '

'You've got enough on your plate, lass, without thinking about me. Go on,' he said gruffly, indicating the tea, 'they'll be – ' He had been going to say 'dying of thirst' and, pulling the words back quickly, he flushed.

'I know what you mean,' she said. 'It's something we'll all have to get used to ... '

Dear God, she thought, while pouring the tea, I'm only just home and those two are squabbling already.

Joseph, who had never found his father interesting, and who had never liked the way he talked to him as though he were still a baby, didn't see why he couldn't go on the flags with his whip and top.

'Stop asking. Mam said we've all to stay in,' whispered Kathleen ferociously,' "cos Dad's back from the war and he's ill, and he wants us round him.' Kathleen added 'the war' to impress him; she had been going to say 'wounded' instead of 'ill' but as there was no sign of bandages, knew he wouldn't believe her. 'I don't know whether you're naturally heartless,' she informed him, 'or bent on getting your own way.'

'You may as well get yer best clothes off, and go out to play' said Tessa, thinking to break up the squabble, but unconsciously proving Kathleen's point, and in the next breath, said 'Ready for more tea, Father Quinn? Kathleen, Father Quinn's cup.'

Joseph skipped toward the stair door. His smile was not triumphant or I-told-you-so, but one of happy relief. Kathleen's heart seethed. There, he'd got his own way again. Every one gave in to him and she wished they wouldn't. She loved him dearly and dreaded to think how he'd suffer at St Gregory's next year.

'Kathleen! Father Quinn's cup?'

Later that night, Finn told her a little of Gibraltar, and she brought him up to date with all the news, including Patrick's job. She told him how she would have to work until October – and in her heart thanked God he didn't flare up – but would then be free to devote all her time to getting him on his feet again, 'Like I did at Downey's barn.'

Although able to get about the house, to sit on the front step, negotiate the three steps into the yard for the lavatory, he would not be able to climb the stairs. When he heard that Kathleen was sharing the big bed with her mother, Finn thought it premature, almost like putting the mockers on his recovery.

'Patrick's fourteen! For shame I couldn't keep him and Kathleen in the same bed. Apart from anything else, he's a working lad, his pride wasn't up to it.'

'And what about my pride, eh?'

*

The following weekend Cormac and Audrey arrived. 'Bearing gifts,' she laughed, struggling through the door with prizes won on the Golden Mile: sticks of rock, furry animals, and a big bouncing ball in a net. Seeing Finn propped up on the Mafeking sofa, she dropped the lot.

'Merciful Lord, you're looking well, the two of you,' greeted Tessa, to hide their obvious astonishment. 'And didn't you pick the weather!'

'And fancy himself coming back the minute me back's turned! God love you, Finn, oh, God love you!'

Finn immediately perked up, and they set to, talking like old army mates, but Cormac could have wept that this should happen to a lovely fella like Finn. All he had wanted was to find a land flowing with milk and honey, but having found it, the supply looked like running out for him.

In the scullery, Tessa told Audrey what the orderly had said, and Audrey, not one for the wringing of hands or slushy sympathy, was at once positive and practical. 'First of all, my dear, you need proper medical advice. I don't mean to alarm you but some of these chest complaints are infectious. The Settlement has invalid funds available to help you out, but above all you must look after yourself, for they depend on you now more than ever!'

'Cormac!' Tessa exclaimed, seeing him at the stage door of the Metropole. 'What the devil are you doing here?'

'Could we alk about Finn? Number Twenty-Seven Loom Street's like Victoria station these days!'

'You two go to the bar,' said Titch. 'Give you a call in twenty minutes.'

Over a shot of Jamieson's and a shandy, he asked all the questions it had been impossible to ask in Finn's presence. 'Would you like a specialist's opinion of Finn's condition? See if we can get him in a sanatorium in Cheshire? It has a good name. Some get cured, and others have lasted for years with medication and treatment. I'm not trying to raise false hopes, mind.'

'I know you're not, but I do feel I need to talk to someone about him. The young orderly was just going by what was on his papers.'

'Has a regimental officer called, or have you received a letter about a pension?'

'No, but Finn said there'd be one.'

'Holy Mother – we do more for our horses. Would you like me to speed things up? Put the fear of God up the buggers!' He knew she would laugh. He clinked her glass, and Mrs Hewitt from the corner shop, on a night out with her sister, spluttered into her gin. Just fancy, her lips pursed. Annie Cooper wasn't far wrong.

Three weeks later a competent-looking doctor specialising in diseases of the lungs spent an hour at Loom Street examining Finn, talking, questioning, doing various tests and taking samples.

'The lungs are in an advanced tubercular condition. Or, in the common parlance, Mrs Collins, your husband is suffering from consumption. Galloping consumption . . .' A sanatorium? He shook his head. Hygiene? He glanced at the fire. Yes, he instructed, Finn must always spit into the fire.

'Christ,' said Finn, 'I'm not a spitting man – never coughed or spat in me life till I joined the army.'

'If for some reason you cannot get to the fire, you must spit directly into this dark blue jar. It has a screw top, easy to undo, and it contains a special disinfectant which your wife will dispose of and replenish. This disease is highly infectious. I'm surprised, Mrs Collins, you were not advised about this when he came home. It's best not to kiss anyone, especially childre.. You have children?'

Tessa nodded, unable to speak. She had wanted medical advice, had wanted to talk about it, but never thought it would be like this.

'You must have your own cutlery, cup, plate.' With a glance at Tessa, he added, 'These must be washed separately.' He saw the packet of Woodbines, reached out, threw them on the fire, and returned to the precautions. 'One more thing you both need to be aware of: tuberculosis is hereditary; there must be no additions to your family.'

'I'm past all o' that doctor.' Finn gave his shy smile. 'I'd be coughing for a week!'

To Tessa at the door, he continued, 'Try to keep him calm. If he gets upset he'll cough, and that causes bleeding and further deterioration. But despite all of this, he must not be made to feel less than a man.'

Finn was a restless patient, and lacking the facility to read, was soon bored. So that he wouldn't be irritated by the sight of her theatrical props and costumes, Tessa removed them to the bedroom and resorted to various subterfuges. It was like history repeating itself, for as a girl she used to smuggle her finery out of her father's cabin in the same manner – and almost for the same reason.

By October, Tessa had given up the laundry because of the steam making Finn cough. She was almost relieved, too, that her contract had expired. It was not the sheer physical effort of looking after an invalid, of being on call twenty-four hours; of emptying the commode now that he could no longer negotiate the yard steps; of washing him, keeping him interested in things, and buying him nice clothes and white shirts so he looked attractive for his visitors. It was not all this which exhausted her, but the emotional strain of the precautions; of tending the dark blue spitting jar; of hating herself for constantly warning Kathleen and Joseph not to use the white cup and plate or towel, not to use the red flannel or cutlery with red wool on the handles; of keeping the family squabbles at bay; of turning the houseplace into a sick room and the problems it caused. Keeping people out, asking people in. Watching they didn't stay too long. Putting up with Father Quinn and Marr the Piper. But no sooner had they all gone and she had sat down with the newspaper, then Finn would ask for something.

It was evident that his condition was deteriorating. Whatever the children did was not right. Patrick, if he followed his usual pattern of going out after tea to football practice with David in the Ancoats Settlement team or to some church activity, or to assist with the Friday-night children's theatricals, would be 'getting out of his dad's way'. If he and David stayed in, Finn said they regarded him as a peep show. 'And when I stayed in with him,' Patrick told his mother, 'just to talk and be matey, he said what's the matter had I nowhere to go, and at my age he was out every night! An' he wasn't, Mam, was he? Not from what you told us of Ennan.' If the younger ones were their natural selves, they were too noisy, and if they made an effort to tone it down he would declare irritably, 'You needn't be creeping about, I'm not dead yet.'

Tessa had to watch he didn't cough over the tea table, and when he was racked with coughing she had to stop Kathleen from running to comfort him. Keeping the children, especially Kathleen, away from their da was awful. He felt ostracised and Tessa felt guilty.

He could no longer keep up conversations, so when they all trooped in from the Sugar Loaf on Saturday night, discussing the Irish question, the coal strike, the German situation, he lay back on the sofa, watching. There was Tess, with her unconscious strength, her easy way of talking and laughing – not too loud for fear of upsetting him. It's a wonder she's not out at the bloody music hall, he thought, lifting her head, pouting her lips with 'How'd You Like to Spoon With Me?'

He began to cough a little and felt the intolerable, tactful pity of his mates crowding in on him. He didn't want their sodding pity. Damn them to hell, all of 'em! He wanted their strength, their bodies, he wanted to be a man again. The coughing continued, hacking at his lungs, the pain piercing his chest like a bayonet thrust. Tessa hurried for the bottle of medicine, pouring it into a cup, the white one. She stooped to put it to his mouth. He jerked up instantly, blood flecking his lips and dashed it out of her hand. 'I'm not a bloody imbecile to be dosed up with goody!'

Visitors were less frequent after that. Cormac came as often as he could, and so as not to remind Finn of army days, came in civilian dress. This for him, meant something 'horsey', dark trousers, hacking jacket, and cravat; sometimes he wore even knee breeches. And as the weather turned cold he wore a soft, white polo-necked jersey. Finn had one as well, she and Audrey had bought them from Lewis's.

But even Cormac had to tread carefully, for Finn had developed the fretful jealousy of an invalid. He envied Patrick and David talking about football; he saw the easy bond between Patrick and his godfather as they talked about horses. He watched Cormac and Tessa with a stab of unreasonable pain. He knew no thoughts of love or betrayal were in either of their minds, but Finn, staring at Cormac's slim, muscular figure, his competent manner, ruffled hair topping his longish face, knew with the amazing insight of the dying, that there lay her future.

At night, if she heard him coughing, she would come downstairs and make tea, sit by him on the sofa drinking it. Just her presence, her warm vitality made him feel better 'Girleen,' he said, stroking her warm hand with fingers cold and withered before their time. 'This is it. The old Aunt's won . . . No, don't stop me . . . Sure, I need to tell ye. When I enlisted I fell right into her clutches. I was away from you and your strength, Tess. If you'd been by my side in that bloody great barn of a hospital in Gibraltar, you'd have cleared the Aunt Hanratty off like you did in the Downeys' barn. You were always more than a match for her. I'm not afraid like I used to be. I dont' care any more, Tess . . . '

The following night she heard the familiar rattle of Finn's cough, and leaping out of bed hurried downstairs barefooted, to be all the quieter. Opening the door at the foot of the stairs, she saw him in the glow of the firelight standing completely naked.

'Oh my God, Finn, you'll catch cold!' She moved toward the nightshirt he had thrown on the sofa. He took her hand limply; there was no strength in his touch. 'You keep me warm, Tess. Here, where you said you'd never make love.'

'What if the kids come down?' she gasped. 'Sure we'd both be mortified.' His wasted hands crawled up the sleeves of her nightgown. 'No,' she said. 'No, Finn . . . God Almighty, and did y'not hear what the doctor said?'

'Bloody doctors,' he gasped. 'I know how to be careful. We've been careful for years.'

Her heart felt cold. The birth-control device had been removed.

'Put yer nightshirt on, Finn . . . The kids might come down, oh, the shame to be caught by our own kids . . . and Kathleen . . . your own daughter mustn't see you naked.'

But he hadn't heard. He wasn't listening. 'What else is there for me now? I've dreamed of this. Love me, Tess, before I die.'

She could have picked him up and carried him to the sofa, dressed him, and gone back to bed. But she couldn't bear to humiliate him. Rejection would kill him as surely as that bloody curse! He had locked his stick-like arms about her, clinging, like the limpets they had seen on the river walls of the Liffy, forcing her beneath him on the sofa.

His hands once dry and rough, were now cold and clammy. She shivered. It was like making love with the dead. He smelt not of machine oil or cotton, but . . . the word leapt into her mind . . . decay. Rottenness. He pressed himself upon her. She turned her head sideways to avoid the sickly sweet smell of his breath, and there on the window ledge crouched the dark blue spitting bottle. Her stomach heaved. He, mistaking the sudden jerk for a response, flared into a blaze of manhood, gave a sudden thrust, and rolled to one side, like a spent match.

Jud Patterson found Finn's body at five o'clock that morning, fully clad in grey trousers and white polo-necked jersey, outside the Sugar Loaf, with a Woodbine behind one ear and the price of a pint clutched firmly in his hand.

Patrick found his mother when he got up an hour later, on the top step of the three leading into the yard. She had leapt from the sofa and run in barefeet and nightgown to the lavatory shared with the Coopers, where, on her knees, she had vomited again and again, and only managed to crawl back as far as the steps before she collapsed.

Chapter Twenty-Five

Due to the nature of his illness Finn's body had been removed to the Ancoats Hospital Mortuary Chapel.

The fumigation had followed. It was a bit like the 'visitation' at Ennan all those years ago. Fortunately, the children were at school and Patrick at work when the two Public Health officials in white coats, masks and rubber gloves went through the houseplace, determined to eradicate every trace of infection. She watched with an odd sense of detachment the blazing fire devour Finn's pillow, slippers, clothes, the new polo-necked jersey in which he had died – everything. What wouldn't burn was carried away in a sack. Finally, one of the men touched her arm.

'Got to vacate the premises now, got yer things have yer?'

She nodded. Kathleen and Joseph were staying on the Settlement premises at the Women's House with her; Patrick would be at David's for the customary twenty-four hours. Outside, the morning was raw; light wisps of fog hung about like wraiths surveying the strange behaviour of mortals. Only months ago there had been bunting round the door and windows instead of sealing tape; a 'Welcome Home' poster instead of a fumigation notice.

'Reet,' said the official. 'You can lock the door now, missus. There'll be no infection when you come back, the fumes o' that gas'll polish 'em off. It's all for the best, missus. A good spring clean, like. All in the public interest.'

Standing in the front pew on the day of the funeral, Tessa could hear that the church was well filled – that should suit Father Quinn, and Finn would be pleased that it did. Her glance strayed to the polished coffin with its canopy of wreaths. There'd be one from the people on the street. She could imagine them.

'We're collecting for a wreath for Mr Collins's funeral.'

'Oh ay, and when are they burying 'im?'

'Wasn't it a funny do, finding him in the street, like that?'

'No last rites and dying in bed for old Finn – best way to go, dressed up for a neet out!'

'Eh, he were a nice fella. Big lad, do owt for anyone, he would.'

And there'd be those who would add, 'Not like her.'

The Mass progressed. David and Patrick officiated at the altar; the organ played; incense was swung, holy water sprinkled. She saw Father Quinn saying 'a few words'. Saw his mouth opening and closing, the bushy eyebrows rising and falling. He'd be saying nice things about Finn. They had got on well; Finn was pliable, easily moulded, as, she feared, were her children. No . . . she corrected herself. Only Patrick was easily moulded. Joseph was her 'free' child, and that she could understand, but at times Kathleen's fierce allegiances and insight were almost frightening.

Effie Wilkins was not in church, she thought Finn would have liked her to lay on 'a little funeral tea', at the house he loved'. As if Effie's teas, God bless her, were ever little! 'Just a few sandwiches, seedcake, and iced buns for the young ones. Oh, and a glass of sherry would be nice – or whisky, and lots of tea . . .'

Sad Sam would be in church, somewhere at the back . . . she must remember to thank him properly for getting her two single beds in exchange for the big brass one with no knobs. In her anxiety not to pass on any infection to her daughter, she had thought this a wise move. But Kathleen, having always shared a bed, felt as ostracised as her father had done.

Sure, it's a funny thing, thought Tessa, people say I'm bearing up too well – it's almost like an accusation, they reckon I ought to cry, to mourn and grieve. Perhaps she would have if Finn had died under any other circumstances, but the man in that box was not the man she had married, and sickness has a way of taking love and changing it.

Tessa was a widow at thirty-two. It scarcely seemed possible to imagine the rest of her life without Finn.

She wondered if he would ever have changed his attitude to the music hall ... Trying to look on the bright side, at least she'd be able to get on with her career openly, unhandicapped by little dreads, cover-ups, and harmless but necessary intrigues. But as Titch Bradley had pointed out, they would have to wait until the panto season ended, when the Broadheads would be 'juggling their bills' for the following quarter.

Shortly after the funeral, she stood in front of the blue-mantled Madonna on the dresser, and gazed for a long time at the softly moulded features, at the smile which continued through to the painted eyes. Then, slowly, with great deliberation, she lifted the figure and put it by the door to be returned to Sad Sam's shop.

In it's place went her beloved Sacred Heart with its familiar air of sadness and its vivid colour. Moving the Heart had dislodged the rent book, and picking it up Tessa realised no rent had been paid since before Finn died. Had she not been in when he called? Those last few weeks had been so fraught she couldn't remember. But anyways, Old Greenledge, now she came to think of it, always gave his tenants a few weeks' grace to collect the insurance money. Come to think of it the man from the insurance company hadn't called either, so the claim had not gone in, and having paid the funeral expenses there was very little money left. It had all been spent on Finn, and she didn't regret a penny of it, but, for the first time in her life, she was owing money.

'Heck, Mam, we're not back on crubeen!' groaned Patrick at teatime.

'We are so,' she declared briskly. 'And it'll be bread and water if I don't get the laundry going again!'

'Bit sudden isn't it? One day we're on the fat of the land, and the next on short commons!'

'With yer da and all, the rent's been let slip – and that insurance fella hasn't darkened the door since.'

'Don't say he's done a bunk, Mam!'

'I'm not, and God forbid. But the thought had crossed me mind.'

'Oh – I nearly forgot to tell you, with the shock of the crubeen, like! I saw Uncle Cormac today. He was passing the stables and called in. Said he'd be over to see you later on about Dad's army pension.'

'Sure, that's a bit o' good news altogether, though they've taken their time about it.'

'But what's all this about laundry? I thought you and Titch would be going back to the music hall?'

'We are – God willing.' Three faces looked at her curiously. She was usually more definite. 'And who'd have thought we'd ever be without your da?' was all she said.

'And who'd have thought,' said Patrick with a grin, 'that our Joseph would have an after-school job.'

Joseph, who had been playing cat's cradle with string spread between his fingers, shot a look of alarm at his brother.

'I've got him in at Bert Flood's as a lather boy.'

'I c . . . c . . . ' he stammered. The cat's cradle collapsed. 'I'm . . . m . . . m,' His face flushed with frustration. 'K . . . K . . . ' Unable to say his sister's name, his face crumpled.

'Mam,' said Kathleen, brown eyes hot beneath her fringe of dark hair. 'Stop our Patrick. Joseph's not old enough to be in a barber's shop of all places. They're always chinwagging in there; I used to go with Dad to get his hair cut.'

'Lather boys don't have to talk, Joe.' Patrick called him Joe when he was being tender. He shortened everyone's name when he was being kind. 'All you have to do is lather soap on bristly chins, sharpen the razors on a strop for Bert, sweep up, keep the stove going, be sure the big ginger cat get's his milk, and there's as much tea as you can drink. Bert knows you're not talkative. "I don't want no one with too much lip," he said. And I said to him, "I know just the lad you're looking for." It's from school till half-past six, and Saturday all day. One and sixpence, with tips. Why, I started at only seven and six for a whole week – and no bloomin' tips!'

What Patrick didn't say, but what they all understood, was that Joseph had spent most of his time by himself and with Audrey, Elfreda and Kathleen. It was time he mixed with his own kind, and Bert Flood's barber's shop was a stepping stone.

Tessa was proud of how her eldest son was shaping up. He looks so like his da, God rest his soul, not that he'd ever be big or broad, but he'd make a fine young man, good looking, and cheerful as the day was long.

After tea, muffled up in scarves and gloves, for Tessa was overanxious now that they shouldn't get chilled, Patrick took Joseph to see Bert Flood. He was going on to David's, afterwards, so Kathleen went along to bring Joseph back, for he was terrified of stumbling over a dead man in the dark, like Jud Patterson had stumbled across his father. Not that Kathleen was trailing into Flood's – no, she waited at the Wilkins' house, talking to Miss Wilkins, David and sometimes his father.

Watching them walk past the lamp and along the street, Tessa wished Kathleen had a friend like she'd had Marie Jane O'Malley and Kate Jarvey. Of course there were girlfriends at school and at the Settlement, but no one special, except David, who was as protective over Kathleen as she was over Joseph.

She closed the door. Dear God, oh dear God, what a muddle. Effie, – whom they always called Miss Wilkins and never 'aunt' as they did Audrey – Effie was having the time of her life with these young people to mollycoddle, and Kathleen, being the only girl, was made a fuss of. But now Tessa had written a note to Effie saying that the laundry was on again, although hopefully for a limited period.

She turned quickly from the door to the table and a strange feeling of faintness came over her, just wafted over and was gone. It would not have merited another thought except it wasn't the first time. She sat down again and remained there, thinking.

A sharp tap on the door made her gather her senses. Getting up more slowly she opened it. 'Cormac,' she smiled. 'Come in out of the cold.'

'Just seen the young scallywags on their way to the barber's. "What, whiskers already," I said to Joseph and they all got the giggles! And will you listen to me now, that boy answered me without a single stammer.'

'He can,' she nodded. 'I've heard him talk to Kathleen

with scarcely a one, but the slightest upset, just anything to throw him off balance, and he's off like a machine gun. So, they all got the giggles?'

'All three,' he replied soberly, closing the door.

'It'll do them good, the past months have not been easy. Dear God, Cormac, who'd have thought all this when you gave us a lift on the Dublin Road . . . ' She paused. 'Here am I blathering on, and the table's to be cleared.' She wrinkled her nose. 'Oh, the smell of that crubeen, ugh!'

'Crubeen,' he echoed. 'The smell of it? God forgive you, woman! The word is savour, aroma, bouquet even . . . '

'They're all fancy words for a smell, and it's yours if you want it.'

He took off his greatcoat. 'Sorry about the uniform. If I'd changed I would have been later still, and we must discuss the pension while the kids are out. Patrick did tell you?'

She nodded and gathered the plates. He made a lunge and rescued the crubeen with a dramatic gesture. 'Oh, it's a fool y'are, Cormac O'Shea!' She hadn't laughed it seemed for months. 'I've got the giggles now!'

'And I've got the crubeen!' He sat by the table scooping it up with a spoon, and it wasn't until he had finished that he realised the apron stuffed into her mouth was not to stifle giggles, but sobs. He thought it best to leave her to it. Audrey said she'd been too damned calm. After clearing the table, he washed the dishes in the neat kitchen, and returned to the houseplace with tea.

'Better?'

Tessa blinked up at him and nodded. 'Sure, I don't know what came over me, at all . . . '

'Have some tea. Y'know if there's anything an army man's good at –' Oh, what a fool, he thought, put me great bog-trotting foot in it.

'You mustn't keep watching your words,' she said simply. 'Any of yous.'

'Very well.' He took some documents from the pocket of his tunic draped over the chair, and sat facing her across the table, which was now covered with a green chenille cloth.

'Tell me now, how much of an allowance did you receive from the army, for yourself and the kids?'

'Nothing regular. Every now and then there'd be a draft for fifteen shillings.'

'Is that all?'

'I gathered there'd been some mix up, with Finn not being good at the reading, y'know. Then he went overseas almost at once.'

'You mean you never made enquiries?'

'I didn't have the time. I was earning good money. I suppose if we'd had nothing I would have. And when Finn came home, he was in such a state that I hadn't the heart to worry him. Y'see he'd joined the army in the first place as a way of providing for us. If he'd known I'd been supporting us while he was away, the blow to his pride would've killed him before the consumption did.'

There was a silence in which the gas hissed softly, the fire spluttered agreeably, and Cormac let out a long low whistle through his teeth. 'Some shifty devil somewhere along the line's taken advantage of Finn, and swindled you – and probably others – of your dues. They made sure Finn got his allowance to allay suspicions about yours – which he obviously thought you were getting.'

'What lousy, cheating swine! They'd see Finn comin', God rest him. He was always a one for the mates . . . I only hope it wasn't that Tatty Entwistle or Nobby Clark. They'd know we weren't short of a bob or two because he told them I was on the halls. You must do something, Cormac – anything – not for me, but to stop some other poor gobeen being swindled?'

'By God, if it were my outfit they'd smart for a week!' He tapped the documents. 'We'll get to filling these in, and what with your widow's pension and a small army pension . . . ' The amber eyes twinkled mischievously, and she continued in the same vein.

' . . . And Patrick's seven and six, Joseph's one and six, laundry money. Oh, and Titch has arranged with Jonty for us to do the Sugar Loaf again till we renew our contract, so that will mean tips . . . '

'Which will make you a very rich woman altogether!'

'Shall we make a start, then?'

He unhooked his new fountain pen from the breast pocket of his shirt and toyed with it momentarily. 'Both pensions,' he said quietly, 'depend on one thing.'

'An' what's that?'

He drew in a long breath. 'Your marriage certificate. You will need it as proof that you are his widow, and the mother of his children. Tessa?' He leaned forward, amber eyes sharp in the gaslight. 'When you returned the borrowed ring you told me you hadn't got round to it, but were going to. That was some time ago. There is a certificate?'

Tessa's mind went blank. The world seemed to stop. 'At first I wouldn't, and then he wouldn't. I thought a marriage at a Registrar's Office would overcome the publicity, but Finn wasn't for it. Y'see, Cormac, when you've been together for so long and reared a family, it is marriage. You feel married.' And in a smaller voice, 'No certificate – no pension?'

'Jesus,' he sighed.

'Thanks just the same. It was decent of you to bother.' She didn't have to ask him not to breathe a word, not even to Audrey. It wasn't necessary. The lack of any pension could be explained by the army pay swindle. Whatever happened, the children, especially Patrick, must never know his parents were not married. He was a proud boy, like his granda, meticulous, liking everything to be right. Anything that would make him lose face was unthinkable. Then she noticed that Patrick had not returned the Madonna. Without saying a word, he had put it on the chest of drawers in the room he shared with Joseph.

'I'm afraid so, Mrs Collins,' said Doctor Louise Harris at the Welfare. She finished her examination. 'You are pregnant.'

'Will it be ... y'know, with Finn having the consumption a' all?'

'With you being so strong, I should say the child will still be delicate. You'll be very lucky if it's as strong as the others, and very unlucky if it has inherited your husband's disease. Look after yourself well, for the child's sake. Plenty of fresh milk, cod liver oil, oranges – and rest as much as you can ...' Her grave eyes met Tessa's. 'You will not do anything foolish, purges or mixtures from the druggist?'

'God, no, Doctor Louise.' She smiled ruefully. 'He was so weak and ill. You'd never think ... '

'It's quite often the case – the perpetuation of the life urge in the dying.'

So, that's what they called it, she thought on the way home. She had refused even to contemplate the memory, now the floodgates were open, and the thoughts poured into her mind . . . A child of despair, frustration, whose begetting had been an almost ghoulish act. To be left without money and in debt was a challenge, but a child . . . It had been very hard to accept, but, after talking to Doctor Louise, she was now just beginning to see beyond that dreadful night. Already she was feeling protective toward the little creature who was destined for such a rotten start in life.

Christmas was a lean one at Number Twenty-seven, but thankfully, Miss Wilkins had set a precedent the year before, and the Styleses, Audrey and Cormac, and Tessa's family flooded into the Wilkins' house after Mass. George, before going to his club stood on the landing, looked down into the hall on their arrival. Tessa had taken off her long grey coat and removed her scarf and gloves, and there she was, elegant in a dark green gown with a white Cavalier collar over her square shoulders, her fingers curled round a glass of sherry. Dear heaven, Effie, he thought, she'd down half a dozen of those in no time!

In the New Year after Kathleen's birthday, Tessa told the children about the baby due in June. Poor Mam, thought Patrick, so that's why she'd collapsed on the yard steps in her nightgown, God save her. Oh his lovely, singing Mam. And what about her and Titch going on the boards? Oh, wasn't life rotten. Aloud he said, 'That's nice, Mam, but you'll have to take it a bit easier.'

Joseph looked uncertain; his beautiful eyes levelled with hers as he muttered, 'It's n . . . n . . . not c . . . coming in our bed.'

Kathleen said nothing. She had resented her mother keeping them away from Dad, going on about giving him peace and leaving him alone or he'd cough and go worse. She had wanted to curl up on the sofa with him, tell him stories, bring him drinks; and now he'd died, gone without a word. 'Toodle-oo' he used to say, and wave the ends of his fingers. He'd gone without a kiss, and Mam had got a baby. It wasn't fair the way she had left him to go to the music hall with Titch. The way she'd suddenly got those single beds, given them all jobs to do. And when Joseph started at St Gregory's, she'd be too busy with the new baby for the rest of them. Kathleen said nothing.

Audrey and Cormac came to the Sugar Loaf, Audrey looking happier than she had ever been, her arm tucked through his in a propriatorial manner. Tessa told them her news, blurting it out over a glass of Guinness.

'Don't be after feeling sorry for me, for God's sake! Cheer up. I have – now. It took a bit of getting used to.'

'But Finn . . . ' began Audrey.

'Before he died . . . ' said Tessa softly. 'I didn't know anything like that would happen. He was so ill. But it did, and here I am, all two of me!'

'Congratulations,' said Cormac slowly.

I bet he's thinking to himself that's bastard number four, thought Tessa.

'Don't want to sound nosey, but how are you for money?' asked Audrey.

'I'd be a lot better off if Jonty wasn't so mean – he doesn't pay me, y'know. I'm back on tips. But God's good.'

'Tessa's affairs must be doubtful,' observed Audrey on the way home, 'for her to be reflecting on the goodness of God!'

Cormac was silent. He had been with Finn toward the end more than most, and now tried to shut his mind to the prospect of that vital woman, warm and enthusiastic for life, clasped in the arms of death. No wonder Patrick said she'd been sick . . . Merciful Lord, she was brave. But, as Effie once said, careless. Careless never to have got around to marriage.

The first intimation of trouble came with Toby Greenledge. He hovered at the corner of the street until Kathleen and Joseph had gone to the children's theatre at Ancoats Hall, and then pounced at the door. It being Friday night, Tessa knew it would be him. The rent was still five weeks behind.

He stood facing her over the square table. 'There's been a delegation of neighbours refusing to pay their rent unless you are evicted. They want you out, Mrs Collins, because they reckon you betrayed your invalid husband with Captain O'Shea. You are in arrears with the rent, and therefore I can evict you. Unless, of course you can prove none of this is true. I may add they have witnesses to Captain O'Shea coming and going, staying for hours, waiting until the children have gone out.'

'Like you have just done.'

He moved to and fro, almost dancing in his agitation, noticing out of the corner of his eye, the improvements done to the property. He was beginning to regret being swayed by the delegation. 'I told them they were mistaken. That your way of life is a bit unconventional for round here, but you were a good wife and mother.'

'Thanks.' The sarcasm was lost on him.

'So, you're not in a certain condition on account of Captain O'Shea?'

She stared at him. He felt the utter astonishment radiating from her, an astonishment that grew into outrage. 'How dare you say such things under my roof? I shall have the arrears of rent on your desk on Monday morning, and if there's not an apology for so slanderous a statement, Captain O'Shea will be consulting his lawyers. God in heaven, Mr Greenledge, you've not heard the last of this!'

He retreated before the fury in her eyes, the red spots of anger on her cheekbones, the vehemence of her soul, and with quick jerky little steps he hurried out.

Shortly after, it was Father Quinn who sat on the Mafeking sofa, carefully turning his biretta round and round. Were they all queuing up at the street corner? she wondered.

'This is all very distressing for me, Mrs Collins,' he added after having mentioned an appeal from certain parishioners.

'And I'm having the time of me life, I suppose!'

'How can you swear this child is Finn's when he was so ill? It's impossible.'

'How do you know what's possible and what isn't? You weren't here.'

'Really, my child, you are quite determined to brazen it out aren't you?'

'Brazen it out? Just you listen to me, Father Quinn. I, who had hoped to resume a promising career on the music hall, am bearing the child of a consumptive man. At best it will be delicate, at worst like its father. My money went on nursing Finn and there is nothing from the army because of a swindle. The insurance man's done a bunk so the policy's void. We get by on what my children earn and the laundry. Through all the gossip, tips at the Sugar Loaf are thin. What I can do without is you coming here and adding to my burdens with tittle-tattle!'

The biretta was turning faster. Its owner stood up wondering how so wilful a woman had produced so fine a son as Patrick. 'You are overwrought . . . ' he said, wishing he had not come.

'Overwrought!' she yelled, jumping up and opening the door. 'I'm bloody furious!'

The following afternoon George Wilkins, sure of finding her alone, called with the laundry money. The surprise showed on her face. He was inside at once. His brown eyes saw not a flushed face and a rekindling of yesterday's indignation, but a glowing, golden figure. He came toward her, rubbing his hands together. 'Marry me,' he said. 'Marry me. I don't care who the father of your child is. Just say you'll have me and we'll go away and start a new life.'

'Sure, that makes a change from the others,' she said with cool civility. 'But, no. I can't. I do not want to marry you. No, don't touch me.' Then quietly and with dignity, she asked 'Will you be going now?' She drew upon herself that marvellous reserve that prevented remonstrance and left him speechless.

When he had gone, she rummaged on the mantelshelf and finding a pencil, hastily scribbled a note. When Joseph returned from Flood's she sent him to the Sugar Loaf with it.

Jonty in the bar served George Wilkins, and indicated the note.

'Tessa Collins is not coming back. Looks as though there's truth in these rumours after all.' Wilkins winced. 'Saves me giving her the push . . . not as popular with all the talk. Now what's got into him!' he asked as Wilkins went out, leaving his drink. 'Titch!' he yelled. 'You're on yer own, Tessa's jacked it in!'

And after closing time, Titch's perky face peered up to the bar. 'Jonty,' he called cheerfully. 'You'll be on yer own again – I'm jacking it in.'

Chapter Twenty-Six

Tessa opened the door. 'Titch, at this hour! You'll be getting me a bad name!' They both laughed as he entered the houseplace. He pulled a bottle out of each pocket, his own brand of light ale and a Guinness. Plonking them on the table littered with song sheets, programmes and designs, he grinned. There were costumes on hooks and props littering the sofa.

'Right lass, celebration!'

'I knew you'd come,' she declared happily, filling the glasses. 'And thanks for the drink. Dear God, do I need it! They've all been here, from Greenledge to Quinn, with rumours and accusations galore! She could not bring herself to repeat the accusation that Cormac was the father of her child. 'I need work, Titch. I really haven't the heart for all this arsing about with laundry when there's good money to made on the boards, and I'm just aching to get back to the limes.' She took a long appreciative drink. 'I'm not prepared to wait until Broadhead's panto's have finished. Greenledge has threatened to have me out, mainly because of all this gossip, but if I'm straight with the rent I can cope with the rest. I think I put the fear of God into him by mentioning the Poor Man's Lawyer scheme at the Settlement! But I want you to fix something, Titch. Somewhere, anywhere, any distance.'

'But –'

'The baby? Sure, I've worked it all out.'

'I thought you might.'

'And it wouldn't be the first to be born backstage!'

'Spoken like a trouper. I've got something fixed.'

'You've not?'

'D'you remember the audition at the Metropole, the manager with a crimson cravat and living off his nerves?'

'I do so.'

'He's come up in the world. I was tuning the old Joanna at the Tivoli when he comes up and cracks a joke about Little Titch. Well, I said we were on the up and up, fed up with the Broadhead circuit. To cut a long story short, we're on at the Tivoli! I was going to tell you after closing time. We start Monday night.'

'Monday! You were taking a chance.'

He shook his head. 'We're a pair, Tessa, professionally our minds think alike. See, I've brought the contract for your signature and it'll be on his desk, personally delivered tomorrow.'

'You're priceless! Where are we on the bill?'

'The middle.'

'Who's top? Who else is on?'

Questions came thick and fast. Titch took out his note-book, she took up her pencil, and over the rest of the Guinness they worked out the songs. Then, over a pot of tea, she outlined her scheme for disguising advanced pregnancy, and over a late supper of bread and cheese they worked out distances, fares, conditions and times.

Annie Cooper saw Titch going across to the lavatory at least twice after eleven o'clock. She told Mrs Hewitt at the corner shop. 'So you can tell how long he was there.'

'Greenledge went, yer know,' said Mrs Hewitt. 'Told her straight. "They are respectable people," he said. "And I won't have my property used as a knocking shop." Now, that's telling her.'

Annie hadn't heard it that way through the wall, but then, Ronnie had been grizzling.

Tessa, looking her best, feeling better and more positive than for some time, was Toby Greenledge's first caller on Monday morning. She placed not only the arrears on his desk but a month's rent in advance. Fancy, he was impressed, being able to lay hands on so much money so quickly.

Titch had been insistent. 'We're a partnership,' he had said. 'We'll regard this as an advance to be deducted from your earnings. Oh, I know you're Proud Riley's daughter and can't help yer upbringing, but this is like a first night again. It's not just to be good, but bloody marvellous. Yer mind's got to be free . . . ' She was still bent on refusal. 'Unless, of course, you want the kids to come home and find their stuff out on the street.' She had accepted the money meekly, thankfully, but with bowed head.

The following day being a Saturday, the accent at the Settlement was on leisure activities. With a gathering of Ancoats folk there, for not all were averse to the Settlement, Tessa dreaded the rumours reaching Audrey before she did. Of course, the rumours might just have been confined to a few streets, but she couldn't take any chances. Joseph was sent to Ancoats Hall with a note of enquiry about Audrey and Elfreda. Apparently both were off duty until the Saturday Social that evening. Tessa sighed with satisfaction. Due to the Sugar Loaf, she had only accompanied the children once or twice before, but she would go down with them this evening. The Social was held every fourth Saturday of the month in the old Swedenborgian Round Chapel adapted by the Settlement people and known as the Round House. Tessa thought the dances dreary affairs compared to the hooleys at Ennan, but the kids seemed to think them fun.

So concerned was she about Audrey's reaction to the rumours that they were halfway down Every Street before she realised Cormac might be present. Dear God, however would she face him again! They reached the Settlement and Joseph, pushing on ahead, opened the door and ran in; Kathleen followed more sedately. The recreation room was lined with chairs along the walls. At the far end was a trestle table, and on a platform was a three-piece band. Dozens of young people stood about in groups or couples. David and Patrick there already, looked smart in their suits, their hair glistening with Rowland's Hair Oil, as Kathleen ran to join them, Tessa, relieved at Cormac's absence, grabbed Audrey by the arm.

'Thank God. You've not heard these scurvy rumours, I can tell you've not.'

'Sounds intriguing.'

'Don't talk to me about intrigue!'

Hesitantly, and choosing her words carefully, Tessa related all the events of yesterday and ended, 'I just wanted you to hear it all first hand. Sure, it's terrible embarrassing . . . Will you ask Cormac not to call without yourself?'

'You mean I'm to be a chaperone, like our aunts had! Oh, you silly goose!' Then more seriously, 'But why not leave things as they are – ignore the whole bloody lot!'

'I just don't intend to give 'em room for more gossip.'

'They have got through to you, haven't they?'

'Yes. I can take anything, but when they're inventing lies about good people like yerself and Cormac – Father Quinn will make it reflect on the Settlement . . . '

'I don't know why you stay there.'

'They'd see it as running away, as driving me out. Besides, people are people. I'm used to Loom Street, and just now with going on the boards and the baby due in June, I couldn't take another upheaval. If I move from here it will be back to Ireland . . . Oh saints preserve us, Cormac's just arrived. Don't tell him anything till I've gone – I'd be mortified.'

The band was thumping out a waltz, and David, who was teaching Kathleen the steps, said proudly to Cormac, 'We have dancing lessons at school.'

'You wouldn't think so!' He winked at Kathleen and walked up the room. 'Merciful Lord, Tessa, did you ever set eyes on such stilted dancers. Now, if you want to see style, wait until Audrey and me do the "Gaby Glide"!'

Tessa said she did not know which would be worse, made her excuses, and fled.

But on Monday, Cormac and Audrey, Nick and Elfreda went to watch Tessa's successful appearance at the Tivoli, and in the bar afterwards, amid congratulations and hilarity, the rumours were discussed in the safety of numbers, and Tessa found her embarrassment gradually dissolving.

Because the baby was due at any time, Tessa did not tag along at the back of the Whitsuntide procession as she usually did; nor would she risk a place in Albert Square. What with twenty thousand walking and as many spectators, it was no place for an advanced pregnancy. She decided to watch from a less crowded vantage point.

Audrey and Elfreda had been delegated to look after a contingent of suffragettes for the silent raising of banners en route, but Audrey had slipped over to Ancoats to help Tessa dress Joseph and Kathleen in their finery. None of the children in the street called at Number Twenty-seven to be admired and be given a Whitsun penny, nor did Tessa's children go to Mrs Barnes or the Pattersons.

When Audrey returned to her suffrage duties, Tessa took Kathleen and Joseph to the Sacred Heart school room where the procession assembled and then boarded a tram to Miller Street, for all the churches on the Ancoats side walked via Pin Mill Brow, leaving Ashton Old Road free for the Ardwick scholars.

The Protestant processions had taken place on Monday, and now, as then, all Manchester was closed, apart from Jewish places of work and the Lyon's Corner tea shops. All traffic was re-routed, barriers erected, areas cordoned off, Red Cross and policeman on duty, and in the distance the sound of the Crossley Motor Works brass band filled the heart with anticipation. The walks took place even if the heavens opened, but today the weather was hot and set for a record number of faintings.

Tessa, standing in the shade of a drapery shop canopy, was thankful for the offer of a chair from the draper's wife. Sitting by the edge of the pavement, she was thrilled at the tableaux and the colour schemes, the formations, the flowers, and the bluster and bustle of the bands.

At the head of every procession was a band. Those churches who could afford it vied for industry's best: Armstrong Whitworth's bandsmen in their blue and gold uniforms; Beyer-Peacock rich in scarlet; and Clayton Aniline leading up St Alyosious. All these made for colourful music, especially when they converged on each other. Sometimes Beyer-Peacock's would swiftly change their tune to compliment Crossley's, others less competent fought it out with venom.

As St Ann's, noted for their all white 'spectacular', passed, Tessa had heard the Sacred Heart Pipe Band in the distance. At the front was Marr the Piper, not on the pipes, but wielding the mace with all the dexterity of his swaggering personality. Kilted, and with white boots, Irish tartan, and black Glengarry bonnet, the size of him called up a lot of admiration – from those who didn't know poor Mrs Marr.

Tessa hoped he would drop the mace, but knew he wouldn't. She saw Tony Cooper, his freckled face already pink, raising the sticks of the kettle drum to just beneath his eyes in a pause.

Behind the band came the massive banner. Tessa stood up. It was a thrilling sight, the great, glowing sacred heart of Christ, elevated, richly embroidered, the tapestry mounted on mahogany poles, and the bearers praying there'd be no wind.

David and Patrick, along with the altar boys and servers, walked with the clerical party, sweating in cassocks and lace-edged surplices. Joseph was one of four pageboys holding the long blue train of a life-sized Virgin Mary, keeping it from sweeping the cobbles. They wore knee breeches of the same blue with white blouses. He saw her, waved and smiled happily. Behind the pageboys and before the infants, who always captivated the spectators, were the Attendants of Mary, half a dozen young girls, among whom was Kathleen. She looked tall and older than her twelve years in the simply cut long white dress, with a sash about her waist and a circlet of blue and white flowers in her dark hair. Tessa was still pondering whether Kathleen had seen her or not when she heard a voice at her elbow.

'And I've taken photographs of them all.'

'Cormac!' Tessa turned. 'What the devil are you doing here?'

'Detailed, ma'am, by my superior, to evacuate personnel immediately after the Sacred Heart contingent had mustered!'

She laughed and shook her head as though despairing of him. He returned the chair and led her along the street.

'I don't know what I'd do without you all.' She was still smiling as he helped her into the cab.

'Corner of Every Street. The Sugar Loaf,' he directed, and then said to Tessa, 'Begod, d'you remember me hauling you on the wagon when you were carrying Patrick!' He tilted his head back and laughed. He had a low, vibrant kind of laugh, which rippled pleasantly over the ears. 'And none of us dreamed I'd be doing it again fifteen years later. I'm nearly forty, y'know.'

'You don't look it. Not a grey hair in sight.'

'I must say I don't feel it.'

It was cool in the cab. Cool and pleasant. Comfortable and nice, thought Tessa. I could stay here for ever. Cormac was very easy to be with, no wonder Audrey was eternally in love with him . . .

'Here we are, my –' Cormac stopped and covered whatever he had been going to say with military parlance. 'Personnel safely at base. Mission accomplished!' In a softer tone he added, 'You promised Audrey to rest up for tonight's performance while the kids were out.'

'I did so, and I will. Thanks for your company, and for taking the photographs. I hope Audrey's not been arrested with her banner!' She stood on the pavement with a tranquil dignity, her height and the long, loose coat taking the look off her pregnancy. She raised a hand. The cab moved off.

Titch would collect her that evening, they had arranged it all; a cab was to be there at half-past six. She still couldn't bring herself to have a cab come to the door, it would seem like showing off, even though they all knew she boarded it round the corner.

While resting on the sofa, with the street and house quiet, and the blind drawn against the sun, she wished that the baby would be born tomorrow night after the show – not that any of hers had been accommodating before at all – so she could have all day Sunday and Monday to rest and care for it. She and Elfreda had chosen a wicker baby basket for easy transport. You couldn't leave a baby from half-past six until gone eleven, but it wasn't fair to make Kathleen responsible, as had happened when Joseph was a child.

She was very much aware that Finn's death had affected Kathleen more than the others, but any attempt to comfort or talk about it was rebuffed in a manner that was chilling in one so young. How would I ever find the courage to face her with the truth of Finn not being her real da, if she had to know? All these reflections saddened Tessa. Never having known a mother's affection herself, she had subconsciously expected the relationship to be there, just like it was with the boys.

Not that Kathleen wasn't helpful. In these last days of pregnancy she had indeed been what Mrs Barnes called 'a little mother, busy in the scullery, making the tea, standing over Joseph while he washed behind his ears, making sure he hadn't a 'tidemark' round his neck and that he wore a clean gansey.

Her mind returned to work. Thank God, anyway, that next week they were at the Tivoli in Peter Street and not as far as Oldham or Ashton. She had disguised her condition fairly well, so far as the management had been concerned. Long flowing draperies, crinolines, frills, cloaks and beautiful big hats; and for these last weeks, she had provided a lavish spectacle, appearing on a float decorated with the theme of the evening.

At seven o'clock the following night, Tessa, knowing herself to be in the early stages of labour, sat in the female dressing room, applying her make-up. It was more of a long corridor than a room, with a black marble slab as a make-up table running the length of the wall, a long, low mirror, and four chairs in front of it. Yes, she thought, these are the pains begod, and I'll just about make it.

She applied the carmine to her cheeks thoughtfully. It was grand to be at the Tivoli where the house was small and intimate, as opposed to Broadhead's stages of fifty or sixty feet. Yet you usually got the same big laugh and a large hand.

'Reeve Sisters coming off!' the boy outside shouted. 'Mr Bush please?'

Tessa inhaled deeply and looked at herself with satisfaction. In the background, drums rolled, the double bass throbbed and Mr Bush ran to the wings. Tessa always gave herself plenty of time, and especially so tonight. Titch had impressed upon her that neglect of the time sheet was a terrible thing. If your time was eight o'clock you had to be in the wings at five minutes to; if you were late on stage there was a fine of threepence a minute.

Tessa and Titch waited in the wings trying to interpret the mood of the audience, wondering whether their new 'Honeysuckle' spectacle would get the house or the bird. Saturday-night audiences were more critical. The seats cost more and they wanted their money's worth.

She had stood in the wings many times before, watching the famous, lost in admiration at the sheer artistry that made star quality. George Formby, Florrie Ford, Gertie Gitina, Kate Gannon, and once, only once she had seen the Queen of them all, Marie Lloyd.

Mr Bush, leaving the audience in a good mood, hurried off and Titch, taking advantage, hurried on with his musical warm-up. The float, propelled on to the stage with a large pole, was beautifully decorated with honeysuckle, and there were artfully illuminated grottoes where bees appeared to hover.

Tessa smiled. The audience took it up and the welcome roared from pit to gallery. It was a smile of excitement and anticipation as the sea of faces, the lights, the atmosphere of make-believe, transported Tessa to a magical world.

Her followers knew she was going to sing 'You Are My Honeysuckle', but she and Titch kept them waiting. He played the opening bars, and switched swiftly to 'Won't You Come Home, Bill Bailey', causing Tessa to rummage furiously amongst the honeysuckle for a Bill Bailey cap and scarf. The audience lapped up the foolery, but the third time, Tessa, feigning the utmost frustration, threw a soft shoe at his head, and while he was supposedly unconscious on the floor, she pitched her voice low and gave them 'Honeysuckle' unaccompanied. Taking them for a brief moment from the sulphur-laden heat of Manchester to the sweetly scented gardens of make believe. The audience joined in the chorus, swaying from side to side in their seats, and when it was over, roared, 'Encore! Encore!'

Titch glanced into the wings, seeking permission, for an encore could throw the timing of the bill. The manager signalled assent, and they launched into a final rendering.

Cormac, with a cab ready at the stage door, waited for Tessa outside the dressing room. This was usually Titch's assignment, but he had agreed to play for a singer at the Gaiety whose pianist had run off with a chorus girl, giving no notice. Getting no answer, he opened the door. 'Tessa!'

She was walking slowly toward him, holding onto the wall. 'How about that for good timing?' she smiled wanly.

'Only second to foolhardiness,' he exclaimed scooping her up. 'By heaven, 'tis a weight, y'are!' he joked, stumbling along the corridor to the stage door. 'St Mary's and quick!'

Getting out on Oxford Road, he supported her to the doorway marked 'Admittance'. As soon as they appeared, the nurse stared at Tessa's crinoline and lopsided coronet of honeysuckle, and then at the dark-haired man who looked even more attractive in his anxiety. She had just decided they were party drunks when the honeysuckle struck a chord of memory.

'It's the music hall star, Tessa Collins, from the Tivoli?'

'It is so, and she's in labour. The child could be delicate. We don't want to take any chances, run any risks. I assure you labour is advanced. Now, for the love of God, will you attend her at once!'

Nurses were called, room prepared, and Cormac waited. They brought him tea, he smoked his pipe and wondered how she was getting on. He thought affectionately of Finn, and decided there was no justice in this world of sin and deceit. He swore, and went out to walk round the block. As a man of action he was not given to waiting about. He wanted so much to give her his arm to hold onto, to wipe the sweat from her forehead, to crack a joke. He couldn't stand it any longer. The corridors were silent, as only hospital corridors can be after midnight. He followed the notices to 'Delivery Rooms', stripping off his coat, scarf and shoes as he went. The rooms were all in darkness, except one. He pushed open the door and stepped inside. The midwife made a lunge to get him out; he made a lunge toward Tessa, legs strung up, lying on her back in a white gown. Her eyes were staring, the smudges of make-up highlighted the pallor and fatigue on her face.

Merciful Lord, he thought, she's given up! 'Get her legs down,' he commanded. 'Out of the stirrups, quickly!' The nurse obeyed. 'She's . . . ' He looked at their clinical, city hospital faces. How could he explain she was a natural creature who responded to the familiar, to whom this kind of thing was alien. She had gone into shock. Given up.

He raised her head and shoulders onto his arm and knelt by the delivery table so his voice was on a level with her ear.

'Tessa . . . ?'

'Really, Captain O'Shea, this is most unethical – '

'Open your eyes, Tessa. It's Cormac.'

'There are laws against – '

'This isn't like you, Tessa. Can you not feel the pains?'

'I will not tolerate such interference in my delivery room!'

'Make the effort, Tessa. You've got the show Monday night. Oh, for Christ's sake, Tessa . . . Tessa, I love you. For my sake, for Finn's sake, think of this baby . . . '

A voice came to her out of the mist . . . Finn? No, Finn was pacing the deck, walking the streets. The mist lifted a little and the lilting voice continued . . . The wandering minstrel with a cane beneath his arm instead of a fiddle. Her hand rested on the muscular arm. The voice came out of the mist, talking to her, encouraging her, coaxing her to feel the pains, to push, push her way out of the mist. Holding his arm for support, she struggled until the mist had cleared.

'Tessa, you and Finn have a daughter, a little colleen. God love you both,' he said as the nurse placed the baby in her arms. 'I'll be back soon,' he said, with a cockeyed smile. 'I'm going on deck for a smoke. Just outside whilst the afterbirth . . . y'know . . . and then I'll take you home for breakfast.'

Tessa sighed deeply and smiled gratefully.

'That was close,' she heard the nurse say. 'Would've been a gonner except for him. You should have seen the midwife's face! She stormed out, threatened to get Matron, and tripped over the coat and shoes he'd thrown off! Who said it's boring on night duty. And she's Tessa Collins, the Irish singer!'

Tessa rested in bed on Sunday, but was up by the evening. None of the neighbours called. No, they were not condoning adultery and loose living by wetting this baby's head. Tessa was relieved. Miss Wilkins and some of the Settlement people called after Mass, the former with a basket of cold chicken and custard pie. 'And a bottle of sherry for your visitors to drink the baby's health.' Audrey came with Cormac in the evening, and Elfreda and Nick called in the afternoon on their way to Boggart Hole Clough. Although tiny, the little face was beautiful, capped with wispy black curls. Her forehead was set wide, and Tessa knew the sapphire-blue eyes would not change colour.

'If I'm going to sip some sherry and drink her health,'

declared Miss Wilkins, looking at Kathleen and Joseph, 'I'll
need to know her name.'

'Tivoli,' said Tessa. 'Tivoli Teresa Collins, what's wrong
with that?'

Everything according to the neighbours. Lovely, thought
Titch. Daft, thought Kathleen and Joseph. Patrick was
embarrassed and refused to tell anyone for days. Father
Quinn thought it in keeping with a character as irresponsible
as to have had it baptised at once by a visiting priest; and with
no godparents. Audrey and Elfreda considered it novel and
wouldn't have been surprised to see it start a trend. Cormac,
looking down at her in the wicker basket, silently promised
Finn that his frail legacy would be treasured. 'Tivvy,' he said
aloud. And Tivvy she became.

'But Annie,' said Mrs Hewitt, 'It's the spitting image
of Finn.'

'That proves nothing,' replied Annie Cooper.

Chapter Twenty-Seven

The birth of a daughter to Manchester's own, very own, Tessa Collins, 'The Colleen from Connemara', was related to the press by Titch Bradley.

'Best-kept stage secret!' ran the caption in the *Herald*.

'Baby named after theatre!' declared the *Chronicle*.

'The show must go on!'

And it went on on Monday night with a flourish. Tessa took curtain calls, the dressing room was filled with flowers, and bottles of champagne were sent backstage. Although Tivoli was not born in the dressing room, it was, said the manager, 'as near as damn it to swearing'.

Little Tivvy, in her wicker basket, was fussed and watched over by dressers, cigarette girls, and those sharing the bill. She was a good baby and slept through endless rolls of drums, stage calls, trolleys trundling and dressing-room tantrums.

Doctor Louise pronounced Tivvy to be a little under-weight; she had not the lusty yell of a more robust child, but with care should outgrow these deficiencies. Nevertheless, it was during periods of growth that an inherited weakness could develop. Children with such a constitution should not be exposed to cold and inclement weather, and should not be allowed to 'outgrow their strength'.

Tessa missed the Connemara shawl, for all her babies had been enfolded in its warmth – as a nest, to crawl on, to be wrapped in and be sheltered under when she had worn it. But Tessa had gone to the Ancoats Mortuary Chapel before the undertakers had fastened down the lid of Finn's coffin and had covered him with the shawl, tucking it beneath his chin as she had when he was ill in Downey's barn. Although he was buried in England, where he had wanted to be, she thought it only right that a little bit of Ireland should be with him at the end.

'Ladies and Gentlemen! We, the officials of the 1914 Lancashire Show, are sorry to inform you that the Gordon Highlanders will not grace this occasion with their magnificent display. We have received a telegram to say they are held back for mobilisation.'

Like a chill wind, the news whistled round the show. There had been one European crisis after another, but the full impact of these crises was only just being realised in Ancoats. A state of emergency was declared, and Father Quinn offered Masses for peace.

Despite, or because of, the situation, Mancunians were determined to enjoy their well-earned bank holiday. On this first Monday in August, commonly known as August Monday – which Tessa would remember for ever as the day Finn came home in a military ambulance – the Sacred Heart outing was to Blackpool. It was to be the last for a long time.

The mills, furnaces and foundries had shut down on Saturday afternoon, and as a consequence the pall of smoke had lifted, and a blue sky with puffy white clouds and a warm sun augured well for the treat.

Extra trains were laid on to cope with day-trippers, and David and Patrick in their best suits and white straw hats stood a little apart, trying not to look involved. Father Quinn, hot already and struggling with tea urns, pushed towards them several large baskets full of teacakes sandwiched together with jam. 'Here, you two, give a hand and get these on board.' With expressions of pain creasing their handsome foreheads they were cajoled into service.

At last everyone was aboard the Blackpool train. Each compartment seating eight on either side instead of the customary six, the long-awaited day trip to the coast had begun. Tessa, with Tivvy in her arms, sat next to Effie Wilkins; Kathleen, sitting with Joseph by the window, looked cool and detached in a sprigged muslin frock and hairband to match.

Tessa, because of the laundry and Finn not being inclined to social events beyond the Sugar Loaf, had never been on the annual trip and was looking forward to it. It was the first time also for Miss Wilkins, who had not wanted to be in the house alone in case war was declared. George, in anticipation of such an event, was spending the day at the office, already working out schemes for increased production. He had ceased altogether to upbraid his sister for associating with Tessa Collins. The ground for such criticism had, he felt, been swept from beneath his feet.

The Coopers were represented by Tony who was sixteen, and as a messenger boy at Pomona docks reputed to earn good money. It was not in his nature to include his mother or one of the younger children on the outing; being one of a large family, Tony had learned early to grab what he could and hold on to it.

Flat-nosed and freckle-faced, he had inherited a cheeky charm from his mother, and a stocky figure which in later years could run to fat. 'Your kid's growing up real nice,' he observed to Patrick. 'Don't see much of her – ' and giving him a nudge ' – Not as much as I'd like to.'

'You'd better keep it that way,' replied Patrick, 'if you know what's good for you.'

'Just 'cos yer ma's on the music hall, you think . . . ' Tony's voice trailed as he noticed Tessa looking at him, and flushing pink over his freckles, he turned to Patterson's youngest, a pale youth whom he could count on to be impressed with his bravado.

'I don't fancy the idea of him running loose on the beach with Kathleen,' murmured David. 'He's a bully y'know – thump her soon as look. Why don't we take her with us up the Tower and everything, she'd like that.'

'No, Dave, not bloomin' likely! If she was your sister you wouldn't want her at your heels. Besides, Joseph would want to come and I have enough of 'em at home! Joseph'll protect her. Uncle Cormac's been teaching him some army fighting – he's a right little tyke when he gets going.'

Tessa found herself wondering, not for the first time, whether Cormac and Audrey were making the bank holiday into one of their illicit long weekends. It would all depend on his duties she supposed. She had only seen him three times in the weeks since Tivvy's birth. And try as she did, she could not ignore the memory of his voice in the delivery room, frantic and husky with emotion: 'For Finn's sake . . . my sake, Tessa . . . Tessa, I love you . . . ' It must have been her imagination, and how foolish of herself to keep dwelling on it . . .

Having arrived at Central Station in Blackpool, the Sacred Heart congregation were mustered into some kind of order, and proceeded to the sands. Marr the Piper and the other big men could have been porters on Shudehill Market, the way they shouldered and jostled great baskets, hampers, tea urns and all the impediments of a congregation on the move. Children, kept in order both by the promise of a bucket and spade and fear of what would happen if they got lost, trotted along obediently. Father Quinn, like Moses bent on the Promised Land, carved his way remorselessly along the promenade and down to the Central Pier, where everyone claimed a patch of sand and became the target of an army of street vendors.

Patrick and David commandeered two orange-striped canvas deck chairs for mother and aunt, which they then erected with difficulty and hoots of laughter in the shade of the pier where the air was refreshing and cool. Tessa and Miss Wilkins, still laughing, sank down gratefully. They watched the young of the parish, giggling, splashing and paddling in pools round the base of the limpet-covered pillars; they fussed over Tivvy; and couldn't help but discuss the terrible likelihood of war.

'We're going now, Aunt,' said David, and, indicating Tony, added, 'Watch he doesn't start tormenting Kathleen.'

'Where are you going to?'

'Oh, round and about . . . ' He leaned down to whisper: 'Anywhere to avoid having to distribute those jammy teacakes!'

She shook her faded honey-coloured head and smiled after them. 'Almost young men,' she remarked uneasily.

Jud Patterson, trousers rolled to the knee and accompanied by his wife, stopped to exchange a few words. 'Eh, little un's comin' on.'

'She is so,' replied Tessa, pulling the parasol aside from Tivvy's face.

'Just like her dad,' declared Jud, and then with concern, 'Are you geetin' over it, lass? It'll tek time, y'know.'

When they had gone, Effie lowered her voice. 'I'm not so sure about time, so far as Kathleen's concerned. She seems to have altered since her father died.'

'Yes, but I don't know what to do about it. She's never forgiven me for keeping her away from her da, or for getting the single beds. But at the time, Miss Wilkins, with all those precautions and worries about infection, sure I didn't know which day it was. And sometimes I wonder if she holds it against me for not giving her some responsibility for Tivvy. Perhaps she feels I'm not sharing her da's baby with her, but out of the three, she's the least interested in her little sister . . . and yet, at the same time, she's so fierce about everything, as if half measures didn't exist.'

'It is difficult,' sighed Miss Wilkins. 'The young can be very hard. They tend to see things in black and white. David certainly does – he doesn't get on at all well with his father, no matter how diplomatically I try to manage them! But you'll never have any trouble with your Patrick.'

'Unless he misses the train!'

The objects of their conversation, feeling like young men about town, were off, determined to spend their money as soon as possible. They soared up the five hundred and twenty feet of Blackpool Tower in the lift, and stood on the observation platform gazing in wonderment at the Fylde coast beneath. Down they plunged into the Tower buildings, goggled at the fishes in the great aquarium, shook hands with monkeys in the zoo, and swaggered round the Italian Gardens.

'This is the life,' grinned Patrick. 'Better than mucking out stables!'

'And better than my father going on about the Archduke Ferdinand!'

Then determined to see everything, from young ladies in Vesta Tilley suits parading under the auspices of the Pier Concert Party, to ridiculous rides on donkeys called Phyllis and Mabel. They were hauled aboard the train by a distracted Father Quinn, just as the guard brought the green flag down with a triumphant flourish.

Tuesday dawned. The seaside was now a memory; people

were back at work and talked of nothing but the likelihood of war. Children who popped tar bubbles and got it on their clothes wondered why parents were too preoccupied to deliver the expected clout. The day seemed long, but eventually the shadows of the mill chimneys lengthened on the flagged streets, and the sun sank.

The air seemed to throb and pulsate. An announcement was expected as to whether war would be averted. Music halls were packed, as were most public places. It was a bit like Mafeking night, thought Tessa; an entire community on the streets, wanting to be together, wanting to share the emotional outcome of the news. The Town Hall clock struck eleven. The Mayor made an announcement. Great Britain was at war with Germany – God Save the King.

If anything quelled the strikes and industrial conflict of the last two or three years, it was the declaration of war. Suffragettes quickly enrolled as nurses, munition workers, or ambulance drivers; strikers worked loyally in their industries or answered General Kitchener's call to arms; and despite the shelving of the contentious Home Rule Bill, Irishmen of both persuasions enlisted in the British Army.

Almost at once posters croped up like mushrooms on a dung heap: YOUR COUNTRY NEEDS YOU. And in Manchester, men, especially the young, queued outside buildings commandeered as recruiting offices, as eager to get to the war as they had been to get to Blackpool. Within three weeks the British Army in France were already retreating from Mons with a loss of fifteen thousand lives.

General Kitchener wanted yet more men to stem the tide of the German advance, and while the public were adjusting their shocked emotions to the losses of Mons, there was at Ypres a fierce battle lasting three weeks which claimed another fifty thousand – and still Kitchener called for more.

By the time Tivvy was a year old, the Rolls of Honour had grown longer; the *Lusitania* had been sunk by German submarines; zeppelins had bombed South End; and almost half of Tessa's audiences were in uniform.

When Tessa looked back, Tivvy's first birthday party was the last time they were all together. They were all squashed in at Number Twenty-seven, packed on to the Mafeking sofa, occupying the four new ladder back chairs, with Joseph perched on a stool, Tivvy in the latest style of what they now called a 'pram' by the open door, and Kathleen hovering by the scullery. But even then, they had not all been there. Nick was in Dover supervising a massive training of shire horses, who, instead of pulling ploughs and haycarts, would now be pulling heavy artillery.

'Poor Little Tivvy,' declared Cormac, as she sat upright in her pram, looking anything but poor, and watching all these people with a lively interest. 'It's the colleen's first birthday and we're all gathered together so solemnly.'

'You'll all be gone,' complained Tessa. 'What with Nick away already, and Elfreda joining the WRAC – what as, Elfreda?'

'Telegraphist, I've volunteered for France,' Elfreda's excitement showed in her smile, her eyes. 'Speak the language like a native, so I'm in with a chance.'

Tessa shivered. If she lived to be a hundred she would never understand this madness that made sane people do crazy things.

'And Audrey, you're after going to London, driving ambulances. Though why you can't drive 'em in Manchester, I don't know.'

'The wounded will disembark at Dover,' Cormac pointed out kindly. 'They'll need transport from ship to hospital.'

'And I,' said Effie, in an attempt to diffuse the seriousness, 'will knit Balaclava helmets and write you all long newsy letters.'

Tessa did not ask Cormac what the War Office had in store for him. He seemed quieter than usual, and if he was going away she didn't want to know until after Tivvy's party.

'Wish I could go,' declared Patrick.

Tessa's heart tightened. He was only sixteen. The war would be over soon. It couldn't go on – with all these casualties there'd be no young men left, on either side.

'Patrick,' said David quietly. 'Chinny's been killed.' Looking about at the others, he added, 'He was one of the masters at school – one of the best.'

'I'm sorry, Dave. I never saw him, but from what you told me, he was real nice.'

'The Head was upset. We all were. Our games master joined up yesterday afternoon, and the science master last week.'

'Same at the stables. All the young chaps have gone. There's only me and a lot of old codgers left!'

Cormac, thinking it time the conversation took a livelier turn, addressed Joseph. 'And how's the champion prizefighter getting on at St Gregory's, eh? Did anyone make the mistake of picking on you?'

Joseph nodded. 'I p . . . punched him on the n . . . n . . . nose.'

The smiles turned into laughter when Patrick added, 'Busted it, he did! They couldn't get over him looking like an angel and packing the punch of a devil!'

'Still lathering chins at Flood's?' asked Cormac.

Joseph nodded.

'Don't nod,' admonished Kathleen. 'It's the lazy way out. When you're at home you're to try and say more. Tell them about the cat.' He stared at her appealingly. 'Go on,' she said sternly. 'Tell them.'

'It's bbb . . . bb . . . big,' he began, and being fond of the cat, he warmed to the subject, and ended with a wide-eyed account of 'www . . . hen I swwweep it attt . . . acks the b . . . brush!'

Tessa went into the scullery to make tea, and David helped Kathleen bring cakes, sandwiches and the much-loved soda bread to the table. Kathleen's slight figure darted among them, offering and serving, receiving compliments, her eyes grave, and long straight hair swinging as she turned to answer for Joseph when he got stuck for words. Her mother, she thought, would never be stuck for words, and little Tivvy would never have to rough it like she and Joseph had. If Joseph had had the attention Tivvy was getting, perhaps he would have expressed himself properly.

'What will you do, Kathleen, when you leave school next year?' Elfreda's voice cut across her thoughts. 'I'll have to think of you doing something while I'm in France.'

'I'd really like to be a nurse, but it's good money at the mill and on munitions . . . '

And so they were back to the war, discussing the way

people called the Germans 'Fritz' instead of the old-fashioned term, 'Hun'.

'What about you, Uncle Cormac? I suppose you'll be off?'

How could Patrick sound so eager, wondered Tessa.

'Soon.'

'Oh.' Audrey put down her cup. 'You didn't say.'

'Saving the best till the last!'

'France?' Audrey's breath was sharp.

He nodded.

David Wilkins was sitting up in his bedroom considering the future – his future. On the dressing table was a sepia photograph of the Sacred Heart football team. Patrick looked fine in his goalie's jersey, and in between stood Father Quinn, a hand on each boy's shoulder. Only six years ago, he thought; it seemed like a lifetime since that breakfast in the presbytery after the nun's early Communion when Father Quinn had asked both boys to consider the priesthood. Off and on, he had done nothing else since then. He had not mentioned it to Patrick, or anyone else, for fear of being influenced. He wanted to be sure it was a call from God, a true vocation – and now it was to be put to the test.

'The headmaster wants to see you, Father, about my future.'

George Wilkins rubbed his hands together. 'Yes, it's time you left and came into management at the mill. Too much schooling softens the brain. It's the practical side you need now.'

David's brown eyes widened, his brows arched to meet the gathering frown. 'What gave you the idea I wanted to go into the mill?'

'Idea! I don't need an idea to know what my son's going to do.'

'You've never given any indication . . . not even to Aunt Effie. You can't – '

'Listen here, young man, don't you tell me what I can and can't do. I've laid out enough on your education and I'm laying out no more.'

'I've never asked you to lay out anything. I wanted to go to St Gregory's with Patrick, but it was you made me sit the entrance for the Grammar.'

'And what for? So I'd have a son with a bit of nouse who could make his way up at Atkinson's instead of mucking out stables like Patrick Collins! Trade's the thing, commerce. That's where Manchester's made its brass. Hard-headed businessmen have made it what it is, not a handful of arty-farty philanthropic jessies running children's theatres and prancing round churches in skirts and lace-edged sleeves!' He paused, then sucked in his breath slowly. 'Oh, so we're coming to it now . . . fancy the church, do you?'

'It's not a fancy,' David was stung to reply. 'It's a call from God, a vocation.'

'Not with my money it isn't! Vocation!' he yelled. 'Vocation my backside!'

'I'm serious, Father.'

'And d'you think I'm not? This is my last bloody word. Do what I say, or get out – that's if anyone'll have you!'

'Oh, I'm in great demand.' David turned at the parlour door. 'The army's crying out for cannon fodder!'

Yes, cannon fodder. He stalked along Oldham Road almost light-heartedly. His future, a few moments ago so clouded, was now crystal clear. Disappointment or bitterness had no place in this euphoric, seemingly predestined decision.

He passed the church. So much for getting high marks in Latin and Divinity! And without a second glance, he hurried to Loom Street, where Patrick would have finished his tea and with a bit of luck ready to go out.

'Kathleen, what are you doing here?'

'Sitting on the step, stupid. What does it look like?'

'Madame is taking the air?'

'Madame is thinking.'

'Am I permitted to know what?'

David was nice. No one else, except Uncle Cormac, talked to her like this, like a grown-up. She glanced at the wave of dark brown hair which fell over his forehead and which he was always pushing back. Patrick was very lucky having such a friend. She had no one to speak of, no one close to talk to . . . about boys, and such like. 'I was thinking that life's a bit rotten.'

'Oh, it's not all that bad,' he said airily, sitting on the top step beside her.

'It's all right for you, boys get more opportunities. I can't see me ever getting away from Ancoats.'

'And why would you want to do that?'

She shot him a withering glance, as though the question was unworthy of him. 'I'm not clever like Aunt Audrey, or gifted like me mam. You've got to have something going for you – You're not listening, David.'

'I am. I'm just remembering that your Uncle Cormac would say that sometimes you've got to give Fate a push to get something going.'

'Right,' declared Patrick, pushing his head between them. 'Let's be getting off, Dave.' Once in the street, he added, 'D'you fancy going to see that new bioscope thing, moving pictures?'

'I fancy going in search of the nearest recruiting centre and offering my all.'

Patrick, knowing by experience that David's flippancy often concealed some kind of trouble, cast him a quick look.

'What's up, Dave?'

David unfolded his story, only to be stopped by Patrick part way. 'You don't have to convince me you've got a vocation. You're cut out for it . . . ' And then, when David reached the end, he gave him a friendly punch on the shoulder. 'If you think you're going to hammer Fritz and leave me behind, you're very much mistaken.'

They stared at each other, momentarily blinded with glory, vision and great purpose. Then they hurried off to the nearest recruiting office, where the flame of patriotism was firmly quenched:

'Come back when you're eighteen, sonny.'

'We're not baby snatchin!'

'You've not got the cradle marks off yer arses, yet!'

It was getting late when they found a recruiting officer tired and fed up enough to sign them on without asking any tiresome questions and demanding to see birth certificates. But first they had to present their bodies to be examined in sack-covered booths by a doctor who was also fed up and anxious to go home, and who reminded Patrick of the vet at the stables. In between opening mouths and filling test tubes, they were rushed from booth to booth half clothed and acutely embarrassed. At last, everything seemed satisfactory and they were addressed by an old Boer War sergeant who, it appeared, was never tired or fed up.

'Get that smirk off yer faces if yer want to be sworn in!' he roared, and the boys meekly swore to serve king and country.

'Bit of an anticlimax!' commented David, as they stood outside, hands in pockets. 'I thought we'd be given a uniform and told to report somewhere for training tomorrow, not be given a number and told to go home and wait till we're sent for . . . ' Home? They exchanged glances. 'Heck, Patrick, I wouldn't like to be in your shoes – your mother'll crown you!'

'What about your aunt!'

'She's not the crowning kind! D'you want me to come with you, while you tell her?'

Patrick shook his head and grinned. 'There are some things a fella just has to do on his own!'

'Sure, I'm not believin' me own ears! You mean you've just gone out and enlisted!' Tessa's voice was reasonably calm, but there was nothing reasonable about her heart thumping with dread against her ribcage. Oh, dear God, poor Miss Wilkins, and David her only one.

'Which office?' she demanded.

'Lime Bank Street, why?' Patrick watched his mother open the dresser drawer with purpose, and rummage in the piled-up mess. With a sigh of relief she drew out a crumpled piece of paper. Whatever else it might resemble now, it was Patrick's birth certificate. Major Mary had registerd him at Liverpool and told her never to lose the certificate.

'You can't do anything about it now,' he said desperately. 'I've been sworn in.'

'If there's any swearing to do I'll be the one to bloody well do it! Now you just stay in and keep an eye on Tivvy till I get back!' The door slammed. Tivvy wailed, and Ronnie next door started crying.

The tired recruiting officer was reaching for his case when Tessa approached. His face lit up in a smile of recognition.

'Wait a minute?' he tapped his forehead to encourage his memory. 'The Honeysuckle and the Bee' – Tessa Collins – the Tivoli. Am I right?'

'You are, and I also happen to be the mother of a sixteen-year-old boy you enlisted a short while ago.' She thrust out the birth certificate. 'You got him in, now you can get him out!'

He was tired, but he still had his wits about him. 'Now don't panic, Mrs Collins. He'll probably be eighteen by the time they send for him, and in any case they don't send 'em to France until they're twenty-one. I'll hold the papers back, delay it a bit, like. How's that suit you? And let's face it, Mrs Collins,' he continued expansively, 'the war can't last that much longer.' Did she believe him, he wondered. Yes, she believed him because she wanted to. Nice woman – as good-looking off stage as on. Wait till I tell the wife I've been talking to Tessa Collins, he thought.

David's aunt said later that the shock had instantly aged her; it had taken years off her life. George Wilkins, suffering from his sister's bitter recriminations, tried to redeem himself by setting up a trust for David to realise his vocation when the war was over.

For several weeks the boys continued at the stables and at school, until informed to report to the Drill Hall. There they learned to march, stand to attention and at ease; they were left-turned, right-turned, formed into fours and right-wheeled until they were dizzy. No uniforms were issued, and their faces were red more with embarrassment than with exertion as gangs of children gathered at the rec – which doubled as a parade ground – to shout rude remarks, since without uniforms, the occasion certainly lacked spectacle.

When Cormac called soon after the talk was all about horses. Patrick, because of his experience with horses, and David, for no other reason than enlisting at the same time, had been drafted to the Veterinary Corps. 'Not much cavalry now, thank God,' said Cormac, when eagerly asked for information, 'but the army needs mules and donkeys, especially out East where the terrain is rough. And we need the big horses, Clydesdales and shires for dragging the heavy artillery to strategic positions.' For Tessa's benefit he added in a louder tone, 'So, there'll be no going over the top for you two!'

He also had to curb Patrick's enthusiasm by whispering,

311

'Will we not tone it down a bit, for the mammy's sake? The women folk are not after looking at it in the same way as us.' Pleased with the inferred camaraderie, Patrick took the hint.

By September they were still not kitted out and Tessa's heart filled with gratitude for the recruiting officer at Lime Bank Street – he was a gent of the first water. But not for much longer.

One Friday night Kathleen and Joseph had just returned from Cunliffe's with meat and potato pies, when Patrick returned from the Drill Hall in uniform and full kit. 'This is it, Mam,' he said as he dropped the pack by the side of the sofa. 'Ten o'clock train at Victoria! It's not been much like army life living at home, but now it's the real thing!' He patted Tivvy's cheek as she pulled herself up on the arm of the sofa, pretended to get Joseph in a wrestling hold, and waltzed Kathleen round the table. They were all as pleased as Patrick, except for Tessa who, as she arranged the pies and peas on plates, was numb to the heart. But when David called the euphoria heightened.

'How do we look?' asked Patrick. 'Will heads turn when we pass like they did for Uncle Cormac and Dad?'

Tessa swallowed hard. Heads had turned for Cormac and Finn because a soldier in the streets had been a rarity. Now there were so many that no one looked twice.

'One thing, Dave,' grinned Patrick. 'We'll miss Cunliffe's pies!' And wolfing down the last crust, they hurried out excitedly to say their goodbyes. Tessa remembered him at seven, showing off his First Communion clothes and coming back with pennies and threepenny bits; later, showing off his Whitsuntide clothes – and now he was showing off a soldier's uniform.

'You do look splendid!' admired Father Quinn.

'Just short of the odd medal and a few stripes!'

'I tried to get in myself,' said the priest, fiddling with the cross at his waist. 'They said my heart wasn't first class – nothing serious, but not good enough for army life.'

'Rotten luck,' said David, thinking how striking Father Quinn would look in uniform. 'Still, I'm glad, in a way. What would Ancoats do without you?'

'Same as Manchester Grammar has done without your dear

Chinny. Now don't be falling behind with your Latin studies, David. You have free time in the army, and here's a letter of introduction to your chaplain, who will no doubt have time to coach you once or twice a week.' After a blessing, he stood at the door, an arm around each boy's shoulders. 'Don't forget what I told you about keeping yourselves decent. There's no place like the army for a young man to lose his purity and faith. Remember – especially you, David – keep yourself pure for the priesthood.'

Having braved the Friday-night hordes of children queuing on the curved drive of Ancoats Hall, David explained their flying visit, and asked if there was any likelihood of Miss Crompton ever returning to Manchester. 'We used to light a candle for her when we were younger, but we don't now.'

Miss Hindshaw, now in charge, shook her dark head. 'We did hear that she was a courier – something to do with Intelligence – but nothing definite. Her horizons have broadened . . . '

'Surely,' said David, 'the government will allow women the vote after the effort they've put into the war? Women have proved they can do everything.'

'Not quite everything,' laughed Miss Hindshaw. 'But I get your meaning!' She accompanied them to the wide doorstep, and waved as they turned at the corner of the drive. Just two of the many grateful young men, she thought wistfully, who have graduated from Shakespeare and Browning to shells and bombs.

Chapter Twenty-Eight

'Pack up your troubles in your old kitbag, and smile, smile, smile . . . ' While Tessa was singing at the Gaiety Theatre, the military band on Victoria Station was playing 'It's a Long Way to Tipperary', and Audrey, Kathleen, Joseph, Miss Wilkins and George were there to wave goodbye to David and Patrick.

'We're going to be less,' said Kathleen sombrely, 'with Uncle Cormac away and Elfreda and Nick already gone . . . ' And our Patrick's going to the war, she thought, and Mam couldn't take time off, couldn't rearrange her order on the bill. She had always said last-minute alterations caused trouble for the other artistes, and the manager didn't like it . . . Mam was scared of losing her pitch, her popularity.

'Just so long as Little Dolly Daydream doesn't go away,' grinned David, taking up her remark, and as the crowd began to sing, she burst into tears. 'Tell you what,' he said in an attempt to cheer her up. 'I'll write to you every week. But you must write to me, mind, about your job, your pals. And when I come back to find you grown into a young lady, we'll go to the Palm Court for supper. Promise to write?'

'I promise,' she answered tearfully. 'Oh, I do promise, David.'

Kathleen had gone home and cried until her eyes were hot and her throat dry. She sat in the dark on the top step of the yard, and thought of David, her Prince. Her mind was full of him, and that he wasn't there, that he wouldn't be calling any more, only made his memory more precious. Oh, God, she stifled her sniffles as one or another of the

Coopers went down the yard to the lavatory; you can't even cry in peace. She wanted to be alone on the steps under the cold stars, and deeply resented the pilgrimage across the yard. The young ones took a candle in a jam jar because they were frightened of ghosts; Tony or Cooper himself came to use the grid; and someone trundled down with Ronnie's slop bucket. Through all this she crouched on the top step, determined to give her grief full reign.

Joseph, who had wept on the way home, more to join her sorrow than anything personal, opened the scullery door, and standing in his nightshirt with a slice of bread and treacle in his hand, said, 'You've cc . . . cried enough, now, KK . . . Kathleen. Mam will be bb . . . back soon.'

'What d'you know about it?' She screwed up her eyes with misery. 'And what's Mam got to do with it? I'll stay here as long as I like. You're heartless, Joseph Collins!' She rose from the step and ran up to her bed where she dissolved at once into another paroxysm of grief.

Tessa, wanting to know about Patrick, had taken a cab from the Gaiety to the Women's House, where Audrey was on duty for the week. She had been listening to the gramophone, and was wearing a full-skirted silk dressing gown. Even with her hair in disarray, she looked beautiful.

'Oh my dear, come in. Your arms must be aching from carrying Tivvy.'

'Wish they were. She's not as heavy as the others.'

'Put her here on the sofa. Shall I loosen her shawl? Isn't she good, not waking up.'

'If she can sleep through the Zampa Overture, she can sleep through anything! I just had to call, Audrey. Tell me about it, how they got off and all of that? Awful it was on the boards tonight. Thought I was going to crack up. The train was going out at ten o'clock – my first born was going to the war – at sixteen, for God's sake. What am I doing here, I thought, and I remembered the look in Kathleen's eyes when she heard I was working . . .'

Audrey made some tea and they sat before the fire in the comfortable sitting room while Tessa heard of the departure with a heavy heart. 'And what of Cormac?' she asked in a stilted voice. 'They wouldn't send him off without you knowing?'

'Lord, I hope not. But large movements of horses to certain areas indicate action, and because of German spies the movements – Cormac's too I suppose – are not advertised. I hope he surfaces for Christmas, for my notice is up then, and I'll be celebrating 1916 down in London. But before I leave, I'm going to pop the question as they say. If he's not for marriage now, he never will be. I mean,' she shrugged her silk-clad shoulders, 'you can't blame a woman for trying, and if it wasn't for the uncertainty of war, I might've been content to go on as we were. Of course, if he refuses my very excellent offer, or side steps the issue, that's us all washed up.'

But Cormac was in Manchester for Christmas Day as Audrey had hoped, and Miss Wilkins laid on Christmas dinner after Mass. They tried to make it a happy occasion, but even Cormac's sense of fun could not lift the cloud which hung like a tinker's tarpaulin over the dining room.

'Wouldn't you think George would have dined here instead of the club?' commented Effie, sipping her sherry, but on slight reflection added, 'Perhaps it's better he didn't – he hasn't much party spirit.'

Tessa quietly thanked God for small mercies.

The three months of David's absence, during which they had received only a few short letters, had made his aunt vulnerable and frail with anxiety. Her once honey-coloured hair was now grey, and while Kathleen and Joseph were occupied in fetching a mince pie from the kitchen and pouring ginger wine, she told them with quiet resignation why David had joined up so suddenly, and how George had tried to salve his conscience by setting up a vocational trust for him for after the war.

'David a priest?' echoed Tessa. 'Fancy Patrick knowing all about it and never saying a word, the little bugger!'

'As if he would – you should know those two by now! Besides, a vocation is a sensitive matter,' said Cormac. 'A private arrangement between yourself and God. And David certainly wouldn't care to be ragged about it – can you imagine what Tony Cooper would make of it?'

'It was all a double shock to me,' Effie continued in a small voice. 'I had hoped that he and your Kathleen . . . Tessa.'

Holy Mother . . . Mother of God . . . Saint Teresa . . .

The names sped through Tessa's mind. No, Effie, she thought in a panic. No. No! It cannot be.

They stayed with Effie until George, who had secreted himself somewhere until it was time for them to go, was home. Strange, thought Cormac, he's a regular Scrooge, too mean even to wish us a happy Christmas!

Although it was late, there seemed to be a general unwillingness to part company on this Christmas night, so almost without consultation, Audrey, Cormac and Titch went on to Loom Street with Tessa.

After Kathleen and Joseph had gone to bed, Audrey made some tea, and Titch produced a light ale for himself and a bottle of Guinness. 'Finn's instructions,' Titch announced. '"Titch," he said, a day or so before died. "Whatever else you do, be sure Tessa gets her Guinness" – and that's God's own truth!'

'Ach, 'tis the darlin' man he was! God rest him. Wine and sherry is all very well, but there's no stamina in it.' And dear God, she thought, after what Effie said about David and Kathleen, I need all the stamina I can get.

'Now, Cormac,' said Titch, 'fill us in about what David and Patrick are likely to be doing in this Veterinary Corps. I've never heard of it and didn't want to upset Miss Wilkins by asking.'

'Sure, I can tell you now, without any breach of secrecy at all, that there's a campaign blowing up out East and the lads embarked several weeks ago for Suez.'

'Suez?' echoed Tessa. 'Where on God's earth is that?'

The subjects of this conversation had disembarked and been transported to the veterinary base hospital at El Zaga, where hundreds of horses and mules gathered to be hardened up and broken into their duties.

Sergeant Major Barton eyed the new intake. He was a fleshy man, not unkind, but a hardened campaigner whose cheek bore a scar which flushed to scarlet as his temper ran out.

'Blimey,' exclaimed Les Butler, a cheerful, chirpy young man who lived near the Metropole in Openshaw and couldn't believe Tessa was Patrick's mother. 'Did you ever see owt like this?' Along with three dozen pairs of eyes, he scanned the lines and lines of tethered horses, mules and camels waiting for treatment. Orderlies and grooms in knee boots and sweat-soaked shirts followed the veterinary officers who were going the rounds.

'That's what Nick'll be doing,' said David. 'Only it's not as hot in France.'

A horsebox drawn by half a dozen mules, stopped in a cloud of dust, and one of the grooms was immediately detailed to lead a shire horse down the plank.

'Blimey!' exclaimed the astonished Les. 'A taxi for his nibs!'

Hands firmly clasped over the short cane behind his back, the Sergeant Major stopped looking over the new recruits to bark out 'Let me tell you, smart arse, that ruddy big 'orse there is on recovery leave. Gone lame through hauling more guns than you're even likely to set eyes on!'

Les waited for him to proceed down the line before risking another comment. 'Honestly,' he began, with a good-natured grin. 'They've had me practising bayonet charges, aiming hand grenades, loading machine guns till I'm bursting to have a go at Fritz – and where do I end up? Nursemaid to a bloody horse!'

'Some people have all the luck!' he grumbled three months later, when, because of Patrick's aptitude for horses and David's superior education, both were chosen to go on a course to Cairo.

'That 'andsome officer's waiting,' giggled one of the 'Two Dollys' in the dressing room of the Gaiety. 'Striding about, swishing his cane against his leg. Wish someone like him would get into a lather about me.'

'It isn't like that,' said Tessa, dolloping cold cream on her face. 'It isn't like that at all.'

'Have I to tell him you've gone, then?'

'No!' exclaimed Tessa, laughing at Dolly through the mirror 'It isn't like that, either!'

'I'll leave you to it then. Goodnight, Tessa – love to Titch.'

'Goodnight, Dolly.'

'Thought she'd never go,' breathed Cormac, as he closed the door and leaned against it. 'Come to report audience reaction! Sure, a fella's got to have some excuse! You and Titch – especially yourself – were marvellous tonight. They were ravin', captivated, enchanted, going wild!'

'Like your imagination!'

'If you don't believe me, ask Titch.'

She asked instead if Audrey had got off to London over the weekend. She had. And when would he be following?

'The midnight train.' He moved from the door and came toward the mirror, lying his cane, cap and gloves amongst the creams and paints.

She paused, eyes wide, staring at him in the dressing table mirror. 'Merciful Lord, so soon?'

'Will I be detecting a hint of disappointment, dismay, sorrow even?'

She sensed the seriousness beneath the surface banter. 'You would so – and why not?' she asked sharply. 'Sure, it's a terrible thing to be going off to the war. Especially for a wandering minstrel.'

'Wandering minstrel?'

'When I first saw you, the uniform seemed so at odds with the jaunty way your cap was tipped and the way your hair was all ruffled. You could have been a wandering minstrel I thought, with a fiddle beneath your arm instead of a cane. Dear heaven, war seemed a long way off then.'

He laughed, pleased with the illusion. 'I'd like you always to think of me that way.'

She shot him a glance. 'You needn't sound so final. Listen to me now, I remember you saying you'd need a shroud before a wedding ring. But could you not find it in your heart to make things right with Audrey? She . . . she loves you, has done for years. Couldn't . . . I mean, she wants marriage. For heaven's sake don't let on I told you any of this!'

'Fancy remembering about the shroud! And when I think of Miss Wilkins supplying you with curtain rings over the years – God, it's enough to make a pig laugh!'

As she stood up, he reached for her coat, holding it while she slipped her arms into the sleeves. Remaining behind her, they looked at each other in the mirror, and addressed the images.

'Forgive my curiosity, but you've not been short of money for some time – why weren't you for buying a ring?'

'What's the point of buying your own? If Finn had suggested it, I'd have had him down to Ikey Solomon's in no time, but, God rest him, he didn't.'

'When I come back, would you consider taking custody of the ring again?'

'You've still got it?'

'Round my neck on a black eye-glass cord ... never been off since it went there, and won't come off until it returns to your finger.' In the mirror she watched his arms slip round her waist, holding her against him, tightly, almost fiercely. His head rested lightly on her shoulder. 'What does the "Colleen from Connemara" say to that?'

'But ... ' Her eyes focused on the strong slim fingers, and her heart began to beat faster. 'But, Audrey?'

'Audrey and I have talked, and although she's the darling girl, and we're very fond of each other, that's all there is to it. I think she'd recognised long ago that you and I were meant for each other. We are Tessa,' he murmured against her hair. 'We didn't know it, but we are so. There hasn't been a day I haven't thought about you in some way or other, whether with Finn, the kids, on certain occasions, or just on your own. I love you, Tessa Collins.' He raised his head from her shoulder, amber eyes brilliant in the gaslight. They continued to gaze at each other in the long costume mirror, as though the images would vanish if they looked away. He brought his mind to practicalities. 'Is Tivvy in safe hands? Have you time to come to the station with me?'

'Sure, I wish to God you weren't going,' she blurted out, and then in a more controlled manner, she continued, 'Yes, Miss Wilkins is at Loom Street with her. It's too cold to bring any child out at night, still less her, and Miss Wilkins seems to like coming – her brother isn't much company, as you'll know from Christmas.'

'I sometimes fancy the old Scrooge has an eye for you.'

'Glory be, what makes you think that?'

'He's at every performance, at least, those I manage to get to, rubbing his hands together as though he's cold.'

For a moment, Tessa, now full of happiness, faced the ghost of George Wilkins. But she rapidly set her heart on course again as Cormac turned her round to face him, tightening his hold. She knew from those lean yet muscled forearms that his embrace would be fierce; from the curve on his lips that his kisses would be tantalising; but, there was nothing to prepare her for the warmth which spread like a fire through her body, at the new awareness between them. Her arms went up to his neck and their lips met in kisses heavy with years of waiting, sweet in swift recognition, sharp with the sense of passing time.

'I want you to know,' he said, on the way to the station in a cab, 'that I'll never be after replacing Finn. We both loved him and he was part of both our lives.' He took both her hands. 'Will you marry me when I get back?'

'Oh, but Cormac, are you sure? What with Elfreda, and then Audrey, and someone in Sussex . . . On your own admission, you're not the kind of man for settling down.'

'Only with you, Tessa. You, me, little Tivvy, God love her, and the auld country, in that order. I'll be an instant family man! The times I've looked round your table on Patrick's birthday teas and thought that I could have had family if I'd stirred meself. But it's no good unless you've the right partner. I wasn't going to say anything yet, thought I'd woo you by post! But the flesh got the better of me! I felt I needed to know whether there was any hope. After all, an attractive young widow, and a star to boot – as I said, thoughts of George even crossed me mind! C'mon, woman,' he teased. 'Will you be puttin' a fella out of his misery. Will you marry me?'

'I will so!' she exclaimed happily. 'And I'm hoping to God I do it properly this time!'

'I promise you,' he joined in her fun. 'There'll not be a broomstick in sight!' And on a more sombre note, 'I'll leave you to tell the family as you wish and in your own time. But I'd like you to wear this signet ring. It was mine but I had it made smaller – with you in mind, of course! But seriously, wherever this bloody war takes me, it'll give some purpose to it to know you're wearing my ring.'

It was made of rich Irish gold with the letter C engraved in an ancient Celtic design. He slipped it on to the third finger of her left hand, and was about to seal it with a kiss when a cab driver yelled, 'Destination, mate!'

Between the cab stand and the station platform they talked fast and breathlessly.

'I love you! I love you!'

'And I love you, Cormac.'

'I knew I loved you the night Tivvy was born. I thought you were going to die – they didn't understand, but I did. Suddenly it seemed as though I'd loved you for ever.'

'Sure, it's an odd thing, but I would have died in the disaster at Ennan if it hadn't been for Finn. I've got a lot to be grateful to my men for! And looking back over the years, I think I've loved you for a long time. Y'see, you're a friend as well. Oh, but all those rumours – I was mortified!'

Heads turned in admiration of so handsome a couple, and sometimes people murmured. 'Eh, wasn't that Tessa Collins the music-hall star?' Tessa enjoyed it: she was sporting her love, if only for a short time, wearing him on her sleeve for all the world to see.

The minutes rushed on apace. Parting . . . he thought . . . such sweet sorrow. The station was packed, trains already getting their steam up, eager to part lovers and families. He held her hard and close as if to impress upon his body the memory of her, the shape of her, the very dearness of her. She couldn't see, only feel him move; she heard him say goodbye, and she was alone.

Miss Wilkins, having just finished writing to her nephew, beamed with pleasure at Tessa's news. 'Oh my dear, I am so very, very pleased for you! But you younger people are full of surprises. I thought he and Audrey – '

'So did I,' she smiled. 'But we thought wrong, didn't we!' She took off her coat. 'Was Tivvy any trouble?'

'Good as gold, bless her.'

Tessa sat down and held her hands out to the fire. 'D'you think I should tell the kids tomorrow or wait a while?'

'Tomorrow. You could have been seen with him at the station. They like Cormac; I think they'll both be pleased, and Patrick will be ecstatic.'

'I'm not sure about Kathleen, Miss Wilkins, not sure at all. She'll no doubt accuse me of betraying her father's memory.'

'Oh, I don't know. Her mind seems to be divided between her work at Ancoats Hospital, the voluminous correspondence you've all embarked upon, and reading those biology and anatomy books.'

'Y'see what I mean – she's never told me about the books, I've not even seen 'em. I think daughters are much more complicated than sons, or nephews . . . ' She eyed the letter. 'How's he getting on? I somehow can't imagine David as a Tommy Atkins!'

'I've been explaining to Joseph and Kathleen, the idea behind all this strategy is for the Allies to clear the Turks out of Beersheba, capture Jerusalem and make the Holy Land Christian again. But, as I was pointing out on the map, what with the hills and heights, the heat and flies, it'll be a tough campaign. And when you've time, my dear, ask Joseph to show you his book-keeping. Very much off his own bat, as it were, he's chronicled Bert Flood's business. It isn't what you'd call a rivetting read, unless you find the price of strops, soap, razors, and the big cat's milk fascinating! He's got the number of shaves and haircuts per day set out, and then weekly and monthly totals. Berts very pleased, and Joseph's a clever child – despite Saint Gregory's!'

Tessa related her good news to her family when they were at breakfast, and the response was as she had expected. Joseph stammered and spluttered in his excitement and wanted to know would Cormac really be living with them like his Dad? Could he call him Dad?

'You can call him whatever you want, he's no stranger to us.'

'But he's *not* Dad,' burst out Kathleen, pouring a look of scorn on Joseph. 'How could you even think of calling anyone else Dad! I've never been able to make me mind up whether you're naturally heartless or just say the first thing that comes into you head!'

'I'm not suggesting, Kathleen – and nor will Cormac – that he will ever take the place of your da. No one can do that.'

Chapter Twenty-Nine

Kathleen looked older in the dark green overall of probationary nurse, her hair was tied back, but she still wore a fringe down to her eyebrows, and was, this morning, raising yet another question of her mother's intended marriage.

'You'll be getting rid of the single beds and buying a big one again, I suppose? And where will I sleep then?' She grabbed a basket and dumped her working shoes and lunch into it. 'Tivvy will be all right in your room for a few years, but if you put me in the back room, where will Joseph go? And Patrick, when he returns? Next thing, we'll be moving to a bigger house. But I don't want to leave the hospital, and Joseph shouldn't be taken from Bert Flood's.' She grabbed her coat from the hook behind the front door. 'It's all right for you, Mam, you can get a cab to your work. That's all you've ever thought of – work!'

'Sure, and if I'd been shiftless like that lot next door,' flared Tessa, 'you'd be happy, would you? Besides, we couldn't manage on the nineteen shillings a week your da earned.'

'And now you're blaming it on Dad!' she yelled, running out of the house.

'She's upset bb...because there's no ll...letter from David,' confided Joseph with a calming smile. Although thirteen and growing up, his nice ways were growing with him. A lovely child, he was destined to be a fine-looking youth. His features were more defined than Patrick's; his hair, like Tivvy's, waved. He was clever, kind and helpful, but very few looked behind the stammer to find this out.

George Wilkins, hearing the news via his sister, shrank into himself again. Why, he reflected, should Tessa be happy? Why, in God's name, should O'Shea be, when he was not? The war wasn't over yet, he thought grudgingly. I hope he stops one of Fritz's bullets or gets trampled on by a gun-crazed horse. If she didn't want George Wilkins, he didn't want her to have anyone else. When Collins had died and Greenledge and the neighbours were turning nasty, he had thought he was in with a chance. But looking back, he had known he would never have a chance with her, just as O'Shea must have known he would have.

The neighbours in Hewitt's corner shop folded their arms, nodded their heads and pursed their lips.

'Didn't take him long to get his feet under the table.'

'Had 'em there for some time if you ask me.'

'Disgraceful the way that woman carries on, and now the Captain's away, she has Titch Bradley in at all hours!'

> *Cairo.*
>
> *Dear Father Quinn,*
>
> I'm writing this among the red plush and gilt of the Sphinx Hotel, where Patrick and I are on a course as part of a Mobile Veterinary Unit. This means we go wherever the fighting is – don't tell my aunt – to attend and make arrangements for dead and wounded horses. At first we felt self-conscious walking about Cairo in our tropical kit of shorts and sun helmets, but we are now used to it. After the first church parade we met Father MacNaughton, who coaches me in Latin twice a week. Patrick and I attend all our religious obligations as promised. Will write again soon.
>
> *David*

David realised no description of his could do credit to the impressive figure of Father MacNaughton, SJ, who swept grandly through European society in Cairo, his purple cassock and personal charm gaining his admission to all that was elite or upper class.

His next letter was more abrupt.

Dear Father Quinn,

> *Only time for a brief letter. Patrick and I have left Cairo and are with the Mobile Unit. We were taken on lorries to enlarge a hospital at the horse lines. This is our first glimpse of war, and there's no glory.*
>
> *David.*

And no mention either, thought Father Quinn, of the illustrious MacNaughton, SJ.

The reason for the omission was due to an incident after the Latin lesson. Darkness in Cairo falls quickly. One minute you can be reading and translating, and the next you can't see a word. David, not having a late pass, and anxious to be back in quarters on time, stood up to take his leave. He felt a hand on his shoulder and found himself held tightly against the purple cassock. Terrified and intimidated by rank, he lifted his head to protest. Thick lips, warm and breathy, closed over his. That's how a man would kiss a woman – and oh, God, here he was with a priest.

'What's the matter, boy?' Low and persuasive, the voice rose in the darkened room.

'Please, sir?' he gasped, throat dry with panic. 'Permission to leave, sir? Let me go! I want to go!'

There was a silence and the chaplain said heavily, 'Permission granted. I'll not keep you, David, if you don't want to stay. I thought . . . Well, the key's in the lock.'

Stumbling over a stool, he reached the door and ran like the wind. Two days passed before he could bring himself to relate the incident to Patrick.

'And there was Father Quinn bellyaching about me keeping myself pure for the priesthood!' He flamed with resentment. 'For the first time in my life I've left the confessional without any sense of peace. Why should God deny me peace? Why did God allow it to happen? That's what I can't get over.'

Patrick had been going to point out it could have been worse, but even to think such a thing smacked of sacrilege. 'How was Father Quinn to know about men like him?'

'Is there something about me, Patrick, that caused a holy Father to sin?'

'No, there's nothing, you great jackass! It's him that's

causing sin. Just look at the state you're in. He's lucky he didn't try it on with someone who'd knee him good and proper, officer or not!'

The Veterinary Mobile Unit left David no time to dwell on the proclivities of Father MacNaughton, SJ. He and Patrick, along with other personnel from the course, were shunted from one battle area to another on salvaging missions where they directed grooms and orderlies and rounded up the survivors back to the horse lines; dispatched the mortally wounded and rigged blocks and pulleys to uncouple useful harnesses, equipment and light vehicles. Occasionally, among the equine corpses, would be a human corpse missed by the stretcher bearers. And always, after every 'engage', the air was filled with the acrid odour of chloride of lime. *It's all so bloody awful*, Patrick wrote to Cormac. *David wonders about God – can you blame him?*

Tessa, like Effie Wilkins, like Kathleen, like thousands of other women, lived for a letter, welcoming the postman, yet dreading the official telegram. Unlike the boys who were out East, and likely to be there until Colonel Lawrence was at Damascus and General Allenby took Jerusalem, Cormac's was peripatetic by nature.

As Chief Veterinary Officer, and responsible for the quality of horses on War Office contracts, he moved between France and Ireland, and had writted from Dublin about the horrors of the Easter Rising. But longer periods between letters began to elapse when instead of shipping livestock out at great expense and risk of being torpedoed, official policy changed to breeding and buying nearer the seat of war.

As a result of these travels, food parcels arrived regularly at Twenty-seven Loom Street: raisins, sugar, tea, rice, and dried milk and cocoa for Tivvy – anything with a long life – to supplement the strict rationing in Britain, which by now had come to include bread.

Tessa wrote long letters every week. She and Titch were now being given opportunities to appear in Liverpool, Blackpool and Birmingham. Titch made jokes and said, 'London next stop!' Miss Wilkins took it upon herself to care for Kathleen and Joseph in these short absences, but the two-year-old Tivvy accompanied herself and Titch, particularly now that the weather was warm and the best accommodation was booked. With all the travelling and coming into contact with different and usually extrovert people, Tivvy was brighter, cleverer and more alert than any of her children. She was a lovely child, with an air of fragility which twisted Tessa's heart, and a skin so delicate that colour blew up and down behind it like a flame in the wind. She moved quickly and daintily like a will-o'-the-wisp.

All this was related to Cormac in weekly letters, but there was one thing Tessa could not tell him, and that was her discovery of a page of a letter destined for David which had obviously slipped out of Kathleen's writing case. Picking it up from the bedroom floor and about to place it on the chest of drawers, Tony Cooper's name caught her eye: *By the time you come home*, Kathleen had written, *the four years between us will hardly be noticeable. Tony Cooper is going out with Hetty Lynch – he is your age, she is mine, so please believe me when I say my liking for you is not a 'schoolgirl crush' as Aunt Audrey would say. I think you knew that when you kissed me goodbye at the station.*

'Oh, my daughter, my darling, my poor little colleen,' cried Tessa, struck to the heart, shocked that Fate should deal such a blow to add to the child's already bitter sense of the wrongs done to her. She obviously did not know that when the war ended David would take up his vocation. Neither Miss Wilkins nor Patrick – not even David himself – had mentioned it to her. But of course no one knew when the war would end. Kitchener had died, but the carnage went on. So many hundreds of lives to advance a few yards, and so many thousands for a quarter of a mile.

The question remained, should this unconscious conspiracy of silence be broken, and who should be the one to do it? Not she, oh, merciful Lord, no! Kathleen bore her enough resentment as it was and why deprive the child of her daydreams? Conscience pricked. If she had been at the station to see them off instead of on the boards, she would have noticed the kiss, or David's attitude. Of course Kathleen had always worshipped him, calling him her prince because he had so often come to her rescue, carrying laundry, and standing up for her against criticism.

Later that night, Kathleen, who always went to bed before her mother came home, was waiting up. Tessa put down her case, and taking off the long, full-skirted coat, threw it as nonchalantly as Elfreda had done all those years ago, on the end of the Mafeking sofa.

Like her da, Kathleen never asked how the performance had gone, whether the House had been full – nothing.

'Thought you'd be asleep by now,' Tessa remarked pleasantly. 'Isn't it the early start tomorrow?'

'About this letter, Mam – you must have read it!'

'Tony Cooper's name caught my eye, and yes, I did.'

'Aren't you going to say something?'

'About what, for heaven's sake?'

'About me an' David. You're not the only one to love a nice man.'

'I realise that.'

'And you don't mind about me and David?'

'Of course not. But don't build on it too much. You're both young yet. War can change people, or something else might.'

'What else is there to build on? He's my whole life, the only good thing, apart from Joseph, to happen to me.'

'You're probably right, love.'

'I am.'

'Sure, it's all settled then. Bed, young woman, or you'll never be at work for six.'

'But what d'you mean by all those veiled warnings that he might change, that war changes people? Do you knowing something, Mam?'

'Will you not leave it, and be getting to bed?'

'No!' Kathleen grabbed Tessa's hand as she went into the scullery to make tea. 'Tell me!'

'And when I've bloody well told you, you'll hate me for it. Honestly, Kathleen, in the name of our Lady, I don't know what's come over you at all.'

Kathleen raised her brown eyes. 'What will I hate you for?'

'David's got a vocation. He's going to be a priest when the war's over.'

'You're lying, Mam. For some reason, you're trying to put me off him.'

'Write and ask him. Ask his aunt, ask Father Quinn. God knows why they all know and you don't!'

'But why didn't he tell me?'

'He's your prince, he's protecting your day dreams. He's always been very fond of you.'

'So he's humouring me. Using me to practise his priestly arts!' She burst into tears and ran upstairs.

'Shut that noise will you!' growled Cooper, banging on the wall. Ronnie screamed in alarm; Tivvy wailed in her sleep. And Tessa stared at the Sacred Heart.

'Oh, heart of Christ,' she appealed, 'what else could I have done?'

Her own mother had died when she was four. The only mother figure she had known had been Mrs O'Malley, and she and Marie Jane were always giving out to each other. She sighed. There was no Audrey, no Elfreda, and it wasn't fair to burden Effie Wilkins, who was worried sick about her nephew, as well as about George, whom, she said, was very quiet these days. 'Not his old hectoring self at all – for which I'm grateful – but I do prefer moderation in all things.'

As the summer of 1917 passed, Tessa came to echo these sentiments entirely. Kathleen, to Joseph's wide-eyed consternation, had taken to throwing David's letters on the fire, unopened.

'Holy Mary!' exclaimed Tessa. 'D'you not think that a bit extreme?'

'But he's been deceiving me, stringing me along. Isn't that extreme for someone who's going to be a bloody priest!'

'Will y'mind your language now, or I'll give you a clout, as big as you are!'

'What about your language, Mam, swearing and blaspheming all your life? It's like everything else – when I come to do it, it's wrong!'

'Out! Get out to work Kathleen Collins, before I lose my temper altogether! God in heaven, you're enough to make a saint swear, y'are!'

The door slammed. Windows rattled. Cooper banged on the wall and Ronnie started up.

'Sshh . . . she doesn't mean it, Mam,' Joseph said, putting his arms about her, comforting his own misery as much as his mother's.

330

＊

Patrick wrote to Joseph faithfully, toning down his news for the boy. He told him of the thousands of mules in big corrals in the hills, watched over by army 'cowboys'; of how chalk marks on the flanks of convalescent horses indicated complaint or treatment: *You've never seen flies like the Sinatic variety – if we don't drink our tea quick, they'll sup it for us! Even the horses are scared of 'em. The Blue Cross have sent us 'flynets' to keep the buggers off open sores, and we've set up tents for the treatment of mange, which if allowed to spread in this heat can kill a horse off in a week. Talking of mange, has Bert still got his cat? And have you decided what to do when you leave St Gregory's?*

Although she was anxious about Kathleen's friendship with the flighty Hetty Lynch, who had been going out with Tony Cooper, Tessa had already contracted to do a four-week tour of the North Wales seaside resorts, grasping the opportunity for Tivvy's sake, to give her lungs a change from the sulphuric air of Manchester.

In Tessa's absence, Joseph and Kathleen went to Miss Wilkins for their tea, and being of an age to cope, lived at home on their own. After leaving St Gregory's Joseph had attracted the attention of one of Bert Flood's customers – a Quaker – who had taken him as a ledger clerk. The office was small and quiet, no one made fun of him, and alone with his figures he was very happy.

On Tessa's return from the tour, Joseph stammered and stuttered his way through 'not wanting to tell tales, but Mam ought to know that our Kathleen's going out with Tony Cooper and that she had him in here to supper and opened that tin of corned beef Uncle Cormac sent.' He was clearly worried.

'She'll never know you told me,' Tessa sighed. 'And you've done right, I need to know.' But short of locking her up, what could be done? In Kathleen's present mood all the talking in the world wouldn't do any good. Tony Cooper, she thought miserably. Him of all people. Drank like a fish, people said. His only claim to respectability had been graduating to the big bass drum in the Sacred Heart band. All the girls, Kathleen included, dashed out on Sunday mornings to stand in groups, watching the band and screaming with

331

delight when Tony threw the drumsticks expertly into the air mid beat, or crossed them over the top of the drum. At nineteen Tony Cooper was a popular young man.

Cormac would know how to deal with the situation. He'd do it with a bit of a laugh, and handle it so diplomatically that Kathleen would look at him with shining gratitude and say 'Fancy, Uncle Cormac, I never thought of it like that.'

Tessa wasn't sure whether it was guilt or sorrow she felt when letters came from Cormac, now that David had given up writing to Kathleen. Cormac's letters, his love letters, were so eloquent they made her cry and long to hold him in her arms. Three or four embraces were all that they had had time for, and she lived off each one, drawing emotional nourishment from the memory.

The charade of Christmas over, the New Year of 1917 dawned to take it's awful toll of lives. War weariness, despite the American declaration of war on Germany, had set in, and shortages of basic essentials did not help morale. Just after her fifteenth birthday, Kathleen reflected gloomily on the state of her hair. She wished her hair was like Tessa's, a cloud of waving tendrils which looked thick and full whatever she did with it – she was destined for rat's tails and a fringe all her life.

But messing about with her hair was just an excuse until Joseph had gone to bed.

'Mam,' she said suddenly, turning from the dresser mirror towards the fire where Tessa was folding Tivvy's clothes. 'I'm going to have a baby.'

The phrase ricocheted round Tessa's head. Her eyes closed, fingers crushing the little lace-edged petticoat. No! her heart shrieked. No! No! She moved her lips, trying to form the question 'Who?' Nothing would come. Then she knew, even as Kathleen said it, that Tony Cooper was the father. At least a whole five minutes later, Tessa said quietly, 'You'd better go to bed, we'll talk about it tomorrow. I'm banjaxed altogether, Kathleen. I don't know what to say. I can't see beyond the ruins – and you only fifteen.'

'Come off it, Mam, you weren't *much* older.'

'I was married to yer da,' she said quickly. 'He was a good man and we were right for each other.'

'And me and Tony aren't, is that it? Why should you think my life is in ruins? Tony's in work, and he's got a tenement in the Jersey Street Dwellings, which is more than you had, wandering like tinkers and living at the Sal Doss in Liverpool.'

'You mean you want to marry Tony?'

'Yes,' she said in a small voice. 'I know I can't without your permission till I'm twenty-one. But if I mean anything at all to you, Mam, don't object. I couldn't stand the shame. "Tessa Collins's daughter" they'll say. "Just fancy." I couldn't bear for people to point the finger – oh, I've done it meself many a time, so I know how it goes. And Father Quinn, God, he'd have a field day.'

Oh, she's right there, thought Tessa, he would so.

'What about David?'

'Well, what about him?'

'Don't you want to . . . let him know?'

'Why? There'll be enough with Father Quinn without David sticking his oar in.'

Thank God Finn had been spared this terrible blow. 'We could go away,' Tessa said desperately. 'Move house, no one would know. The child could be brought up with Tivvy.'

'Oh yes, I can just see you carting two of them round the music halls. And what would Uncle Cormac say to that? Besides, I told Tony and he wants to marry me.'

'D'you love him?'

Kathleen shook her head.

'Does he love you?'

The dark, lustrous head shook again. 'And no, it didn't happen here, or at his tenement – I've never been there.' Tessa closed her eyes wearily. 'It was only meant to be a bit of a lark. It was on Helmet Street rec, standing up with me knickers down.' Tessa knew Kathleen was aiming to shock, to hurt, but it was understandable; she kept silent. 'Hetty Lynch said if you stood up, you didn't get caught. She's done it many a time, and she's never got caught.'

Tessa, despite having a heavy day on the morrow with a matinee and evening performance, sat up all night, mechanically folding and unfolding Tivvy's clothes. 'Aladdin and his Wonderful Lamp' . . . She could just do with a genie to put everything right for Kathleen. David and Patrick would be terrible upset. They had never liked Tony Cooper. Finn had never liked him either. She suddenly felt tired; not the exhausting tiredness that came at the end of a busy day, but a tiredness that drained the spirit right out of her.

Chapter Thirty

The banns were put up in the second week of the New Year. Father Quinn and all the neighbours guessed there was a reason for the marriage; Tessa Collins would never have consented otherwise. People tended to marry young in wartime, but fifteen was pushing it a bit.

Tessa felt deserted. What wouldn't she give for the practical advice of Audrey; for the breezy lift of a chinwag with Elfreda; for Cormac's good-humoured wisdom. You're supposed to be able to turn to your priest for help and advice, she thought, and the blue-mantled Madonna, smiling away on Patrick's chest of drawers, was supposed to bring comfort. But when it came to the crunch, you were on your own.

Tony and Kathleen were married at the end of January. Tessa hired the recreation room at the Round House for a reception and laid on barrels and bottles of beer. Food was even more strictly rationed, and with only six weeks' supply of corn left in the country, there was no flour to make even soda bread, even if she had had the heart for it. With Kathleen being so young she had never even thought of weddings, but if she had, it would have been something far above this, with her godparents, Audrey and Nick, watching proudly, and Patrick to give her away, and the church awash with flowers . . . as for the groom, she would never have envisaged Tony Cooper in a thousand years.

But the uneasy alternative filtered through her mind. If David had not had a vocation, it may well have been, as Effie Wilkins had once envisaged, David and Kathleen – and that could never have been. If anything was to be salvaged from this mess, it was that her secret, God forgive her, was safe. David being a priest was one safeguard; Kathleen being married, a double seal.

Titch gave the bride away – bride, she looked more like a little waif with so pale a face and those enormous eyes. Joseph was best man, and two of Tony's sisters bridesmaids. Even though Tessa did not approve of the wedding, she did her best, in memory of Finn. Basic clothing, still less finery of any description, was in short supply, but knowing some theatrical costumiers, Tessa was able to hire a simple but fetching bridal gown, as well as bridesmaids' dresses of pale yellow.

There was an air of grim determination about the wedding, as though the Coopers had, in duelling terms, demanded satisfaction, and because she was Proud Riley's daughter, Tessa felt bound, for her own daughter's sake, for Finn's sake, to provide it.

She recalled her own wedding in the auld country. A broomstick wedding, out in the open air on a fine, sunny St Patrick's Day, with Spider Murphy in his embroidered coat and gold chains, and Martin and Kate Jarvey holding the broomstick, gay with ribbons and bright with gorse petals. Afterwards there had been music and feasting, dancing and drinking until people dropped in their tracks ... Tears gathered in her eyes. What a mournful place the world had become.

At the Round House, Titch opened the proceedings with a toast to the bride and groom. He had been going to make a short speech, but could think of nothing which could be said with any degree of sincerity. To see all the Cooper tribe gathered was not a pleasant sight, and the youngest strapped into the bassinet equipage which Finn had helped to make did not help. These undesirables were now Kathleen's in-laws.

Tessa, in a smartly cut, heather-coloured costume with purple boots, gloves and toque hat – none of it hired for the wedding – had not heard the toast. She was still stunned from overhearing Annie tell Mrs Hewitt, "'Marry her', I said. "Time you had someone to look after you, keep that pigsty of a tenement clean and have your tea ready when you come in. It won't affect your little jaunts," I told him.

"She'll be tied with the kid. And Tessa isn't without a bob or two. If their Kathleen gets fancy ideas of new clothes, her mother'll stump up rather than see her without. The kid will have a wealthy grandmother, especially if she lands the Captain. Oh, yes, our Tony," I said, "Get her to the altar as quick as yer got her in the club.'"

'Eh, lass,' said Titch. 'I've never known you off your Guinness.'

'I've a mind to throw it over that swine of a son-in-law!'

'Keep your voice down, lass. We don't want trouble for Kathleen.' He ushered her toward the door. 'Tivvy, love, come here while I get your coat on. Joseph,' he called, 'yer mam's going home. You needn't come if you're not ready.' Joseph glanced toward his sister and decided to stay to the very end.

Miss Wilkins could not have attended the wedding. She had hoped Kathleen would take her elementary exams at sixteen, and once she was eighteen, become a student nurse wearing a blue cloak, David would call at the Nurses' Home to bring her to tea with his aunt. They would have made a lovely couple. No . . . she could not possible attend.

As the U-boat war increased, the delivery of mail was sporadic and sometimes several letters arrived together. David's were frantic and full of frustration:

> Why have you allowed her, Mrs Collins, to go ahead with so undesirable a marriage? Why did she stop writing to me? I don't understand any of it. I'm in the dark, and this bloody war is getting on my nerves. Write to me soon. You have no idea. Patrick is wild and threatening to kill Cooper.

And from Patrick:

> Mam, I couldn't believe my eyes when Miss Wilkins wrote to David about Kathleen's marriage. She's only fifteen, for God's sake. David is distracted, Mam. He was and is truly fond of Kathleen. We can't understand why you gave your permission? Where are they living? Write soon.

337

Tessa knew this fling with Tony had been a direct result of knowing David would never be her prince; her priest maybe, but never her prince:

Kathleen had romantic ideas, she wrote to David, which were dispelled when I happened to mention your vocation. You had not told her this, and she felt you misled her. You should have told her, David. I'm sorry it had to be me.

And to Patrick she wrote:

I had to give my consent because your sister is expecting Tony Cooper's child, and she couldn't face the humiliation of not being married. I hope you see my position was a difficult one. It's easy for you to tell me what I should have done, but if you'd both been here instead of joining up under age, it might not have happened.

A few weeks later David wrote again:

Dear Mrs Collins,
Will you tell Kathleen I am not becoming a priest. My faith has taken a rare old hammering. I don't think I've any left, not with what's going on here and no doubt being repeated in France. Will you ask Kathleen if I can write to her at your address?

But Tessa could only reply:

I cannot do as you ask, David. If Tony found out it would be awful. In Kathleen's eyes I have been responsible for everything that has gone wrong in her life. I cannot add to the list.

At the end of August Kathleen gave birth to twins, a boy and a girl she named Francis and Florence. They were plain babies, with nothing about them to cause the beholder to search for superlative adjectives.

One baby was complicated enough to the uninitiated, as Tessa well remembered – but two! Not that Kathleen was as ignorant on matters of welfare and hygiene as she had been, but Kathleen was not as robust. She was slender and growing tall like her grandmother Teresa, but there the resemblance ended. Kathleen was as tough as old boots really, but the privations of rationing, without extra meals from Miss Wilkins, Cormac's food parcels, and the odd chunk of black-market cheese from Titch, had depleted her strength and sapped her energy.

Tony had forbidden her to be 'always round at yer mam's', not that she wanted to be; neither did she want her mother to see how she lived. Joseph was always welcome, so long as he left before Tony came home. He used to take eggs, cheese, and occasionally some soft white bread, until he discovered she was giving it to Tony to keep him in a good humour. Joseph could understand this, for the one time he had stayed too long, Tony, yelling 'I married Kathleen not her bloody family!', had threatened to throw him over the balcony, but, thankfully, had thrown him downstairs instead.

The Dwellings, as they were known, were an obsolete cotton mill, horribly converted for a good profit into a hundred and forty tenements. Each one, equipped with meagre gaslighting, and one gas ring, consisted of a bedroom, living room, cold-water tap, and a coal bunker. It was the latter, Titch said, which had introduced beetles into the premises; when all was dark, a vast army of the insects, like prunes with legs, swarmed from every crack and crevice. Each tenement was rented off, and the Dwellings had rapidly become dirty and overcrowded. The whole business had become a social problem which the Settlement had been tackling since the turn of the century. The advent of war had slowed progress down, but conditions which were shocking when Elfreda had been compiling the report had rapidly worsened. Tessa, winding her way up the iron stairs, was glad Elfreda, God love her, was spared the knowledge of Kathleen having come to this. No wonder Tony had never brought her here! But to him, she supposed, anywhere was better than the squalor his parent's house had descended to.

Tessa's quick efficiency only served to heighten her daughter's helpless resentment. The strain of giving birth had taken its toll, but Kathleen, unable to breastfeed sufficiently, wouldn't listen to the voice of experience, especially when the experience was her mother's, and so the babies were constantly hungry and wailing.

Tessa, knowing young Cooper wasn't the most tolerant of men, decided it was time for action. Although the Settlement staff came and went, and its policies were changing to meet the needs of the times, its machinery was still as efficient as ever.

Tessa explained the family situation and asked that a Welfare visitor should call and advise Kathleen about bottles. 'Send someone tough,' she added. 'Mr Cooper's a swine of the first water.' Then she called on the Little Sisters and explained the family situation to Sister Boniface who, thankful for a donation to their charity, promised to call weekly and report anything suspicious.

Somehow Florence and Francis survived, due mainly to Mrs Bryant from the Welfare, a big woman, who, in her navy-blue uniform, puffed and panted up the iron stairs of the Dwellings, and was motherly and tyrannical at the same time, the scourge of neglectful mothers and violent husbands.

Kathleen never asked about David, and Tessa felt it would only make her feel worse to know that he had abandoned his vocation. Sometimes Tessa felt uneasy that he had. At other times she hoped Kathleen's marriage would get better as both she and Tony grew older. Then again, she wondered, ought she to tell David and indeed Kathleen of the blood bond?

No, it could only be revealed if absolutely necessary; Kathleen would never forgive her. 'What an excuse!' She could hear the young voice, shrill and full of bitterness. Yes, she reflected, it would seem a likely tale all these years hence. How could she try to describe the effect of the Aunt Hanratty's curse on Finn, and how it had driven her to George Wilkins' sofa? A likely tale; the stuff of music-hall jokes . . . No one would believe it now, especially not Kathleen.

Chapter Thirty-One

In the New Year of 1918 Mrs Hewitt suffered a particularly bad bout of influenza. When Mr Barnes died of the same illness, people began to be worried. The manager at the Tivoli went down with it, and there were several gaps on the programme. The winter was hard, food strictly rationed, and the rapidly spreading 'flu was declared an epidemic. Jud Patterson and Mrs Marr scraped through, but by the time Mrs Hewitt survived and said she'd never be the same again, Mrs Barnes, lost without her verbal sparring partner, gave up without a word. Tessa increased Tivvy's dose of cod-liver oil and sent a bottle with Joseph for the twins; surely that wouldn't find its way down Tony Cooper's throat!

But in March, further tragedy struck:

27, Loom Street.

Dear David

     I bring you terrible news and there is no way to make it sound easier. We have a 'flu epidemic raging here and your aunt has died. She had scarcely taken to her bed, and it happened very quickly and was a great shock. We all loved her, and feel for you hearing such bad news at so great a distance. Your father has taken it terrible bad, you wouldn't believe the state of him. I've had to arrange for a housekeeper, recommended from the Settlement, a Mrs Horrocks, so all is taken care of until you are home. Surely, dear David, the war cannot go on much longer?

Patrick had written a short, jubilant note dated late April: *On our way home, in Alex awaiting a convoy. All finished here.*

341

Will bring what food we can, and telegraph on arrival on England.

As the troopships waited for a convoy on the quayside at Alexandria, Sergeant Major Barton, addressing the Veterinary Corps, and the Mobile Units in particular, summed it all up. 'Jerusalem would never have fallen, nor Beersheba and Gaza been taken, without the cavalry. In fact, this war, this long and bloody war could not have been won without those noble beasts, the horses, donkeys, mules, asses, and camels. All my men engaged in their welfare did a magnificent job.'

But where is Cormac? Tessa asked of the Sacred Heart as she fixed her hat before setting off for the Ardwick Hippodrome. Was he, too, awaiting a convoy from one of these Godforsaken places? Oh, please, she begged, don't let anything happen to any of them at this late hour; I couldn't bear it.

'Call a Tune' had been a popular spot on Tessa and Titch's bill since the beginning of the war. Patrons in uniform would call out names of favourite tunes, but they had to be prepared to come on stage where anything could happen, from joining in the song to flirting, joking, and sometimes a kiss.

'The 'Full House' boards were up early tonight at the Ardwick Hippodrome, for at the top of the bill was the famous male impersonator Hetty King, who, stunningly dressed in a sailor suit, swaggered about to 'All the Nice Girls Love a Sailor' and 'The American Ragtime Octette', which set feet tapping and ready for 'Waiting for the Robert E. Lee'.

It was a measure of the professional esteem in which they were held that they were sharing to illustrious a bill, for Tessa and Titch were the only other musical item, the rest being acrobats, illusionists, clowns and comedians.

Appearing with top stars brought out the best in Tessa. She and Titch were so attuned they could immediately improvise or add to their material, giving the act a spontaneity and sparkle which kept audience anticipation finely honed. Their followers had come to expect the unexpected.

But tonight it was Tessa who faced the unexpected and the tables were turned when, on the 'Call a Tune' spot, she picked out a voice from the stalls yelling for 'Cockles and Mussels'. No, she thought, it couldn't be. The constraints of theatrical expertise calmed her down. Had that been his voice? He always had preferred the stalls. Shading her eyes against the lights, she stalked along the front of stage in a predatory manner, heart beating madly beneath the silk-fringed yoke of her gown. It was Cormac? Dear God, it was Cormac!

'"Cockles and Mussels"!' he demanded, as their eyes met.

'He wants "Cockles and Mussels"!' She rose to the occasion, with an exaggerated air of incredulity.

Titch, expert in the timing of innuendo, took it up and turning from the piano, nodded knowingly, 'I know what he wants!' The giggles mounted. He studied the house, and at just the right moment added, 'He wants "Cockles and Mussels"!'

'Doesn't this fella know we're rationed?' Tessa peered out over the pit. 'No . . . He's an officer, they don't know about anything!'

Titch, still from the piano stool, shaded his eyes to the stalls. 'He seems to know a lot about Molly Malone!'

'I think he means the song, Titch.'

Titch let them have it. They knew what he was going to say, and they loved the anticipation. 'Don't tell me what he means!' he roared. 'We all know what he means!'

'Well, if he means what I think he means, you'd better go and winkle him out!'

And there he was before her. She'd never seen him bashful, never thought it possible, but it suited him. His skin was tanned, sable-coloured hair as glossy as a horse's flank, his amber eyes . . . merciful Lord, she mustn't look. Mustn't touch.

'You're not shy, are you?' They were the stock-in-trade opening words.

They laughed about it afterwards, but how they ever got through all three verses and choruses without even a touch of hands, neither of them knew.

'Oh, 'tis the devil of a fella, y'are,' she teased as they sat on the sofa in the parlour of the Men's House at the Settlement. 'No one can accuse you of being predictable!'

His arm was comfortably about her shoulders and her

head rested against his. She hardly felt recovered from the delicious turmoil of their first embrace, which seemed to have lasted from the dressing room, to the cab, to here. And still, after a pot of tea and some army crackers spread with canned jam, they exchanged glances, reached out to touch, and then continued the exchange of news.

Nick had been killed in France, caught in an ambush after freeing some horses from a corral too near the gun lines. Elfreda had joined Intelligence, and Audrey, still in London, was hot on a more political career. They discussed Miss Wilkins' death and the 'flu epidemic.

'As for me, all I want is to marry the "Colleen from Connemara" and whisk her and little Tivvy away from the filth of industry to the sweet air of the auld country. They do have music halls over there you know, lots of openings, concerts, ceilidhs and wakes!' He glanced down, hugging her shoulders, 'What's up love? Changed your mind about the wandering minstrel?'

'As if I would – I've waited too damn long! But I can't really leave Kathleen to that swine, Tony Cooper. The twins are not yet a year old and she's expecting again – at sixteen begod. Honest, it makes your heart bleed to see her . . . ' She glanced sideways at him, mouth twitching into a smile. 'You did say you were looking forward to a ready-made family, and you can't have a family without one bloody problem after another! And where would Joseph live? Tony won't have him in the house. Did I say house? More like a hovel. Reminds me of the shiftless at Ennan! No, Joseph wouldn't survive without his sister.' She glanced at the clock. 'Oh, wait till you see him, he's a broth of a boy – well, hardly a broth, but you know what I mean!' She patted his knee and got up. 'Time I went. Not that Tivvy's alone for Joseph looks to her at night. She's good for his talking – too young to realise he's slow, so he's not embarrassed.'

He opened the door onto the passage. 'I'll walk home with you. Have I to kiss you standing on the bottom step? It'll give the neighbours a whirl!' He pulled on his tunic and held her coat, whispering, 'Another excuse for a cuddle.'

'Sshh . . . ' She put her finger to his lips. 'Remember the rules, no females in rooms after ten.'

'What makes them think anything immoral can't happen before ten!'

Once on Every Street he tucked his arm through hers and they strolled along together, thigh to thigh, voices low. The houses were all in darkness, and the street-corner lamps glowed like large chrysanthemums.

'How long are you staying at the Men's House?'

'Just for this month's leave, then it's back to quarters at Regent Road Barracks, until my term of service is up at the end of December. I've always fancied going into breeding bloodstock with Doyle's y'know, so there's no rush to leave Finn's land of milk and honey. But Tessa, I want us to be married soon, when the boys are home.' He gave a short laugh. 'Fancy waiting for a convoy in Alex, poor sods!'

'Will David and Patrick be getting a month's leave, or will they be home for good?'

'Ah the ranks, the backbone of the British Army. They get demobbed. Issued with a new suit, given a few pounds, and it's goodbye Tommy Atkins, till next bloody time.' She noticed the bitterness creep into his voice but said nothing. What could she say, she who had never seen the horrors of war? 'As for the thousands of horses we shipped out there, those that survived, with their knifeboard backs, staring ribs, sunken eyes and the shuffling amble of the incurably lame, they'll finish up at the knacker's yard.'

It was another month before the welcome telegram arrived. *Coming Wednesday afternoon – be in.* Tessa had not minded the month's wait. It had given her time to be with Cormac, to talk about the future, for him to call and see Kathleen without being intrusive, and for him to become acquainted with Tivvy and re-establish his relationship with Joseph. And in doing all this, he became less tense and the outbursts of bitterness came less often. They no longer cared about the neighbours in Loom Street. The 'library' atmosphere of the Men's House was not, especially after ten, a suitable place to discuss arrangements for Patrick's homecoming, or, with Titch, the evening's performance. Titch was taken with the idea of crossing the water, and had already received interest from Dublin and an enquiry from Cork. But, as yet, the war was not over.

345

Cormac often stayed late with Tessa, for if she had been out of town in Oldham or Bolton it was already late when they arrived at Loom Street. Sometimes, especially now that they had fixed their wedding date, he didn't want to leave her, and she too yearned for him to stay. She had never thought to feel this way about anyone after Finn died, but now, as Marie Lloyd would have said, she had to 'batten down the hatches', which she did. Besides, there was always the sneaking feeling that he may think her easy, what with not being married legally to Finn and all. For Cormac's part, he did not want her to think he was continuing the Audrey tradition. Their love was something special and after all, what was another three or four weeks.

Wednesday finally arrived, and to David and Patrick the muck and mills of Manchester could have been the gates of paradise. The light summer rain and grey sky were a welcome change from the unremitting rays of blazing sun.

'I can see Titch and Mam have been raiding the props again!' joked Patrick as they struggled through the red, white and blue bunting round the door and pointed to the 'WELCOME HOME' posters. Neighbours hung about, people from the next street, Jonty from the Sugar Loaf, all shaking hands and thumping shoulders.

'Just look at the sight of you both!' exclaimed Tessa as, with their kitbags and greatcoats, they seemed to fill the room. Patrick, she thought, catching her breath, was the image of his da, although smaller and not as broad, but he was a grown man and reminded her of Finn by the chapel when they had been young. As for David, the ravages of war had gone deep; he was thin, his face was thin, his smile thin.

After a big hug from Patrick, Tessa exclaimed. 'Lord, I can't get over the sight of you . . .' She held him at arm's length, eyes brimming with tears of happiness. Then, welcoming David, she whispered her sorrow that his aunt was not here.

'And obviously the old man didn't think it worth his while.'

'Sure, you know he's not one for the big scene,' she said softly. Neither knew any such thing but she felt an answer was called for.

'Joe still at work?'

'He is so, and can't wait to see you.'

'And Uncle Cormac?'

'Been home a month already. He's moving into quarters at the Barracks so won't be coming till tomorrow. I think he wanted us to have time to . . . get to know each other a bit. After all, four years is a long time.'

'Too long,' said David.

'Now,' teased Patrick, 'where's Tivvy, where's that little sister of mine?' He was looking at the stair door, which was open slightly, and at the bluest pair of eyes peering round.

'Not that she's shy at all, but you're grown men, and for all that I've talked about you, it'll be a bit overpowering for a little one.'

Patrick made a rush at the stairs and carried her into the houseplace, laughing. She buried her head in his shoulder for a minute. 'Eh,' he said, 'you must be all of what? Three, or is it four?'

'Four,' came the indignant reply, and they all laughed.

Setting her down, he sighed. 'I'd almost forgotten what it's like to belong to a family again. Here's a threepenny bit, go an' get yourself some dolly mixtures while Mam gets the tea.'

'Coat!' said Tessa.

'It's only up the street,' declared Tivvy, sidling toward the door.

'Coat,' came the unrelenting reply. 'And fasten it.' To the young men, she added, 'It's the damp, can't take any chances. What d'you think of her?'

'I think she's going to be fine, Mam, not as tough as us lot, but fine. Now, where's our Kathleen? Thought she'd be here to welcome the wanderers . . . ' He glanced at David who, having dumped his coat, had found salvation in putting the kettle on. While he was in the scullery Patrick added, 'Oh God, Mam, I could weep for our Kathleen. You must have known she was seeing Cooper. Couldn't you have stopped her?'

'Like I tried to stop you going to the war! None of yous takes a blind bit of notice of your parents.'

'I'm not blaming you.'

'Are you not? Well, that makes a nice change. I thought she'd be here by now. It takes her a while to get the twins ready and the bassinet down all those stairs . . . '

The front door, already open, was pushed further. Kathleen stood on the top step. Patrick stared momentarily at the large, mournful eyes in so pale a face; her hair was cut short to below the ears, and she wore a coarse, woollen shawl.

'Mam said you were coming home . . . oh, it's good to see you, Patrick!' She rushed into his arms and burst into tears. The sight of him had brought back the old times . . . Church, Cunliffe's pies round the table, all going off to the Settlement . . .

David came in from the scullery. 'Have you got a kiss for me?'

She had, all the kisses in the world, but it was too late.

'I'll take me gear upstairs, make a bit more room. Am I still in the back with Joseph? Come on up, Mam, and show me.' He gave her a significant wink and as Tessa followed him, she heard him call down, 'Give you twenty minutes, if Tivvy comes back, send her up.'

'What's all that for?' she asked, sitting on the edge of the bed.

'They've got to talk, Mam. She wouldn't write to him, remember? And they were such pals. Just give her time to explain. And while I've a minute, I may as well tell you now, that I'm staying on in the Veterinary Corps. Dave isn't, he's had a bellyfull one way and another. But I'm in with the horses, probably got a fancy for 'em from Uncle Cormac. I wouldn't be able to settle at the stables, and I'd be wasted with all the knowledge I've accumulated. You'll never guess where I'm stationed.'

She wouldn't try. Merciful Lord, was there no end to it?

'I've volunteered for service in Ireland, peacekeeping or something. Thought you'd be pleased I was going to the auld country you're always on about – after all, there's not much doing in Ancoats, is there?' He glanced at the door. 'Tivvy? Come and show me what you bought.' As she settled between his knees, he asked her, 'What are they doing down there, still talking?'

'Crying,' she replied.

'Crying, oh my God!'

'Five more minutes,' said Tessa uneasily. 'Then she'll

need to eat before making the journey back. Oh Patrick, sure I feel for her – but she's so obstinate.'

They descended the creaking stairs noisily, making clear that talking time had ended. Kathleen was still tearful but with a little trace of radiance. Her prince was back.

'I'll go and fetch the twins,' said Tessa. 'It's time they're introduced to their Uncle Patrick.' She lifted the twelve-month-old babies from their pram. There was not much weight to them; like Cormac's shandies, no bant, no body. They were pale-faced from being indoors, freckles over their noses and a big yellow dummy sticking out of their rosy little mouths. They were tired-looking infants and sat propped up on the Mafeking sofa with listless eyes . . . It was only then the suspicion crossed her mind. Surely, oh, surely, Kathleen hadn't been dosing them with 'goody'? But who could blame her, for Joseph said Tony had threatened to throw them from the balcony if they didn't stop yelling.

Tessa had made sultana scones and soda bread with ingredients saved over a long time just for this occasion. The twins chewed on crusts hungrily, and Kathleen ate so heartily that Tessa couldn't swallow for the tightening of her throat. The boys – she'd have to get out of that, but to her they'd always be boys – were big, and Patrick strong, and sitting between them, Kathleen was wedged like one of Tivvy's dolls.

'Thanks, Mam,' she said. 'That was nice. I'd better be off to get Tony's tea.'

'I'll come with you.'

'No, David, there'll only be trouble.'

'Not to the hearth, Dolly Daydream, only to Jersey Street corner! Can I leave me kit here till later, Mrs Collins?'

'Yes, but don't be too long going to see your father.' At least, she thought, seeing David's old protective manner, he's brought sanity back into her life – and there's no danger of marriage because she already is.

Despite the neighbours, and especially the Coopers, being on the front, David took the handle of the pram, with a 'D'you want to hop on as well!', he dismissed her protestations, and they set off down the street.

'David's going to have to be careful,' Tessa warned Patrick. 'You must make him aware of this. Annie's a right old spy, she tells him her every move in this direction. Not that I'm bothered about David – he can stick up for himself – but I'm always afraid Tony takes things out on her.'

'He only married her to bring her down to his level, y'know. She was set on being a nurse, studying her books, and growing up real nice. I'll never forgive him.'

'Neither you nor David gave any thought to that when you swanned off to Lime Bank Street. All he thought of was getting one over on his da, and you – God alone knows what you thought of! Sure, you've got more than a shot of yer da in you, with all this fascination with the army.'

They sat and talked while Tivvy emptied his kitbag upstairs; not so much talked, as skirted about issues, feeling their way over the absence of four years. And at six o'clock, Joseph was home.

'Eh, look who's here, the smart city gent! I wouldn't have known him!'

Joseph smiled his pleasure. He was shy still and could not have uttered a word if he'd been paid. His brother and David were men. They had seen the world, seen death and no glory. Been perched on the waves of the sea, tossed in boats; borne on lorries over expanses of desert. Brushed shoulders with Turks and Arabs. They had travelled in the flesh while he read it all in books.

It was late when David returned, and Tessa was almost ready for the Palace.

'Nearly sending a search party out,' laughed Patrick. 'Thought Cooper had done for you!'

'Take more than Cooper to do for me, the mood I'm in!' He threw himself on the sofa and surveyed their questioning faces with an air of satisfaction. 'It's good to be home and doing positive things with my life,' he breathed.

'Listen to him, and he's only been home a few hours. There sits the human dynamo!'

'To start with I went to see the old man, and as you said in your letter, Mrs Collins, he's gone to pieces. Just shows you. I never thought he was that gone on my aunt, either. If he doesn't pull his socks up I can see Atkinson's giving him the boot! Now,' he leaned forward from his lounging position, elbows on his knees, the chestnut hair across his brow, 'I'm staying the night at the Men's House. I'm working at the Settlement – it's got to go through official channels, but it's all sewn up – and at the same time going for my degree. When I get it I shall apply to be warden. In the meantime, I shall take tramloads of kids out to Didsbury for some fresh air and do all the things Miss Crompton and Miss Hindshaw did – when I'm warden, who knows where it might lead on the educational front. I feel this great urge,' he told their astounded faces, 'to rebuild and consolidate.'

'By all the saints, Dave, you're not letting the grass grow beneath your feet!'

'There's more. I called on Father Quinn. Thought it the decent thing, really, to tell him I hadn't a vocation after all. I told him why . . . ' he looked directly at Patrick, acknowledging the Father MacNaughton affair. 'He was naturally upset and angry and promised to look into it. I told him he needn't bother on my account . . . ' David's face looked positively elfish in his glee. 'I can tell you, Patrick, I left a very bewildered and white-faced Father Quinn.' He inclined his head to a rakish angle. 'I did tell him that good old Patrick would be round at confession on Friday and to serve at one of the Masses, if not all!'

Patrick flushed. His faith was still whole. The carnage had been very terrible and God's ways not easy to understand, but although no thinker, he did not see that humanity had any right to expect to understand. Knowing David's sensitivities he never ribbed his friend, and was just a little hurt that the courtesy should not be extended to himself.

'Well, there's a day's work,' he said.

'And I'll tell you another thing – yes, why not? – I went to the Dwellings with Kathleen, and dear God, it was awful. How you could leave her there, Mrs Collins –'

'Mam's had it all,' Patrick warned. 'Since Dad died it's been all uphill.'

'Sorry, Mrs Collins.' He was contrite. 'I am truly, truly sorry. I didn't mean to imply blame.'

'It's a good thing you didn't – none of you are too big to get a clout!'

'Anyway, I wasn't leaving her there. We collected her things, what bits there were, and I took her and the twins to Oldham Road, to the old man's.'

351

'You did what?' Tessa sank onto one of the ladder back chairs.

'He wasn't sold on the idea, but at the sight of Kathleen he told Mrs Horocks to get everything sorted out for them. I've done the right thing, Mrs Collins. Living with that brute would have done for her, and as for the kids . . . The upshot of it was that instead of Kathleen waiting with his tea ready, Tony found me. He wasn't pleased. I told him what I'd done and that she was under the old man's protection. I know you'll raise hands in horror, but we're going to live in sin until such time as she can get a divorce. It shouldn't be too difficult to prove his adultery as well as his cruelty. And then we are going to be married legally according to the law of the land – Patrick, quick, your mam, she's going to faint –'

Tessa did not faint, mercifully. Somehow she kept a hold on herself and mind whirling with the ramifications of David's rebuilding and consolidation programme, she arrived at the Palace just in time to stop Titch falling prey to a stroke.

Stepping onto the stage was like stepping out of herself, and when she stepped back into herself, her next move was clear. No matter how the blame would crush her, she could not allow this marriage to take place. It was not only a mortal sin – and of that she had no right to talk – but such a marriage could be incestuous. Thank God Cormac was not with her tonight.

She hoped George Wilkins would not be asleep and that Kathleen would. Her hopes were realised. George opened the door; he was still fully dressed and with a cigarette between his fingers. They looked at each other, suddenly terrified.

What does she want?

What will he say when I tell him?

He did not say anthing at first, but walked about rubbing his hands together. 'You mean that Kathleen is my daughter . . . when you and me . . . ' He walked the length of the room again. 'But you told me you were already –'

'I was, with her. That night. I know it all sounds very unlikely, but I assure you Finn would have cracked. I *had* to do it.'

'Deceive me for him?'

'Yes.'

He could still wince at her matter-of-fact rejection. 'Why are you telling me this now, and at so late an hour?'

'Because I want you to use your influence with David to stop this marriage.'

He stopped walking. 'David is not my son.'

It gave him great satisfaction to see her slowly sink onto the sofa.

'Effie's will relates that Sylvia was already pregnant when she married me. Our courtship was brief for I was busy making my way and had no time for long drawn-out affairs. David's real father was thrown off a horse and killed before she had chance to tell him, but Sylvia told Effie before she died in childbirth. So it seems, Mrs Collins, that I have lost a son and gained a daughter.' He was talking in a matter-of-fact voice, taking it calmly. Yet inside his heart was thawing, warming, he could feel the mellowness spreading. What people had mistaken for grief at Effie's death had been rage ... at being deceived ... for bringing up a total stranger's child, and in the end nothing. No one to come into the mill – not even a priest in the family. No family. Nothing. God, how that rage had burned, how it had scorched and seared, leaving a whole tender area which was now being soothed.

'Leave it to me, Mrs Collins. But I shall tell Kathleen the truth first thing in the morning. I insist. She's all I have.'

'I can't expect her to forgive me for deceiving Finn or herself, not yet, anyway. She has a lot of growing up to do and I'm glad she's got David to help her.'

They were each talking, beginning sentences, trailing off. Tessa moved toward the door. 'I'm going to marry Captain O'Shea in a few weeks, and we are returning to Ireland with Tivvy. Can I take it that as Kathleen's father, you'll look to her until she marries David?'

She need not have asked. She knew he would.

Tessa left quietly and quickly. George Wilkins had talked of his daughter and future grandchildren; there would be someone for a lonely old man to make plans for, someone to rule whatever little empire he would leave.

Tessa walked along Oldham Road, a lonely silhouette against the flare of the street lamps recalling the sense of

353

purpose and exhilaration of that fateful night sixteen years earlier. She had the same feeling now, only this was topped up with relief that her secret was out in the open. She'd had enough of schemes and strategies and knew that with Cormac there would be no need. There was also the inner assurance that Cormac would understand the realness of the Aunt Hanratty's curse on a man like Finn.

A few days later Patrick passed on a note to David from Father Quinn:

I have made enquiries and discovered that Father MacNaughton, SJ was killed in action. His death, it would appear, was more glorious than his life, for it saved the lives of a patrol, and for that he was awarded a posthumous medal for gallantry. In view of his decease I have decided to terminate enquiries.

But David was no longer interested in the past. By the time the war had ended and the Armistice was signed on the eleventh of November, Cormac and Tessa were married, not in the Sacred Heart church by Father Quinn, but in the military chapel at Regent Road barracks by the regimental priest. It was to have been a quiet, family affair, but things began to escalate, from Cormac's fellow officers arranging a Guard of Honour to Titch providing a grand reception at the Midland Hotel, attended by the manager of the Tivoli, the Two Dollys, and other artistes with whom she and Titch had worked. George Wilkins, although invited, did not attend. He could not have borne it, and was not even lurking on the edges of the crowd that watched Tessa leave Number Twenty-seven Loom Street in a turquoise-blue gown and wide, Elfreda-style hat.

It was a measure of something that Wilkins had invited Joseph to stay with his sister. 'They are all catered for,' Cormac had said softly. 'Which leaves you and me and little Tivvy to spread our wings and fly away home across the water.'

Midnight found them standing together in the first-class area on the deck of the *Hibernia*. Tivvy, in velvet coat and scarf and gloves, sat on a capstan swinging her legs, turning to smile at passengers who came up the gangway. Then, impatiently, she skipped down the deck, asking questions and singing little songs to herself. Tiring of this, she squeezed between Cormac and Tessa and holding each of their hands, watched the last-minute drama of embarkation, the shouting of the shoremen, the pulling and shoving.

The quayside was crowded with familiar faces, friendly faces, family faces. The more formal cries of 'God Speed' and 'Write soon' were offset by Titch, who was following a week later for their debut in Dublin, yelling 'Don't do anything I wouldn't do!' and the inevitable response, 'That doesn't leave much scope!' Music-hall cracks faded in the blare of the hooter; propellers thrashed, and the air throbbed with the pulses of powerful engines. Tivvy, startled at the noise, clung to Cormac, who picked her up, and from the shelter of his arms she waved madly and confidently.

As the boat moved away in the darkness Tessa and Cormac looked at each other with the incredulity of two people who couldn't believe their luck, and as the shore receded, his free hand met hers under the shelter of her tweed travelling cloak.

Joyce Bentley
Proud Riley's Daughter £3.99

With *Proud Riley's Daughter*, Joyce Bentley begins her magnificent
and haunting saga, rooted in the threatening landscape of
nineteenth-century Ireland.

When the Tinker's Fair comes to the wild and isolated valley of
Ennan it is Tessa, beautiful, headstrong daughter of the peat-digger
Riley, who is drawn to the handsome Finn Collins, nephew of a
woman rumoured to be a witch.

But Finn must shake off his dark inheritance of superstition to
declare his love – a love threatened by a father's proud ambition . . .
and by the turbulent events that will engulf them all. For in the
lonely crofting community there are those who still seek revenge for
past wrongs.

As progress threatens the destruction of an ancient way of life, Tessa
and Finn must build a future together amidst the ghosts and spirits
of the past . . .

'A powerful story, liltingly told' YORKSHIRE EVENING POST

Anita Burgh
The Azure Bowl £3.99

For Alice Tregowan, daughter of a wealthy mine owner, the Cornish estate of Gwenfer still holds the dreams of a past long buried: the wealth and privilege she sacrificed in her fight for freedom . . . and love.

But for Ia Blewett, daughter of a drunken and penniless miner and Alice's childhood friend, Gwenfer is the symbol of all that she could never have; and all that she will struggle to gain in her relentless quest for wealth and vengeance.

From the sweeping landscape of rugged Cornwall, to the brothels of Victorian London and the grim tenements of turn-of-the-century New York, theirs is a story of passion and conflict, of courage and desire.

Nomi Berger
So Many Promises £4.50

Behind the glamour of the world's musical arenas – one woman's victory over the memories of her shattered past . . .

Kirsten Harald flourished under the good love of her immigrant parents: a love that the harsh poverty of life in New York's slums could not stifle. Musical excellence was Kirsten's passport to a life beyond the dreams of her upbringing, and becoming the protégée of a wealthy and sophisticated art patron the reward for the gruelling demands of her talent.

But all too soon she learns her first lessons about the greedy passions – and the crushing power – of the music world élite. All too soon she learns of the cruel choice she will have to make: music or love. Never both.

Still Kirsten dares to have it all. With Michael Eastbourne, renowned conductor, she finds the passion of forbidden love. With Jeffrey Powell Oliver, society physician, she finds the contentment of marriage and the joy of motherhood . . . until tragedy strikes.

Betrayed and alone, Kirsten vows to triumph again – to fulfil the greatest promise of them all . . .

Ann Victoria Roberts
Louisa Elliott £4.99

In a passionate world of loyalty and betrayal would true love win the ultimate victory?

In the ghostly shadows that lay between the flickering gas lamps of the City of York the past was ever present, binding cousins Louisa and Edward Elliott with the stigma of their illegitimacy.

Until out of the mists emerged Robert Duncannon, an Irish officer with the Royal Dragoons. Dashing and impetuous, he is everything that worthy, steadfast Edward can never be.

Obsessed by an overwhelming love, Louisa sails to Dublin to be with Robert. But in Ireland she encounters hostility – and the mysterious Charlotte who threatens to shatter Louisa's dreams for ever.

'A magnificent novel . . . a portrait of an extraordinary woman of her time – for all time.' CATHERINE GASKIN

All Pan books are available at your local bookshop or newsagent, or can be ordered direct from the publisher. Indicate the number of copies required and fill in the form below.

Send to: **CS Department, Pan Books Ltd., P.O. Box 40, Basingstoke, Hants. RG21 2YT.**

or phone: 0256 469551 (Ansaphone), quoting title, author and Credit Card number.

Please enclose a remittance* to the value of the cover price plus: 60p for the first book plus 30p per copy for each additional book ordered to a maximum charge of £2.40 to cover postage and packing.

*Payment may be made in sterling by UK personal cheque, postal order, sterling draft or international money order, made payable to Pan Books Ltd.

Alternatively by Barclaycard/Access:

Card No.

Signature:

Applicable only in the UK and Republic of Ireland.

While every effort is made to keep prices low, it is sometimes necessary to increase prices at short notice. Pan Books reserve the right to show on covers and charge new retail prices which may differ from those advertised in the text or elsewhere.

NAME AND ADDRESS IN BLOCK LETTERS PLEASE:

....

Name ————————————————————————

Address ——————————————————————

————————————————————————————

————————————————————————————

————————————————————————————

3/87